Taryn Belle is the pen name of Cea Person, a bestselling Canadian author who wrote about her unconventional childhood in two memoirs, *North of Normal* and *Nearly Normal*, both published by HarperCollins. She is a former international model and a businesswoman, running a swimwear company with merchandise popularised by celebrities such as Jessica Alba and Kate Hudson. She loves playing board games with her husband and three children, hosting dinner parties in her Vancouver home and crafting out.

New York Times and *USA TODAY* bestselling author **Cathryn Fox** is a wife, mom, sister, daughter, aunt and friend. She loves dogs, sunny weather, anything chocolate (she never says no to a brownie), pizza and red wine. Cathryn lives in beautiful Nova Scotia with her husband, who is convinced he can turn her into a mixed martial arts fan. When not writing, Cathryn can be found Skyping with her son, who lives in Seattle (could he have moved *any* farther away?), shopping with her daughter in the city, watching a big action flick with her husband, or hanging out and laughing with friends.

D0231194

If you liked *In For Keeps* and *Under His Touch*
why not try

Teach Me by Caitlin Crews
Getting Dirty by Rachael Stewart

Discover more at millsandboon.co.uk

IN FOR KEEPS

TARYN BELLE

UNDER HIS TOUCH

CATHRYN FOX

MILLS & BOON

All rights reserved including the right of reproduction
in whole or in part in any form. This edition is published
by arrangement with Harlequin Books S.A.

This is a work of fiction. Names, characters, places, locations
and incidents are purely fictional and bear no relationship to
any real life individuals, living or dead, or to any actual places,
business establishments, locations, events or incidents.
Any resemblance is entirely coincidental.

This book is sold subject to the condition that it shall not,
by way of trade or otherwise, be lent, resold, hired out
or otherwise circulated without the prior consent of the publisher
in any form of binding or cover other than that in which it is published
and without a similar condition including this condition
being imposed on the subsequent purchaser.

® and TM are trademarks owned and used by the trademark owner
and/or its licensee. Trademarks marked with ® are registered with the
United Kingdom Patent Office and/or the Office for Harmonisation
in the Internal Market and in other countries.

First Published in Great Britain 2020
by Mills & Boon, an imprint of HarperCollins*Publishers*
1 London Bridge Street, London, SE1 9GF

In For Keeps © 2020 Cea Sunrise Person

Under His Touch © 2020 Cathryn Fox

ISBN-13: 978-0-263-27750-0

MIX
Paper from
responsible sources
FSC™ C007454

This book is produced from independently certified FSC™ paper
to ensure responsible forest management.
For more information visit www.harpercollins.co.uk/green.

Printed and bound in Spain
by CPI, Barcelona

IN FOR KEEPS

TARYN BELLE

MILLS & BOON

To Remy, my real-life love story.

PROLOGUE

"THIS DRESS," DEV SAID, trailing his hands beneath it up to the lacy edge of her panties, "needs to be on the floor."

Kiki laughed and squirmed away from him to the other side of the sofa. "You said you were going to show me around, rock star," she said, gesturing toward his studio equipment.

Dev gazed longingly at the woman he'd known for less than an hour. Their eyes had met across a room full of people—*his* room full of people—and her pull on him had been as irresistible as a rare earth magnet. She was obviously gorgeous, but it was her confidence that had attracted him to her. A brief conversation had revealed a quick wit and a straightforward, no-games personality. The habit she had of pulling her hair to one side to bare her neck, the way she parted her sensual lips when he spoke to her, had had his mind going to lustful places within minutes.

"Later," he said. "Right now we've got way better things to do."

"But you're missing your own party," Kiki said, bringing a finger to her mouth. She held it there, licking the tip suggestively while electricity jolted down Dev's spine. She was making him fucking crazy, but soon she would be his. He only hoped he wouldn't crush her. At six foot two he was tall, and he kept his body muscular with regular workouts. She couldn't be a shade over five-three, a perfect china doll in a pink minidress. Her large blue eyes, freckles and long strawberry blonde hair added to the effect of innocence.

But he already knew from what had led them here, desperate for privacy, that she was anything but. Thirty minutes of making out on his private beach like a pair of hormonal teenagers had nearly brought him to his knees. By the time she'd taken his hand and pressed it to her pussy in a silent plea, he'd actually been worried about his own control. No—this woman was no innocent doll. She was red-hot, in charge and fully attuned to both of their gratification. "This *is* my party," Dev said. "We've got everything we need. Music, fun and the best fucking present I've ever gotten."

"Oh, yeah?"

"Yeah," he said, unbuttoning his shirt.

"That's a lot of pressure. I guess I'd better deliver."

"Somehow I'm not too worried."

He dropped his shirt onto the sofa, not missing the hungry rove of her eyes over his chest. Drawing one knee up, she let her leg fall open just enough for him to catch a glimpse of her thong: black silk edged with a cream lace border. His cock surged forward in his shorts, aching for her touch. She licked her lips, which were swollen and pink from the intensity of their kissing. He leaned toward her and took them again. She yielded to his tongue, and he let it build until she was biting ravenously at his mouth. A sharp charge zapped up his thighs. The pleasant, dull ache in his groin was becoming a throb. He *needed* her. Needed her breast in his mouth, her long hair wrapped in his fist, his cock thrusting into her, her moans of pleasure in his ear. His entire body was vibrating with anticipation, an insane urgency to claim her. Something told him he was in for the fuck of his life, and it wasn't just because he hadn't bedded anyone in over a year. He had chosen her when he'd had no intention of sleeping with anyone tonight, and that in itself was a dangerous thing to consider.

Throwing her head back, Kiki slid a hand into her panties. "Ohh…" she moaned as she touched herself. He watched her, so overcome with desire he was practically trembling. "Was this what you wanted?" Pushing a finger inside herself, she closed her eyes and sighed rapturously.

It was too much to take. Dev grasped her wrists and pushed her hands above her head. Then he slowly lowered himself between her legs until he was pressing his cock, still caged in his shorts, against her pussy.

"This is what *you* want. Trust me," he said, pushing into her rhythmically. He knew he'd hit her sweet spot when he was rewarded with a helpless whimper. Her wrists strained as she tried to reach for him, but he held them firmly in place. Then he brought his mouth down on hers for another slow, sensual kiss, ending it before it became too urgent. He wanted to prolong this delicious moment for all it was worth—not his usual MO. Normally he preferred quick and impersonal, but this tiny creature was bringing something out in him that had his head spinning. He wanted to fuck her like a wild animal and caress her gently at the same time. But most of all, he wanted her to experience the same pressing need that was melting his brain and firing up his insides like an inferno.

"It looks like you have a present for *me*," Kiki said, looking down at his shorts. "Shall I unwrap it?"

"That would mean I'd have to let you go," Dev replied, rubbing his thumbs in slow circles on the insides of her wrists. "And I happen to have you just where I want you."

Her wide blue eyes teased him back. "I promise I won't try to escape."

Dev loosened his grip, and she unzipped his fly. He let her get a good look at his cock, perfectly outlined against his black boxers, before he reached for the hem of her dress. "Me first."

He tugged the garment over her head and stared at her in wonder. Her breasts, encased in a bra that matched her panties, were the perfect size— still small, but not as tiny as the rest of her. Lightly dusted with freckles. Her rosy nipples strained toward him when he unclasped her bra. He hooked a finger around one and tugged, thrilling at her sharp intake of breath. "Yes, please." Her hands, finally freed, went to the back of Dev's head to bring his mouth to her breast. He flicked his tongue over it mercilessly until she was gasping. When she pushed her pussy harder into him, he pulled back. She made a frustrated sound.

"Oh, I'm sorry," he said, looking down at her face. He was pleased to see that her pupils were dilated with need. "Was there something else you wanted?"

"There sure is, rock star. Your tongue." She brought his hand down to her panties. He could feel her wetness through the thin fabric, sending another jolt straight to his cock. "Lick my pussy just like that."

He hooked his fingers around her thong, and she eagerly raised her bottom off the sofa. He slid the silky triangle down to her ankles. She was beautiful down there, too, a wet dream come true. "You mean right here?" he teased, hovering his hand an inch above her pussy.

She drew toward it like a magnet. "*Yes*, right there," she gasped, grabbing his fingers and pushing them inside her. The intoxicating moan that escaped her lips was almost his undoing, but it was nothing compared to the feel of her warm wetness. *Jesus.*

It was time. But his body wanted to rush forward and pull back at the same time to prolong the delicious tension.

Sliding his hands under her ass, Dev trailed his tongue up the inside of her thigh. When he reached the tense muscle that led straight to heaven, he stopped, making her wait for one more torturous moment. Then he flicked his tongue across her clit. "God, you're sweeter than a strawberry," he whispered. Before long, he found the exact pressure that brought those arousing moans of pleasure to his ears.

"Please, Dev. *More, more, more—*" Kiki gasped. He saw her hands open and close, open and close, like it was the last part of her body she had control over. Then she started to tremble, and he knew she was dangerously close. He pulled away from her. "Oh, no you don't. Not without my cock inside you."

Her eyes were wild with desire. "Give it to me. Now, Dev. *Fuck me.*"

He couldn't have waited any longer if his life depended on it. Kneeling on the sofa with his hips at her eye level, he let his shorts drop to his knees. Her hips, which were squirming on the sofa in anticipation, stilled when she set eyes on his cock. "That's a very nice instrument you have there, rock star."

"Just wait till you feel it," he said, rolling on the condom he'd snagged from an old stash on his way in the door.

"I'm dying to," she sighed, back to gyrating her hips. He grasped them firmly to stop her, gripping her with the same claiming energy he felt charging through his cells. Her eyes widened a bit, and then her face relaxed into a smile. "My God, where did you come from?"

"I've been wondering the same thing about you," he said, letting her feel his weight on top of her. "You ready?"

"Never readier."

He wanted to go slowly, but his consuming need for her halted that idea in its tracks. *Next time*, he thought above the roaring in his head. He positioned himself and entered her in one forceful thrust.

"That's it," Kiki moaned. "God, yes. That's it. *That's it!*"

It felt heavenly. Better than he'd even imagined. It took all of his control not to drive himself forward in pursuit of his own pleasure, and he could tell by her face that she'd been transported to a similar place. As he moved, her legs went around his waist and her hands went to his ass, pushing him in deeper. He could already feel a thin sheen of sweat coating his body, the result of passion and forced restraint. It felt so good that he never wanted it to end, he wanted to fuck her until his party was over and the guests had cleared out and morning came. And then he wanted to do it all over again.

"Fuck me harder, Dev," Kiki cried breathlessly, her eyes hooking into his like talons. "Give me everything you have. *Everything. Please.*"

She's there with me, Dev thought triumphantly.

His to bring to the same heights of ecstasy he knew he was about to rise to. At his mercy.

Or was he at hers?

He slid a hand up her neck and over the bump of her slightly pointed chin. When her lips parted, he pushed his fingers inside her mouth. She made sweet sounds of greed as she sucked them. He quickened his pace, feeling the promising heat build at his center. Her moans spurred him on as their bodies slid, skin against skin. They were too perfect together. As different as their bodies were, they were made to move as one, made to leave each other gasping over and over again. And it made no sense that he was thinking that way. Who was this woman he suddenly wanted to know everything about, to feel the same desire that was consuming him? An hour ago Kiki had been a temptation, half an hour ago an object of lustful anticipation, ten minutes ago the best fuck he could remember. But now, as she pitched beneath him with a sharp cry and her pussy tightened hard enough to bring him over the edge with her, all that filled his head were three little words: *more of her.*

CHAPTER ONE

"EARTH TO DEV," Alex said, waving a hand in front of his face. "Nicola will be here in a few minutes. You want another beer?"

Like an earsplitting record scratch, Dev's mind snapped back to the moment: Pablo's bar, late afternoon on the patio, a casual drink with his little brother.

And two days before his descent into hell.

Remembering that night with Kiki had been so much more pleasant—even if it did fill his entire body with frustrated, overheated longing.

"Sure," Dev said to the waiter, trying not to look over his shoulder as he slid his bottle across the table. Because that was where the bar was, which also happened to be where Kiki worked. Not that she was here today—ever since their night together three weeks ago, she seemed to have developed the magical power of avoidance. And on a three-square-mile island that they both called home, that was nothing short of miraculous.

"Hey," Alex said, working his thumbnail under his beer label. "Did I tell you Brissoli's being sued? By one of your party guests—the son of the judge, I think."

"Good for him," Dev said dully. It wasn't the first time he'd wondered if things might have turned out differently with Kiki if Brissoli had never happened. It should have been a perfect night—a gathering of Dev's friends, along with Alex and his girlfriend Nicola, to celebrate his thirty-sixth birthday. The same night he'd been with Kiki. That part had been a dream, but the next morning they'd all been pitched into a cold and dark reality. John Brissoli, hungry for fodder for his celebrity-chasing website, had found the perfect target with Moretta. This tiny island of only ninety-two estates was where celebrities came to get away from the spotlight, and they paid dearly for that privacy, but occasionally the bottom-feeders still crawled onto land. Brissoli had not only crashed Dev's party, he'd managed to get photos of several of the guests in compromising situations. Drugs, sloppy drunkenness, sex in risky places—he caught all of it that night, including footage of Dev and Kiki's encounter in the studio. In the end he, Kiki and Alex had managed to head the disaster off, but it had taken a serious toll on all of them. Dev didn't think it was any coincidence that he'd barely laid eyes on Kiki since.

"Just in time. I ordered you a margarita," Alex said, looking up to greet Nicola. She kissed him passionately on the mouth and sank down into a chair between the two men. Dev gave her a quick grin to hide his irritation, which had nothing to do with Nicola herself. A month ago Alex had come to Moretta on business and ended up meeting his dream girl. It wasn't that Dev wasn't happy for them, it was just that things were so damned simple for Alex: meet a woman, decide she was the one, cue happily-ever-after.

Things could never be that easy for Dev. Being the fifth-bestselling recording artist of all time had always made relationships complex. In the beginning the female fans had done the trick, but he'd left that scene behind a while ago. Sure, he still let them hang around, but it was more out of habit—and loneliness, if he was completely honest with himself—than anything else. A stretch of celibacy had followed after that, when he found himself less willing to spend time with anyone he saw as temporary. Ready for a real relationship but without the right woman to fill the role, and that mostly came down to a matter of trust. Finding someone he wanted to go to bed with every night was one thing, but in his experience, finding a woman who wouldn't fuck with either his head or his money was an even bigger problem.

Until Kiki. The girl who'd handled the sex-tape scandal like a pro, who clearly had no interest in fame or fast money, who'd been in his corner every step of the way. The girl he'd broken his year of celibacy for, who drove him to obsessive, cock-stiffening thoughts every night when he tried to sleep.

It was torturous.

"Alex tells me you're off on tour in a few days," Nicola said, plucking the menu from between the salt and pepper shakers.

Dev felt himself crash down to earth yet again. *The tour.* His heart slammed once, twice in his chest. "Yep," he said with simulated lightness. "Back to the grind."

"We'll miss you."

"Speak for yourself." Alex grinned.

"Aren't you supposed to be gone?" Dev asked his brother in annoyance.

"Nicola keeps asking me the same thing," Alex said, cupping a hand around her face. "I'm still trying to convince her to move back to LA with me."

Dev's beer had arrived. He took a long swig and set the bottle back on the table, aiming his gaze at the view beyond the patio to calm his roiling gut. The clear Caribbean Sea lapped gently at the sandy white shore. Palm trees swayed to the mellow reggae music coming from the bar's speakers. It should have been enough to soothe anyone's frayed nerves, but none of it worked on Dev. He may have lived in paradise, but his mind was in hell.

His phone started vibrating on the table. He glanced down at the screen and almost laughed out loud. *Bix Jenner.* The guy's timing was uncanny. Flipping his overgrown dark hair out of his face,

Dev grabbed his phone and stood up. "Bix. Give me some good news," he said as he strode toward the end of the deck.

"I didn't need Viagra to bang my wife last night" was Bix's gravelly response.

"Not quite what I had in mind," Dev replied with a grimace. Bix had managed Dev's career since the day he'd called him up seventeen years ago and congratulated him for attracting the interest of the best manager in the business. Despite his immodesty, Bix's claim wasn't without truth, and Dev trusted him with his life. But Bix's crass manner came with the territory, and even on a good day it grated on Dev's nerves.

"You never did appreciate real humor, Stone."

"It's not that you're not funny, it's that I don't believe you," Dev responded dryly, hooking a flip-flop over the railing.

"You're goddamn killing me. How about this, then—Jerry Farr's guy is looking to move on. Said he'd take on the assistant job."

Dev nearly dropped his phone. "What the fuck are you talking about? Vanessa's got it covered," he said, referring to his assistant of two years.

A beat. "You're kidding me. She hasn't told you?"

"Told me *what*?"

"She quit. Sent her notice in three days ago. She really didn't—?"

"*Quit?* Why the hell would she do that?"

"Wouldn't give a reason. But between you and me, I heard she's moving to France with her boyfriend."

Dev slapped a hand to his forehead. Vanessa was the best assistant he'd had in a long time, and with their high burnout rate they were hard to come by. "Nice of her to clue me in. We kick off rehearsals in two days!"

"You don't have to tell me. Lucky for you, your fairy godfather found you a solution before you even knew you had a problem."

"I've met Jerry's guy—he's a wet freaking noodle."

"A noodle's better than jack shit."

"Is that what your wife says, too?"

"Screw you, Stone. He'll get the job done."

Dev shook his head tiredly. "I'll have to think about it." He paused, considering his next question. When it came to his career, offers went one way—they came to him. But it was making him crazy that a producer had recently dangled a carrot and then never followed through. "Listen, you ever hear from Larry Weatherby again? He seemed pretty hot for me to write for a few of his artists a couple months ago."

"Nah. Reality probably kicked in—someone as big as you, he had to know it was a long shot. Besides, you've got the tour to focus on now."

Dev suppressed a sigh. He'd started his career by writing songs for other artists until Bix had taken him under his wing and brought him into the spotlight, insisting that Dev was way too talented and easy on the eyes to keep hidden. Bix's promises of fame and fortune had all delivered, but sometimes Dev wondered if he would have been better off staying where he'd been. Even a platinum album at the age of twenty hadn't settled the beast of anxiety he tangled with onstage each night. The voracious crowds he'd dreamed of as a kid had turned out to be the stuff of nightmares. It wasn't always like that, of course. When he managed to control his nerves, the adrenaline high from a great show could leave him buzzed for hours afterward, better than any drug. But more often than not, touring meant sleepless nights of worry, a hammering heartbeat and cold shakes as bad as any junkie's.

"Listen, Stone, I know what's on your mind, okay?" Bix continued, as if he were right inside Dev's head. "And I want you to take all that worry and put it into Uncle Bix's back pocket. We'll handle it—you and me. Don't we always?"

"Sure," Dev said flatly. It was true—Bix was the only person in the entire world who knew the price Dev paid to get up on that stage night after night, and he made sure he had everything he needed to get through it.

"I'll see you in London. And, hey—nice job on the *Rolling Stone* piece. If that doesn't put you down in history as rock god of the century, I don't know what will. People are eating up the new album. They

love it. They love you, and don't you goddamn forget it."

"Thanks, man," Dev said, and hung up. He knew
Bix's assurances should make him feel better. In a
world being taken over by rap, EDM and sugary pop,
Under My Skin, his tenth rock album, was selling
almost as well as his first. His career was a resound-
ing success, the one thing in his life that he'd always
been able to depend on. And he knew he had to take
the good with the bad; it was time for him to go out
there and be a superstar again.

Back at his table, Alex and Nicola were deep in
conversation and his beer was still waiting for him.
Dev traced a finger through the condensation. *Enjoy
it while you can*, he thought. In a few days he'd have
to stop drinking altogether if he was going to get
through his tour alive. He brought the bottle to his
lips.

Six weeks of anxiety-filled days and nights. A
woman he couldn't get out of his head. And now
no assistant.

Dev drank long and deep.

Victoria O'Hare, Real Estate Agent.

Sitting in her golf cart outside Pablo's, Kiki
Becker stared down at the woman's face on her
phone. Blue eyes under wispy brows, a ski-jump
nose and reddish bobbed hair. Did Kiki bear a resemblance to her, or was she just trying to see some-

thing that wasn't there? Not knowing the answer to that question had been driving her crazy since she'd come across the photo a few days ago. A search of the website hadn't revealed anything further about her other than her recent home sales, and there was nothing else on the entire internet about any Victoria O'Hare who looked like this woman. Her picture mocked Kiki, daring her to reach out—which was completely out of the question.

Kiki clicked her phone off and shoved it into her handbag. The emptiness swelled in her chest, spread to her belly, threatened to spill tears. But she would not succumb to it. She swung her legs out of her golf cart and walked toward the entrance to Pablo's. It had taken all of her strength to drag herself to work, but at least today she had a plan. Three weeks of feeling down in the dumps, tossing and turning through the night and mainlining junk food had been more than enough for her. It was time to accept that there would be no encore to her encounter with Dev Stone and move on with her life. And she would do it the best way she knew how: by getting laid tonight.

Entering the noisy bar, Kiki did a quick scan for potential victims. Several heads turned her way that she supposed would do the trick. Eventually, she'd choose one on the criteria of being unattached, relatively sober and preferably on their way off the island in the next twenty-four hours. It was how she'd operated since she'd moved to Moretta after her divorce two years ago. Just because Dev Stone had

brought her earth-shattering pleasure for one un-
forgettable evening didn't mean she couldn't return
to her old ways.

Dev—*damn him.* Kiki pushed his face out of her
mind as she lifted the door to the bar, praying he
wasn't here. She'd managed to avoid him almost
completely since their night together had blown up
in their faces, and she planned on keeping it that way.
If she couldn't have him for herself, the last thing
she needed was a direct comparison to any other
guy in this place.

Tossing her handbag under the bar, Kiki stole a
quick glance at her reflection in the mirrored back
wall. She'd spent the past three weeks in shorts and
baggy T-shirts, forgoing her daily makeup routine
and throwing her long hair into careless ponytails.
With her plan in place this morning she'd made a
bit of an effort, but the dark smudges under her
eyes still revealed her truth. She looked like shit.
Her skin was pale, and she'd put on a few pounds.
It was the one thing she hated about her roommate,
Nicola—while she lost her appetite under stress,
Kiki reached for the late-night cookies as if she
could tame the ugly monster that raged inside her
with refined sugar. Crouching behind the bar, she
slicked on some lip gloss, adjusted the straps of her
sundress and stood up.

"Strawberry."

Jesus. Dev was standing right in front of her.

Kiki's groin went mushy as the memory of their

entangled bodies came crashing over her. His kiss, demanding and soft at the same time. His eyes on hers as he'd latched his mouth on to her clit. His beautiful body and perfect cock, his urgent breath as he'd driven into her again and again, ripping sweet cries of ecstasy from her throat. The way he'd touched her like it *meant* something. As they'd lain on the sofa recovering, she'd seen it in his face—the same question she wanted to ask him: *When can we do this again?* The answer had been twenty minutes later, but even that hadn't been enough for her. In a few short hours Dev turned her into an insatiable sex monster. She'd wanted to break all of her no-strings rules for him, and looking back, she was almost grateful for the near scandal that had derailed them the next morning. That whole experience had sucked her libido dry, which had probably saved her fucking life. Because Dev Stone was dangerous, addictive and a straight arrow to only one thing: heartbreak.

"Hey, rock star," Kiki tossed out, reaching for a bar cloth to occupy her hands. But it was no use—she could feel her fingers trembling as they swept past his. Her cheeks were warm. She was certain her nipples were straining against her dress.

"You've been busy," he said as he leaned into the counter. Those aqua eyes. That square jaw. That dark lock of hair that always flopped over his brow. She could smell his spicy aftershave, the same one that had been on her skin the next morning. *Damn it.*

"Busy avoiding you," Kiki said, scrubbing hard at an invisible spot. "It's a full-time job."

"Then I'll talk to your boss and get you fired."

"Very funny," she said when a snappy reply failed her. His eyes were all over her, *devouring* her—why? Dev was a rock star god who had his choice of any woman on earth. From where she stood, Kiki could throw a champagne glass at at least three gorgeous household-name females. And she was a divorced executive-assistant-turned-bartender from Atlanta, guaranteed to fall short of any man's expectations.

"I was hoping you'd be in today," he said.

"Oh, yeah?" she replied over the sound of the blood rushing through her ears. "And why is that?"

"You want the real reason, or the PC one?"

She stopped scrubbing. "Let's start with the PC one."

"My tour assistant quit today. I'm just gonna say it—I'm a little desperate for a new one. Any chance you'd consider taking the job?"

She put a hand out to steady the martini glass she'd almost knocked sideways. "The job?"

"Yeah." Dev's fingers skimmed hers as he reached out to catch the glass with her. She pulled back as they buzzed with electricity. "You'd be perfect for it."

"I pop beer caps for a living, in case you hadn't noticed."

"But you used to be an executive assistant."

"I worked with CEOs. I don't even know what a—*a rock star assistant* does."

"That's easy." He winked. "Whatever I want you to."

Her belly flopped over. "That's what I'm afraid of."

"Why, Kiki? What are you so scared of?" Dev's aqua eyes were unblinking. He leaned closer to her and lowered his voice. "I haven't been able to get you out of my head. It's been three weeks, and I can still feel you under me. That's the real reason I wanted to see you again, Kiki. I leave in two days, and I want to take the memory of you with me. I want to be inside you again. Don't tell me you don't want the same thing."

Her knees unlocked, threatening to collapse her onto the floor. God, did he really just say that? She could feel her face overheating as she measured honesty against fake indifference. As usual, honesty won. "I do, Dev, trust me. But that's not a road I can travel down."

"Why not?"

"Because—because it's just not. It's complicated. And accepting a job where I had to work anywhere within a one-mile radius of you would pretty much undo me."

"I feel like things would have been different if Brissoli had never happened."

"They wouldn't have been."

"Why not?"

"Stop asking me that."

He shook his head. "Even if I can't have you, I still want your skills. What if I promised to keep anything personal out of it?"

Kiki laughed. "After what happened between us? I think that's beyond wishful thinking."

"Who said anything about wishing for it?"

"You see?" Kiki stopped the banter with a loud thud of a wine bottle. She poured a glass out and slid it to the end of the bar for pickup.

"I can be a perfect gentleman when I set my mind to it," Dev persisted. "Even with you."

"Jesus, would you stop? So I get to see you with your groupies instead? No, thanks."

"It won't be like that. How about this…" He laid his hands flat on the counter. "The first leg of the tour is six weeks long. You're the boss. We keep it strictly business unless you decide otherwise."

When she didn't come up with an immediate protest, he pushed on. "Listen—I'll pay you whatever you want. Have I mentioned where we're going? We start in London. Then Paris, Italy, Germany. And then onto Australia. Sydney, Brisbane—"

Sydney. The word bounced around in Kiki's head. Home to Webber Real Estate Agency, employer of Victoria O'Hare. A chance to solve the mystery. A chance to fill the empty ache that had been gouged into her at six years old.

But only maybe. Only if Victoria O'Hare was really who Kiki wanted her to be, which she probably wasn't. And then there was the matter that she would be halfway around the world with Dev, a man she wanted to make her sex slave for all eternity. Who, in her most secret dreams, sang a song of his undying love to her.

Very bad idea.

"…anyway, you need a change," Dev was saying.

Kiki felt her jaw tighten. Even if she did, the only person who was going to make that call was her. "How would you know what I need?"

"You moved from Atlanta to LA to go to university. You changed your major halfway through. You came here on your own two years ago. You switched from being an executive assistant to a bartender. Clearly you like to mix things up."

Kiki couldn't help her stunned look. On the night of his birthday party, Dev had been surrounded by groupies. Kiki hadn't imagined he would even glance at her, but his eyes had stroked her all the way from her face down to her toes, lighting her body up like she'd been zapped with electricity. After that he'd suggested a walk on his private beach, and he hadn't even made a move on her—instead he'd actually *talked* to her, asked her about her life and her family, until she'd grown weary of waiting and gone in for the kiss. She hadn't imagined that he'd retained anything she'd told him, and yet he'd just recited most of it back to her. She squared her shoulders.

"So, what—you think I'm just going to drop everything because Dev Stone asked me to? Sorry, but I'm not one of your worshipping fans."

"Obviously." He waited, sexy grin still in place, as if her protests were mere pebbles to kick away on her inevitable path to acceptance.

God, he was actually serious. It was true that Kiki had been a career girl once upon, making her way steadily up the ladder in LA, but that was before her ex-husband had crushed her dream of marital bliss and made building a new life her number one priority. She could see returning to the real world one day and starting over, but making the switch as Dev's assistant? With him night and day, in hotel rooms with him, in his dressing room, on his tour bus, seeing him perform in all his hot glory?

"No way," Kiki said firmly. "And that other thing you mentioned? That's not going to happen, either. You're leaving in two days, and I'm going to make it my mission to stay away from you until then. Just so you know."

Dev gave her a slightly amused look, as if he knew something she didn't, and then he slapped a hand down on the bar. "The offer is open until Tuesday morning."

As Kiki watched him walk away and disappear into the crowd, she finally began to breathe normally again. His face remained etched into her brain, as did the words she knew she'd turn over in her head over and over again in bed tonight: *I want to be inside you again.* Dev Stone, the man who had ruined her for all others.

So much for getting laid tonight, Kiki thought.

CHAPTER TWO

ONLY SIX COOKIES LEFT? How the hell had that happened?

Kiki stared guiltily at the Chips Ahoy! package beside the open, crumb-riddled jar of Fluff on her coffee table. She didn't even have the decency to binge on *quality* junk food—not that she had much choice. Her monthly shopping trip to neighboring Barbados was due next week, and in the meantime she was forced to make do with the paltry selection at the island's tiny, overpriced grocery store.

A key rattled in the front door of her cottage and Kiki's roommate, Nicola, walked in, trailed by Alex.

Kiki reached for another chocolate chip cookie.

Nicola gave Kiki a teasing smile as she tossed her work satchel onto the kitchen counter. "I thought you said you were cutting back?"

"This *is* me cutting back," Kiki said grumpily, sinking her teeth into the dry, crumbly sweetness. She hoped to hell that enough time had passed since her recent crying jag to allow her face to return to normal. Nicola was the best friend she'd ever had; the women had known each other for a decade, meeting in LA long before Nicola had followed her to Moretta six months ago. And Kiki was genuinely thrilled that her friend had found true love with Alex, but she really didn't feel like explaining herself to him or anyone else right now. She must have still looked a mess, though, because Alex cleared his throat as he stood at the door. "Nicola, didn't you say you were out of coffee? I'll just run out and grab some. Need anything else?"

"Nothing that comes from the store," Nicola said, giving him a lingering kiss before he slipped out the door.

To her horror, Kiki felt tears pricking at her eyes again. What was it about her friend falling madly in love that made Kiki feel like a total loser? Just a month ago she'd been proud of her attachment-free sex life. And then Dev had come along. Now she knew for sure that she could feel the kind of mind-blowing passion she thought only existed for others, like Nicola.

And Kiki couldn't have him.

"Okay," Nicola said, kicking her flip-flops off and dropping down on the sofa beside Kiki. "Talk to me."

"It won't help," Kiki said stubbornly, stuffing the last of the cookie into her mouth.

"Neither will eating your way into oblivion," Nicola pointed out, using her toe to push the package away from Kiki. "Or keeping everything bottled up inside."

Kiki snorted. "It's kind of what I do—you should know that by now. Talking might help some people, but it doesn't help me."

"I guess that explains why we've been living together for nearly seven months and you still haven't told me why your marriage ended," Nicola said archly.

"I told you exactly what happened. Jack was a world-class prick," Kiki responded, turning her face away. No—*that* was not a conversation Kiki was willing to have right now, if ever. "Anyway, it's not true that I don't tell you anything. I told you all about my sad-luck childhood that night we drank way too much tequila. And it didn't make me feel any better, FYI. Just saying."

"That's because you had a hangover the size of planet Earth the next day. Just saying," Nicola retorted. "Now tell me what's going on with you. You've been acting weird ever since that night at Dev's—which is understandable," she added quickly. "I mean, I was traumatized, too. But it does make me wonder, is it those slimeballs that've still got you down, or is it Dev?"

"*Dev?* I'm a little smarter than that, but thanks. Even if I was looking for a boyfriend—which I'm definitely not—he's pretty much the last person on earth I'd get involved with."

"Oh, yeah? And why is that?"

"*Why?* Are you even—"

"Dev is a good guy, Kiki—he's Alex's brother! And you like him." She shook her head. "I mean, have you ever noticed that the term *rock star* is not synonymous with single? Have you ever noticed that they get married and have kids just like everyone—"

Kiki felt herself flush. "Oh, my God! Will you please shut the fuck up?" She took a deep breath. Dev was only one of her problems, and Nicola clearly wasn't going to let up until she spilled *something* to her. "Okay, fine. It's…it's my mother."

Nicola looked at her in shock. "Your *mother*?"

Kiki nodded rapidly to stop the threatening tears. There were only three people she'd ever shared the story of her mother with—her ex-husband, her high school best friend Laina, and, during a late-night drinkfest years ago in LA, Nicola. "Yes. I… I think I might have found her."

Nicola jumped up excitedly. "Oh, my God! Are you serious? That's amazing! How? Where is she? Have you gotten in touch—"

"No, no, no." Kiki waved an impatient hand. "This just came up. I found a website for a real estate agency, and one of the agents is named Victoria O'Hare. That's her maiden name, and it's possible she stopped going by Vicky. And—I don't know, but there's a photo of her. The last picture I have of her is from twenty-four years ago, but…this woman has red hair." Kiki shook her head and then dropped it into her hands. "I'm terrified, Nic," she said through her fingers. "Freaking terrified. I wish I never looked. I didn't—for two years I didn't, and then I had to go and start again."

"That's because she's half of you," Nicola said gently, placing a hand on Kiki's arm. "You moved here to heal, but this place also allowed you to bury the things in your life you didn't want to look at. But they come back—they always come back. You need closure with her."

"But what if she wants nothing to do with me? I'm too scared to email her. What if she doesn't write back? Or what if I scare her off and she goes into hiding again? What—what if she just doesn't want to hear from me? I mean, she knows my name—*she named me*! If she wanted anything to do with me, she could have reached out anytime. It's been twenty-four years, and *nothing*."

"Oh, honey..." Nicola reached for her hand. "You for a daughter? She doesn't know what she's missing."

Tears flooded Kiki's eyes. "But that's the whole point—she *does*! She's the one who left me, remember? I was six years old. She knew exactly what she was doing."

"But she didn't leave you alone," Nicola reminded her. "She knew you had your father, and he's an amazing dad. Listen..." She tightened her grip on Kiki's hand. "You need to meet with her in person—just show up at her work and force her to see you.

I'll go with you, okay? Where is she? She's not still in Atlanta, is she?"

"That's the thing." Kiki shook her head in disbelief. "This woman is in *Sydney*, of all places. As in Australia. Which makes me think it can't be her—why would she travel so far, unless it was to get as far away from me as possible?"

Nicola looked thoughtful. "Well, that is strange," she admitted. "But it could happen. People end up all over the world for all sorts of different reasons. Just look at us—a couple of girls from the States. Who would have thought we'd end up living in the middle of the Caribbean?"

"Yeah, I guess so…" When Kiki pulled her T-shirt up to dab at her eyes, Nicola went to the kitchen to grab her a paper towel. Then she sank down on the sofa beside her again. "What?" Kiki asked when she felt her friend's eyes on the side of her face.

"Just waiting, that's all. There's something else you're not telling me."

"My God, you're a pain in the ass." Kiki sighed deeply. "Okay. This is kind of crazy, but Dev offered me a job today. His tour assistant just quit and he needs a new one. Would you please stop fucking smiling?" Kiki threw her hands up in annoyance. "I said no, of course. But here's the crazy part. His tour will take him to Sydney. And I—I really can't afford to go otherwise. I mean, to spend that kind of money to go and check out a remote possibility? It's just not going to happen on my bartending tips."

"So it's a sign!" Nicola said, clapping her hands together. "Come on—you have to accept!"

"But I can't! It's—it's *Dev*! We had a…a *thing*, and that messes everything up. I mean, watching him get swarmed by groupies for weeks on end? No thank you. And besides, I have a life here…" she ended weakly, thinking that *did have a life here* felt more accurate right now.

"Listen, sweetie. I know it might not be the perfect scenario, but this is a lifetime opportunity. Eventually you have to get back to the real world anyway, and this is your chance to start a new career. Remember— the Kiki I met in LA was a go-getter with big career goals! But more important, this is a chance to find your mother, and you can't pass that up. No matter what may or may not happen between you and Dev," she added when she saw the protest forming on Kiki's face.

Oh, God. Nicola was right, Kiki knew, but just the thought of it—leaving the safety of her island world and her easygoing job, working side by side with Dev, confronting the woman who had abandoned her as a child—was enough to tie her stomach in knots.

"You are a survivor," Nicola went on, her voice strong with emotion. "And you've never been one to take the safe route. Even if I don't know the details of what happened between you and Jack, I know that by moving here and shaking your life up, you took a huge risk to find happiness. This might scare you more than anything you've ever done, but fear won't stop you. It never has."

"Thanks for the pep talk, Brené Brown." Kiki smiled weakly as a knock sounded at the door. Knowing it was Alex back from the store, she quickly flicked her tears away and ran a hand over her hair. Nicola rose to greet him, but though the aqua eyes belonging to the man on the landing were identical to Alex's, this man had a power over Kiki that his brother didn't have.

Dev.

"Hi there," he said, transferring the Beats he was wearing on his ears to around his neck. His gaze rested on Kiki, making her belly flop over. "I hope I'm not...?"

"No, it's fine," Kiki said. Nicola stepped aside, and Dev walked over the threshold. There was a rock star in her house. Kiki almost laughed aloud as she cast a glance around, comparing her tiny combined kitchen, living and dining area to his sprawling beachside home.

"Listen," he said. "I just—there was something I didn't say to you today, and I couldn't leave without being honest."

"I think you were pretty damned honest," Kiki said as she stood. "If I recall."

Nicola grabbed her handbag from the coffee table. "I'll just—"

"No," Dev said quickly. "You're her best friend, and I'm fine for you to hear this. Just..." He took a breath. "A tour is a really intense experience, and I need the right people to get me through it. I know I've just sprung this on you out of nowhere, but I want you to know that the real reason I want you with me is because I trust you. And that's hard for me to come by."

Kiki absorbed his words. "But…you don't know me well enough to trust me."

"I know, and that's the crazy thing. I can't explain it, but I felt it the moment I met you." He shook his head. "I'm making this weird for you. I don't want you to accept because you feel obligated to. But if you do, it's your terms, okay? Business only—if that's what you want."

Kiki swallowed hard. There were so many reasons to accept and only one reason not to. But that reason was huge, because it was Dev. It would take every bit of her strength to make it to the end of six weeks with her virtue intact, not to mention her heart. The only way this would work would be for her to develop a resolve of steel.

Dev was looking at her with something close to pleading in his eyes. *It's still a no*, she opened her mouth to say, but it didn't come out. "I, uh…"

"—accept your offer, for double my regular salary," Nicola coached her with a mischievous grin. "Right, Kiki?"

Kiki nodded slowly as Dev's mouth turned upward into a grin. Holy shit—was she actually going to do this? "I guess so," she said hesitantly. "But I'll have to meet up with you in a week or so. I have to tie things up here, make sure my boss can get someone to cover for me…" She stopped when she saw the sheepish expression on Dev's face. "What is it?"

He squeezed his eyes shut as if he were in pain, and then he directed them at the floor. "I might have just come from talking to him. And I might have also arranged to cover your portion of the rent while you're away. Which means you can theoretically fly out with me on Tuesday…" He finally lifted his eyes to Kiki, cringing as if he expected her to hit him.

Which was exactly what she should do. She jumped up furiously. "You have got some nerve. Let's make one thing perfectly clear, okay? You are *not* in charge in my life. And if you ever pull something like this again, I'll be on the first flight back here—no matter where in the world we are."

"Of course," Dev agreed. "I'm sorry, I just, um… so this means I'll see you on Tues—?"

Kiki made an exasperated sound in her throat and marched toward her bedroom, slamming the door behind her. Then she leaned against it, trying to process what she'd just committed to. A new job. The possibility of finding her mother. And Dev… *oh, God.*

Just breathe. You'll be fine. Just breathe.

Dev repeated the mantra in his head as he stood in the bathroom of the private Learjet 40 en route to London. But the familiar feeling of panic was setting in even earlier than it usually did. He hadn't even begun rehearsals and he was already a mess. A month ago he'd entertained the idea that he might get through this tour drug-free, but the futility of that thought was now all too obvious. In his whole career, he hadn't made it through a single performance without some kind of helper.

No point in suffering with relief so close at hand, Dev thought. Reaching into his jeans pocket, he pulled out the bottle of pills. He spilled them onto his hand and counted five. This batch was left over from his last tour, and the label informed him that the tablets had expired a month ago. But they would do until Bix gave him a new supply in a few days. Dev could always count on Bix to take care of the details. Sure, he could have gone to a doctor for the prescription himself, but that was how secrets got out—and this was one he planned on taking to the grave.

He dropped four pills back into the bottle and held one in his hand. Xanax. His little helper for the past three years, ever since he'd built up enough tolerance to Valium to make it lose its effect. On show night he'd mix it with two propranolol to get himself on-stage, and more often than not he'd need to take an Ambien to come down afterward—the classic combo for anxiety-ridden housewives and celebrities that more often than not led to addiction.

But Dev couldn't worry about that right now.

He knew that as long as he kept his helpers under

control he'd be fine. He always got off the stuff as soon as his tours ended, and it wasn't like he was doing *real* drugs. His were legal, regulated, doctor prescribed. He even avoided alcohol when he was on them like the label said. He was nothing like many of his peers, who combined booze with the hard stuff night after night. He may have done some of that indulging in his early days, but now he couldn't imagine taking anything like that before a show—the drugs revved him up enough to keep him awake for hours afterward. That's where the Ambien came in, and when he didn't take it he paid the price. The dead of night was when the dark monster of his reality came crashing into his bed. *Other musicians can handle the stage, so why can't you? How long do you think you can go on like this before you're hooked?* the monster asked him with its ember eyes. Having a warm body in his bed had always helped keep the monster away—until about a year ago, when the emptiness he felt each morning when he awoke to women with names long forgotten was worse than any empty bed.

And then she'd come along. Kiki. Not only the hottest fuck of his life, but gorgeous, independent, totally unaffected and unimpressed by his career. Offering her the job had probably been a mistake. He'd be up close with her day after day, which meant his secret was in danger—and she was the last person on earth he wanted to discover it. He hadn't been thinking straight that day in the bar, when he'd been overtaken with lust at the sight of her. And then he'd laid all that shit on her about trust. All of it was true, but it was a wonder she hadn't run away screaming. People didn't just come out and say things like that when they barely knew each other, but it was like she'd messed with all of his wires to turn him into a raging, sex-starved honesty machine. And the real hell of it was that she hadn't said no to his strictly business proposal. All the same, he promised himself, he would leave it up to her—no matter how wild she drove him.

Dev left the bathroom, slipped the bottle of pills into his carry-on and walked back to his seat. Kiki was sitting exactly where he'd left her, deeply engrossed in her notes. God, but she was something. He knew she had to be at least a little dazzled by the private plane, but she hadn't even commented on it. She may have been fiery, but she was also down-to-earth. Grounded. The exact opposite of him.

"It's still four hours to London," he said, sliding into the leather seat across from her. "It wouldn't kill you to take a break."

"I have a lot to learn to get up to speed," she replied without looking up. "Now, where were we?"

"I was telling you about Bix. He'll meet us for the first show on Sunday night," Dev said, tapping two fingers on his armrest. They were seated across from each other with a small fold-down table between them. His legs were long enough that his knees would touch Kiki's if they both faced forward, but she had angled hers away from him into the aisle. She was wearing a simple black dress that screamed *First day on the new job*, but its conservative cut was hopeless at hiding her sexiness. She still had her eyes aimed at her notebook, so he let his eyes drift down to her bare legs.

The crazy thing was that Kiki wasn't even his regular type—he normally preferred his women tall and willowy. But Dev loved her tiny frame, the curve of her hips, the way her small breasts strained beneath her modest neckline. The way their bodies had moved that night had proven how perfect they were together. And now she was close enough to touch, not to mention all alone with him. When he thought about what they could be doing right now, what use they could make of the sleeping quarters—it was killing him.

"…road crew?"

He jerked his eyes up to find her looking at him expectantly, pen poised. Those wide blue eyes under delicately arched brows. That long hair falling over her breasts in a smooth curtain. The crease in her dress right between her legs.

Focus.

"Uh, yeah. You'll meet them in London," Dev said. "Scotty—my bassist—is flying in from Chicago today. He and Stuart will—"

"Stuart?" Kiki interrupted.

"My drummer. He's flying into London from Brussels."

"Got it. Speaking of which…" She lifted a sheet of paper up from the small table between them. "According to this itinerary, you're staying at The Connaught with the rest of the band. Is that a mistake? I'd imagine you'd want to stay at home while you're in town."

Damn—she didn't miss a thing. Dev had moved from LA to London a decade ago, but his Kings Cross penthouse felt less and less like home since he'd bought the house on Moretta. His flat screamed of the bachelor days and rock star nights of his twenties, and that just wasn't where his head was anymore. "It's just easier if the band is all together," he said, which also happened to be the truth. "I'll pop by at some point to make sure the place is still standing, pick up some clothes. By the way, we're only staying in hotels in London and Paris. After the Paris show we move to tour buses for the remainder of the European leg. Once we're in Australia we'll be in hotels again."

"I know. I've already confirmed all the bookings," she said, glancing down at her notes. "What about rehearsals? I don't see anything about that."

"The three of us will spend the rest of the week rehearsing at Ryder Studios. We already put in a good round a month ago, so we're pretty tight."

Tight. Good God, could he really not say such a banal word without thinking about how Kiki's pussy had felt around his cock? How old was he, fifteen? He seriously needed to get a grip, but now that the door had been opened, his cock was all in. All he could think about was stripping her down and fucking her until she screamed, flight crew be damned. He shifted in his seat to hide his raging erection. This line of thinking wasn't going to help anything.

The drone of the engine filled the silence as a flight attendant entered the cabin. "Something to drink, Mr. Stone?" she asked, holding out a cheese board.

"A club soda, please," Dev said, plucking a cracker and a wedge of Brie from the platter.

"What, no champagne?" Kiki asked without looking up. "Pretty impressive for a rock star."

If you only knew, Dev thought. "Would you please stop calling me that?"

"What? Impressive?" She looked up at him under long lashes, uncrossing and recrossing her legs. He caught a brief glimpse of zebra-print panties.

He was going to fucking lose it. He hit a button on his armrest, filling the cabin with the sound of Coldplay.

Kiki tilted her head at him. "You don't like silence, do you?"

Dev started. Didn't he? He'd never thought about it before. "I'm a musician. I think it makes sense that I enjoy listening to music."

Kiki gazed back at him until he felt like squirming. Her eyes held a knowing look, as if she could see all of his secrets. Like she knew shit about him that he didn't even know himself. No one had ever known him like that, and it was unnerving.

Suddenly she stood up and stretched her arms to the sides. "I didn't get much sleep last night. I'm going to try out my bed."

And with that she walked away, leaving Dev alone with his club soda and his tortured imagination.

CHAPTER THREE

BY THE TIME the night of the first show rolled around, Kiki was regretting the day she accepted her new job. The work was more demanding than she'd expected, but that wasn't the reason. She'd assumed Dev would slip into a different persona when he was in celebrity mode—high-maintenance, egotistical, absent, no longer interested in her. She was wrong. Dev was exactly the same guy he'd been on Moretta: fun, relaxed, kind to his staff, a natural leader. It seemed like he was everywhere she was, and he always had that heart-stopping sexy smile for her. In the hotel elevator. At the catering table. At the rehearsal studio. And now backstage, where he'd winked at her as he passed her in the hallway. Every time his eyes met hers she felt like she'd been electrified—which made keeping her boundaries in place even more important. She couldn't afford to weaken, especially now that she was on the road with him. Like it or not, Dev was a man she was willing to break her rules for, and Kiki knew exactly what would happen if she got involved with him—he'd leave her when he found out the truth about her, just like her ex-husband had.

So why hadn't she made this arrangement strictly business when she had the chance? He'd put it out there—*your terms*—but she'd left it alone. Dev was a man of his word, and she had to admit that a part of her hadn't wanted to shut that door completely.

She walked along the side of the hallway, trying to stay out of the human traffic jam. She knew Dev was in his dressing room. Her pulse quickened as she thought about the stage outfit she'd laid out for him an hour ago: a white button-down Armani shirt and black leather pants. The thought of seeing him onstage had her nerves on edge. But was it because she was about to witness the hottest performance on Earth, or because of what she was afraid might happen after it? Everyone knew that was when the groupies showed up. Dev might not flaunt them in her face, but she wasn't naive enough to think that one night with her had changed his ways forever.

She reached the main artery of the backstage area, which was controlled chaos. Roadies shouted orders to each other, organizers zipped around with clipboards and iPads in hand, a bored-looking caterer tapped away on her phone behind a table laden with food. A heavyset man shouted loudly into his cell phone while he paced inches from Kiki's toes. Scotty lounged on a nearby sofa, tossing Skittles into his mouth one by one while Stuart walked the floor in

front of him, tapping a beat out on an invisible drum
set. And above it all was the roar of the twenty thousand fans filing into London's largest concert venue,
O2 Arena.

Kiki was good at hiding her intimidation. Sinking down into a plastic chair, she took her phone out
to tick the day's tasks off: meals organized; media
interviews booked for the following day; assorted
shopping trips done; fan mail answered; backstage
photos posted to Instagram and Twitter; a Snapchat
story of the band warming up for the show made;
water, towels and snacks set out for the band.

She was about to click her phone off when it rang
in her hand. *Laina Rose.* Kiki grinned. Laina was
her best friend from high school, and the whole reason she'd moved to Moretta in the first place. Her
friend had grown up spending her vacations on the
island with her super-wealthy family, so when Kiki
called her in tears after Jack left her, Laina had come
to her rescue by offering her the guesthouse on her
parents' estate. Kiki had thought she'd spend a few
weeks there recovering, but instead she'd found herself getting a job at Pablo's and renting a staff cottage. Laina had visited her several times over the
years, always staying with Kiki instead of at her family estate. Laina was one of those rare people who
chose to separate herself from her family's wealth,
but Kiki knew there was more to the story than that.

Standing up, she glanced around for a quiet place

to talk. She hadn't spoken with her friend since she'd announced her engagement, one that Kiki proudly took credit for because it was she who'd introduced the pair back in Atlanta. Wedding chatter wasn't number one on Kiki's list right now, but a little girl talk might get her mind off things...like Dev.

Kiki dashed into an empty bathroom and closed the door behind her, dulling the sound of the mayhem. "Banger!" she said when she picked up, using Laina's old high school nickname.

"Mash," Laina replied dully.

Kiki gripped the phone. "What's wrong?"

A sniffle, and then she blurted, "He fucked another girl in our bed, Kiki."

Kiki's blood froze in her veins. *"What?"* she gasped.

"I caught them. And then he tried to blame it on me." Laina let out a choked sob.

Kiki slapped her hand down on the sink. "Oh, my God. The fucking *prick*! I am so, so sorry, honey."

"Me, too."

"And I introduced—"

"Stop. It's not your fault. It's—it's better this way. He said I was boring in bed, Kiki. It's better that I found out what a cocksucker he is now."

Kiki inhaled deeply to settle her boiling blood. What Jack had done to her had been scathing, but she couldn't imagine the intensity of what Laina had just experienced.

"Tell me what I can do for you, Laina. I'm not on Moretta right now, but I'm here for you. Do you need anything?"

"You mean besides something to castrate Ward with? No, I'm good. Just—I need to get away. Are you up for a visit?"

"Of course! Except that I'm away for another five weeks," she added guiltily. Laina had been a rock-solid friend to her when she desperately needed one, and it bothered her that she couldn't reciprocate in the same way.

There was a pause on Laina's end. "Five weeks? Where are you?"

Not now. Revealing where she was would lead to a conversation about Dev and/or her mother, and this wasn't the time or place. "Long story. This is about you, honey. Can you come in late November?"

"I'll have to check with my boss. She's a bit of a bitch."

At least her sense of humor was intact; Laina had started her own architecture firm two years ago. "That's not what I've heard about her," Kiki replied. Then she fell silent, wishing there was a sure way to convince her friend that everything would turn out fine. But she remembered what it was like to be in her shoes, and she knew that the only real cure was time.

And that as soon as she got over him, the next complication would enter her life.

"Ten minutes," a male voice crackled in Kiki's back pocket. Damn it—she'd forgotten about her walkie-talkie, and part of her job was to keep Dev on schedule. She killed the volume and turned her attention back to Laina.

"It's going to be alright, okay? I promise. And you are *not* boring in bed."

Laina managed a laugh. "How would you know?"

"Because Ward seems pretty damned boring himself, if you ask me. Someday you'll meet a *real* man, and…" Dev's face filled her head. That's what he was, wasn't he? One of only a few real men out there. Or maybe that was just what she wanted him to be.

"And what?"

"Nothing. You just focus on you right now, okay?"

"Okay," Laina sniffed.

After she hung up, Kiki made her way to Dev's door, preparing herself for the onslaught on her senses. And sure enough, her breath caught in her throat when he appeared. He looked every inch the rock god he was and more. His dark hair was mussed and his shirt was left open at the top, revealing a hint of his muscled chest. She could smell his after-shave, that ever-present reminder of the traces he'd left on her skin. Against her will, her eyes dropped to his leather pants. She felt a jolt shoot straight to her pussy at the sight of his generous bulge.

Stop it.

But her face was already flushed. Damn, but being a redhead was an unfair disadvantage.

Through the walls, the crowd had reached a fever pitch. *"Twitch! Twitch!"*

"It sounds like they're ready for you," Kiki managed. "What's that all about?"

Dev leaned against the doorway, arms crossed. "Just a nickname. Maybe because I like to play my guitar hard and fast."

His aqua eyes caressed her body, telling her exactly how he'd rather be applying those two adverbs. She could feel the heat creep down from her cheeks to her breasts.

Cool it.

She tried for a casual stance, hands in front pockets. "So, uh…you good to go? I mean, do you have a routine you like to do before you go onstage or anything? I've heard some musicians like to do scales, tai chi, snort a few lines, whatever…" She cringed as she trailed off. Did she really just say that? She was nervous as hell, and she always babbled and said stupid shit when she was nervous.

And yet Dev, the person who *should* be nervous, seemed perfectly calm. "Never readier," he replied with a wink—the same two words she'd spoken right before he drove his cock inside her for the first time. *Jesus.* He wasn't making this easy.

In her peripheral vision, Kiki saw a crew member

approach. "Hey, Chester," Dev said when he stopped near them.

"Hey. Bob was wondering if you wanted us to scout for you tonight. He just took a walk and said to let you know there's plenty of good material in the crowd."

"Nah, I'll pass. Just like I did on the last tour," Dev replied pointedly, his eyes never leaving Kiki's.

Kiki watched as Chester took his baseball cap off and replaced it on his head, turning the visor backward. Then he crossed his arms over his chest and rocked back on his heels, as if waiting for Dev to come to his senses. "You sure, man?"

"Sure of what—that he's the best goddamned musician since Springsteen?" a man said as he appeared beside Dev. Kiki felt herself stiffen. It was the heavy-set guy with the cell phone she'd noticed earlier. He wore his long white hair slicked back, and his paunch strained at his shirt buttons.

"Bix, it's about time," Dev said, giving the man a back-pounding embrace. "Bix, I'd like you to meet Kiki Becker. Kiki, Bix is my tour manager."

Kiki nodded. "Nice to meet you."

"Pleasure's mine," Bix replied, but his eyes only lit on her briefly. She watched as Chester cleared his throat, trying to remind Dev of his presence. It was an interesting hierarchy dance, Kiki observed— Chester was clearly at the bottom, and a minute ago she would have put Dev at the top. But Bix's entrance into the picture had made her less certain of that.

Dev turned to Chester. "Thanks, man—I'm all good."

"Hey, you're the boss." Chester shrugged and turned away. Bix's cell phone rang, and after he walked off, Kiki burst out laughing. "'Plenty of good material'?" she said to Dev. "I take it that's code for hot chicks."

"I would never use such a disrespectful term," Dev replied. "But yes. There is a certain tradition among certain musicians that involves inviting a certain type of female backstage. It's not something that interests me."

"No?"

"Anymore," he clarified with a smile.

Kiki gave him a skeptical look. "So all those lovely ladies I see you around the island with are— what, your sisters?"

He grinned. "Just because I let them hang out with me doesn't mean I let them into my bed. But point taken. Old habits die hard, I guess."

Kiki busied herself with adjusting her necklace. So she wasn't going to be tortured by the sight of him with another woman…not tonight, at least. But how long would he hold out? The guy was only human, after all.

"Listen," she said hesitantly. "I, um… I just want

you to know you don't have to do this. This is a professional relationship, and—"

"Is it?" His aqua eyes bored into hers.

"Um…" *Yes. Just say it and everything will be so much simpler*, she thought. "Well, I think it's easiest if we just… I mean… I have no expectations," she stammered.

That sexy smile. She wanted to melt into a puddle on the floor. "I appreciate that," he said, stepping a little closer to her. The crowd had grown louder than ever with their frenzied chant, forcing Dev's lips to her ear so he could be heard. "There's just one problem."

He was so close she could feel his breath on her face. Toothpaste and lemon. She wanted to brush against his mouth with her fingers, feel him suck them before she replaced them with her hungry lips. "Oh, yeah?"

"Yeah. The only woman I want is you," he whispered, sending shivers down her spine.

Kiki swallowed hard. She finally turned to face him, but he was already backing away from her with his arms over his head. He gave his hands three loud claps in the air. "Alright. Let's fucking *do this*!" he shouted. A roadie handed him a guitar, and then Dev slipped the strap over his head, ran up the steps and disappeared through the stage door.

Blinding strobe lights. Sweat dripping from his face. Stuart pounding the drums, Scotty beside him on the mic. Lightning ripping from his fingertips on the guitar. The whole scene magnified behind him on a massive screen. And the feverish crowd, the lifeblood of every show, singing every word along with him. This was one of the moments Dev could acknowledge that the dreams of a ten-year-old boy with an air guitar and a bed for a stage had come true. If only they weren't so few and far between.

The encore was the one time onstage Dev could actually enjoy himself. During that short golden window between having the worst behind him and the end in sight, he suddenly felt like he could play all night. By all accounts, his first performance of the Up All Night World Tour had gone well. Along with his little helpers, his usual coping mechanisms had worked. He'd launched into his first song, "It All Starts Here," with his back to the audience, only turning around two choruses in when his hands finally stopped shaking. The wild cheers when the crowd saw his face assured him that his secret was safe; they thought it was all part of the act. After that he'd kept his eyes either on his guitar or on the front row of the crowd, and by the third song he was nearly relaxed enough to give the audience what they wanted: everything. All of him. His very flesh, heart and soul. And though his stomach still churned, he'd done it. Worked the stage, riffed with his bandmates, sung hard. He'd never gotten used to having his every move blown up a thousand times, but when he caught a glimpse of himself onscreen he looked okay. He looked perfectly in control. And now here he was on his last number of the night, "Stand Your Ground," one of his midcareer chart-topping ballads that always got the audience singing along. As Dev drew out the last, endless note, twenty thousand cell phones glowed back at him. Only then did he allow his eyes to lift to the back of the stadium, where they settled on the reassuring sight of a fully packed house.

It was over. Relief pulsed through his body as he ran off the stage with his guitar. A waiting roadie took it from him and handed him a bottle of water. He took in the compliments.

"Great show, man."

"You killed it."

"They loved you."

The voices and the roar of the crowd fell away as he looked into the darkness backstage.

Where is she?

Dev's eyes finally adjusted, and he saw her near the back wall. She was turned away from him in conversation with a crew member, allowing him a perfect view of her beautiful ass. Predictably, his cock jerked in his pants. Dev took two steps toward her—and caught his foot on a cable, sprawling him across the wooden floor. "Goddamn it!"

His left elbow throbbed dully as two crew members ran over to help him up to his feet. His first reaction was embarrassment, but then the monster was right up in his face. *That's what Xanax does to you, Stone—makes you clumsy. Maybe you should have stuck with one.*

But he'd needed two tonight, and anyway, that was only the paranoia speaking. Someone had forgotten to cap the cable, that was all. It could have happened to anyone.

"Are you okay?" It was Kiki, looking at him with concern.

"Just a little bump on my pride," he replied, though his elbow hurt when he stretched it out.

"Let's get you into your dressing room." Placing a hand on his good arm, Kiki gave him a gentle push toward the door that led backstage.

The roadies trailed after her. "Should we call a medic?" one of them called.

"I'll let you know," Kiki responded, leading Dev through the door. They crossed the hallway and entered his dressing room. "Sit down. I'm going to roll up your sleeve and take a look."

"Look, if you want to undress me, all you have to do is—"

"No jokes, okay? There might be some swelling happening here."

"You're telling me."

Fuck. What was wrong with him? He was acting like a juvenile, and Kiki looked suitably annoyed. But, Jesus, how was she so resistant? "Look, I'm sorry, okay?" Dev said. "I'm always a little wingy after a show. I make dumb jokes, say the wrong things."

"Why don't you just stop your spewing so I can take a look?"

Dev held his arm up obediently. He watched as her pink-tipped nails pushed his sleeve up. She'd worn a similar shade of polish that night, when she'd wrapped her hands around his cock and stroked him until he was ready for round three. And then she'd taken him in her mouth and sucked him until his entire world had tilted on its side.

Dev saw Kiki's eyes drop to his pants. There was no hiding it anymore—he was rock hard for her. She licked her lips and met his eyes.

"Dev, I—" Kiki dropped his arm and took a step back. It was the only thing she could do to avoid climbing into his lap and rubbing herself against his cock like a desperately horny I'll-do-everything-but-that virgin. Her panties were wet. She'd never wanted anyone so badly, and it all had started the moment she'd seen him onstage. Ninety minutes of excruciating torture where she'd imagined every sweet thing she'd love to do to him after the show. Certain she wouldn't be able to resist him if he so much as breathed on her again. Dangerous. Addictive. So fucking sexy. And such a bad idea.

Both of their sanities depended on her getting her head straight right now.

Dev pounded his good fist onto his thigh and flung himself out of his chair. "Jesus, Kiki! *Fuck!* This is messed up! You want me, I want you, we both know—"

"Don't fucking tell me what I know!" she shouted. He looked at her sharply, and she took a breath. Her anger had taken her by surprise as much as it had him, and it wasn't his fault. She was pent-up, frustrated, desperate to act on the feelings she knew they both had. But she couldn't. She wasn't worth sticking around for—she knew it as well as she knew her own name—and she wasn't prepared to have her heart shattered again. "I get it, okay? No woman on earth has ever refused you."

Dev raked a hand through his hair. When he spoke, his voice was low and furious. "That is *not* what this is about and you know it. Stop throwing that shit in my face, Kiki. How many times do I have to tell you it's you that I want?"

She turned her face to the side. "This was a mistake. I never should have accepted the job."

Dev bent down so his face was inches from hers. "Then define it, Kiki," he said between gritted teeth. "Tell me you never want me to fuck you again right now, and I'll be all business from this moment on."

Kiki lifted her chin. "I'm not going to lie to you, okay? I'd love nothing more than to be with you. But you have to stay away from me, Dev. Believe me, it's better for both of us."

Dev didn't move a muscle. She stared back at him, not daring to let her chilly expression melt.

The door flung open. Kiki glanced toward it and saw Bix striding toward them with an ice pack in his hand. "You okay, buddy? I heard you took a spill. Not going to affect your guitar playing, I hope?"

Dev returned his gaze to Kiki. "I'm fine."

"Glad to hear it," Bix said, slapping the ice pack on Dev's arm. "'Cause you got a hot lineup outside just dying for a piece of you."

Kiki searched for her voice. Never mind Bix's ill timing—her job was to look after Dev, and it was time for her to be professional. "Dev really isn't in any shape to be meeting anyone right now."

The smile dropped off Bix's face. "He just said himself he's fine. And here's the thing—autographs make for happy fans, happy fans tell their friends, they all buy more records, and that—"

"Let them in," Dev interrupted, his eyes still boring into Kiki's. "Go ahead. I'm happy to meet them. And, Kiki, I'd like you to stay."

Panic filled her chest. She'd shut him down once and for all, and now he was going to show her exactly what she was missing. As her feet stayed rooted in place, she realized she was holding her breath. *This is going to be so bad.*

Bix opened the door, and two burly men leading a barrage of skimpily dressed women streamed into the room. Kiki was sure they'd crush Dev completely if it weren't for the handlers, who stood protectively in front of him and shouted for the fans to approach one at a time. The room was so small that Kiki had to practically push herself against a wall to avoid getting crushed. She tried to catch Dev's eye as he signed autographs with his good hand and smiled for selfies, but it was as if he'd already forgotten about her. *Oh, God, what have I done?*

Finally, Dev stood up from his chair. A few of the pushier ladies crowded in even closer to him, cleavage and pouting lips on full display like a Discovery Channel mammalian mating ritual.

Kiki couldn't stand it any longer. Looking for an opening in the throng, she started pressing her way toward the door. She was almost there when she heard Dev's voice behind her.

"Thanks for coming in, ladies," he said. "Kiki will show you out."

She froze, meeting his eyes as the women reluctantly started filing out the door. Several of them threw her jealous glances as they left, and she couldn't help it—she felt a surge of power. It was written all over Dev's face—it was her he wanted. Kiki Becker, strawberry blonde, freckled, currently several pounds over her ideal weight—and he wanted *her*.

Even if she could never let him touch her again.

When the room was clear, Dev slowly walked toward her. Kiki watched him approach, pressing herself backward again. He stepped close enough that she could feel the heat of his body, and then there was nowhere for her to go. He placed his good hand on the wall right beside her shoulder, and then he reached up to brush a strand of hair off her face. He smiled sadly at her. Then he pushed himself off the wall and left the room.

CHAPTER FOUR

"DID YOU SAY PARIS? You must mean the town in Texas, right?" Kiki's father, Lawrence, chuckled over the phone.

"No, Dad, I mean the real deal," Kiki said. Moving toward the window of her hotel room, she pulled the gauzy curtains wider to take in the nighttime view. The Eiffel Tower, lit up in the dark, was framed in the distance as perfectly as a postcard. She still couldn't believe she was in the city she'd only ever dreamed of going to, staying at the famous Hotel George V no less. If only she could be experiencing its romance with Dev at her side instead of just in her head.

She banished the thought.

"I wish I could show it to you, Dad. Do you know what I had for lunch today? Two chocolate croissants. Well, it might have been three—"

"Three croissants, huh?" Lawrence cut in. "Is that just 'when in Rome,' or has something got you stressed out?"

Kiki sighed; she should have known she couldn't get one by her father, who understood her better than anyone on earth. It was 5 p.m. back in Atlanta, and Kiki could just picture him sitting in his favorite armchair with his *Time* magazine and his black coffee. She could see the lines around his eyes that fanned out like rays of sunshine, the head of hair that was now fully gray. Looking at photos of him from when she was a toddler, it was hard to believe the person with the smooth skin and sandy hair holding her up like a prize was the same man. She knew her mother's departure had aged him, even if he rarely talked about it. Lawrence Becker was a man of action more than words; when it became clear his wife wasn't coming back, he'd simply risen to the task, doing his best to raise his only child on his own until he'd eventually remarried.

Kiki sighed. "I'm fine, Dad. My new job is… interesting. It's just…" She paused, wondering how much she should say. Though she longed to spill her guts to someone about Dev, that was a conversation better saved for a girlfriend. But there was something else on her mind that she knew she could unload on her father. "This is a little crazy, but I found a woman who could be Mom. I haven't reached out to her yet, but I will soon. And I guess I'm a little scared."

Kiki knew there would be silence, but it seemed to stretch on forever. "Well. I know how important this is to you," Lawrence replied finally. "I'll say what I've always said about it—that if you find her,

your life will never be the same. That's not neces-
sarily good or bad. Just be prepared, that's all. She
might not be what you're expecting."

"I know. And this woman is in Sydney, so it's
probably a dead end." She hesitated. "Unless—
unless you can think of any reason she'd end up
there?" Kiki knew the question was as good as hy-
pothetical, but she still had to ask it. Her father had
always refused to say much about her mother—
especially when it came to possible reasons for her
leaving them—and while she admired his neutrality,
she sometimes wished he'd be more forthcoming.

"Nothing comes to mind, honey. Sydney isn't a
place she ever mentioned."

Kiki nodded resignedly. "That's what I thought.
But since I'm going to be there anyway…"

"Indeed. It's worth a try." When he paused, Kiki
knew the subject was closed. "Deirdre will be sorry
to have missed you," Lawrence said after clearing
his throat. "Why don't I have her call you when she's
back from the library?"

"No, Dad, it's okay. It's almost midnight here and
I have an early morning." Kiki sank down on her
bed, trying to ignore the familiar tug of guilt she
always felt when it came to her stepmother. Her father had married Deirdre when Kiki was ten, and
she'd tried hard to form a bond with her stepdaughter.
But back then Kiki was still convinced her mother
would return and that when she did, Deirdre would
go right back to where she came from. And though

logic and reason told her adult self that it was a ridiculous notion, wasn't there a tiny part of her that still wanted it to be so?

After she hung up, Kiki sat on her bed staring at the wall in front of her. She'd booked the hotel rooms, so she knew Dev was on the other side of it.

Or was he?

She'd been avoiding him as much as she could since that night in his dressing room. It was an impossible situation. Sleeping with him again was sure to end in heartbreak, and watching him move on would be excruciating—either way, she lost. But she had to stop kicking herself for getting into this situation and keep her eye on the prize: Sydney.

Dev started awake from a thin sleep. How long had he been out? His bedside lamp was aglow and the Netflix show he'd been watching was still playing, showing a young couple in the middle of an argument. He'd probably only dozed off for a few minutes, as per his regular pattern of sleeping and waking throughout the night after a show.

Staring up at the ceiling, Dev focused on making sure his head was straight. One by one he recited the facts. He was in Paris. Tonight's audience had been wild enough to get security involved when two women tried to climb the stage. His hand had been sore, so he'd taken a non-opioid painkiller along with his usual pills. After the show he'd downed two bottles of water and greeted a few VIP fans. Then he'd taken a limo to the George V for his last night in a hotel; as of tomorrow the band would be using their tour buses for the remainder of the European dates. And even if the idea of being on a metal tube for hours on end filled him with dread, at least it was familiar. It was something a little closer to home than this damn hotel room.

An Ambien would put him out. He should take one, he thought. But the fact that he hadn't cracked that bottle yet felt like a small victory—even if it meant lying in bed drowning in regret and self-doubt. He gave his pillow a hearty punch and closed his eyes, wishing for oblivion. But instead, memories of his first tour tumbled through his head. Twenty years old, nearly a solid year on the road, homesick and scared shitless. After his first show, he'd learned to dull his nerves with whatever he could get his hands on to keep from disappointing anyone. He'd discovered that there were so many people to keep happy—his record label, his booking agent, his business manager, his tour manager, his fans, the press. He would have dropped out right then and there if it hadn't been for the money he owed his record label. Something no one had told him before he got famous was that the million-dollar advance that had seemed so huge would get eaten up by recording fees, management, lawyers and taxes, leaving him with almost nothing. On the day his first album went platinum, he had less than five thousand dollars in his bank account and an increasing debt to his record label, forcing him to continue touring to pay it off. After that he'd figured out that even the most successful musicians didn't get wealthy by playing music—they got it by accepting endorsements. Pushing everything from watches to guitars to foreign cars were what had padded his bank account over the years. That took care of his money troubles, but nothing could fix the homesickness and loneliness.

Dev opened his eyes again. On TV, the same couple who had been arguing were now furiously ripping each other's clothes off, evidently having made up. Dev nearly groaned aloud. For a guy with a near-fucking-permanent hard-on, a year and a half minus his one night with Kiki was a hell of a long time to go without. Sometimes he thought it would be easier to just go back to his old ways, when he'd stay up all night partying with the band and fans before taking his pick from the gorgeous women presented to him to bring home. But everything had changed. After the shows everyone went home to their families now, even Scotty and Stuart, who got on to FaceTime with their wives and kids the moment they could escape. But for Dev, after being showered by attention all day long, home was an empty hotel room or tour bus. And he was so goddamned tired of it. He wanted his room, his bed, his life to be filled with another body—with *her* body. He rolled sideways, grabbed a pillow and chucked it across the room in frustration. The monster was raging hard in his head tonight, and fans were such an easy Band-Aid. They threw their numbers at the handlers, who always tucked them into their pockets for their own use if Dev wasn't interested. One phone call to Chester would be all it took. Within thirty minutes, he could have three women in his bed if he wanted to.

Fuck it. He wasn't going to get through to Kiki. Or was he?

Dev sat up in bed. He knew one sure way to find out.

CHAPTER FIVE

KIKI WAS AFRAID she might get sick.

Bringing a hand to her stomach to steady herself, she left her tour bus and started across the underground parking lot of Milan's San Siro Stadium. The last person in the world she wanted to see right now was Dev, but unless she was prepared to get on a plane back to Moretta she had little choice. Her job revolved around him, and she wasn't about to sacrifice her entire reason for coming on the tour when Sydney was just around the corner. So she would face him and get her revenge by pretending his little stunt last night hadn't even bothered her. She'd dressed for the occasion in a plunging V-necked pink sweater, a short denim skirt and knee-high boots. Her plan was to make Dev feel like the shit stain he was by being her usual friendly self with a little added sexiness, and then tonight she'd have a little fun herself. There were plenty of hot guys around—she was in Italy, for Christ's sake, where she couldn't cross a street without twenty men tripping over their dicks at the sight of her.

So she told herself, but Kiki had never been good at tough self-talk. Her heart hammered with each step that brought her closer to him. She tried to calm herself by listening to the sound of her heels clicking across the concrete. The bus drivers, off duty until the end of the show, leaned against a pillar smoking cigarettes. She was still recovering from her first tour bus commute, which had taken nine hours and all of her strength to refrain from strangling her twelve fellow crew members.

The buses themselves were built for comfort—hers even featured an entire second floor for the sleeping quarters—but the living space made for a forced sociability that was absent on airplane travel. Upon arrival, she'd barely ejected herself from the bus when the crew swung into high gear. The logistics that went into getting a show up and running were mind-boggling. Dev traveled with a convoy of eight tour buses to transport his team of nearly a hundred people including audio, video, stage and lighting managers, riggers, technicians, carpenters, electricians, wardrobe, security, catering and management staff. The equipment arrived separately and was met by a locally hired crew of workers at each city, who had to work at a relentless pace to get everything ready on time. Right now the crew was setting up inside, and Stuart and Scotty had chosen to hang out in their bus until showtime. But Dev was waiting for her in the building, and as Kiki headed up the stairs to the backstage maze, her stomach twisted hard enough to make her whimper aloud.

She fucking hated him.

Last night, as the first moans of passion had reached her ears, she'd thought she was literally going to vomit. Even if she *had* told him he needed to stay away from her, she'd also admitted how much she wanted him—and he'd slapped her right in the goddamned privates with it. As she lay in bed listening to the agonizing sound of his desire for someone else, she told herself that she'd been right all along. She'd known he'd go back to his old ways, and the only thing that had surprised her was the dizzying heights of his insensitively.

She clacked up the stairs and wove her way through the hive of backstage activity to Dev's dressing room. Then she smoothed her hair over her shoulders, willed her heart to stop beating like a war drum and knocked on the door.

"Come in!" Dev shouted. She entered the room and forced a carefree smile.

Dev was sitting on a sofa, casually strumming an acoustic guitar as if he *hadn't* busted her world apart last night. She took in his dark jeans, his studded belt and bare torso. Against her will, her eyes fell from his broad shoulders to the light hair on his pecs. To her fury, she felt a jolt shoot straight to her clit. How could she possibly still be attracted to him after what he'd done?

Kiki pulled her iPhone out of her handbag. She'd

been planning to put on a bit of a show—look at him under long lashes, slide a hand suggestively up her thigh to remind him of what he'd never have again—but now that she was here it was all she could do to stay upright. Her emotions had her in complete turmoil. For the first time ever, she found herself wishing for the game-playing revenge skills she knew some women possessed. "Uh," she began awkwardly. "We didn't have time to do a post before last night's show. A quick shot of you on your guitar is fine." She lifted her phone, ready to take the picture and make a dash for the door, but Dev put his instrument aside and walked over to her.

"I can't get my photo taken," he said, stopping right inside her personal space. "I'm not even dressed."

She narrowed her eyes at him, willing them not to drop to his chest, his biceps…the same body he'd shared with someone else last night. *Fuck him.* He'd *known* she was in the next room, and whatever their relationship may or may not be, what he'd done was downright cruel. Worse, he'd ruined the memory of their one beautiful night together. To Kiki's horror, she felt tears spring to her eyes. She blinked them back furiously and held her phone up in front of Dev's face. "Then tell your manager that—he requested it."

Dev flicked his gaze to the text from Bix: Get Dev in his DR for snap. "Bix would have me promoting myself while I sat on the toilet if he could," Dev responded.

"Have it your way." She was turning toward the door when Dev caught her by the arm.

"Hey—"

Kiki ripped out of his grip. "Do *not* fucking touch me!" She was shaking with a fury she didn't even know she had in her. Dev's face registered shock as she backed away from him. "I actually thought you were a great guy. To think that—that I had feelings for you! That I actually thought our night together was something special!"

"Kiki—"

"And then you fuck someone in the room right beside me? And you don't even have the decency to keep it quiet? You *knew* I was next door! Jesus Christ! I was so wrong about you!"

"But I—"

"Groupie days behind you? As if! Maybe you can fool yourself into thinking you've changed, but it's pretty obvious that once you're back on the road you haven't! How can you even—?"

"Kiki, please! Stop! I was an asshole, okay? I went too far." She paused her tirade long enough to see that he had real regret in his face—as if that could make a difference. "Yes, you did, and you're despicable," she spat as her walkie-talkie blared to life.

"Thirty minutes," came a male voice from her back pocket. Kiki pulled the device out. "Copy that,"

she said, and then she shoved it away again and went
for the door handle.

"Wait. Please." Dev's voice was pleading. "It was
stupid. I just… I don't know, I thought it might remind you what you were missing out on."

The fucking audacity. Her jaw dropped as she
turned back to him. He was looking down at his cell
phone, swiping at the screen furiously. "What I was
missing out on?"

"Yeah. Here." Dev hit a button on his phone and
held it up. On the screen was a bird's-eye view of a
woman straddling a man, going for it full throttle.
And the sex sounds were the exact same ones she'd
heard last night. "It was a movie," he said sheepishly.
"I might have cranked the volume up a bit. It was a
total jackass thing to do."

"You…?" Kiki brought a hand up to her mouth
as her mind busily reordered everything she'd believed. So he hadn't slept with anyone, but— "You
tried to *trap* me?"

"I just wanted to know if you care, okay? I'm
so—Jesus Christ, Kiki! I'm so fucking frustrated!"
He punched his phone through the air.

Kiki wasn't sure if it was because of relief or
anger, but the tears she'd been holding back started
spilling over. She did care—*of course* she did. And
it had never been more apparent than in the past ten
minutes. "So am I, Dev. And I…" A tear tracked
down her cheek. He reached out and traced it with

a finger, and then he slipped a hand under her chin. His eyes probed her face.

"What is it?" he asked.

Kiki's chest filled with emotion. His voice was so gentle, gentle enough to make her want to spill all her secrets. She couldn't do that, but she also couldn't deny her desire for him any longer.

Standing on tiptoe, she reached up and pressed her lips to his. His mouth stayed firm for a moment, like he was waiting to see if she was really sure about this. And that just made her want him more. That he hadn't made a move on her. That he'd been totally respectful of her, even if he couldn't help what might have gone on in his pants. And that he'd gone about trying to prove her feelings for him in such a ridiculous, juvenile way.

She broke away from him and started laughing. Dev looked at her in surprise, and then he started laughing with her. He picked her up and lifted her off the floor, burying his face in her hair. "Jesus, Strawberry, what are you doing to me?"

"I don't know, but I seriously need to get off this emotional roller coaster."

He brought his forehead to hers. "You don't need to ride it anymore," he whispered. "All you need to do is let this happen."

Then his mouth was on hers, confident this time. And so hungry for her, as if he were wrapping all the longing and uncertainly of the past five weeks into one perfect kiss. Hard and demanding, and yet soft at the same time. She brought her legs around his hips, pressing her body into his as if she could meld them into one. The bare skin of his chest felt heavenly against her. She opened up to him, making a ravenous sound in her throat as he bit at her lips with increasing urgency.

"I thought I'd never get to do this again," he whispered hoarsely into her mouth. "Do you have any idea how much I've dreamed of you?"

His words were sweet music to Kiki's ears. All the reasons she thought they couldn't be together fell away into the abyss of their passion. "I couldn't stay away from you if my life depended on it," she rasped, throwing her head back as she dissolved under his touch. Dev's tongue trailed down her neck. Still holding her around him with one arm, he made an animal sound when his other hand found her breast. She could feel his erection pressing into her groin. She forced herself not to rub against it like a desperately horny fifteen-year-old. "I'll make you late," she breathed.

"We've got plenty of time," Dev replied, applying just enough pressure with his hips to make her lose her mind. "If I can't walk on that stage tonight smelling like you, I'm not going on at all."

"Then I guess you'll have to cancel," she teased.

"Are you really prepared to be responsible for disappointing fifty thousand fans?" His hand was sliding up her thigh now, making its way toward her panties.

She dropped her hand from his neck to his cock, which was now straining against his jeans in all its glory. She plunged her hand into his pants and watched his face go slack with lust as her hand wrapped around him. "Okay, rock star, you win."

CHAPTER SIX

FIFTEEN MINUTES. THAT'S how long Dev knew he'd have until his stage manager came knocking on his door. But right now there was only Kiki and him. Dev's entire world shrank down to this small room where their intense longing was all that mattered.

More of her. Finally.

When her ass hit the dressing table, she'd already yanked her skirt up around her waist. With her boots still on, she brought her feet up on the table and leaned back against the mirror. Then she spread her legs wide to give him a perfect view. Hot desire ripped through Dev's synapses when he saw the wetness on her thong. He rubbed a hand over his erection, which was straining painfully against his jeans.

"That tight pussy," he murmured, reaching for her panties. "Do you know how many nights I've pretended my hand was you?"

"I've had a few sleepless nights myself," Kiki breathed, squirming as he cupped her right there. She bucked into his hand and let out a tortured moan when it hit exactly the right spot. "Rip it. Just fucking rip it off," she choked out. "I need you *now*."

"If you insist," Dev said thickly, curling his hand around the pink garment. He yanked hard, and he heard the thin fabric snap as it pulled off in one swift motion. Then he dragged her hips toward him until she was balanced on the edge of the table with full access to her beautiful sweet spot. Like a man possessed, he brought his mouth down on hers again while his fingers went inside her.

She moaned as he drew her wetness up to circle her clit. Her body started to tremble as she arched backward, her chest heaving with barely controlled desire.

"My sweet little strawberry, I can't wait to taste you again," he whispered into her ear.

"Next time. Please, Dev. Just fuck me. I'm dying for you."

Next time. And just when he thought it couldn't get any better.

Kiki's hands were at his belt buckle. He heard the arousing sound of his fly unzipping, and then he was in her hands, so hard he ached.

"Tell me you have a condom somewhere," she pleaded.

Dev fumbled a drawer open on the dressing table. He'd yet to occupy a dressing room that wasn't fully stashed with condoms, and thankfully this one was no exception. He snatched one, ripped the package open and got it on. His heart was pounding like an animal in heat. That face, that body, that pussy—he wanted to possess all of it. He pressed himself into her so his cock was lying against her clit. "Do you remember how I felt inside you?" he murmured, locking his eyes on hers.

"Perfectly. Now fuck me, Dev, or I swear to God I'll finger myself again. But this time I'll make you watch until I—" The words died on her lips as he moved his cock to her opening and pushed himself inside her.

Something akin to savageness overtook his body as he felt her heat envelop him. She felt even better than he remembered, the most incredible heaven on earth he could imagine. They were perfect together—so fucking perfect it defied all logic. Leaning forward on his arms, he drove into her again and again, ripping sweet whimpers from her swollen lips. His belt buckle banged loudly against the table, punctuating every amazing thrust. Kiki's head fell to the side, her hair sweeping over his shoulder. "Yes, yes, yes!" she cried, meeting him thrust for thrust. Her breath was as quick as his as they desperately chased their long-overdue release. "Don't stop, Dev. *Do not fucking stop.*"

He had no plans to, but the sight of her was driving him dangerously close to the edge. Beautiful. Primal. Completely consumed by pleasure. It was almost too much, and yet not enough. When his desire threatened to topple his control, he grabbed her hands and brought them above her head. She gasped, laid open, and brought her legs around his hips to pull him in deeper. The feel of her leather boots on his bare ass urged him ever forward. Every muscle in his body strained toward his own pleasure, but it wasn't nearly as important to him as hers.

"Five minutes," cracked the walkie-talkie. As Dev slowed his relentless pace for one stroke, Kiki grinned at him devilishly. "Should I tell them you're coming?"

"I'd rather just do it," he said breathlessly. He was so close, but he didn't want it to end yet.

"Good. Because I'm about to," she moaned.

Dev watched her face as he circled his groin against her clit. Her mouth fell open, her body tensed and she contracted around him, bringing him to the point of no return. He exploded as he anchored into her, riding crest after crest of melting heat that singed his synapses all the way to his fingers and toes.

The best fucking orgasm of his life, and all he wanted was to do it all over again.

His breath was gone. As he recovered, he let Kiki's hands slide down. Then he picked them up and kissed her palms, one after the other. "I want you there with me tonight," he said. "Right where I can see you."

An hour into Dev's show, Kiki could still feel him between her legs. Her climax had been close to an earthquake, but it had done nothing to tame her raging libido. Of course, the fact that she was wearing a thigh-skimming skirt with no underwear didn't help matters. She felt naughty and wild, built for pure pleasure. Every cell of her body was hypersensitive, culminating at her clit, where she felt like she could come again at the brush of a hand. *Dev's* hand. No other man could make her feel the way he did, which meant she was in very deep trouble.

In the wings, the roar of the crowd was deafening. Thick smoke from cigarettes, marijuana and the dry ice that was part of the show clogged the air. Kiki stared at Dev, mesmerized at the sight of his fingers flying over his red Gibson. He played his instrument just like he'd played her body, building and building the excitement until it practically begged for mercy. But it wasn't just his charisma that was so sexy—it was his utter comfort up on that stage, like he was born to do this. For Kiki, who quaked at the thought of giving a mere dinner toast, the idea that he could handle such a relentlessly bright spotlight was a massive turn-on. Which was just one reason the rest of the world loved him—not just her.

"It's one of his greatest talents," a voice said loudly in her ear. She turned to see Bix beside her, hands shoved in his pockets as he looked out at Dev. Fuck. If there was one thing that could put a damper on her arousal, it had just shown up. She grasped the hem of her skirt and yanked it down.

"What is?" she replied, shouting above the noise to be heard.

"His ability to make every woman out there feel like she's the only one in the room."

Kiki looked away. She didn't know if Bix somehow knew about Dev and her or was only guessing, but his message was clear: there was nothing special about her. She recognized a cheap attempt at relationship sabotage when she saw it, but why should Bix care? Did he just make a habit of treating anyone who dared get within arm's length of his best client as if they were so much trash?

"I hadn't noticed," she replied, attempting to make her shouting voice indifferent.

"He makes it look easy out there, but no one appreciates how hard he works. Harder than anyone I know. I'd hate to imagine how empty his life would be without that stage." Kiki felt his eyes on the side of her face before he turned on his heel and exited through the side door. She rolled his words around in her head, searching for their true meaning. Even if she wasn't exactly sure what it was, it was clear Bix wanted her to keep her distance from Dev. But she'd tried that. And even if she felt pathetically weak to have given in to him again, right now she hardly cared. It's not like they were talking marriage, they were both just enjoying the fuck out of each other's bodies.

Except that it was more than that, and Kiki knew it.

She pushed that knowledge from her head.

The crowd was losing its shit. The last song had ended, and Stuart was now starting in on a drum solo. She saw Dev toss his guitar aside and stride off the stage under the cover of darkness. He came straight for her, grabbing her hips to bump her back against the wall. "You're fucking killing me. I'm rock hard up there from thinking of you," he growled into her ear.

He wasn't lying—she could feel it pressing into her belly. She went wet all over again. "I wish you could fuck me again right now."

He made a tortured sound in his throat. "This drum solo is four minutes long. Just enough time to make you come."

Her belly flopped over. Was he serious? She'd barely got the thought out when his hand was under her skirt. "I could get used to this easy access."

Kiki took a quick look around before her intense arousal could sweep all good sense away. The space was dark and sparsely occupied. To anyone around them it probably just looked like he was leaning in close to her to be heard.

At least that's what she told herself because she was helpless to stop anything that felt this good. As Dev sunk a finger into her wetness, she felt like she might collapse with desire. Her body went rigid as he massaged her clit with expert strokes, driving her toward her orgasm with breakneck speed. She couldn't help another glance around. Was she really doing this? It was loud onstage, but what if someone heard her?

As if reading her mind, Dev moved so his shoulder was against her mouth. She inhaled the heady scent of his sweat and aftershave. His cock pressed firmly into her thigh. "Think about how good I felt inside you," he said hoarsely. "Think about how hard I'm going to fuck you later. And then let me feel you come."

She was almost there. Dev's fingers moved in and out of her with a rhythmic thrust while his thumb maintained just enough pressure on her ultrasensitive clit. The heat built until it burst at her center, bucking her against the wall. Goose bumps crawled up her spine. *Jesus.* She muffled her whimper with an open mouth against his shirt.

"Exactly what I needed," Dev said, gently slipping his hand out of her. "Meet me in my bus after the show."

He didn't even wipe his hand off before reaching for his six-string Fender.

CHAPTER SEVEN

CLIMBING UP THE two steps to Dev's tour bus, Kiki took a quick glance around to make sure no one was watching before she opened the door. She knew exactly how it looked, and the last thing she wanted was for the news to hit the crew that she was Dev Stone's new little piece of ass. Today had been amazing, but the reality of her situation had set in a bit. She'd slept with Dev on tour, just like countless other girls before her had. Was her status really that different from any other hanger-on groupie? Kiki wasn't here to make a new best friend, but she didn't want to become the laughingstock of the crew, either. *Just keep it under wraps. Whatever* this *is.*

Her legs felt shaky as she stepped inside the bus. She knew it was from the sex—she was out of practice—but she was also exhausted from her sleeplessness the night before. She could hear the shower running. Even the image in her head of Dev naked had her going again, but it wasn't just his body she ached for. The way he touched her, like she really

meant something to him…it was addictive, and she
had to keep her head together. She'd already broken
two of her soft rules by mixing business with pleasure and taking things beyond one night, and she was
dangerously close to breaking her hard rule of keeping her emotions out of it. In fact it was ridiculous
to try to fool herself that she already hadn't. Dev lit
up something in her that no one else had come close
to, not even Jack.

While Kiki waited for the water to stop running
in the bathroom, she glanced around the bus. The
space was generic looking with no personal touches,
but it was nearly as big as her cottage on Moretta and
a lot more luxurious. She was standing in a lounge
complete with two leather sofas and a large-screen
TV. The dining area opened to a kitchen with glass
countertops, a dishwasher, fridge, range and built-in
espresso machine. The bathroom door stood open,
displaying a marble vanity. Beside that was a small
gym with weights and a treadmill. And at the end
of the hallway she could see the bedroom, complete
with a closet and queen bed. Her gut clenched. This
wasn't a rental, it was Dev's personal bus that he kept
in storage and brought out for his European tours. It
pained her to think of how many women he'd taken
to that bed over the years.

Dev stepped out of the bathroom with a towel
wrapped around his hips. Her eyes went to the muscular indentations at his hips that pointed down to-

ward his perfect package. A jolt fired through her limbs. God, but he was fucking ruinous.

Wordlessly, he pulled her toward him and claimed her mouth with his. She yielded against his chest as he ran a hand up her back and into her hair. His tongue slid against hers with the promise of more to come, causing her belly to go molten. What the hell was happening to her? She'd become insatiable. "I thought you'd keep me waiting all night," he said against her mouth, running his tongue over her lip.

"You got off stage twenty minutes ago."

"Longest twenty minutes of my life."

Her knees went weak as their kiss deepened. She pounded a hand on his back and broke away from him breathlessly. "You are too much for me, rock star," she gasped. "I don't even know what to do with myself."

"Then don't do anything. Leave it all to me." He was back on her, relentless. His need of her, his demand that she be his—it was so intoxicating. She curled a leg around his knee to bring him in closer.

"Let me show you the bed." As he spoke with his mouth pressed to hers, he pushed her back bit by bit until the mattress hit the backs of her knees. She collapsed onto it, and he braced himself with his arms to lean over her. "Is it comfortable? Good enough for me to fuck you on?"

Kiki couldn't resist. "I think you'd know better than me."

He reached for her sweater and yanked the gaping neckline open, exposing her bra. "Not really," he said, running a hand over the thin fabric. Her nipple went erect. "It's brand-new."

Kiki dropped onto the mattress, laughing. "It's okay, Dev, you don't have to bullshit me. I know you've had this bus for a decade and I still like you."

His hand freed one of her breasts. He took it in his mouth, flicking his tongue across her nipple. She tried to bite back her whimper, but it was impossible. The sight of his cock tenting his towel had her coming apart. Dev lifted his lips long enough to speak. "If I'd known you wouldn't mind it, I would have spared Chester the hassle," he said, trailing kisses down her belly.

"Hassle?"

"Yeah. I put in an order to have the bed switched out just before I went onstage tonight."

Kiki laughed deliriously. Dev's show had started at 8 p.m. in a European city, whose businesses weren't obsessed with twenty-four-hour shopping like they were in the US. How the hell had he managed to get a new bed purchased, brought in and made up in the past three hours? He was Dev Stone, that was how, and his world was as different from hers as another planet.

But more important, he had done it just for her. It was a piece of information that caught in her chest almost painfully. This was happening too fast. It was never meant to happen at all…because it couldn't last. She exhaled, determined to rein herself in. "I guess I shouldn't have doubted it. I forgot that you have people for that kind of—"

Her words froze in her throat as she felt his tongue sweep across her clit. She looked down, meeting his eyes as he shoved her skirt up roughly. He gripped her hips tightly enough to inflict mild pain, but his mouth on her was so gentle it made her cry out with a feeling she couldn't quite name. The contrast of his desperate need for her and his soft mouth—it was mind-bending.

"The sweetest thing I've ever tasted," Dev whispered before he sunk his tongue all the way inside her. And then his mouth was fastened to her clit, licking and sucking her toward her third climax of the night with the strength and power of a freight train. Before she even knew what was happening, it was washing over her, taking her breath away as her whole body tensed and shook. Finally, she released with a long sigh and collapsed onto the mattress.

And yet she still wasn't satisfied. No—she was voracious, made of pure lust, and she'd never needed anything more than she needed him.

It was insanity.

Dev stood up and tugged at his towel, dropping it to the floor. His cock was so hard it barely fell forward. "See what you do to me?"

The sight of him naked kicked her heartbeat up even further. His wet hair lay over his brow in that way she loved, highlighting his aqua eyes. His abs rippled as he braced his arms on the bed on either side of her. "Are you ready for me to fuck you?"

She thrust her chest up and spread her legs open. "Never readier."

As Dev reached for a condom and put it on, her pulse jumped with delicious anticipation. God, he was going to make her scream—

Her mind screeched with a sobering thought. "What about that?" she asked, gesturing to the cab up front.

"Soundproof," Dev assured her.

"A must for any horny rock star."

"Stop calling me that," he said, reaching for her waist.

"So you're *not* horny?"

"What does it feel like to you?"

Before she knew it, he'd flipped her onto her front like a rag doll. She gasped as he pulled her hips back and filled her opening with the tip of his cock. But then he stopped, teasing her as he moved those two inches in and out of her. A fresh wave of lust gripped her like a fist. "Dev. *Fuck*," she moaned.

"At your command," he said, and with that he slammed himself into her up to the hilt. When he paused for a moment, she turned around to look at his face. It was the picture of ecstasy, driving her extreme arousal even higher. He locked his eyes onto hers, and then he leaned over her back and bit her earlobe. "Are you getting this, Kiki? How we feel together? It's not just me, is it?"

Being filled with him was so good she could barely speak, but she tried. "No," she managed just before he started to move. And God, *how* he moved. Every beautiful muscle in his torso tensed as he thrust into her mercilessly, driving himself toward what she could only imagine was his own pent-up pleasure. And she was the lucky recipient of his urgency. She dropped her chest to the bed to allow him to go deeper. "Yes!" she cried, countering his every movement with a stroke of her own.

Dev's hands went to her shoulders, caressing them gently as he plunged into her with one final, impossibly deep thrust. She heard a low growl come out of him as he trembled behind her, lost in the climax of their passion.

At last he collapsed onto her back. "Jesus, Strawberry. How did I live without you for even one day?"

"Shit!"

The word, spat out furiously, jolted Dev awake. He bolted upright in bed, nearly banging his head on the overhead shelf. The bedside light was still on, illuminating the panic on Kiki's face as her eyes darted around the room. Beneath them he could hear the low whine of the engine as the bus made its way steadily south toward Rome.

Dev put a hand on her arm, stroking it soothingly. "I should have warned you that it can take some getting used to. Pretty soon you'll find that the movement will actually help you sleep."

"It's not that!" Kiki said, swinging her legs out of bed and reaching for her bra. "I should be on *my* bus!"

Dev shook his head as discouragement filled his chest. After everything that had happened yesterday, was he really back to square one with her? "I want you to stay with me. I thought that was obvious."

"That's not—"

"Do you need something? I have toothbrushes. Contact lens solution. Even pajamas with teddy bears on them if you want." His eyes were on her face but hers were everywhere else, like a wild animal preparing to flee.

What's wrong? Everything had been going so well, but maybe he'd let things go too far. Kiki had fallen asleep within minutes of their last encounter, and he'd justified not waking her by telling himself she needed the rest. He knew she was exhausted from the stupid prank he'd pulled the night before, and even if it had led her back to him, he was still feeling guilty about it. But in his heart he'd known he was being selfish—he'd just wanted to have her there beside him. To keep her in his arms where he could pretend his life was something resembling normal as long as she was with him. What was it about this woman, with her skyscraper-high walls and infuriating independence, that made him want to delve into every part of her? Not just her body, but her mind, her likes and her dislikes, her dreams and fears?

Kiki was fastening her bra and pulling the straps up over her shoulders, *snap snap.* "You're kidding me, right? Have you forgotten that I'm supposed to be your *employee*? How do you think I'm going to feel doing the walk of shame back to my bus?" She glared at him. "You've never even thought about that, have you? How I'm going to look in front of everyone now. It's fucking embarrassing, if I have to spell it out for you."

Jesus—she was furious, and she was also right. Dev hadn't considered for a moment how any of this would impact her life. Overtaken with a consuming need he could barely control, he'd only been thinking about his own desires—*as per usual*, as his brother, Alex, would have said.

"Look, Kiki, this isn't just for right now, okay? I want you with me." When she continued to ignore him, he grasped her chin gently and turned her face toward him. "Will you look at me, please? I want you, Strawberry. For the whole tour." *And longer*, he thought, but he stopped himself. He had to keep his head sane and take this one step at a time—for both of their sakes.

"Fine," she said, reaching for her skirt. "But I still have a job to do, and the line between work and play is looking pretty damned blurry to me right now. I can't just—"

"So I'll find another assistant! The last thing I want is for you to be uncomfortable. But we can find a way to make this work, okay?"

The quick tensing of her mouth told him he'd said exactly the wrong thing. "By quitting my *job*? I know it may not seem important to you, rock star, but this is my life! And what do you mean, make this work? *This* was never even supposed to happen!" She was making a lunge for her sweater when he caught her around the waist. She strained against his grip, but he refused to let go. He landed a soft kiss on her tensed shoulder blade and spoke to her softly.

"Yes, but it did," he said, moving her hair to one side so he could kiss the back of her neck. "Kiki, listen. If you want to leave because you don't want to be with me, you never have to set foot in this bus again. But if it's just because of what you're worried other people will think? Life is too short."

"Easy for you to say when the whole world loves you," she said hotly, crossing her arms over her chest.

"Funny, that's what Alex always says to me. Only it's not that simple."

When she didn't respond, he took her arms and gently uncrossed them, and then he slid his hands down to entwine them with hers. "When I was younger, I used to stress out a lot about my career. My mother was still alive back then, and she used to quote me this old saying, that I could please all of the people some of the time, or some of the people all of the time. I tried going with option two because to me my fans and my managers were all the people

I thought I needed. It worked for a while, until I discovered that the one person I wasn't pleasing was maybe the most important."

"And who was that?" Kiki asked, her voice still edgy.

"Myself."

"Oh, yeah? So what did you do about it?"

Dev shook his head. "I'm still working on it. Money might buy me a new bed in three hours, but it doesn't solve most problems in life that really matter."

Kiki was silent for a moment. "So why weren't you pleased with yourself?"

Dev took a slow breath, metering his response. He certainly wasn't about to tell her the whole truth, but for the first time in his life, the idea of sharing his burden with someone was profoundly tempting. Not just someone—with *her*, the person he'd come to trust in a terrifyingly short amount of time. "I made some compromises to have the career I wanted," he began carefully. "When I first started out, being up onstage wasn't what I thought it would be. I'd loved performing since I was a kid. I used to put on shows for my friends—you know, get up on my bed and pretend it was my stage. When I finally got the chance in real life I thought I'd kill it, but I was scared shitless. So I turned to some calming methods I shouldn't have."

"You mean drugs," Kiki clarified.

"Yes. And way too much bourbon."

"But that was a long time ago, right? You *own* that stage now."

His gut clenched. *If she only knew.* "Sure, but it still comes at a price. And I've gone through my whole life feeling like I never had license to verbalize any of it, because I knew I was the luckiest bastard alive. Most people have to starve for years before they make it big, and my dream came true at twenty. So a few years ago I started talking about it. Doing interviews that brought the image of the infallible, glamorous rock star down to earth. I wanted people to know that we have just as many problems as anyone else, they're just a different variety. That was more important to me than public adoration." Except that he still hadn't admitted the worst of it, hadn't exposed the true depth of his weakness to the world—and he never could.

"I guess that's why you hate it when I call you that," Kiki said. Her back was still to him, but there was a hint of a smile in her voice. "Rock star."

"Sure, but you know what I love about you? That you know none of this about me. You haven't read a single article or watched a single interview with Dev Stone. I don't impress you, and that's exactly what I need."

She finally looked over her shoulder to meet his eyes. "Need for what?"

Too much. Too soon.

Dev kissed her shoulder one more time, scooted

to the end of the bed and tugged his boxer shorts on. "You know what would be good for us?"

"You mean besides the obvious?"

He grinned, relieved to see that her sense of humor had returned. He trailed a hand up her thigh. "Don't get me started."

Kiki batted his hand away. "Tell me. What do we need?"

Dev grabbed a navy robe from a hook on the wall and tied it around himself. "Say you'll stay with me tonight and I'll tell you."

"That's blackmail."

"You're absolutely right. Will you stay?"

She hesitated a moment, and then she nodded. Relief filled his chest. He placed his hands on the bed, leaned toward her and kissed her. "What we need is our first proper date."

She snorted. "On a tour? How do you think that's going to happen?"

"We have tomorrow off, in case you've forgotten. Now, no more questions."

Dev stood up again and made his way to the front of the bus. He was about to do something he could have done with a hundred women over the years, and yet he'd never had the urge to—and suddenly he knew exactly why. Allowing his cock or his ego to choose a woman meant the fun was over the minute the orgasm was. But with Kiki, he got the feeling it was just beginning.

CHAPTER EIGHT

WHEN KIKI AWOKE from a much deeper sleep than she'd expected to have, the bus was still and she could see light around the edges of the blackout blinds. Her ears slowly tuned in to the sound of cars passing outside and Dev's voice down the hallway. He was in the lounge, she realized, talking to someone on the phone in a tone that told her he was trying not to wake her. She grabbed the same robe he'd put on earlier and walked to the front of the bus to find him.

The gorgeous sight of him sprawled in a chair was almost surreal. Wearing only a pair of charcoal boxers, he appeared to be in the middle of a slightly heated conversation. But he flipped his hair off his forehead and gave her that smile when she walked in. Jesus, but he was hot. Just the memory of last night had her body zinging. Still talking, he beckoned to her with his finger. She walked over to him and he pulled her down on his lap. "Yeah. Uh-huh," he said into the phone.

When the person on the other line started speaking, Dev went for her mouth. She sunk into the kiss, loving how important he made her feel. As if the only person in the world who mattered was her, and everyone else could get fucked.

So dangerous.

Ending the kiss, Kiki jumped up from his lap and walked into the kitchen. Two lattes sat side by side on the counter. She picked one up, brought it to her lips—and froze when she caught a glance out the window. She had a sudden urge to rub her eyes to see if the image would go away, just like Alice in Wonderland. Instead, she stepped toward the door and threw it open.

"Oh, my God!" she screamed, forgetting Dev was on the phone.

The bus was parked on a narrow cobblestone driveway mere inches from a three-foot drop to the water. Across that water was a row of the most beautifully ornate buildings Kiki had ever seen. To her left, a bridge arched gracefully over two passing gondolas.

She was in Venice.

Covering her face in disbelief, she turned toward Dev, who was just putting his phone down. He walked over and wrapped his arms around her. "Surprised?"

"You think? It's amazing! But we're supposed to be in Rome. How…?"

Dev shrugged. "I caught the driver just in time.

We were just approaching Bologna, so it was an easy detour to have him head east."

"Wow. I—I don't know what to say."

"Don't say anything. Just thank me later," he said, sliding his hand into the robe to palm her breast. The way he touched her—insistent, powerful, claiming. Enough to turn her world inside out and upside down over and over again. *Fuck*.

She batted his hand away. "If you wanted to spend the day doing *that*, you shouldn't have brought me to the most gorgeous city in Europe. Right now no offense, but Venice wins."

Dev grinned. "None taken. Let's get dressed—we've got lots to do."

"Holy fucking shit," Dev said to Kiki when she stepped out of the dressing room. He licked his lips hungrily. "Turn around."

Kiki did a slow turn in front of him. Watching the rows of herself reflected back in the three-way mirror, she willed her tell-all cheeks not to blush. She wasn't used to being on show, especially for a pair of eyes like Dev's. Though she knew how to play up her round blue eyes, unique hair color and tiny figure, she hadn't been blessed with height, large breasts or the world's slimmest hips. And yet Dev, who'd been with more Victoria's Secret models than she could count, didn't just make her feel beautiful—he made her feel like an absolute sex goddess. It made zero sense, but maybe that was just part of the dream.

Because today, Kiki was letting herself pretend her life was a perfect fantasy.

Dev stopped her spin with two hands on her waist, then he pressed his groin into her backside. The saleslady turned away, discreetly busying herself with folding a thousand-dollar T-shirt. "My cock just decided this is the dress," he said quietly into Kiki's ear.

"I noticed," she said as he pulled her against himself firmly. Sure enough, she could feel the beginning of a healthy erection between her cheeks.

"Think anyone would notice if I took you into that change room and fucked you senseless?" His mouth was at the back of her neck, trailing shiver-inducing kisses along her shoulder. He brought a hand around and cupped her breast. God—here he was, so famous that three people had stopped him for his autograph today, and he didn't even care who saw them. With *her.*

All part of the fantasy, she thought. "My screams of passion might give us away."

"Then I guess I'll have to settle for taking this dress off you later. And this time, we're going to go slowly."

Hot anticipation pulsed through her. "Promises, promises."

Dev finally released her after tipping her face sideways for one last deep kiss. Blushing like a pre-teen, Kiki stepped back into the change room and shut the door. She closed her eyes and took a deep breath. It was all so goddamned perfect—too perfect. Dev was a dream come true, and she was riding the wave as if this could last forever.

Just pretend it can.

When she opened her eyes again, the mirror showed her exactly what she was: a woman in the grips of a passionate affair. Flushed, happy, sexy. And the dress suited her new persona. Made of cream silk, it hugged her body just enough to show her figure without being too overt. A draped neckline fell open above her breasts, and below the midthigh hemline she wore a pair of patent-leather nude heels. And beneath it all was a set of lacy white lingerie so luxurious she could barely feel it against her skin. Pure Prada, and together worth more than she made in two months. She felt like she was in *Pretty Woman*, minus the prostitution part.

Kiki gathered up the tired clothing she'd worn into the store. She should have known she'd lose the battle that had started the minute she and Dev stepped away from the tour bus. Looking at the same skirt and top she was stuck wearing from yesterday, Dev had insisted on taking her shopping for something new. Kiki had felt weird about him spending money on her, but he'd finally convinced her that it was a very dangerous idea for her to go out for dinner with no panties on. She'd given in on the condition they find an H&M, but instead he'd run with her compliance and directed their gondola to the high-end Le Mercerie shopping district. There he'd steered her into the Prada store, watched as she tried on dress after dress, and found so many excuses to caress and kiss her that her whole body felt scorched by his touch. All she could think about was getting to their hotel later and burning up the sheets with their insatiable desire.

She smoothed her hair with her hands and refreshed her lip gloss before she exited the change room. Dev took her skirt and top and dropped them into the Prada bag. "Thank you," Kiki said, dropping a kiss on his mouth.

"I'll collect my payment later," he murmured.

By the time they'd settled into a gondola to make their way to dinner, the sun had dropped low in the sky to bathe the entire city in a magical golden light. Kiki sat on the bench with Dev's arm around her, trying to enjoy the quiet. Dev had orchestrated the entire day—a tour of Doge's Palace, the most incredible *ravioli al formation con salvia* at an intimate trattoria and watching the pigeons at Piazza San Marco. Kiki had learned about Dev's hilarious delinquent high school antics, the family media business his brother had taken over, his mother's passing from a heart attack four years ago and the details of the renovations he'd put into his Moretta home. Each story grew her attraction to everything he was—funny, principled, intelligent and humbler than she ever could have imagined. She loved the sexy way he leaned back in his chair with one elbow hooked over the back of his seat, the way he stroked his chin when he was trying to remember something. She could have filled her entire day with *him*, but she knew her time to do that was coming to an end. She'd already dodged his inquiries into her divorce and her family with a few humorous cracks. And now, as Dev held her against him in the boat, the silence wasn't uncomfortable to Kiki—it was dangerous.

"Your call sounded a little heated this morning," she said, running a hand up his back. "Everything okay?"

"Hmm?" Dev seemed to be reeling his mind back to her. *What is he thinking about?* she wondered. *Does he still like me after spending a whole day with me?*

She banished the thought, hating the jab of insecurity. He'd done more than enough to reassure her of how wanted she was. Why was her default to assume she wasn't worthy?

"Oh, it was just Bix," Dev replied dismissively. "Trying to keep me under his thumb as usual. Maybe one of these days he'll figure out that I'm the one who pays *him*."

"I take it he didn't approve of your little detour?"

"Bix likes me where he can see me. Like I'm going to blow the whole tour by taking one day away from the schedule. You'd think he'd have learned that isn't my style after seventeen years of working together, but there you go." He shook his head. "I shouldn't bitch about him so much. He can be hard to take, but his heart's in the right place. I owe him my life."

Kiki glanced at Dev's profile. It was a statement bordering on heavy, but she got the feeling it was a topic he didn't enjoy discussing. She watched a seagull circle and dip overhead as the gondola pulled up to their destination.

"Grazie," Dev said to the man after he'd paid, and then he offered Kiki his arm. She giggled at the old-fashioned gesture. "You're going to love this place," Dev said as they strolled along the water. "They have the best *pomodoro* ever. I used to come here whenever I was in town, but that's not too often anymore."

"Why not? Venues here too small for you?" Kiki teased.

When he didn't answer, she laughed. "I'm right, aren't I? I guess playing for less than twenty thousand isn't really worth your while."

"It's a matter of economies of scale. I love it, though—the intimacy of a smaller room. Bix used to book a few of those along the way, but lately he's all about the big box."

She shook her head in wonder. "Where was your first-ever performance?"

"You really want to know?" he asked with a sideways glance.

"I do."

He sighed deeply. "Hollywood Bowl."

Kiki's jaw dropped as they stopped in front of a restaurant called *La Columbina.* "Are you serious?

Your *first* show? Most artists get years to warm up in front of club audiences. How did you even deal?"

Dev held the door for her. "I admit it wasn't my most enjoyable night. I actually felt like a total failure, if you want to know the truth."

Something in his voice pulled her eyes toward his face. There was that distant expression again; was she reading too much into it?

"I think you should see it differently," she said as she stepped inside the restaurant. "You did something that scared the shit out of you and you conquered it. And look at you now—you refused to let fear stop you." She gave him an admiring smile, but Dev was busy looking for the maître d'. The restaurant was pure charm, with pale yellow tablecloths, white peonies on the tables and hurricane lamp lighting. A pianist played a classical piece in a corner of the room. Kiki glanced down at her outfit; it was perfect.

Abandoning his conversation when he spotted Dev, the maître d' rushed over to them with a huge grin on his face. "Signor Stone, what a pleasure," he said in a heavy Italian accent. "It has been too many years too long since I made your acquaintance."

Dev shook his hand. "Hello, Giorgio. It's wonderful to see you again."

The man's eyes switched to Kiki. "And who is the most beautiful young lady?"

"This is Kiki. And she's all mine, so hands off," Dev joked, pulling her into his side. Kiki's belly flopped over. *All mine.* It was what she dreamed of, wasn't it? To belong to Dev, and for him to belong to her? For today to be only the first of a thousand spent strolling exotic cities hand in hand, for the two of them to find that special combination of heat, compatibility and shared values that pointed toward forever?

No, not to find it—to simply acknowledge it. It was already there, plain as day for both of them to see. And tomorrow she would remind herself of the reason that could never be. But not tonight.

At their small table, Kiki settled into the chair Giorgio pulled out for her. "Too far away," Dev announced the moment the maître d' left, and swung his chair around so he was sitting at a ninety-degree angle from her. Her belly warmed pleasantly. She couldn't ever be close enough to him, and that he felt the same way made something inside her ache. He pressed his knee into hers and stroked her thigh as she started scanning the menu. She was down to *secondi piatti*, trying to figure out what *controfiletto di manzo* might be when she felt Dev's eyes on the side of her face.

"Kiki?"

She looked up into his mesmerizing eyes. "Yes?"

"Would you mind telling me what's wrong?"

Her brows drew together as her heart thumped. "Wrong? What are you talking about? This has been the best—"

"I'm not saying you're not having a good time," he

said, pushing a hand flat against hers. "But the Kiki I know is rarely at a loss for words, and I've heard way too much of my own life story today."

She kept her gaze steady. "I guess… I've just been really enjoying getting to know you."

Dev flipped her hand over and traced a spiral on her palm. God, how did he make every little touch feel so good? "I want to do the same thing, Kiki. Getting to know your body has been…*incredible*. I can't even sit beside you without thinking about what I want to do to you next. But there's so much in here—" he tapped a finger to her temple "—that I want to learn about you. And I feel like you're afraid to tell me."

Kiki opened her mouth, but words failed her. Dev's ability to see right into her and call her on her fears, his desire to truly know her was something she'd never experienced. This was a man who wouldn't allow her to replace painful honesty with humor or deflections, who would block her escape attempts and force her to confront her issues. She understood in that moment that the intimacy of their bodies was a mirror for the raw truth Dev wanted from her, and for the trust he was already handing over to her.

It was terrifying.

Only two people in the world knew Kiki's deepest, darkest secret. But she didn't need to spill that tonight, she told herself. All she owed him was the very best she could do right now.

She sat back in her chair, creating a little distance between them. "I've never been great at talking about myself. Just ask Nicola—it drives her crazy. But I... I want to be. With you, I mean. But it doesn't come naturally."

Dev gave her a disarming smile, lightening the moment. "It's easy—just tell me all your hopes, dreams and fears. Or if you want, you can start by telling me about your family."

She let out a sharp laugh. "Can we talk about something else, maybe? Like how badly I failed calculus?"

"Sure. But after that I'll still want to know about your family. So unless you get really turned on by math talk, you might just want to skip it."

Her hands spread out on the table as if she were bracing herself. She nodded. "Okay, then. Well, I'm an only child, and I have a wonderful father. I mean it—he's like the Rock of Gibraltar. He's a bridge engineer, but he retired a few years ago. He's not wealthy, but he was always smart with his money."

Dev smiled. "So the father isn't the bad guy in your picture—I'm glad to hear that. What's his name?"

"Lawrence."

Dev passed her the bread basket, which was laden with rosemary focaccia. Kiki took a piece and poured olive oil onto her side plate. Just then the waiter stepped in to take their order, which Dev managed to rattle out in charming broken Italian.

"What about your mother?" Dev asked the moment the waiter stepped away.

"Dad remarried when I was ten. Deirdre's... great." Kiki quickly dipped a piece of bread in her oil.

"I sense words unspoken."

She shrugged. "She is, really. Just...we never bonded as well as we should have. I blame myself."

Dev raised an eyebrow.

"I guess I wasn't the most accepting stepdaughter," she continued. "She wasn't my real mother, and..." Kiki trailed off. Since she'd only talked about her family dynamics with a handful of people in her life, she didn't have the go-to phrases ready to explain everything neatly the way some people did.

"Your birth mother. Is she not in the picture?"

Kiki took a breath. "She isn't. She, uh, left when I was six." She reached for her water glass, wishing the waiter would show up with her wine. Dev had passed on the alcohol, as usual. Though she respected the hell out of him for staying sober while he was on tour, she had a sudden desire to get stupid drunk with him like she had the night she'd told Nicola her story. But was that really what she needed to talk about her mother? There was something not quite right about that, but she'd never allowed herself to look at it too closely.

"That must have been so hard," Dev said, his expression pure empathy. Then he fell silent again, waiting.

"Sure it was. But I had my father," Kiki assured him with a bright, don't-pity-me smile. "It could have been so much worse."

Dev pushed a strand of hair off her face. "Don't do that."

"Do what?"

"Discount what you went through. Tell yourself you don't deserve to feel ripped off or sad or angry about it because some kids lose both parents in a car accident or get beaten or don't have enough to eat. Of course it could be worse, but it could also be better. She could have *not* left you."

Once again, Kiki felt paralyzed by his words. How could he know that she'd never allowed herself to feel cheated? That she'd always filed the whole thing away in her mind as a character-building experience that she had no right to whine about? And he was still looking into her eyes so intently she wanted to squirm. "Do you think it would have been better if she'd stayed?" he asked gently.

Kiki shook her head. "I've asked myself that question so many times, but I guess I don't have enough information to base an answer on." She paused, wishing she had something to occupy her hands—if not a drink, at least a cocktail napkin to rip up. But there was nothing to hide behind at this table, no protection. Only Dev's aqua eyes, the promise of a safe haven that she instinctively knew she could trust. She opened her mouth and let her story out. "That morning, I... I remember she insisted I wear my favorite outfit. A pink dress with a big gold heart on it. I didn't get new clothes very often, but I'd begged her for that one. After that, I don't remember what she made me for breakfast. I don't remember her... saying goodbye to me."

Put your shoes on, angel.

Those were the last words Kiki could remember her mother saying to her. Just an everyday instruction, but given softly, without the usual impatience Kiki was accustomed to. Did her mother know that her daughter had spent the past twenty-four years wondering if there was any meaning in those last words, that last clothing choice, that last hug? Wondering if they contained any evidence as to why she'd left her?

Kiki's eyes blurred over with tears. She brought her fingers up to stem them, breathing deeply. "She used to call me 'angel.'" Her voice caught in her throat. "But...she was depressed. I know that much. Not always, but before she left it seemed like she was always angry. But I still...loved her so much." Kiki took a steadying breath. "I think she planned to leave that day. That's why she wanted me to wear that outfit. I think she wanted me to think of her each time I wore it."

Dev wiped a tear away. "When did you know she wasn't coming back?"

Kiki's amarone had arrived, so she picked the glass up gratefully and took a sip. "After school. My mother had arranged for a friend's mom to take me until five o'clock that day. When six o'clock rolled around and she still hadn't shown up, the mom took me home to my father. I think—I knew the minute I walked in the door there was something wrong. He didn't look surprised. My mother was never late, so he should have been, but it was almost like he was expecting it." Kiki's nose was running now—*God, no*—but if Dev noticed, he didn't seem to care. He was sitting forward in his chair, absorbing every one of her words as if there were no one else in the room.

"And does he know why she left?"

"No. At least—he may have had his suspicions, but he never shared them with me. And I respect that so much, that he didn't want to ruin what few memories I have of her."

"But you never saw her again."

"No. Never." Kiki reached for her wine and swallowed a large gulp.

Dev finally leaned back in his chair, his expression thoughtful. "So you never found out why," he stated slowly. "And you've spent your whole life wondering."

"Yes."

"It's left a huge hole in your life. In *you*. I can't imagine what that must feel like."

Kiki placed her glass on the table. Her eyes flooded with tears again, but she made no move to wipe them away. So this was it, she thought—this was what it felt like to share your burden with some-

one who really cared. Sure, she'd told Jack about it
and he'd said all the right things, but she'd just been
reciting the facts. Leaving the conversation feeling
as emotionally impacted as if she'd told him what
she'd eaten for lunch that day. But now, as Dev circled a protective arm around her neck, she felt ripped
wide-open in a way that was perfectly *right*. As if
there was a precious gem at the bottom of her pain,
and all she had to do to claim it was allow her heartache to fill her.

Right in the middle of a Venetian restaurant, with
the rock star god of her dreams sitting across from
her. It was fucking crazy.

Dev lifted her hand to his mouth and gave it a long
kiss. His lips were warm and dry, but still so sensual.
"I will tell you one thing for sure, Strawberry. She's
missing out on so much."

Kiki's tears were still there, blurring her vision
and barely contained. *I may have found her. In Sydney*, she nearly blurted out, but thankfully she had
enough good sense left to stop herself. Telling Dev
that part wasn't an option. If Victoria O'Hare didn't
turn out to be her mother then no damage would be
done, but what if she did—and what if she told Kiki
she wanted nothing to do with her? Being rejected
by her yet again would sting, but reporting that fact
back to Dev was an admission so ugly Kiki hardly
dared contemplate it. He would be forced to look at
her differently, in the same worthless light that both
her mother and her ex-husband cast her in.

Dev was still holding her hand. "Kiki?"

"Yeah, rock star?"

"Thank you."

Thank you. For telling him her sad story, for dumping her huge burden on him. He was so damned different from any man Kiki had ever known.

"You're welcome," she said quickly just before their plates were placed before them, breaking the precious moment. Kiki breathed a silent sigh of relief. What just happened may have been magical in its own way, but she was more than ready to get back to the fantasy.

Giorgio swept in after the waiter left. "I hope you enjoy, Mr. Stone," he said, flourishing toward their plates.

"Thank you."

The man clasped his hands together. "And please to not make obligation for you, but the invitation…" He gestured toward the piano. "It is always open."

Dev grinned. "Thank you, Giorgio, but I think your crowd might be a little rowdy for me."

The man's face fell slightly, but he gave a bow as he stepped away. "As you wish."

Kiki looked at Dev in wonder. "Wait. Do you mean to tell me you play the piano, too?"

"Hardly," Dev responded. "I use real pianists in the studio."

"But you can carry a tune."

"I guess so—"

"Then *oh, my God*, I want to hear it!"

"But—"

"No buts. You said yourself you miss smaller venues." Kiki gave him a devilish grin. "I promise to make it worth your while." She batted her eyelashes at him playfully, but instead of relenting as she'd expected him to, he just reached for his water. He took a sip and set it down.

"Another time, okay?"

"It's just that I'd love to see—"

He cut her sentence off by leaning forward and kissing her. God, but he had a way of silencing her with his body—not that she was complaining. As his tongue slid against hers, he slipped his hand up her dress and applied firm pressure right where it counted. "It's been twenty-two hours since I've been inside you, and I'm about fucking ready to combust. We're not staying here a minute longer than we have to."

CHAPTER NINE

THE OUTSIDE OF the grand palazzo was breathtaking from the water, but it was nothing compared to the interior. For their night together Dev had chosen The Aman Canal Grande Hotel, the stuff of sixteenth-century dreams. As Dev climbed the stairs to their room with his arm wrapped firmly around Kiki's waist, he took in the intricate architecture, the silk-covered walls and crystal chandeliers the size of small cars.

He opened the door to their room with a flourish, smiling as he watched Kiki enter and spin around in wonder. On their left was a graceful carved fireplace, on their right a luxurious bathroom big enough to hold an armchair and settee, and above it all was a domed ceiling painted with angels. Bouquets of fresh flowers sat on the bedside tables, the desk and the bathroom vanity. The four-poster king bed was the centerpiece of the room, made up with a gray velvet duvet and a mountain of charcoal and white pillows.

"It's incredible," Kiki breathed. "Like a fantasy."

"You're the fantasy," Dev said. Pushing an arm behind her back, he pulled her to him tightly by the waist. Her mouth eagerly reached for his as she pressed into him unrelentingly, as if she could meld their two bodies into one. His need for her was consuming, but where it had once been for her lips, her body, her hot pussy, now it was for so much more. This woman was a fascinating study in contrasts that he'd never experienced. Organized and logical with endearing scatterbrained moments and a tough-talking sense of humor he couldn't get enough of. At the same time she built up his sexual energy to a fever pitch, she also calmed his soul like a soothing caress. And her fragile frame belied the incredible strength of her interior. She'd given him a window into the reason for that tonight, and now that it had been opened he wanted *everything*.

"You promised to get this dress off me," Kiki whispered into his mouth.

"I also promised to take it slowly."

As Dev turned her around to unzip her, he tried to bury his regret in the soft feel of her skin under his hand, the spicy floral scent of her. She'd opened up to him, and he should have done the same. He'd had the perfect opportunity at the restaurant—he could have told her about his first piano recital, that spring day when he was nine years old that he could trace back to the root of his anxiety. But it was so damned hard to let go of being Dev Stone, the guy who'd been born for the stage. That's what everyone thought about him, what Kiki believed, too, and he'd never let that image slip for any woman. He sensed that with Kiki he eventually would, but not yet. For now he still wanted to keep the persona intact. Confident and assured, commanding, powerful. These were the adjectives he'd built his career on, the ones that burned at the very core of his being.

Still balanced on her sexy heels, Kiki's dress dropped to the floor to expose her lingerie. Dev's cock, which he'd been making a steady effort to control all day, surged to life. He wrapped his arms around her from behind, murmuring into her neck as he captured a breast with one hand and her pussy with the other. "You're so beautiful and sexy you've got my fucking head spinning. All I want to do is lock you away and make you mine."

"Dev…" Her chest heaved as she tipped her head back into him, pressing his hands tighter to her with her own. "You're too perfect. It terrifies me," she whispered.

"I am not perfect," he whispered back, grasping her wrists to turn her toward him. "But we are perfect together."

Her eyes hooked onto his. "I know." He kissed her deeply, loving the wine-chocolate taste of her, almost frustrated by the limitations of his mouth to express his true yearning for her.

She reached for his shirt buttons and got the garment open, and then she slid her hands around his waist. "Take your pants off," she said, pushing his shirt to the floor.

Dev obeyed, tossing them aside. She looked down at the tented front of his boxers and back up at him, her pupils dilated with desire. Slowly, she worked her hands into his underwear and slid them down his hips, freeing the part of him that had been dying for her touch all day.

"The most beautiful cock ever. Award winning," she said, stroking him firmly. He shuddered as he focused on control. *Slowly.* It was so hard, but they both needed it. A chance to finally explore each other's bodies without a time limit or a screaming sense of urgency that pushed both of them to their physical limits. Dev knew there would be plenty more of that to come. "Would you be okay with me blowing your mind?" Kiki asked, looking up at him with those big, innocent eyes.

Dev's cock jerked in her hand. All that hot experience combined with that doll-like face—it was too much. "I could definitely handle that. But…"

"I know," she said, already trailing kisses down his torso as she lowered herself to the floor. "I'm so tiny. But I can handle you, believe me." Giving him a sweet smile, she grasped his cock firmly and swirled her tongue around his head. The sight of her on her knees, still wearing her heels and lingerie, was almost his undoing.

Dev planted his feet, feeling his balls pull in tightly. Kiki brought her hand up to cup them, and then she started licking and sucking his entire shaft with alternating pressure. He let out a low growl and started a restrained pumping into her mouth. It felt incredible, but he was still afraid of hurting her.

She reached for one of his hands, placed it firmly on the back of her neck and looked up at him. "I've felt you fuck me hard, Dev, and it doesn't feel like this. It feels like you're driving into me like it's the last fuck of your life. I want the same thing from you right now. Don't hold back."

He pulled a strand of her beautiful hair up and wrapped it around his shaft. Just the thought of fucking her mouth with abandon was bringing him closer to the edge. "It feels so good. I just… I don't want to hurt you."

She gave him a sassy grin. "Then let me surprise you. Oh, and, Dev?"

"Yeah?"

"Come in my mouth. I'm dying to taste you."

Dev's eyes widened. Those dirty words coming from that sweet mouth released something savage in him. Keeping one hand at the back of her neck, he brought the other to the side of her head and started moving, faster this time. His hands wound tighter into her hair as his breath became increasingly labored. "So good," he gasped. "Fucking amazing."

As Kiki still held his cock with one hand, Dev felt

her grab his ass with the other to make him move
even faster. He was gasping for breath now, the sound
filling the silent room as his desire raised him to a
place so heavenly that it brought goose bumps to
his skin. He needed this so badly. He needed *her* so
badly. With a final driving thrust and a loud curse,
he emptied everything into her—all of his longing
and hopes and failures, the very man he'd been before her and never wanted to be again. In that moment his mind opened along with his body, and all
he saw was her face.

In Kiki's dream, Dev wasn't fucking her. He was
making love to her, moving inside her, behind her,
with one finger massaging her clit with perfect
strokes. As the heat within her built, she heard him
whispering to her, "There's no one else. Only you. I
never want to be without you."

She was awake. The bedside lamp burned dimly
beside the bed, which was still piled high with
charcoal pillows. A low gas flame flickered in the
gracefully carved fireplace. Kiki was lying on her
side, and Dev was behind her with his cock deep
inside her. She moaned as she realized her dream
had turned to reality, that the intense passion building at her center was real and not imagined. She
reached her arms over her head to sink her hands
into his soft hair. His face nuzzled into her, and
then, without missing a stroke, he rolled her onto

her front so he was lying on her back. She spread-eagled her legs.

"I was having such a good dream. But this is even better," she sighed, loving the heavy feel of him on top of her.

"Oh, yeah? Did you get wet in your dream? Because I woke up hard for you, and you were ready for me."

"I'm permanently ready with you around."

"What were you dreaming about?"

She turned her face to the side so she could see him looming over her. They were still in Venice, which meant the fantasy wasn't over yet. She could still pretend that this was her life, that she could actually have a future with a man as wonderful as Dev.

That they could fall in love.

So dangerous, the thoughts she was having. But Dev was too amazing not to become addicted to, like a potion that had put a spell on her. "You," she answered simply.

He breathed the words into her ear, sending a shiver down her spine. "I'm not a dream. I'm real, and I'm yours." And then, before she could reply, he was pushing her hips into the mattress forcefully while he drove into her. The abrupt change in pace brought a cry of pleasure to her lips, and within seconds the pressure of the mattress on her clit did her in. She spiraled up, up, up, verbalizing her ecstasy in a long moan before she crashed back down again, filled with every sweet and wonderful part of him.

God, but she was in so much fucking trouble.

CHAPTER TEN

CHICKEN MARBELLA, MASHED POTATOES and green beans on the table. Crème brûlée on the counter, ready to be finished off after dinner with the small torch she'd borrowed from catering.

Kiki happily surveyed the results of her efforts as she heard the treadmill winding down at the other end of the bus. Dev was finished with his workout, and after a quick shower they would sit down for yet another of her home-cooked meals.

Over the past week, she and Dev had fallen into a routine that broke all of her rules with its undertones of coupledom and domestic bliss. On the way from Venice to Rome, Dev had asked her to stay in his bus with him for the remainder of the tour, and the rest of the crew had even treated her as if nothing was amiss, likely too intimidated by their boss to do otherwise. During the mornings she and Dev worked side by side on the bus, with him stroking her thigh as she tooled on her laptop or covering his phone to kiss her while he was on a call. After that they either spent the travel time in a state of fevered lust or, if it wasn't a travel day, went their separate ways for a while and came together again for dinner, conversation and sex before Dev's show. Each day was finished off with a final round of passion and another night spent entwined together on the bed he'd bought just for her. It was heaven, perfect, better than anything she ever could have dreamed of.

Each day of this is just bringing you both closer to disaster and heartbreak, the voice at the back of her head kept reminding her. And yet here she was yet again, successfully blocking it out.

Dev came out of the bathroom wearing a pair of sweatpants and a T-shirt. Kiki couldn't help but stare as he pulled up a chair and grinned at her offerings. Even dressed completely down, he was the epitome of sexy. "You've outdone yourself again," Dev said as he circled his left arm backward.

"Are you okay?"

"Just my shoulder. It gets sore sometimes when I play a few nights in a row and forget to correct my posture."

"Sounds like you need a massage."

"I could see that going sideways very fast." He grinned as he loaded up her plate for her.

"That's the whole point."

"So, what, this morning and—" he glanced at his watch "—two hours ago wasn't enough for you?"

"Not nearly."

"Not that I don't appreciate the offer, but would

you believe I'm the only living being who doesn't like massages?"

"You're kidding. What's that all about?"

"I don't know. Maybe it's because Bix is always hounding me to get them."

Bix. Kiki weighed her response carefully before speaking. "Finally something he and I agree on."

Dev lifted his eyes. "Like I said, he's not exactly Mr. Charisma. But he does care about me."

Kiki decided to drop it. Bix had always been standoffish with her to say the least, avoiding eye contact and refusing to acknowledge anything positive about her working relationship with Dev, such as the streamlined press communications she'd implemented and his huge social media boost since she'd taken over. But even if she found Dev's words hard to believe, she had to accept them at face value. He'd known Bix a hell of a lot longer than she had, and she had to assume that anyone in Dev's position would have learned to weed out the leeches from the tried-and-true pretty quickly.

Dev cut into his chicken and took a bite. "This is incredible."

Kiki waved his compliment away. "I cheated today and took the chicken from catering because I didn't have time to get to the grocery store. Speaking of which, do you ever find it weird being in all these cities and not really experiencing them?"

Dev laughed. "I forget where I am sometimes."

"That happened to me for the first time today. I

got in the taxi and forgot what language I was supposed to be trying to speak. I had to look around at the street signs to remember I was in Hamburg. It was so weird."

"Welcome to my life."

"Really, I don't know how you do it."

"I've heard there are worse jobs out there," he said with a half smile.

"Yeah, but still. To do what you do and not collapse under the pressure? It's a miracle." She gave him an admiring look, but he was busy salting his mashed potatoes. *Modest as usual*, she thought.

"Is that truffle I taste?" he asked as he tried the potatoes. "Seriously, where did you learn to cook like this?"

"I don't really know. It seems like I just always knew how. Dad worked long hours, and after Mom left…" She shrugged. "There was a lady down the street who used to watch me after school. I remember standing on a stool in her kitchen and watching her cook, and after that I started asking Dad for cookbooks. I think the responsibilities made me feel like a big girl. On the weekends I started taking over the laundry and vacuuming. I remember the first time I tried folding Dad's clothes. I must have been around seven, and they were probably a mess. But he hugged me hard enough to crush me. I didn't understand then why he had tears in his eyes, but I do now."

Dev shook his head. "That's incredible. So much

responsibility for a little girl, and yet you never complained."

Kiki laughed. "Yeah, well, I probably created more work for him in the beginning, but eventually I figured it out. And then Deirdre came along. I guess I never really thought about it until now, but she probably made me feel a little bit replaced in my dad's life. Even though she was only doing exactly what she should have been doing, which was giving me my childhood back. Anyway…" Kiki searched her brain for a change of topic. For someone who'd never been big on talking about herself, she was doing an awful lot of it these days.

"Do you ever think about trying to find her?" Dev asked suddenly.

Kiki's heart skipped a beat as she stalled for time. "She was living with Dad last time I checked," she said, forking her green beans.

Dev smiled patiently. "I mean your mother, Strawberry."

Kiki took her time chewing. Even if she wasn't ready to tell him the exact truth, she wasn't going to lie to him, either. "I've thought about it. I mean, I've looked, actually. But she doesn't seem to want to be found. Nowhere obvious, anyway. My father— he always says that I might not like what I find. I mean, what if I meet her and she's this person I totally can't relate to, or she's downright horrible, and I regret it? You can't unsee or unknow something once you've crossed certain lines." Her mouth felt dry. She took a sip of sparkling water, wondering if she dared tell Dev the one piece of information she had on her mother. But a glance at his face told her she was going to do just that. He was looking at her intently, not just like he wanted to absorb every word she was willing to share with him, but like he wanted to pull all of her pain into himself so she wouldn't have to feel it anymore.

It was wrong. She was letting him have feelings for her when all she had in store for him was disappointment. But she was so far gone herself that the thought of either telling him the truth or ending things sent her down a hole of emptiness so deep she hardly dared contemplate it. Appetite suddenly gone, she put her fork down.

But Dev remained undeterred. "You have a theory about why she left, don't you?"

God, how did he do that? How did he know things about her that she barely acknowledged herself? "I, uh…" She lifted her napkin to her lips, dabbed at nothing and replaced it in her lap. Her heart was thudding. "I have a cousin who's a few years older than me. James—his mother is my mother's sister. They were the last link I had to my mother after she left. James and I used to talk about her a lot, and he was so patient with me even though I'm sure I drove him crazy asking the same questions over and over again. Anyway, he let it slip once that about a year before my mother left, she called his mom one night in a panic and asked her to come and meet her. She was a single mother, so she had to drag James along with her—he was about eight at the time. They ended up in this really dodgy apartment in a bad part of town, and James said my mom was…acting really strangely. Like as in, totally skitchy and freaked out and asking for money." She shook her head, lost in thought. "James told me he thought she was on drugs. I asked my father about it, but all he would say was that you never know a person completely, something like that. And then I guess he had a word with James, because he wouldn't talk about it after that. It was all just shoved under the rug."

Dev's gaze didn't waver from her face. "So you think she might have left you because she had a habit?"

"Sure. I mean it doesn't explain why, exactly, but it's the only thing that makes any sense." She shook her head. "I don't know, but that conversation really affected me. I never did drugs. Even as a teenager— I didn't even try pot. I wondered if I might have some predisposition to getting hooked, and that terrified me."

Dev put his knife and fork down. Moving his chair to one side, he patted his thighs. "Come here." Kiki walked over to him, and he pulled her into his lap so she was straddling him. "Can I tell you something?"

"A deep, dark secret hopefully. Something that makes me feel a little more normal."

He moved his forehead to touch hers, making his face go blurry. "I admire you so much," he said hoarsely. "Everything you've been through makes you even more amazing. There's nothing about you that's normal, and I love that."

Kiki's throat felt thick. God, how she longed to give herself over to this man, to succumb to the constant pull toward him she felt in her body, her mind and yes…her heart. But she couldn't. Doing so would be horribly unfair to him, and the longer she waited to put an end to this, the harder it would be for both of them.

But not tonight, she thought. *Tomorrow.*

"Can I tell *you* something?" Kiki asked, moving her face back and cupping his jaw with her hands. "You need a flaw. Seriously. I'm getting kind of sick of looking for cracks and not finding any."

Was it her imagination, or did a shade pull briefly over his eyes? He brought his mouth to hers and kissed her deeply. "Maybe you just bring out the best in me, Strawberry. Now, you promised me a massage."

"I thought you didn't like them."

He grasped her hands and pressed them flat to his, pushing her back playfully. "I'm willing to let you change my mind."

She could already feel him hardening at the place their groins met. "I see I'm not the only one hoping for a happy ending," she said, rocking her pelvis back and forth against his growing thickness. "Can I even ask if you have any massage oil on hand without your mind sinking into the gutter?"

"Not a chance. And no massage oil."

"Well, I noticed coconut oil in the kitchen, but it's kind of…not a good idea."

Dev raised an eyebrow. "How come?"

"It breaks down condoms."

"Now whose mind is in the gutter?"

"Guilty." She grinned.

"Okay, so…" He trailed off, and it took her a moment to understand what his silence was suggesting.

"Um, are you—?"

"You're the only woman I've been with in over a year," he said, his aqua eyes electric. "And I'm clean. You?"

Kiki's mind was spinning. She wanted to feel him like that—*God*, how she did—but it was another step that would bring them closer together. Another promise made with her body that the rest of her wouldn't be able to fulfill.

"Kiki?"

She cleared her throat. "I was tested recently," she said, her voice catching slightly. "All good."

Dev nodded at her slowly. "And…birth control?"

She forced herself to keep her gaze steady. He wanted this. She wanted this. In the morning she'd tell him the truth about herself. But tonight, she was going to enjoy him as if they could last forever. "It's taken care of."

"You're not going to make this easy for me, are you?" Dev said as Kiki pulled her jeans off, revealing the baby-pink thong that matched her bra. He was sitting on the bed, stripped down to his boxers as she undressed.

"I'm just making myself comfortable. Now lie down," she commanded, pushing him backward. As she straddled his waist, Dev looked at the ceiling, determined to keep himself under control for at least a few minutes. Kiki dipped a hand into the coconut oil, rubbed her hands together and smoothed it over his shoulder. "How's this?" she asked, holding his arm up to access his traps. "Torturous enough for you?"

"Sure, but for all the right reasons. You get one more minute before you're riding my cock," he groaned. Predictably, he was already rock hard as the slippery strokes brought to mind another part of his body he'd much rather she be stroking. And thinking about fucking Kiki was so much better than thinking about what she'd just told him about her mother. So much better than lying here trying to convince himself that prescription drugs were nothing compared to the hard stuff she'd probably been into, and that Kiki never had to find out because he was going to quit anyway.

Just as soon as the tour was over.

He closed his eyes, determined to push everything but *her* out of his head. It didn't take much. Just the thought of what they were about to do, of how it would feel to be inside her with no barrier between them, had his mind exactly where he wanted it to be.

He opened his eyes in time to see Kiki unclasp her

bra and toss it aside, apparently having given up the pretense of anything therapeutic coming out of this session. Using the oil she still had on her hands, she brought them to her breasts and started circling them teasingly. He went to reach for her, but she pushed his arms over his head. "Stay still," she commanded. He watched her, prepared to have his mind blown.

Inching herself backward, she slid over his aching cock until it was in front of her. Then she started stroking him with her slippery hands as she landed her flickering tongue on his head. He bucked up as her hands came down again and again, one after the other, pulling at the base of his erection to make it stand perfectly upright. She spoke to him softly. "Do you know how good you feel inside me? How perfectly you fill me up? It's going to feel so amazing when my pussy is wrapped around your cock. It's going to take all your control not to come as soon as you feel how wet I am for you."

It was too much, just right, not enough. He opened his mouth to tell her how much he wanted her, how incredibly beautiful she was, how he never wanted to be without her, but she brought a hand over his mouth. "Shh…this is all about you, rock star. All about how much I worship you. I never thought I'd say that, but I do. I wish we could just fuck all day long. Are you ready for me?"

He nodded mutely, afraid of what might come out of his mouth if he dared open it. He was always the one in control. Feeling his power was what enabled him to do everything in his life—write songs, perform, deal with other people's expectations, fuck. But right now, giving all of his power over to this woman felt like absolute perfection.

Kiki rose up and leaned forward, positioning her pussy over his face. "No touching, but I thought you might be curious to see how wet I am." He looked up at that glistening beauty, aching with every cell of his body to feel her. To make her experience the same desperate need that was pulsing through him with every agonizing fill of his lungs.

But he knew she was, because her barely controlled breath told him so. "Kiki, God—"

"Shh…get ready. Here it comes."

Straddling his hips, she slowly lowered herself until his head was buried inside her. A groan escaped his lips at the incredible feeling. "More. Please—"

Kiki cut his request off by driving herself downward on his cock. She rose up slowly, and then she repeated the motion again and again—up slowly, down hard—until he was ready to lose his mind. The slipperiness of the oil was like the icing on the sweetest cake, bringing him closer and closer to what he knew was going to be the biggest and best fucking orgasm of his life.

"You like that?" she panted, anchoring herself to his pelvis and rocking back and forth with subtle movements. His balls were begging for release.

"God, yes."

She pushed her fingers into his mouth, and he

sucked them hungrily. "I could do this all night," she teased, slipping a nipple between her fingers. "Or I could let you get on top of me and fuck me for all you're worth."

That was it, just the golden ticket he needed. Moving with the speed of a man possessed, he rolled her until he was on top, and then he grabbed her thighs and squeezed them together so her pussy felt even tighter on his cock. He was gasping for air along with her now, their panting breaths mingling as one as each cry brought them closer...and closer...

The world shrank to just the two of them, each climbing toward their ultimate pleasure and yet knowing it could only be reached because of the other. In that moment, sex took on a new meaning for Dev. When he closed his eyes he knew without a doubt that it was Kiki. Now and for always, the only person on earth he wanted to feel this close to. And together they reached that earth-shattering moment of mutual release, driven by their entwined minds and hearts as much as their physical bodies.

CHAPTER ELEVEN

"THIS IS AMAZING. I can't believe they threw it together in just two hours," Kiki said to Dev as they sat down at a rustic wooden table. She glanced around the outdoor space. Though mere steps away from the tour buses, the gravel parking lot had been magically transformed into a charming beer garden by Dev's catering and construction staff. The restaurant was complete with seating for the entire crew, authentic German food and even massive steins of beer, which were being circulated by buxom waitresses hired especially for the occasion.

Dev grinned. "It's kind of a tradition on my tours. Since it's not always easy for us to get out into the world, every now and then the crew brings the world to us."

Kiki didn't comment, knowing full well that Dev was up to his modest ways again. Germany was home to his most numerous and rabid fans, and she knew that he simply couldn't go out in public here without being mobbed.

She turned her attention to her beer, hoping it might take the edge off her nagging guilt. The late afternoon air was chilly, but the setup even included heating lamps—and since tonight was the last European date, the crew's mood was celebratory. Everything was perfect. *Dev* was perfect.

And she was a fucking fraud. It had been almost twenty-four hours since she'd promised herself she would tell him the truth about herself, and yet here she still was. She was selfish, cowardly, avoiding the truth just so she could keep the man she was falling so deeply for close to her. And she couldn't escape the distinct feeling that it was all about to blow up in her face.

"I can't believe we're in Munich already," she said, trying to keep her mind off the churning in her gut. "And that in just two days we'll, uh, be in Sydney." Quickly, she reached for one of the large salt-speckled pretzels sitting in a basket. She could feel Dev's eyes on her as she squeezed mustard onto her side plate.

"Have you ever noticed that you occupy your hands when you're talking about something that makes you uncomfortable?"

Her heart skipped a beat. "No."

Dev tapped a finger on the table. "Is there something about going to Sydney that's got you nervous?"

Jesus. There it was, point-blank. How could he know her like that? She *wanted* to tell him about Victoria O'Hare, she realized, but why? Not only was a journalist due to show up any moment to interview Dev for a magazine article, her admission would just be one more thing to bring them closer. And she didn't think it was possible to feel any closer to him than she already did.

She settled for a partial truth. "I guess it just symbolizes the beginning of the end. Australia's the last stop, and then it's back to reality."

Dev traced his finger up her arm. "I don't know about you, but I'm loving my reality right now."

Her belly flopped over. *Loving*. There was no point in denying it—it was exactly the way she felt.

Fuck.

"Dev Stone, as I live and breathe."

Kiki glanced up to see a heavyset woman looking down at Dev with a smile. Her hair was pulled back into a tight ponytail that made her head look too small for her body.

"Petra," Dev said, standing to kiss her cheeks. "Wonderful to see you again. This is... Kiki Becker."

Kiki extended a hand, not missing Dev's omission of her title. Even if she still worked for him, her place in his life was firmly established as something else now. Yet another reminder that she'd let this whole thing go too far.

"I'm Dev's assistant," she clarified. "He asked me to be here for the interview."

"Of course. Petra Niemer, *Connect Magazine*," the woman said with a light German accent, seating herself beside Dev. Kiki knew the magazine from

the newsstands, a continent-wide European publica-
tion and the direct competition to *Hello!* Petra with-
drew a small recorder from her briefcase. "I know
you have a show to prepare for tonight, Dev, so I'll
cut right to the chase if you don't mind."

"Fire away."

Petra started the recorder and started tossing out
questions to Dev about his early beginnings, the difference between the European and American music
scenes, his impression of German fans and the in-
spiration for his latest album. And somehow, with
Dev being Dev, he was able to turn the whole thing
into something that was about Kiki. Instead of looking at Petra as he replied to her questions, he gazed
intently at Kiki like she was part of his answer. He
flipped his hair back and trailed a hand up his bare
arm so deliberately she could almost feel it on her
own skin. He turned his hips toward her and opened
his legs, giving her a perfect view of his package.
The nonverbal exchange was even obvious enough
for Petra to pick up on, judging from her glances at
Kiki. She felt heat sweeping up her body. She was
so distracted by Dev's arousing body language that
she hadn't listened to much of anything he'd said,
and that suited her just fine. She'd made a vow to
herself not to read his press when the tour began.
She'd told herself it was because she wanted to get
to know him for herself, drawing her conclusions
about him by her own experience rather than by a

collection of filtered statements, but that wasn't the whole truth, was it?

She *had* watched one interview early on, after their very first night together. And it was the reason guilt weighed on her as heavily as a backpack filled with stones.

Dev broke eye contact with her for a moment, and she was jerked back into the present.

"...but the time comes for new ideas," he was saying. "Sure, I think of retiring sometimes. I started off writing, and sometimes I think I'd like to go back to that. Producing, maybe. Seventeen years has been a long run."

"So you'd like to settle down? Have a family?" Petra asked, leaning forward in her chair.

Kiki froze.

No.

She was certain that the mild blush on her cheeks was turning to the shade of a ripe tomato. She felt sick. She could feel Dev's eyes boring into her, but she couldn't meet them. Using her fingertip to fish a nonexistent speck out of her beer, she waited.

"Definitely," Dev said.

Definitely. The word reverberated in her head.

"I think I've always known I'd want a family someday," he continued. "The whole shebang—wife, kids and dog. Musicians love to complain about how hard it is to hold a relationship down, but the truth is that it's just a matter of priorities. If you get to that point where meaningful connection with someone feels more important than everything else that's going on in your life, then you make the leap." He paused. "Of course, it helps if you finally meet the person."

Kiki couldn't have helped lifting her gaze to Dev if her life depended on it. She found his face and there were those aqua eyes, directly on her. Her cheeks burned hard enough to tingle. A wave of panic washed over her. She wanted nothing more than to get out of there, but she was trapped. Dev's assistant by day, his lover by night, and destroyer of his dreams if she kept up this charade any longer.

She forced herself to stay in her seat with a promise: as soon as the interview was over, she would walk away from him for good.

As Dev watched Petra's retreating back, he could feel the dull thud of regret beat in his gut. He was a fucking fool to have answered her question honestly. He should have hedged it, played it cool, told her questions about his personal life were off-limits. But he'd walked right into it, made brazen by how amazing things had been going with Kiki for the past week. There was no way she couldn't be feeling what he was feeling—he'd been sure of it.

But he'd forgotten one thing, that the Kiki he'd had to talk into taking a job with him was a serious flight risk. Beneath the amazing sex, the honest revelations and the deep emotional connection, she was still as skittish as a prey animal. And her expression had told him everything he didn't want to know.

He turned to her. She was already gathering her belongings up, her face etched with that jumpy look that he'd thought was gone for good. "I think I forgot my phone on your bus," she said as she scrambled around in her bag.

Your bus. Not *our* bus, not even *the* bus.

Dev stood up with her, and together they walked in a silence so unbearable he finally had to break it. "Leave it to me to make everything awkward," he said as they reached the door to the bus.

"Hmm?" Kiki responded distractedly, taking the two steps up and entering the lounge. She immediately started searching the room for her phone.

"I said that was a little awkward," Dev repeated. "Do you think you could stand still for a minute?"

"Sure! It's just that I'm supposed to be in a meeting with Wardrobe right now, so maybe..." She glanced at her watch and frowned.

"Kiki."

"Uh-huh?" She reached for her phone, finally located on the bookshelf, and dropped it into her bag. Still not looking at him. Wanting to get away from him as fast as humanly possible. As if Venice had never happened, as if the past week of domestic bliss and deep conversations and the kind of earth-shaking sex that had him feeling things he'd never felt before had only happened in his imagination. And she had felt it, too—he *knew* she had. So why was she so god-damned resistant?

He placed a hand on her shoulder to still her. "I should have told Petra to mind her own business. But…" He shook his head, searching for the right words. "I've made it my policy to be honest when I do these things. It's all part of what I was telling you before—putting the celebrity on an even playing field with the public, at least as much as I have the power to." He squared his jaw. Screw it—he wasn't going to play games, and he certainly didn't see a future with any woman who was going to, either. "I guess I thought you were the kind of person to appreciate that."

"What, brutal honesty?" Kiki snorted. "Believe me, I got plenty of that in my last marriage and I can handle it just fine."

"Then why don't you try being honest with *me*? What are you so afraid of, Kiki? Why does the idea that I have feelings for you freak you out so much? I mean, Jesus Christ! Have I been alone in those bedrooms? I thought you were there with me, I really did! Or was that all just regular sex and casual conversation to you?"

"You know it wasn't." Her voice trembled.

"Do I? How?"

Her eyes were shiny. "Listen, Dev, I… I'm just not a commitment kind of girl, okay? And you made me change my mind about that. I saw…something with you I've never seen with anyone else. But I've tried the commitment thing, and it just didn't work out for—"

"Why?" The word was out of Dev's mouth before he could stop it. Fuck it. An explanation—after everything that had happened between them, she owed him that much at least.

Kiki's brow tensed and then smoothed again. "Why? Because I thought I was cut out for that kind of life, but I'm not. You made me break all my own rules, Dev. I'm already falling for you—I mean, Jesus, who wouldn't? Any woman would walk to the ends of the earth for you. And I'm so sorry that when you decided you want a different kind of life, you chose the wrong woman to think about doing it with."

"But you're *not* the wrong woman!" Dev slapped his fists down on the table in frustration. "My heart is yours, can't you see that? I've already given it to you, and guess what? I don't want it back! So you need to give me a reason, Kiki—a *real* reason. Because you are really good at avoiding the questions that matter. And after the time we've had together, you owe that much to me."

But Kiki was shaking her head wildly. "I never should have let it go this far. I never should have moved into your tour bus and gotten all cozy with you. It just—*this* doesn't feel like the real world. Being on tour, living on four wheels—I fooled myself into thinking it didn't count."

"Didn't count?" His throat worked up and down.

Was this really happening? Had he really opened his heart and soul up like he never had before to a woman who told him their time together *didn't count*? "A reason," he repeated furiously. "Give me one."

Kiki drew herself up, crossing her arms over her tiny chest. She looked like she was going to break for a moment, but then her expression steeled again. "All you need to know is that you're much better off without me."

"Oh, yeah?" He whirled around, paced a couple of times and then stepped close to her again. "Then say it, Kiki. Tell me right now that you're fine with going back to a life without me. That you're fine with never feeling our bodies move together again. That you're fine with not waking up and looking at me and knowing that what we have is fucking magical. And then I'll let you go, no more questions asked."

She squirmed under his gaze, her defiant expression finally wilting. But still she said nothing.

Dev forced his voice to be calm. "I get it, Kiki. Your mother rejected you, and apparently your ex-husband did, too, which proves nothing other than that he's the biggest asshole on earth. *But I won't do that to you.* Can't you get that through your head? If you would just let yourself trust—"

"Trust?" Kiki spat the word out like it was poison. She was backing away from him now, clutching her handbag to her chest as she moved toward the door. "Believe me, Dev, okay? You just have to be-

lieve that this is for the best." Her back hit the door, and she reached around for the knob as he watched helplessly. "I'll stay on as your assistant until the end of the tour. But you don't want anything more from me other than that."

And then she was gone and Dev was watching the door bang shut behind her. He clutched his hands to his head, wanting to scream at the top of his lungs. Instead he spun around, stalked toward the lounge and stopped cold in his tracks.

On the bookshelf next to the sofa, Kiki had placed two souvenirs from their day in Venice together: a colorful vase of Venetian glass and a caricature sketch they'd had done by a street artist. He picked up the drawing. In the picture, a hotshot-looking Dev was playing his guitar while Kiki stood beside him rolling her eyes. They'd giggled like a pair of teenagers when they'd seen it. The kitchen was tidied up the way she liked it with the dish towel folded into a neat square. Hanging on the bathroom door he could see his robe, the one she'd taken to wearing each morning. This bus had always felt like a prison cell to Dev, requiring all his strength to not climb the walls or crawl right out of his skin during the endless commutes. But when Kiki had been with him it didn't feel like that. For one short week, this strange place had felt exactly like home. Which was only one reason he wanted to insert that maddening woman into his life and keep her there forever.

And she had stuck around day after day, letting him believe that could happen.

Dev let the drawing fall to his feet, resisting a childish urge to stomp on it. A sick feeling was bubbling up from his belly to his chest. *Helplessness.* He was used to dealing with his problems alone, probably a result of feeling he had to pretend everything was wonderful since he'd made it big. In the beginning he'd hinted to his family and friends that his life wasn't as rosy as they imagined, but their unsympathetic silences and dubious looks soon brought that kind of talk to a grinding halt. Dev learned that it was better that way anyway, because as much as they couldn't relate to him, he also couldn't relate to the stability of their world.

Trust started to erode as friends he'd known his whole life suddenly showed up asking for business loans or a celebrity introduction. Meanwhile, the wall between him and his family grew. Though he knew his parents were immensely proud of him, their main focus always seemed to be on their media empire. Dev remembered feeling a flare of jealousy when his father announced that Alex would be taking over the family business after their mother died. And it wasn't just because they'd be working together, it was that Alex was so damned self-assured. His little brother was fine with working behind the scenes. He didn't need an audience to feel worthy, and Dev desperately envied him that.

Right now Dev would have traded a thousand audiences to have Kiki. The calm he felt when he was with her was worth so much more to him, but the situation was completely out of his control.

He had to do *something* or he was going to lose his mind. He could call his little brother for some advice, he thought. Even though the brothers had never been tight, Alex's recent visit to Moretta had cleared the air between them, and he seemed like someone Dev could turn to.

But no. He'd given Kiki every chance to explain herself, to make things right again, and instead she'd just walked away. If he was going to break a thirty-six-year habit by reaching out to his brother for support, it better be for a really good reason—not a woman who'd let him believe she had feelings for him and then dropped him like a hot fucking potato.

CHAPTER TWELVE

DURING HER SHATTERING conversation with Dev, the last things on Kiki's mind were the ramifications of returning to her own tour bus. But she'd definitely failed to consider one thing: the crowded space was very inconvenient for emotional meltdowns.

By the time she stepped into her temporary home for the first time in a week, it was seven o'clock at night and she'd managed to hold it together for three hours while she completed the day's tasks. Whatever was happening with Dev, unprofessionalism wasn't an option for her. After she'd left his bus she'd immediately swung into action, blanking her mind out by helping to fix a wardrobe emergency, answering a slew of fan mail and taking a taxi to three stores to look for Scotty's beloved Skittles. *I can fall apart later*, she kept telling herself.

But now later was here, and she realized for the first time how her bus mates would probably look at her: Dev's assistant-turned-lover, pitched out of his bed just like all the others. There was no mistaking the lull in conversation that her entrance caused, but she didn't even care. Kiki knew that what she'd had with him was special. No other man would ever compare to Dev—she accepted that as fact. The only question was whether she'd be able to get over him enough to even consider letting another man touch her.

Her tears were dangerously close to falling. *It's for the best*, she reminded herself as she climbed up to the sleeping quarters in search of privacy. *You got the worst over with, and now you just have to stand your ground. If he found out the truth about you later, it would be even worse.*

Her bunk was still there, seemingly untouched, but there were several people lounging on their own beds. She dropped down on the mattress, grateful for the curtain she could pull around it. Her hands went to her face as silent tears coursed down her cheeks. Images flashed through her brain—Dev's eyes meeting hers in the beer garden, his fists slapping down on the table, his incredulous expression as she'd walked out the door.

It was the hardest thing she'd ever done. But she wasn't willing to make a man like Dev compromise his dreams to be with her—and that was exactly what he'd do if he knew the truth about her. He'd tell her they'd find a way to make it work, that all he really needed was her, and she'd let him talk her into it because he was the only man on earth she wanted.

Then one day reality would set in, and he'd wake up and realize he'd made a huge mistake.

She couldn't bear it.

From the handbag at her feet, Kiki heard her phone ringing. She lifted her face from her pillow, which was now soaked in tears and smeared with mascara, and stared at it miserably. The only person in the world she wanted to hear from right now was Dev, but she knew that was both an impossible and unfair expectation. Hooking the handle with her foot, she brought the bag to her hand and halfheartedly dug her phone out.

Nicola Metcalfe, the screen informed her. Kiki sighed. She hadn't talked to her friend since she'd left for the tour, only sending her a few texts along the way. And she hadn't said a word to her about Dev. But it was Sunday afternoon on Moretta, and Nicola was likely calling for a full download—which was the last thing Kiki was up for right now.

She let the call go to voice mail, but a minute later a text came through. Call me the minute you get this.

Kiki suppressed a groan. Nicola wasn't in the habit of bossing her friends around, so it had to be something important. Wiping her tears away, Kiki focused on making sure her voice was steady when she hit the call button. She was almost starting to panic, thinking something might really be wrong, when Nicola picked up and addressed her in a stern voice. "Becker. What the hell is going on?"

Kiki pulled the phone away from her ear and then replaced it. "Nice to hear from you, too, Nic."

"This isn't a hangout girlie call, okay? Alex just got off the phone with Dev. He's seriously devastated, Kiki. Do you know how often Dev calls his brother for advice? Exactly never. Well, I guess you can make that once now."

Kiki's heart skipped a beat as she ducked out of her bunk. If she was going to have this conversation, she needed at least a little privacy. She made her way down the steps and across the lounge, ignoring the eyes that followed her. She let the door shut behind her as she stepped down to the parking lot. The October evening air felt refrigerated. Kiki pulled her cardigan around her as she tried to come up with a snappy response to her friend's admonishment, but her mind stayed blank. It seemed that the most devastating experience of her life had a way of locking her wit away. "Thanks for letting me know, but I really—"

"Don't want to talk about it?" Nicola interrupted. "What a surprise. For someone who never seems to run out of shit to say, you have a funny way of keeping all the stuff that really matters to yourself."

Kiki's mouth fell open. Of the two women, Kiki was the one with the edge. Nicola was softer and more laid-back, but right now their roles felt firmly reversed—and Kiki didn't like it one bit. "What the hell would you know?" she blasted back. "I made a mistake and slept with him again—so sue me. I finally came to my senses, okay? Like I said before, the last thing I need is to get involved with someone like Dev."

"'Someone like Dev'?" Nicola mocked, sounding pissed off enough to spit. "Please. If Dev hasn't proven to you he's a changed man, then it's only because you're purposely not seeing it. Don't forget how long I've known you, Kiki. You might want to *think* you're all about the one-nighters, but you want the real deal. You never would have gotten married if you didn't. Hell, you never would have let Dev into your bed again if you didn't. So what's the big secret, Kiki? Why would you send the man of your dreams packing right after he admitted he saw a future with you?"

Kiki swallowed hard. "Dev told Alex that?"

"Yes, you dimwit! He told him about the interview, and about how you walked away without giving him one good reason why. And—and I'm not even supposed to be calling you, but I crossed my fingers behind my back when I told Alex I wouldn't. Because as your best friend, I'm not going to sit around watching while you throw away the best relationship you've ever had!"

"Oh, my God, it was *not* a relationship! We've just been hanging out—"

"*Hanging out?* Would you do me a favor and listen to yourself? Get real, honey—you've been hot for each other since August, and whatever's transpired between you two over there doesn't get to be labeled as *hanging out*. It's a lot more than that and you know it. Dev knows it. So I'll ask you again—what's the big fucking secret?"

Kiki's shoulders slumped as she stopped her pacing in front of the bus. An overhead lamp shone a yellow pool of light on the ground, so she sank down in the middle of it. The pavement was cold on her backside, but she didn't care. It matched her mood. It reminded her of the way her blood had frozen in her veins when Jack told her he was leaving her. And now she'd spent over two years keeping the reason to herself, and the tumor of resentment and disappointment had barely shrunk in size. "You asked me why Jack left me," Kiki started, her voice catching. "Well, it's the same reason any man would leave me."

"What are you talking about? You're amazing and Jack was an asshole. Whatever happened with him has given you a warped view of reality."

Kiki squeezed her eyes shut. Outside of her father, she'd never told another soul what she was about to say. "Nic. Do you remember that time I went to New York for a job interview?"

There was a beat of silence. "Right. Didn't I say something about you not seeming very excited about it?"

"Yeah. Because I wasn't really going there for that." Kiki took a deep breath. "I went there to meet with a fertility specialist. The best one in the country, Jack and I were told. Back then, I still had hope that they could find out what was wrong with me. Or fix it."

Nicola inhaled sharply. "Oh, sweetie. So you were—"

"Trying to get pregnant, yes," Kiki pressed on, knowing that if she stopped too long she'd lose her nerve. The reality was that her story could be summed up in a few sad sentences, but now she felt the sudden urge to spill the details to her friend. "For two years we tried, and nothing. At first Jack was worried it was him, so he got tested. Everything came back fine, so I was next. It didn't take much to find out there was something very wrong with me, but it took over a year to get in to see the specialist. Jack was so supportive—he kept saying we'd figure it out. He even said he was okay with not becoming a father if that's what it came down to. I thanked my lucky stars every day to have such an amazing husband. But I guess that was when he still believed I could get pregnant somehow." Kiki paused, waiting for Nicola to throw in a comforting word, but she stayed silent. Just listening as the best of friends did, just waiting for Kiki to release the beast on her that she must have known was coming.

"Anovulation due to premature ovarian failure— that was my diagnosis. They prescribed Clomid. I tried it for a while and then moved on to other drugs. Nothing worked. There was some hope that they could still use my eggs for IVF, but that was eliminated, too." She fell silent at the memory of that last thread being cut; she'd spent nearly a week on the sofa afterward, comforting herself with cookies and Hallmark TV specials...while Jack suddenly found the need to work overtime. "I think the worst part of it was... I talked to my father about it. He told me my mother had had fertility problems, too, and that she had to get a hysterectomy after she had me. But she still left me! So there I was, trying to have something she hadn't even ended up wanting, and it just brought it all home to me in the worst way."

"I...oh, my God," Nic said. "There are no words, except that I'm so, so sorry. I had no idea."

Kiki shook her head. "Nobody did because that's how I wanted it. I kept telling myself that I wasn't going to tell anyone anything until I was too pregnant to deny it. And Jack..." She drew a shaky breath. "I don't blame him, you know. He just wanted to be a dad, and he didn't want that to happen with anyone's DNA but his wife's. And I was awful to him. Since I was so determined not to let the rest of the world see my pain, I just took it out on him. I guess I always thought that someday we'd get back to where we were after a baby came, but that never happened."

"He should have stuck with you. A real man—"

Kiki held up a hand, as if Nicola could see it. "No. It's better this way. When you've been through something like that with someone, you see things in each other that you can't unsee. And in a way, walking away lets you erase those ugly parts of yourself."

Kiki could almost hear Nicola considering her words. "Still, he abandoned you. Just like your mother did. And now—now you leave before anyone else can leave you. Before Dev could leave you."

Kiki heaved a sigh. Her phone was hot against her cheek now, not to mention wet from her tears. "Look. Don't get me wrong, Nic, I'm glad I finally told you all of this. But my phone is about to burn a brain tumor into my head, and I really don't feel like being psychoanalyzed right now."

"I get it. Sorry."

"It's okay. Just…" Kiki hesitated, hating the admission she was about to make.

"Yes?"

"I knew, Nic. I watched an interview with him on YouTube after the first night I slept with him. And he said it right there—that he'd always been a family man at heart and couldn't wait to have kids. And I still—"

"Kiki, get a grip. So you lusted after the guy— you didn't know it would get serious!"

She sighed. "That sounds fine on paper, but that's not how it was. I *did* know. I knew from the moment I kissed him again that I was in for the long haul. I started imagining a future with him that very night. And I didn't say anything to him about my…" She trailed off. *Infertility.* The word was too ugly.

"You need to stop beating yourself up, honey," Nicola said. "Remember that Dev isn't Jack. Even if he might have told some journalist he wants a family, it might not be as much of a sticking point for him as you think. And there's always adoption—"

"Sure. Which is a huge compromise to your own flesh and blood, not to mention years of waiting and—"

"Would you stop? Let Dev decide what he wants—don't decide for him before you've even given him a chance. Opening up to me was a huge step for you, but I'm not the one who counts. You can't move forward with your life if you don't tell him the truth."

"Sure," Kiki said unconvincingly. "What you said."

"I mean it. And I love you."

"Love you, too."

There. I told someone, and I don't feel any better, Kiki thought after she hung up.

But maybe that wasn't entirely true. She could feel relief creeping through her body, but it was blended with a strange sense of recklessness. Opening her hand, she let her phone drop facedown on the pavement. Then she picked it up again and examined the screen, almost hoping it was cracked.

What is that all about? she wondered. Was she looking for somewhere to redirect her pain? Was an inanimate object supposed to represent her hopeless, throw-in-the-towel attitude? Was she testing how far she could go before something important to her broke? Was she really that self-sabotaging? And was it just Nicola's attempt to counsel her that had her thinking this way, or was she actually taking the first step toward dealing with a huge issue in her life?

She rubbed a sleeve over the screen to polish her fingerprints off. In the darkness, her face was barely reflected back at her. No cracks. Despite her best efforts at damage, both she and her iPhone remained intact.

Completely drained, she stood up and went back into her bus.

Shut away in his dressing room, Dev glanced at the clock as he paced the floor. It was fifty minutes until showtime, and he desperately needed…*something*. If not a solution to the nightmare raging through his head, then at least a distraction from it.

He'd tried having a conversation with his brother about Kiki, and even though Alex had said all the right things, it hadn't brought her back to him. Nothing would, as far as Dev knew, and the raw emptiness of that bare fact chewed at him, practically screamed at him to fill it. But a drink was out of the question, as were a full dose of his meds. He'd made that promise to himself last night, when Kiki had told him about her mother's suspected drug habit. Up until then he'd felt guilty enough keeping his pills a secret while Kiki was staying with him on his bus, but her admission had forced his hand. She might be done with him for now, but if she ever came back to him, he didn't want her discovering something about him that would drag her back into her painful past.

Tonight, knowing that quitting Xanax cold turkey could lead to hallucinations or seizures, he'd taken only half his dosage—and now he was paying the price. With less than an hour to go until showtime, he had no idea how he was going to calm himself the fuck down enough to get on that stage. His hands were visibly trembling. His mouth was cotton dry and his underarms were sweaty. He felt like a man tied to a palm tree on the beach, watching helplessly as a tidal wave closed in on him. Sure as shit, it was going to crush him as easily as a sand castle.

Dropping down on the sofa, Dev rolled his head from side to side a few times and shook his hands out. Inhaled through his nose. Closed his eyes. Tried to blank out his mind. If he'd had to name what he was doing, he might have called it *desperation meditation*. It wasn't the first time he'd tried holistic methods to control his panic button. He'd worked with a naturalist several years ago who, after signing a Bible-thick nondisclosure agreement, had suggested meditation, daily exercise, chamomile tea, aromatherapy, breath control, herbal supplements, nature walks, buying a dog and watching a list of TED Talks on the topic.

None of it had worked. Only one thing had ever eased Dev's anxiety, and it came straight out of a medical manufacturing plant. But now more than ever, the idea of giving in to his little helpers filled him with shame.

A knock sounded at the door. It had to be Bix,

who always checked in on him before showtime. Dev didn't feel like seeing anyone right now, but he knew his manager would just come barging in if he didn't answer. He pulled the door open and froze.

It was Kiki, looking extra tiny in a gray cardigan that nearly swallowed her. Her hair was scraped back into a loose bun and her face looked weary, but the sight of her was like an oasis to Dev. Familiar, beautiful, calm. The love of his fucking life, if he were completely honest with himself.

His heart leaped hopefully until he saw her expression. Distant and aloof, not much different from when he'd told Petra he wanted a family.

She stood at the doorway instead of stepping into the room. "Sorry to bother you, but you didn't answer my text about Prague tomorrow."

Work talk. He felt like puking. "My mind isn't exactly on work right now."

"Mine, either, but I still have a job to do. I need to know if I'm going with you."

He gave a humorless laugh. "As my assistant, or as the woman who just gutted me?"

She drew herself up. "As your assistant. Attending charity events is part of my job description. If you'd rather I didn't, then it's probably best for both of us if I move on. I could help you find a replacement."

Dev stared at her. How could she be so goddamned impersonal right now? Because he was the emotional one in this ex-relationship, that was how. Kiki was the one who could bury her feelings and deny her attachments. Her mother's abandonment of her had prepared her well for that. He suddenly felt furious at the woman he'd never met. She'd made Kiki like this out of necessity, and because of that, she was pushing away the man who worshipped her. Who would do anything for her, who could have made her happy for all time.

Dev shook his head. The sight of her had him coming apart in pieces he wasn't sure would ever fit together properly again, and that wasn't something he could afford. He needed to straighten his head out, which wasn't going to happen with her in the room. "I'm about to do a show, and I am exhausted. Do what you want, Kiki. I'll see you when I see you."

She stepped back as if she'd been stung, and the surge of regret he felt when he closed the door was worse than any beating he could have imagined. But screw it. She was done with him, and he had a show he had to do.

He walked over to the dressing table, grabbed up the Xanax bottle and knocked a second tablet back with a fierce shake of his head.

CHAPTER THIRTEEN

JUST ONE HOUR, Dev thought as he followed two foundation organizers through the doors of Prague's Motol University Hospital. *I can put on a smile for that long.* He stepped into the elevator, and one of the organizers pressed the button to the third floor.

Dev hadn't slept. His stomach was churning worse than it did before any performance, but that couldn't matter right now. The only thing that was allowed to matter was the nine-year-old boy he was about to meet. This was both the best and the worst part of his job: the children who decided that meeting him was their dying wish. The request had come in a week ago, and even though it had meant sacrificing his day off, Dev hadn't hesitated to accept it. He'd never declined one. But he'd also never had to spend an hour beforehand in a private plane with the woman who'd led him down the garden path of sweet fucking possibility and then dropped him for a reason she didn't even have the decency to share with him.

She'd been there waiting in his limo this morn-

ing, busying herself with her laptop so she wouldn't
have to look at him. The plane ride hadn't been
much different, with him burying himself in the
lyrics of a song he was working on to avoid eye
contact with her. It had been excruciating, and to
top it all off he was furious with himself for caving
to his meds last night. By the time they landed in
Prague, he'd had enough. He'd stalked off the plane
before Kiki had even risen from her seat, telling
himself he didn't care whether she followed. *Let
her stay here waiting for me. Let her feel some of
the gutting rejection I'm feeling*, he'd thought, as if
that could dislodge the Pluto-sized ball of pain sitting in his chest.

But right now it was time for Dev to focus on
someone who actually deserved his attention. As
he stepped off the elevator, he blocked all thoughts
of Kiki from his head to prepare for the task ahead.
He had been briefed by the foundation organizers
on the ride from the airport to the hospital. Konrad
Novak had terminal brain cancer. He'd been diag-
nosed two years ago, in and out of hospitals ever
since and currently in hospice care, not expected to
live for more than another four weeks. Knowing how
much he loved Dev's music, months ago his parents
had bought him tickets for the Milan concert, but he
hadn't been able to attend. On a hope and a prayer,
they'd reached out to the foundation that granted
wishes to terminal children on the off chance Dev
might be able to make a personal appearance.

Room 318. Dev stopped in front of the door. It was only then he realized that in his rush to escape Kiki, he'd forgotten his guitar.

Looking through the window from the visitors lounge to the third-floor corridor, Kiki placed her hand on the door, but she didn't push it open. Her heart was racing, and it had been since the moment Dev had walked off the airplane and left her in his wake. She knew she deserved it—she'd been as standoffish with him as a stranger for the entire flight. Last night when she'd shown up in his dressing room, she'd told herself she would open up to him if he seemed receptive to her. He hadn't, of course, and as she'd walked away she'd had to fully face the cop-out she was. Walking in on him right before a show, gauging his reaction to her when she deserved absolutely nothing from him, expecting him to lay his heart out yet again when he'd already done so, so painfully—it was despicable and cowardly of her.

But it was still better than the alternative, which was setting both of them up for the lifetime of misery her infertility was sure to inflict. Things may be fine between them for a few years, but she knew how this kind of thing rotted a relationship from the inside out until it was a decayed mess. She'd experienced it firsthand. No—she would keep this burden to herself, even if losing Dev was killing her as slowly and surely as arsenic poisoning. She'd barely slept a wink last night, shedding silent tears in her bunk until her entire being was sucked dry. A shell of the passionate, vibrant woman she'd been just a day ago when she'd allowed her life to be filled with the most incredible thing that had ever happened to her. Her eyes had been so puffy this morning she'd scared herself when she looked in the mirror. Cucumber slices, eye-drops and carefully applied makeup masked her painful truth as she'd climbed into the limo.

The hell of it was she still had a job to do, and that job involved close proximity to the man she adored. After Dev had left the plane, she'd noticed that he'd forgotten his guitar, so she'd taken a cab to the hospital. But now she was losing her nerve. He was in there doing something few people had the strength or stamina to, and she admired him deeply for it. She didn't want to interrupt such a personal moment, but she also wanted him to have what he needed to do it properly.

She walked through the door. Maybe the moment wasn't so personal after all, because it was easy to spot where Dev was from the small crowd of nurses and staff gathered in the hallway. As Kiki approached, she saw that the wall to the child's room was made of glass, and that the curtain had been pulled aside to allow viewing from the hallway. She peered inside and saw Dev seated beside the bed. He was smiling down at a hairless boy, whose thin body was swallowed by his hospital gown. His mother stood nearby, recording the interaction on her phone.

Kiki stepped back. Even though the moment was being witnessed by many, the intimacy of it still made her feel like a voyeur. She clutched the handle to Dev's guitar case tightly, wondering what to do. Maybe Dev didn't need it. Maybe he'd even left it behind on purpose.

"You saved my butt," Dev said.

Kiki looked over to see him standing in the doorway with a guarded expression. The crowd gave an appreciative laugh. She stepped forward and handed the case over to him, being careful not to let their fingers brush. He went back into the room. Kiki stood rooted to the spot as Dev started tuning his guitar, asking the boy for his request.

"'Destroyer'?" she heard him tease, strumming the familiar opening chords. "Or 'Up All Night'?" He switched chords again. "Wait—did you say 'Desert Heart'?" He transitioned into the new song, continuing until he was playing a full medley of his greatest hits. The boy grinned ear to ear. But his mother…in Kiki's emotional state, the sight of her was almost too much to bear. She was smiling as she watched the scene unfold, stroking her son's arm with her free hand. Kiki may have experienced the death of her motherhood dream, but she couldn't imagine the pain of losing a child she'd raised and loved. She felt a sudden flare of anger toward her own mother. The unfairness of it all—that this woman's child was being taken from her when Kiki's mom hadn't even loved her enough to stick around—

hit her full force. An ugly needle of envy pricked at her gut. Why couldn't she have had a mother who stayed with her through thick and thin?

Dev moved to the end of the bed, as if he were onstage, and held up a pretend microphone. "Ladies and gentlemen, this one's going out to a very special boy. Put your hands together for Konrad!"

Caught up in the moment, Kiki found herself clapping along with the rest of the crowd. Dev finally launched into the boy's request, "Make Me Care," putting as much energy into it as he did for any show. During the chorus he came closer to the child so he could join in singing with him. The whole world focused down to that one room, where the power of music could make even the most heartbreaking situations wondrous, where sorrow and joy entwined inseparably.

This is who Dev is, Kiki thought as tears came to her eyes. More human and compassionate than any person she'd known, and he was doing it all with a huge spotlight on him under an ocean's worth of pressure. In that moment, her yearning for him filled her heart with a pain so palpable it took her breath away.

The drone of the engine filled the cabin as Dev sat across from Kiki, who had her phone in both hands as she furiously typed out the day's social media posts. He sipped his club soda listlessly. For the first time since the tour had started, he truly wished he could just drown his sorrows in binge drinking. Performing for the boy had been uplifting, but also depressing as hell. And the frustration of sitting next to the woman he was so close to just yesterday, who now treated him like a practical stranger, had his gut twisted into knots. There was no cure for any of it; there was only temporary numbness and forgetting, and even that wasn't an option for him.

Pulling his eyes away from Kiki, he stared out the window at the blank whiteness. In an hour they would be back in Munich, and tomorrow they would fly to Sydney. Twelve days after that the tour would be over. He and Kiki would return to their separate lives on the same tiny island. This was the worst part of it all—that he would have to coexist with her, and that the home he'd so carefully built there would be spoiled for him. He would run into her, hear about her, even see her with other men. The thought was agonizing enough to make Dev's toes curl in his shoes. He may have to move back to London, he realized, or even LA. Anything but face the excruciating reminders of what he'd once had.

In his peripheral vision, Dev saw Kiki put her phone down and look over at him. He stared stubbornly outside. "You're amazing with kids."

"Thanks," Dev said flatly. His dejection was making him feel reckless; what did he have to lose now? "The only audience that doesn't make me nervous."

He expected her to laugh—*as if*—but instead she looked at him sharply. "Really?"

But she no longer deserved to hear his secrets. "No," he said.

Her eyes were still on him. "Three kids, huh?"

"What?"

"You want three kids. You said it on *In the Studio*."

"I thought you didn't pay any attention to that shit."

"I don't. But I happened to see that one." She picked her phone up from the table and started turning it end over end. *Occupying her hands*, Dev thought. *This conversation is hard for her.* "I always wanted one child. Just one."

One child. But not with him, obviously. He stayed silent.

"I guess because they say we all subconsciously try to replicate our family of origin," she continued as if he'd asked. "Maybe I thought having one would allow me to be the mother I never had. Or that giving my own kid the childhood I'd missed out on would restore my faith in the family unit."

"So you don't believe in the family unit?"

She shrugged. "My father did an amazing job raising me without my mother. Maybe it would have been worse if she'd stayed, I don't know. But I've also realized it's a lot to ask from one kid. Having them change my worldview, fix my childhood, prove that I'll never be my own mother. Maybe I need to do all of that on my own."

Dev shook his head at her. She was so damned mature and insightful, and yet she wouldn't do the one thing he was certain would actually heal her. Why couldn't she see that what they had could have changed her entire fucking world? "Is that why you don't want me?"

Her eyes widened. "Don't say it like—"

"Why not? It's the truth. We were in a relationship, Kiki, even if it was short. You hide behind generalizations and vague explanations. I know you don't want to hear this, but this is how much I care about you. I want you to actually learn something from this so you might be able to be happy with someone one day."

She was shaking her head. "*No.* God, Dev, I don't want anyone else. I—you've ruined me for anyone else. Things are just…complicated for me."

He couldn't keep the fury out of his voice. "Then enlighten me, Kiki. We have forty-five minutes of air time ahead of us, and I am all ears."

He saw a blush rise to her cheeks as he pinned his eyes on her face. She shifted uncomfortably. The pause stretched into a silence. He tamped down his boiling frustration. What the hell was she so afraid to tell him?

That she has a prescription drug dependency, maybe? the monster whispered.

Dev crammed it back into its dungeon.

"I've found a woman who might be my mother." Kiki brought her hand up to her mouth after she said it, as if the sentence had fallen out against her will. Then she dropped it again. "I'm, uh, going to look her up. I was afraid to tell you, because I'm so scared she'll reject me again."

"Kiki. God." He shook his head. "You were afraid of *that*?"

"I also happen to have an ex-husband who left me." Her chin was trembling. "Rejection has been a bit of a running theme in my life. It took me so long to—to accept that you saw something special in me. And I didn't want anything to change your mind."

Dev's hands gripped his armrests. Kiki was dabbing at her eyes, but he didn't dare move. "I could never change my mind about you," he said slowly. "The way you kept me at arm's length for so long, I'd be a fool to at least not try to. But I couldn't. I can't."

Kiki nodded, her eyelashes wet. "She's in Sydney. It's why I took the assistant job—partly, anyway." She wiped a tear away with the back of her hand. "The other part was because of you. I tried so hard, Dev, but I couldn't deny how much I wanted to be with you. And—I don't know, it's still not simple for me, but I want you so badly. I can't let you go. This… you…" She waved a hand at him. "I *need* you." Her voice caught with emotion.

I need you. Dev felt a warmth spread throughout his body, like ice melting. He unbuckled his seat belt and walked over to her. He crouched down beside her chair and cupped her cheek, wiping a tear away with his thumb. "You *have* me, Kiki. Jesus, you *so* fucking have me. And I will not abandon you. Ever. Do you understand me?"

"Yeah," she whispered, bringing a hand up to cover his. "Okay." She reminded him of a child, tiny and vulnerable. But inside, she was so incredibly strong. Stronger than he'd ever had to be in his life.

Kiki leaned toward him and paused, as if asking for permission, and then she landed a light kiss on his mouth. Dev's lips stayed soft but closed, still afraid to trust this was real. She pulled back again and looked into his eyes. "Dev, I..."

He read her mind. Everything he felt, too, but it wasn't the right time. That perfect sentence, uttered for the first time, deserved the perfect moment. He knew she felt that, too.

"I know," he said quietly, bringing a finger to her lips. "Let me show you." He slid his hand into her hair to cup the back of her head. He tipped her face back so he was above her, and drank her in with his eyes. That fringe of reddish hair above long lashes. That slightly pointed chin. Those freckles and that beautiful mouth. Her lips parted as her eyes searched his face. Dev felt his chest fill, his heart reconnecting to hers. His need for her filled him bigger than ever. Bigger than anything tangible and more potent than the most precious elixir.

When his lips came down on her, they were already open.

Kiki yielded to him immediately, her tongue sliding against his as their mouths communicated everything unsaid between them, bringing them further and further into each other. His arms slipped around her waist, pressing her to him tightly enough to crush the breath from his own lungs. An unintelligible sound escaped her throat, something accepting and yearning and tortured all at once. Something that revealed the depth of the moment to both of them, completely unhinging them.

Kiki slammed her hand down on her armrest and arched backward, exposing her throat to him. Dev attacked the hollow beneath her jaw, pressing his tongue into it and trailing his stubbled face down to her chest hard enough to make her cry out again. "*Dev*. Oh, God—"

Her hands came up to fist his T-shirt, and then they were everywhere. Yanking it up to touch his skin, sinking down the back of his jeans to grab his bare ass. As he moved over her, her leg came up onto the small table and swept it clear, knocking her phone and their drinks off in a tumble of spilling water and fluttering napkins. But they didn't even pause. Her legs wrapped around his hips to pull his pelvis closer. The raw strength of her passion sent a delicious shock wave up Dev's spine. Every thought that entered his head came out of his mouth in a breathless, guttural voice he barely recognized as his own. "Jesus Christ, my sweet little strawberry, I need you so much. So perfect…never stop…give me that beautiful fucking mouth, it's all mine." Her boots were digging into his back so hard it hurt, her nails clawing at his back. Dev ripped her jeans open so forcefully the button snapped off. He yanked her black thong down far enough to give his fingers access, and then he sunk them into her wetness, grinding the heel of his hand against her clit. Her hips rolled into him, and she threw her head back and let out a long, ecstatic string of words. *"Yesyesyes—"*

Through his fervor, a blurry thought took shape in Dev's head: he needed to get them out of there. Somewhere private. And if he didn't do it right this second it would be too late because he would fuck her right here and now, flight crew be damned—and it would not be quiet.

He got his arms around her waist again and lifted her out of her seat. Kiki's legs and arms wrapped around him as her mouth crashed to his. He considered his choices. There was the bathroom, but it was cramped. The sleeping quarters were more comfortable, but less soundproof. He headed there because as much as he needed to fuck her, he also needed to feel her body close to him. He walked them to the back of the plane, ripped the privacy curtain open and lowered Kiki onto the narrow bed.

Kiki was feverish, delirious with desire, barely cognizant of where they were in time and space. In a plane, on a bed made up with a duvet traced with the airline's logo. Nothing but a thin curtain separating their intense greed for each other from the airline crew. Kiki didn't care what they might think. She didn't care that she'd let down her carefully constructed guard to allow the man she des-

perately needed back into her life. She didn't care
about the conversation that would have to come tomorrow as a result. All she cared about was feeling
Dev deep inside her again, and hearing the rasping
breath of his desire for her as they moved together as
one. That first kiss had opened something in her she
didn't even know existed, a chasm of need so deep
that only one person on earth could ever fill it. Dev.

She still had the pink top on she'd carefully chosen that morning: feminine but not too sexy, because
she hadn't wanted to flaunt what Dev couldn't have
in front of him. Her jeans and thong were around
her ankles, and Dev, still fully dressed, was reaching for her boots. They were tight, requiring effort to
remove, especially in these cramped quarters. "Forget them," she panted as she writhed on the mattress,
desperate to feel the pressure of his body, his hand,
his mouth—any part of him at all—on her aching
clit. "Just fuck me, Dev. *Please.*"

He practically dove on top of her, crushing her
beneath him as his mouth came down on hers again.
Their teeth knocked together. She could sense it for
both of them—that control was a long-ago-deserted
notion buried by their mutual fervor. Pointless, and
completely unnecessary.

Kiki got her hands between their torsos and
opened Dev's belt buckle. He lifted off of her long
enough for her to get his pants open and pushed
down his hips along with his boxers. Dev shoved her
thighs apart mercilessly, causing her ankles to strain

against the binding force of her jeans. She grabbed his rock-hard cock greedily and positioned it at the part of her that could never lie to him. She could push Dev away as much as she wanted to, but here, her lush wetness revealed her true feelings for him.

Dev drew up on his hands to look down at her. *"Now,"* she said urgently, and then bucked her hips up to envelop his cock in one swift movement. Dev gasped, pulled out—and then began to fuck her in a way she'd never experienced. It was brutal, so urgent and unrelenting that it made their bodies slick with sweat, and yet restrained at the same time in a hopeless attempt at discretion. Dev's eyes locked on hers as he drove into her, taking her straight to heaven, and his scent was the most arousing thing she'd ever known. His belt buckle banged against her thigh again and again, and she relished the idea of being marked by him. She could feel it in every rapturous thrust—Dev's need to possess her, meeting her need to be his.

Kiki's climax was woven into every sensation of her body so that she was barely aware of where it began and ended. She heard herself saying Dev's name over and over again, and it was only when she felt his mouth on her shoulder, pressed hard against her skin to muffle his release, that she knew he was coming with her.

When she returned to her body there were a hundred things she wanted to say, but the words jumbled in her head so that all she could do was listen to the

sound of their breathing. Dev shifted her sideways
with her back against the padded wall of the plane,
and then he wrapped his arms around her head and
pulled her into his chest. He caged his legs around
hers so that she was immobilized against him, their
bodies and breaths melding together. There wasn't
a sentence in the world that could describe what had
just happened between them. And as she felt her heartbeat in every part of her body, she was exactly where
she wanted to be, her entire world shrunken down
to a three-by-six-foot space floating over Germany.

CHAPTER FOURTEEN

IF KIKI THOUGHT she and Dev had hungered for each
other before their brief breakup, it was nothing compared to afterward. Their desire was so unrelenting
that she actually began to fear for her mental health.
Their encounter on the plane had been followed by
another the moment they were back in Dev's tour
bus, and another after dinner that night. The next
morning they'd flown to Sydney, where Dev had
made the ultimate sacrifice: after Kiki had refused
to switch to first class, thinking it unfair to the rest
of the crew, Dev had given up his seat and flown
cattle class with her for the two flights totalling over
twenty-one hours. They'd spent most of it in a state
of aching need for each other, which drove them into
the cramped bathroom together when masturbating
each other under the blanket wasn't enough.

In Sydney they'd checked into their hotel room,
and despite their jet lag and exhaustion, they'd barely
made it out of the elevator with their clothing still
on. She simply couldn't get enough of him. One foot

away was too far. His cock inside her was only the beginning of the connection she felt to him. Her entire private area thudded with the pain of overuse, but it was the most amazing feeling she'd ever known. It meant that Dev was hers. Her entire world was *him*, but she knew she had to get a grip on herself if she had any hope of doing the two things she still needed to: find out if Victoria O'Hare was her mother and tell Dev the truth about her infertility.

On her first full day in Sydney, Kiki rose after noon to find Dev gone from her side. She smiled as she left their bed, still feeling him between her legs from their dreamlike, half-asleep early morning session. Now he was in a meeting, so it was the perfect time for her to formulate a plan for contacting Victoria O'Hare. Given all the distractions with Dev, she hadn't thought about it much recently, but she was also surprised to realize that her sense of urgency had waned. Maybe it was just because the moment was finally here after so many years, but instead of reaching for her phone and dialing that number, she found herself puttering around the room, unpacking, ordering brunch and generally avoiding the whole situation. But she was only in Sydney for three days, so she knew she had to get moving on it.

After showering and dressing in a simple blue dress for the spring weather, Kiki sank down on the sofa with her phone. The Sofitel Sydney Darling Harbour was as luxurious as hotels came. She'd never been one to be impressed by what wealth could buy—the values her father had raised her with were much more nonmaterial—but she had to admit that staying in world-class hotels wasn't horrible. Her and Dev's room overlooking Sydney Harbour had windows wide and deep enough to make her feel like she was suspended over the water. And the city was as beautiful as promised, an alluring mix of North American and European architecture with a unique flavor all its own.

Pulling the real estate website up on her phone, Kiki contemplated her options. Sending Victoria an email made no sense—Kiki could have done that from Moretta—and showing up at her workplace and springing the big question on her seemed awkward and inconsiderate. The only option that made any sense was to pretend to be a client interested in buying a home, meet up with her and suss out the situation. Of course it meant she'd have to come up with a fake name, but she couldn't do much about that— there wasn't much point in coming halfway around the world to do this just to give herself away now.

Kiki's heart started to thump as she planned out her opening words. Even if she was feeling slightly less invested emotionally, the idea of playing a role and the great unknown that would come afterward had her nerves going.

She dialed the number and a woman's voice picked up. "Hello, you've reached the office of Victoria O'Hare. Please leave me a message and I'll return your call at my earliest convenience." Voice mail. Kiki was glad she didn't have to fake a conversation quite yet. She tried to analyze the woman's voice. There was a bit of an accent, but it was hard to place. A mix of Aussie with something else, but was it American?

Kiki realized that the beep had sounded and that she was breathing into a void. "Uh—hello. My name is Katherine Jones, and I'm interested in one of your listings. If you could call me back at 555-890-2900, I would appreciate it. That's, uh, a US number. I'm just visiting. But interested in a house. In Sydney. Um, thanks."

Kiki cringed as she hung up. The voice mail robot hadn't given her the option to rerecord her message, so she was stuck with what she'd left—and she'd sounded like a mess. She tapped a fingertip on her phone's screen. She still had no idea what she was going to say to the woman if they met. Was she going to play it cool and delicately try to pull information out of her, or was she going to confront her head-on? *Maybe she won't call back*, Kiki thought, and suddenly she wasn't sure if that would be a disappointment or a relief.

But perhaps that was just because she had more important things on her mind. Dev was due back any minute, and Kiki had made herself a promise she swore she wouldn't break. She'd run out of excuses, and it was time to tell Dev the truth about herself.

As Dev made his way across the hotel lobby toward the elevators, he grinned at passing strangers and even exchanged a few words with the concierge. It wasn't like him to extend himself in public, but he was so fucking happy that he could barely contain it.

Being with Kiki again was more than a dream come true—it was the most incredible reality he could imagine. They couldn't keep their bodies apart. He'd gotten used to walking around with a permanent semi-hard-on that could swell into a full-blown problem if he let himself think about her too much. All he wanted to do was fuck her in every possible position and location, but the sex was only a by-product of his feelings for her. Her every laugh, smile, tear, insight and observation was worth a grand-scale celebration to him. Sure, she still had some rough road ahead of her if she actually ended up meeting her mother, but Dev would be there for her every step of the way. He would do *anything* for her. He wanted to pull her entire being into himself, where he could keep her safe and spoon-feed her pure happiness for the rest of her life. Without a doubt he knew he had found her—the woman he would spend forever with, build a family with, have hot sex with until he was old and gray. He loved her with all of his heart, mind and soul, and he couldn't wait for the right moment to tell her.

And he could, now that he was practically free and clear. This morning, before leaving their hotel room, he'd finally done it—flushed his meds down the toilet. Well, his Ambien at least. He wasn't stupid; he knew the dangers of quitting Xanax too quickly, so he'd kept just enough for a comfortable withdrawal, safely tucked away in a pocket of his suitcase. It wasn't the end, but it was the beginning of the end. He'd taken action, which meant he didn't need to divulge anything to Kiki about it, after all.

Dev tapped his foot as he pushed the button for the elevator, anxious to get upstairs and indulge in their second session of the day. But there was one thing he needed to do first, something he should have done a long time ago—get in touch with Larry Weatherby. He'd been a fool to let his pride stand in the way of a collaboration that could lead to a switch within his career. Slipping behind the scenes to write and produce for the music industry's hottest talents was more appealing than ever to Dev. It would mean he could leave the road behind, spend more time on Moretta with Kiki. He pulled his phone out and typed a quick email to the producer.

The elevator dinged, and Dev was about to step inside when Bix stepped out. "Just the man I wanted to see," he said.

Dev gave a silent groan. He knew he'd been distracted on this tour, that he hadn't been giving Bix his usual amount of attention, and that Bix wasn't a man who took well to that. Dev had managed to push aside his mild guilt over it, but standing in front of him brought it all back. Bix had been in his corner since day one, and there were very few people Dev could say that about. He clapped him on the shoulder. "Bix, my man. What's up?"

"You tell me. You've been pretty scarce lately. Everything good?"

"Everything's great. Just busy chasing the dream, you know?"

"I do." Bix shoved his hands in his pockets and gave him a meaningful look. "Nice hotel room? You got everything you need?"

"Yeah." Dev flipped his hair off his forehead as he glanced around for eavesdroppers. Tomorrow night he was going onstage with only half a dose in his system. He knew the nerves might show up later, but right now he was feeling good about it. Calm. And part of changing his habit was making the commitment to more than just himself. He lowered his voice. "Actually, I'm glad I ran into you. I wanted to let you know I've made a decision. The stuff I take—I don't like what it does to me. I'm going to spend the next couple weeks getting off it, and then I'm done."

Bix rocked back on his heels. "Done? You really think that's a good idea? Big show tomorrow night."

Dev shrugged. "I've done the Super Dome enough times. It's familiar territory, I'll be fine."

Bix looked skeptical. "Just five shows to go. Why not stay comfortable till you're finished?"

"Because I'm stronger than that." Dev set his jaw. "Look, I really do appreciate your concern, okay? You've always had my back. But this is something I have to do. I'm not twenty anymore. Times have changed, I've changed, and I'm ready for my career to look different, too."

Dev didn't like the downward slant of Bix's brow. "And does that difference include your little assistant?"

Dev felt his mouth tighten. "Kiki is not my 'little assistant.' And whether she has anything to do with it or not is irrelevant. I'm making some changes I should have made a long time ago."

Bix jingled his change in his pocket, and then he broke into a smile. He clapped Dev on the back. "Hey. It's your life, Stone, and you know I'm here for you no matter what."

Dev grinned back at him, feeling more relieved than he cared to admit. It was hard to imagine any aspect of his career without Bix's support. He stepped inside the car and jabbed the elevator button. "Thanks, man. I'll see you later."

He was back. Kiki's pulse started to race as she heard the beep of Dev's key card at the door.

Steady. You can do this. Maybe it won't be as bad as you think.

But it would be. Kiki knew all too well what it was like to go through life assuming that one day you'd pass your genes on, blend them with the person you loved to create a life, bond over the beauty and pain of pregnancy and childbirth. That reality would never be theirs. She would never bear a biological child, and Kiki knew that was a deal breaker for many men...like Jack.

"Hey, beautiful," Dev said when he came into the room.

"Hey, rock star," Kiki tried, but her throat clicked closed. She could hear her heartbeat in her ears. Dev took her in his arms and gave her a soft kiss. Kiki could feel his want for her press into her waist, but he made no move to act on it. It was one of the things she loved about him—he sensed her moods and seemed to know exactly what she needed, and right now it wasn't sex. "You're trembling," he said, drawing back to look at her. His expression turned serious. "You called her, didn't you?"

Kiki nodded wordlessly. *Yes, but that's only the beginning,* she thought.

"And?"

"And it went to voice mail."

"Did you leave a message?"

"Yeah, but I wish I hadn't. I had to pretend I was an interested buyer, and it came out sounding so dumb. I don't know, I guess I didn't think I'd be so nervous. But I was a wreck—I could barely think straight."

"That's totally normal."

"No, it's not!" Kiki pressed her face into Dev's chest. She was seriously on edge, and it wasn't just because she was about to spill her guts to the man she was indescribably crazy about. She was on an emotional roller coaster. She may have tried to convince herself that her interest in meeting her mother had faded, but she recognized a protection mechanism when she saw it. She *did* care, and the thought of sitting down across from the woman, of searching her face for a physical likeness and probing into her past for clues, seemed like an insurmountable task. She looked up into Dev's face. "You perform in front of fifty thousand fans and you're fine. I can't even make a phone call without feeling like my heart's going to hammer through my chest."

Dev smoothed her hair back from her face, and then he looked down at her for so long she started to squirm. "What?"

"I was just thinking about my first piano recital. It was also my last."

Kiki tilted her head. "But I thought you knew how to play."

"I do, but I learned in my teens. My recital happened when I was nine."

"And, let me guess—you killed it."

"Not exactly." Dev kissed the top of her head, and though he was holding her tightly when he spoke again, his expression was faraway. "I sure thought I would, though. I practiced for hours. I was so excited—it was going to be my big moment, the day I finally got a real audience instead of just a few friends cheering me on while I danced around on my bed. I mean, I dreamed about that applause—it was going to be *thunderous*." He gave a short laugh as he stroked her back absently.

"Uh-huh?" Kiki prompted when he stayed silent.

Dev shook his head. "I didn't get a single note

out. My mind went completely blank. I sat down on that bench, and the notes on my music sheet just… blurred together. The next thing I knew my father was standing beside me. When I saw him, I stood up hard enough to topple the bench and ran off the stage."

"Oh, my God," Kiki said slowly. "So that night in Venice…it just brought it all back to you. And I was so pushy!"

"No, you weren't. You just wanted me to play something for you, and I—I really wanted to. I pictured myself going up there, doing the big serenade for my dream date just like in the movies." His chin dropped. "But I couldn't."

Kiki slid her arms around his neck, thoughts of her mother and even her pending confession forgotten. A few days ago she would have taken this story at face value, but now she sensed a deeper meaning to it. She knew Dev so much better, as if their bodies had revealed secrets to each other that went beyond the physical. She thought back to a conversation on his bus, when he'd told her about his early stage fright. And other times, she'd put it down to modesty when he'd cut her admiration for his performance confidence short. But was it something else that had silenced him?

Kiki had to let him know he could trust her. That she was the warm, comforting space he could step into whenever he needed it, and that she would never turn him back out into the cold. "It took so much strength for you to get up there on that first night, didn't it?" she said carefully. "The Hollywood Bowl, I can't even imagine."

Dev kept stroking her back. She saw his throat bob as he swallowed.

Kiki's phone rang from the sofa. They both looked down at the screen: Webber Real Estate. She brought a hand to her mouth and looked at Dev with big eyes. The timing was ridiculous—the last thing she wanted to do was break this moment. But Dev was already snatching her phone off the sofa.

"Answer it," he said as he held it out to her. He gave her cheek a quick stroke. "I'm right here."

Kiki had little choice but to accept her phone. Reminding herself of her fake identity, she hit the green button. "Hello?" Her voice came out in a rasp. She cleared her throat and tried again. "This is Katherine speaking."

"Katherine, it's Victoria O'Hare from Webber Real Estate. Thank you for your message."

Kiki focused on the sound of the woman's voice. Pleasant and businesslike. Australian with a touch of…what? "I—thank you for calling me back."

"Of course. Which listing was it you were interested in?"

Kiki's mind went momentarily blank, but then she pulled it up from the file in her head. She'd researched it this morning. "The one in Freshwater. On Bay Street."

"Oh, yes, the condo. Beautiful home, fully renovated, though it does overlook a busy part of the street. Are you familiar with the area?"

"No. I mean—I'm just visiting. But my, uh, partner and I were thinking of buying a second home here."

"How exciting! I'm open to show it to you on Sunday morning, does that suit? I just have to double-check the time with the seller."

Sunday. Three days from now. Kiki would be gone by then, preparing for a show in Adelaide. "Sure," she lied, her brain finally kicking in. "But I was wondering if we might meet beforehand. Like I said, I'm new to the area, so I was hoping you could help me get the lay of the land. Describe the market, different neighborhoods, things like that. Maybe we could meet for coffee tomorrow or Saturday?" She held her breath.

"Certainly, I'd love to," Victoria replied brightly. "Only I'm leaving for a convention in Brisbane this evening. But I'd be happy to get someone else from my office to meet with you in my stead, and then we can catch up on Sunday." *No.* Kiki was wracking her brain for a new angle when Victoria spoke again. "Unless, of course, you'd like to meet right now. I'm open for the next hour or so."

Kiki's heart stopped. *Right now.* Her voice caught again when she spoke. "Yes. I could meet you right away," she said, shifting her eyes to Dev. She could almost feel her pupils dilating with anxiety as he gave her an encouraging nod. Kiki exchanged location details with the woman, and then she hung up.

"I'll go with you," Dev said immediately. "If you want."

Kiki shook her head. "I'd love that, I really would, but… I don't know. I think I need to do this on my own."

"I totally understand," Dev said, stroking her arm. "I'll be waiting right here for you when you're done."

Kiki nodded. She wanted to find a way to get back to their earlier conversation, but the pending meeting had her mind in turmoil and her stomach in knots so tight it was cramping.

"I should go, but…" She slipped her arms around him. "I want to know every little thing about you. Can we continue our conversation later?"

Dev smiled. "Of course."

CHAPTER FIFTEEN

BREATHE. JUST BREATHE, Kiki told herself. But she was an absolute mess. As she sat waiting at a waterfront café done up in shades of pastel, she actually wondered if she might start hyperventilating. Her heart was beating so hard she was certain the waiter had seen it thumping through her T-shirt when she placed her order. Her voice had trembled slightly, and right now she could feel sweat gathering under her arms.

She couldn't remember the last time she'd been this nervous. All the times she'd envisioned this meeting, she'd never even considered this aspect of it, and it narrowed her approach options down to one. There was no way she was going to be able to sit here and play it cool with this woman. Her only choice would have to be direct honesty.

Trying to wash away the cotton feeling in her mouth with a sip of water, she glanced at her watch. Four minutes before three o'clock. She'd arrived a few minutes early, and now she wished she hadn't. It gave her too much time to think, and right now she was thinking that this whole scene was a very bad idea. If Victoria O'Hare turned out to be her mother, things would never be the same for Kiki. Her father had always told her that; why hadn't she listened? Despite the hole her mother had left in it, she'd always had a good life. Right now she was the happiest she'd ever been, and it wasn't just because that empty ache had been filled by Dev's presence. It was because Kiki had learned to see the value in what her mother's absence had given her, and because she'd started to acknowledge her own unshakable strength. Dev had helped her recognize that, but he hadn't given it to her.

Kiki was squeezing her lime wedge into her water when the realization hit her like a tidal wave: Dev would never desert her. She knew it in her soul, just as sure as she'd known her father would never follow in her mother's footsteps. It was what Dev was always telling her, and all she had to do was believe him. She could trust him with everything she had. Victoria's call had come at the best and worst moment, putting the big admission she'd been ready to lay on him in perspective. It wasn't the end of the world. Her body's flaw might have made her think of herself as a failure, but that didn't mean Dev would. He would tell her they'd find a way to make it work, and they would—it was as simple as that. And she didn't need a mother who hadn't wanted to be a part of her life for twenty-four years to complete her. All she needed was who she already had—Dev.

She had to get out of there. Kiki stood up, scraping her chair back loudly, and snatched her handbag up. She dug a ten-dollar note out of her wallet with shaking hands and dropped it on the table. She was hurrying toward the door when a middle-aged man walked toward her with a tentative smile. "Excuse me, are you Katherine Jones?" he asked in a thick Aussie accent.

Kiki stopped in her tracks. "Yes."

He extended his hand. "Brad Silver from Webber Real Estate. Victoria sends her regrets, but she had to deal with an auction that fell through at the last minute. I'd be happy to answer any of your questions."

Kiki gave him a lopsided smile. *Abandoned again*, she thought. "I'm sorry to have wasted your time, but that won't be necessary." She dug a business card out of her handbag and held it out to him. "Please pass this along to her."

And then she left the café, walking through a door that held her past behind her and her boundless, uncertain, beautiful future right over the threshold.

CHAPTER SIXTEEN

KIKI COULDN'T GET back to Dev fast enough. She couldn't wait to tell him that he was all she needed, that she loved him desperately and wanted to be with him and only him for the rest of her life. After she told him about her infertility, which she'd blurt out the moment she saw him. She wasn't even afraid of saying the words anymore—in fact, she wondered now what she'd been so afraid of. Dev would understand. He would barely even care—she was certain of it.

Her phone rang in her handbag as she was exiting a cab in front of her hotel. She dug the device out and looked down at the screen. "Dad," she said when she picked up. "I'm so sorry I called, but I completely forgot about the time difference. I was hoping I hung up before I woke you."

"It's okay, honey. You know you can call me anytime."

Kiki's throat felt thick. She'd phoned her father the moment she'd gotten into the cab, eager to tell him about her aborted meeting with Victoria, her decision to let her search for her mother go…and especially Dev. But her heightened emotional state was making her sentimental. "I know. All those times in my teens, the calls you must have gotten from me in the middle of the night. You've always been there for me, Dad."

"That's a father's job. But you've made it easy, honey."

Kiki inhaled deeply to pull herself together. The doors to the lobby opened in front of her, and she passed through them. "Thank you. Listen, I just wanted to tell you… I decided not to meet with that woman, after all. The one who might have been Mom."

"Well. That was a big decision," Lawrence said in a measured tone. Calm as always, steady as that famous rock.

"I guess so. But you know, it's funny. It didn't *feel* big, somehow. It felt…like my life is full enough without her. Like I had to come all the way here to find her just to realize that I didn't need to come all the way here to find her, if that makes sense."

"It does."

"And…there's something else," Kiki said, unable to keep the manic smile off her face. "I've met someone. And, Dad, he's so amazing." She inhaled again to keep her emotions under control. She was so full of love for Dev right now, it was as if her body couldn't contain it. It needed to spill out of her, to surround him and pour into his heart, and she couldn't wait for that magical moment. "I just know you're going to love him."

"That's wonderful, Kiki. Does he have a name?"

"He sure does. Dev Stone."

There was a brief pause. "Now, why does that sound familiar?"

"Does it?" Kiki grinned; that was a conversation that could come later. "You know, Dad, I was actually hoping to talk to Deirdre."

"Deirdre?" He sounded surprised.

"Yeah. I know she's sleeping right now, but I'll try her tomorrow."

"Of course." He paused. "Was there a message I could give her?"

Kiki gripped the phone. Delivering this message through her father would be a cop-out. It was a conversation she needed to save for her stepmother's ears, but her father was part of it, too. Over the years she'd seen his frustrations with their relationship, had known that it hurt him just as much as it hurt Deirdre to see Kiki push away the woman he loved. The woman who had only been doing her very best to bond with her stepdaughter and give her back her childhood. "Just…maybe you could tell her that I'd really like to spend some time with her next time I'm home."

"Why, certainly, honey." Kiki could tell by the smile in his voice that her words had made their point.

"I have to go, Dad. I love you."

"I love you, too, bunny."

Kiki hung up, practically vibrating with excitement at the thought of what she was going to do next. But as she turned toward the elevators, her perfect mood snagged. Bix was striding across the lobby with a small white bag in his hand. She flicked her eyes away, hoping he wouldn't see her—or more likely, just ignore her—but no such luck. He veered toward her.

"Ah, Kiki," he said with uncharacteristic friendliness. "Would you do me a favor?"

Dev stared at the email on his laptop, still wanting to believe it was all just a misunderstanding. But it wasn't. In his gut, he'd known the truth about Bix for longer than he cared to admit. All these years. Had he really been so desperate to have someone on his team that he'd allowed himself to be completely blind? It was a thought that made him sick to his stomach.

Dev read the message once more line for line. It was a reply from Larry Weatherby, saying that Bix had told him that Dev had zero interest in songwriting for anyone but himself. Larry had been disappointed but not surprised, so he'd let it drop. And now he was informing Dev that he not only wanted him to write for his artists, he'd also like to discuss Dev moving into a producing role with him. It was exactly the change of gears Dev had been looking for, and Bix had kept it from him. How many other communications like this had he kept to himself?

At the door, Dev heard Kiki's key card beep. He closed his laptop and took a breath to reset his mood. He would deal with Bix later—nothing was more important than this. Kiki had possibly just had one of the most life-changing experiences a person could have, and he would be there for her with every fiber of his being.

She stepped into the room with her eyes down. *It didn't go well*, he thought, feeling a punch to his gut. He rushed over to her. He was about to take her in his arms when she finally looked at him. What he saw in her face stopped him in his tracks. "What…?"

"Bix wanted me to give this to you," she said, holding up a paper bag. His heart stopped as he stared at it. *No.* "He said you might want it tomorrow if you change your mind."

Bix again—*Jesus.* Dev felt like punching something. His manager had seen a potential weakness in Dev and Kiki's relationship and tried to kick it wide-open because she represented everything that was a threat to Bix's income: reassessing his life and his career, settling down, quitting the road. Dev knew now that was really all he'd ever been to him—a money train.

His legs felt weak. He dropped down into an armchair. "Kiki, I…"

"I wasn't snooping. The label is stuck right on the bag." She took a seat across from him.

Dev felt like puking. His mind was crawling, searching for the right words to make everything better again. He'd messed up. He'd known she was his forever girl, and that was what you did with the person you wanted a future with. Why hadn't he just told her?

Because he'd never had his heart at stake before. Not like this. And now he had damaged their trust. He'd told Kiki she could trust him completely, and he'd held this back from her.

He leaned his elbows on his knees and put his forehead in his hands. "I decided to quit. Just this morning, how's that for irony? But I've been wanting to for so long. I was just afraid to tell you, especially after what you told me about your mother. The drugs…" He tipped his face up to meet Kiki's eyes, but she was staring out the window at the setting sun.

She shook her head. "You don't have to feel guilty, Dev. Please don't. I—maybe I already knew. It just didn't seem possible, that you could do what you do without some kind of…help. There isn't one part of me that thinks any less of you because of it." Her eyes were on him now, intensely blue, filled with empathy. He longed to lose himself in them, to believe it was all going to be alright between them. But he couldn't shake the feeling of foreboding crawling over his skin. "Do you know what happened to me today?" Kiki continued. "I was sitting in that café, waiting for the woman who might be my mother to show up. And, Dev, I had a total panic attack. You should have seen me—I was a wreck. I've never felt that way before, and all I could think was, *How does he do it?* That kind of stress was nothing compared to what you face night after night—all those rabid fans, so many people to please—but you do it! I know it scares the shit out of you, and that makes you the strongest person I know."

Dev felt pressure well up in his chest. Kiki was so evolved, so compassionate that it made him want to cry. There was no other woman in the world who even came close to her, and he would do everything in his power to keep her. His throat felt like it was closing. He almost gasped aloud for air. He needed her as much as he needed oxygen. "You're the first person who ever made me feel that way," he said in an unsteady voice. "I always thought of myself as weak. I thought if you knew the truth about me you'd think of me that way, too."

"You see? It's the same way I thought you'd see me in the way my mother and ex-husband did. God, our false perceptions of ourselves can fuck things up." She stood up and walked over to him. Dev watched as she lowered herself onto the floor until she was kneeling in front of him. He longed to reach out for her, to wrap her in his arms, to have her tell him nothing had changed between them. But something in her face stopped him.

As Kiki looked up at him, a tear tracked down her face. She reached her hands out and laid them flat on his thighs. "There's something I need to tell you." Her voice caught. "You want a family, Dev, and I can't have kids. That's why my ex left me. I'll never be able to get pregnant, not even with IVF. There will never be a child who carries my DNA. So you see, if you choose me, a big part of your dream will die."

Dev tried to make sense of her words. Four weeks. That's how long they'd been together, how long he'd been falling deeper in love with her every single day. She'd known he wanted kids, and she'd taken this long to tell him. Because she'd been terrified to lose him, just like he had her. Afraid to reveal the most vulnerable part of herself.

It was all so familiar.

He shook his head. "Jesus, Strawberry. I don't fucking care." He leaned forward and took her face in his hands. He'd imagined telling her he loved her at a romantic restaurant, maybe, or in bed right before he entered her. But life wasn't a fairy tale, it was messy and heartbreaking and soul-destroying at times, and he wanted to experience every part of that with her. He looked deeply into her eyes. "I love you, Kiki. I love you so much it hurts. My need for you tears me apart. There's nothing in the world that could change that."

Kiki's tears were flowing freely now. "Oh, Dev…" She choked out a sob that wrenched his heart in two. "I love you, too. I think I've loved you from the moment you admitted that stupid prank you pulled on me in Paris. Or maybe even from the first time I felt you inside me. Or even that first kiss on the beach.

I never in a million years dreamed I could ever feel this way about anyone."

Dev's tears joined hers. There was something horrible coming, there had to be. And as much as he was being ripped apart as if his very flesh were tearing, even more than that he couldn't bear to see Kiki in pain. She squeezed his hands. "The thing is, is that...this isn't how it should go, Dev. Right now we're looking at each other with big hearts in our eyes, shot by Cupid's arrow. But that's not real life. A real life together would mean me getting on your case about quitting the road, because I know that's what you want even though you don't say it. It would mean me being secure enough to make a life with a celebrity that every woman on earth wants. It would mean you being patient while I try to fig-ure out my next career. It would mean me saying *no more* to those pills you take, because they scare the shit out of me. It would mean you having a child with another woman's egg, or maybe years of heart-break and waiting if we chose to adopt. And all of that might seem doable right now, but time takes its toll. Believe me, I've experienced it firsthand. In a few years, the last thing I want is for you to regret who you chose to make a life with."

Dev's tears were flowing now, coursing down his face in an endless stream. He'd never felt so exposed and vulnerable, and yet he wouldn't trade it for any-thing. It was the kind of pain that reached the very deepest part of him, the part of him that he knew no other woman would ever touch. "Oh, God, Kiki, I would never—"

"No." She gripped his hands tighter. "I *can't* let you reevaluate a lifelong dream in one day. If we're going to be together, you need to be a thousand percent sure of what you're getting into. And the only thing that can guarantee that is time." She paused, and Dev sensed it: another piece of devastating news. "I'll help find you a replacement for the rest of the tour. I'm flying home tomorrow."

A fresh wave of sorrow crashed over Dev. She was leaving. He'd go back to Moretta for a few days after he was done in Australia, and then he'd be on to the North American leg of his tour—without her. Time and distance loomed ahead of him, a lonely and gaping emptiness he wanted to smash into a million pieces.

He shook his head helplessly. "Can't you see how this is killing me? You are my home, Kiki. You're my *everything.* You told me once that I didn't like the sound of silence, and you were right. I hated the chatter that went on in my head. It sounded like a monster was trying to fucking devour my brain. But I've been working on it. I'll never be perfect, but I know I'll never change my mind about you. You have to trust me." His last statement fell on his ears guiltily. Trust. Both of them had proven the extent that theirs was damaged in the past hour, and Dev knew there was no way to put that faith in someone else until you'd put it in yourself.

Kiki held a hand up to him, and Dev grasped on to it like a man going under. "If we're going to work, we need time," she repeated. "I never told you what happened today. I walked out of the café before I met that woman, and you know why? Because I decided that the only person I need to complete me is you. But it took me twenty-four years to realize I didn't need my mother in my life, and about a month to decide you were the one I needed instead. That's beautiful, but it's also dangerous."

They looked at each other. The neckline of Dev's T-shirt was wet with his tears. Kiki's face was streaked with mascara. There was nothing he could say to change her mind, he knew that now. He had to let her go, lay himself at fate's feet and trust that time would bring them together again. But for now, all he could do was sit here and feel the heaviness of his heart in every cell of his body.

When Dev reached for Kiki, she stood up and scrambled into his lap like a child, straddling her legs over him. He took her face in his hands, studying her while she did the same to him. Memorizing every plane of his face, those electric eyes, that errant lock of hair. "I love you so much," Dev said thickly.

"I love you more," Kiki whispered, her eyes huge with emotion. What people said about heartbreak was wrong—you didn't feel it in your heart. You felt it in your stomach, a tight, squeezing ball of pain that told you nothing would ever be the same again. That all the love in the world didn't matter if it was built on a foundation she knew could collapse at any moment. But she had to believe they would be together again, that time and distance and uncertainty would be their allies because it would make them stronger than they could ever be right now.

Kiki brought her mouth down on Dev's. She slid her face against his, letting their tears mingle together. Dev wrapped his arms around her tightly and buried his face in her neck. He inhaled and exhaled over and over again, trying to come to terms with the agonizing future she'd just laid out for them. Kiki couldn't get close enough to him. She pushed into him harder, as if she could absorb all of his pain into her. And now she could feel him between her legs, a thickness growing in spite of, or maybe because of, their sorrow. She rocked her hips back and forth ever so slightly.

It was all the encouragement Dev needed. He reared his pelvis up, and a dam inside Kiki burst. She pressed her hands to his face and kissed him fiercely, so filled with need for him she could barely breathe. She wanted him to make the sweetest, slowest love to her and fuck her like an animal in heat at the same time. "Dev," she whispered into his mouth. "I need you. One more time. *Please*."

He made a savage sound at the back of his throat as his mouth opened completely, his tongue finding hers. He sucked her lower lip, wound her hair around his hand and pulled her head back so he could bite her neck. She gasped, wanting more. It could never be enough with Dev. She could be with him for a thousand years and it wouldn't be enough. The way he claimed her, she knew without a doubt she could never belong to anyone else.

Trying to take this slowly was pointless. No foreplay was needed or wanted. Her pussy was already achingly wet, and she could feel him rock hard through his pants. They reached for each other at the same time, so frenzied with desire they nearly collided. She opened his zipper and pulled his cock free while Dev reached under her dress and moved her thong aside. Fully clothed, desperate for each other, consumed with one thing—being together as one. And then Dev was entering her, the sheer force of the incredible feeling knocking both of them back so that he was lying prone in the chair while Kiki fell backward with her hair brushing the floor. She threw her head forward again, her hair flying over her face as she looked down at the arousing place they were connected. Dev grabbed her by the hips, immobilizing her, and started thrusting into her like it was the last fuck of his life. Neither of them spoke. There was nothing left to say that they hadn't said already, nothing that could bring them closer or further into love with each other. Just their bodies working together perfectly, Dev's heavy breathing and Kiki's small cries of rapture as they climbed upward together.

Suddenly Dev stopped with her anchored onto his cock, and then he rose up from the chair and laid her out on the floor. The rug was thick enough to cushion her back, but Kiki loved the raw, slightly painful feeling of the hard wood beneath it. She wanted rug burns on her back tomorrow, a painfully stretched pussy, Dev's bite marks on her neck.

The added depth and thrust caused by the firm floor was driving both of them close to the edge. Dev was up on his hands driving into her like a madman. She wrapped her legs around his waist as she fell over the edge with a cry, feeling her body tense and shudder while time stood still. On and on her orgasm went, crest after crest of heat, as if her body knew this was the last time.

When she finally opened her eyes, Dev was looking down at her with the tenderest expression she'd ever seen. His body was perfectly still on top of hers.

"I'll wait forever for you, Kiki," he said hoarsely, and then he landed the softest kiss on her lips. She felt him thrust once, twice, and then he came with a brutal, almost violent force that seared their spirits together for all time.

EPILOGUE

"WELL, I GUESS that's it," Kiki said, sealing the last box with a length of packing tape and standing up. She rubbed at her lower back, sore from packing since early that morning. She hadn't wanted any help with it, but her move had happened to coincide with one of Laina's visits, so she had insisted on helping. Kiki glanced at her watch. "The movers should be here any minute to pick everything up. Thank God you wouldn't take no for an answer—I had a lot more stuff than I thought I did. Amazing all the shit you collect over time."

"Well, you had a real life here," Laina said gently.

Kiki nodded sadly as she looked around the tiny cottage. This place had offered her solace for three pivotal years of her life. She'd laughed and cried here and spent countless evenings solving all of life's problems over cookies or wine with Nicola. But now everything was changing. Two months ago Nicola had moved back to LA to be with Alex, and Kiki had even quit Pablo's for a new career.

Kiki put a hand on Laina's arm. "Thanks again for being here. I know this isn't your favorite place in the world anymore."

Laina shrugged. "I still love the island—it's just my family that makes me crazy. Things have been better since I started avoiding them," she finished with a lift of her chin, but Kiki couldn't help but wonder if that was really true. The important thing was that her friend had recovered from the heartbreak that had rocked her nearly a year ago, and she seemed to be getting on with her life—at least to the rest of the world. Kiki knew all too well the strong currents that could lurk beneath a life that looked calm on the surface.

She shook her head. "I can't pretend that I'd be as big a person as you in your situation. Staying in my little hovel when you could live like a Kardashian just up the hill?"

Laina grinned. "That's the whole point. Even staying at the guesthouse—the emotional price is too high with my family. I guess I'll just have to find a new best friend to stay with now that you're moving."

"Yeah." Kiki felt tears prick at her eyes as she looked around the room one last time, but she fought them back.

Laina touched her arm. "Are you okay?"

"No." Kiki's face lit up. "I'm fucking ecstatic, actually."

Laina laughed. "I am so proud of you, Mash. Ev-

erything you've been through, and now look at you."
She shook her head. "I couldn't be happier for you."

Kiki's chest filled. "True love is out there, Laina."

"For some, yes."

"No. For *everyone*. It just takes such a ridiculous
leap of faith." She grasped her friend's hand. "I know
it's out there for you, too."

"I don't think so. But that's okay," Laina added
quickly. "I'm not looking for it. My life is good right
now—I don't even want it."

Kiki nodded. She remembered exactly what it was
like to be in that place of denial, but she also knew
that it wasn't her place to tell her friend that. Everyone had their own journey, and love wasn't something that could be picked up along the way and put
in your pocket. It was a road you found yourself on
with breathtaking hairpin turns and soul-swallowing
potholes and the most aching beauty that existed.
And getting through it sometimes meant hanging
on for dear life.

She walked to the door and turned toward her
friend. "Ready?"

Kiki felt Dev before she saw him. Sitting in the lobby
of The Palms with her iPad in hand, busily typing
an email, she jumped when she felt something bur-
rowing into her neck. *"Shit!"* she cried out, and then
she laughed when Dev turned his face toward her.

"You're late," he said, nibbling at her ear while

his hand slipped discreetly up her shirt. "Everyone's already in the restaurant."

"And I'm going to be a lot later if I don't get these emails done." Kiki tried batting his hand away, but she knew it was pointless. If Dev wanted to touch her, he was going to touch her. That insistency was one of the things she loved most about him. It was what got her into bed with him each night, made her climax more times than she'd thought humanly possible, reminded her daily of her beauty and worth, forced her to deal with her issues and even kept her from working too hard. But most important, it was what had brought them back together after eight excruciating months apart.

Physically apart, that was, because Kiki hadn't been separated from Dev emotionally for even a second. They'd talked every single day while he was still on tour, after agreeing to put the subject of "them" aside and just focus on what grew outside of their insane sexual chemistry. After Dev had returned to Moretta full-time, he'd announced some big changes in his life: Bix was history, and so was touring. He'd moved into the role of songwriter and producer, doing most of his work from his home studio, and he'd never been happier. That's when he'd come to Kiki with a proposal—that she work for him as his publicist with a very specific goal in mind. Together they'd mapped out a plan that Kiki could only describe as incredibly courageous and perfectly Dev. It began with an article for *Rolling Stone* about his lifelong anxiety. He'd laid it all out—his early substance abuse, the panic attacks, the prescription drugs, the secret shame and debilitation he thought he'd never be able to get in front of. After that Kiki had made his social media a platform for anxiety, using discussion prompts and old photos of him on tour to help crack the image of the infallible rock star—already part of Dev's passion, but taken a big step further. The outpouring of support had been overwhelming, with other celebrities coming out of the woodwork with their own stories. The offshoot result had been a brand-new career for Kiki as a social media manager to the stars. It was the perfect job, allowing her to work from Moretta, and she could barely keep up with the demand.

At first, Kiki had wondered how she and Dev would manage a professional relationship without crossing any lines, but they'd done it by keeping most of their communications remote. In the meantime, their companionship had only grown. They'd spent hours talking, laughing and sometimes crying on the phone, until one night Kiki realized that her fear was gone. Dev was as rock-solid as they came, and there was nothing that was going to scare him away from her. In the middle of the night, she'd taken the caricature drawing they'd had made in Venice and taped it to his front door along with a sticky note with two little words: "Never readier." Dev had shown up at her door the next morning with a smile bright enough to light up the whole island, and they'd spent the next twenty-four hours in a relentless, fevered state of reconciliatory bliss.

Dev rubbed a thumb over the thin fabric of Kiki's bra and tugged on her hair lightly, a promise of what was to come later. "I'll meet you in there."

"I'll be fast," Kiki promised, giving him a quick kiss before returning to her work. She finished the email, details for a media tour one of her clients was starting in a few days, and clicked off her iPad. There was plenty more work she could do, but tonight was special. It was Dev's birthday, and he'd only wanted one thing besides Kiki wrapped up in a bow. By the time she and Dev got home from having dinner, his gift would be waiting for him: his house filled with her boxes. It was a step she never imagined she'd take again with any man, but with Dev it wasn't even scary. It felt perfectly right, because she knew there would be a million imperfect moments ahead and that they would handle them all together.

Kiki entered the restaurant and glanced around, looking for their table. It was busy tonight, as it always was at The Palms, with loud chatter competing with the classical music. Kiki spotted Laina, who was sitting with a few of Dev's and Kiki's other friends. "Where's Dev?" she asked Laina as she sat down, and then she did a double take. "And what's that funny look on your face?"

Laina gave her a mischievous smile, but she didn't answer her. Kiki followed her eyes to the corner of the room. Dev was standing there with a microphone in his hand, clearly waiting for her to notice him. "What…?" Kiki's jaw dropped as he caught her eye and gave her that carefree, sexy grin she loved so much.

Dev stepped forward, and the room immediately quieted to a hush. He tapped the microphone jokingly before speaking into it. "Hi, everyone. I'm Dev, and it's my birthday."

A roar of approval and applause filled the room.

"I'm just hoping you'll bear with me for a few moments. There's a woman in this room whom I love with all of my heart, and I happen to owe her a song."

Kiki couldn't breathe as she watched him move across the room and take a seat…at the piano. A shiver of emotion ran up her spine. *Oh, Dev…*

"A while ago she asked me to play the piano for her, but I couldn't do it. But now I can, and it's all because of her. So I hope I don't break all of your ears, because I'm extremely rusty and I'm going to play a new song. But, Kiki, this one's for you. I love you with every part of my heart and soul, Strawberry."

Kiki watched, mesmerized. Dev began to play a slow melody, and then he started to sing. A beautiful ballad about kisses on the beach and everlasting passion and trust and heartache and eternal love. Kiki's hand stayed frozen to her heart for the entire song, her eyes glued to him. It was too incredible. He was too incredible. To her the song sounded flawless, but maybe that was because she knew it was just for her.

When it was over, she stood up amid the clapping

and cheering and went straight for him. She wrapped her arms around him and kissed him deeply enough to embarrass the entire room, but she didn't care. One year ago today, on a sofa in his music studio, Dev had made her his. It had been the beginning of forever.

* * * * *

UNDER HIS TOUCH

CATHRYN FOX

MILLS & BOON

This one is for you, Amanda W.

You are a gem! So glad to call you my friend.

CHAPTER ONE

Megan

"HE WANTS YOU to do what?"

Heavy spring rain pummels the Manhattan streets, along with the café's windows as I sip my mocha latte and take in Amanda's wide-eyed stare. Thick, black lashes blink rapidly as she works to absorb this crazy turn of events; and for God's sake if she doesn't pick her jaw up from the table, she's going to catch the fly buzzing around her jelly-filled doughnut.

"I know. Insane, right?" I say to my best friend, and give a slow shake of my head, still unable to believe what billionaire James Carson has asked me to do. Although, I have to admit, I'm more shocked that I actually agreed to do it. I mull it over for a second and a burst of unease moves through me as I think about putting his plan into motion. Am I making a big mistake? Maybe I shouldn't have agreed to it at all.

Amanda lifts her mug to her mouth and looks at me over the rim before asking, "Is the man losing his mind?"

"He's ninety." I flip my hand over. "So, I get why you'd think that, but after talking to him it's clear he's as sharp now as he was when I met him back in high school. Hard to believe he's playing with a full deck, though, considering what he wants me to do."

Every time the bell over the door chimes as it opens, my stomach does a little somersault. I'm far more nervous about this afternoon's meeting than I thought I would be. It's been eight years since I've set eyes on Alec Carson. Eight long years and I've never stopped thinking about him. Never stopped wanting to stab him in the eye with a fork.

"Okay, so let me get this straight," Amanda says. "James Carson wants you to find his grandson a wife?" She rubs her finger between her eyebrows, one of her cute quirks when she's trying to wrap her brain around something. Her nose crinkles. "But you're an event planner, not a matchmaker."

"I know, and I don't know the first thing about matchmaking. Cripes, the last time I used a dating site, I ended up with a narcissistic lawyer who probably feasted upon the dreams of innocent children." I give a low, slow whistle. "Not going there again."

Amanda laughs, and my stomach comes alive when the bell jingles again. By the time Alec arrives, I'm going to be a jittery mess. I need to keep it together, but facing the boy I once loved, the boy

I gave my virginity to, is messing with my mind and body in the worst kind of way. Then again, he's not a boy anymore and I'm not some innocent, naive love-struck teen. Truthfully, I never expected the grand-son of billionaire magnate James Carson—a sweet, generous old man who always put family first—to walk away from me after a beautiful prom night in St. Moritz, without so much as a backward glance. We spent nearly all of senior year together, and I thought he was different. I thought we had something special. Thought he didn't care that I was from the wrong side of the tracks.

I thought wrong.

He always teased that I was the girl-next-door type, and I thought he liked that about me. In the end, however, it was just another thing I was mis-taken about. I guess bigger and better, more glam-orous, was waiting for him at Harvard. He didn't want the poor, parentless girl from Philly holding him back. Now he's a financier at Blackstone Ven-ture Partners, working his way through the ranks at the multimillion-dollar holding company, one harsh corporate takeover at a time.

Ah, what was that you just said about feasting upon the dreams of innocent children?

"And Alec actually agreed to this?" Amanda asks, her damp blond hair brushing over her shoulder as she shakes her head, incredulous.

I run my hand over my own curls, a frizzy mess from the weather, and work to make myself presentable. Jesus, am I seriously preening for the jerk? Suppressed anger surfaces as I reach for my latte, take another fast sip, irritated with myself.

"His granddad set this up, and Alec is meeting me here, so he must have agreed," I say.

"I get why you're doing it. You find him a wife and throw him the royal wedding of the century, no expenses spared. That will take you from obscurity in the event planning world to the most sought-after consultant in Manhattan, but why would *he* agree? What's in it for him? From what I've read about 'Manhattan's most eligible bachelor' in the tabloids, he doesn't seem like the settling-down type."

Not only does Amanda know him from the tabloids, as my best friend since college, she knows how close Alec and I once were, and how he ditched me after prom. I look past Amanda's shoulder, and my heart jumps into my throat when Alec walks in. The air of authority about him draws the attention of every single woman in the room, and some not-so-single ones. Then there's the impeccable suit he's sporting, one that was undoubtedly tailor-made for his tall frame and athletic body. The men in the room begin to posture in his presence, but there's no point. Alec is breathtaking, the most impressive guy here, and for a moment I can't think, let alone breathe as he smooths his hands over his tie in much the same way his grandfather did during our meeting. With a laser focus, he casts a quick glance around the café. Intense blue eyes find mine, and the muscles in his square jaw ripple as he clenches down, giving me the impression that he had no idea it was me he was meeting.

Wouldn't James have told him?

As our eyes hold and lock, my insides burn like I've just been hit with a high-voltage Taser. Damn, he hasn't changed a bit. No, that's not true. He's grown from a boy to a man, his body wider, thicker, filling out his clothes in a way the young Alec never could. I swallow. Hard.

"I guess I'm about to find out what's in it for him," I squeak out.

Amanda's eyes pop open again. "I take it he just arrived." Her head angles, and I touch her hand and stop her before she can turn and gawk.

"Yes, he's here. Right on time, as I suspected." He always was conscious of the time, a stickler for the rules. Except now, something in my gut tells me he no longer plays by them. "Please don't look."

Amanda picks up her mug and half-eaten jelly doughnut. "Then I'm gone. Text me later," she says. "I can't wait to hear all about this."

I stand with her, and run my damp hands over my skirt. No need to greet him with a wet palm and let him know what the sight of him is doing to me— even after all this time. It's best I give a professional vibe, and the appearance that I'm completely unaffected by him.

If only that were true.

He nods to Amanda as she walks past him to put

her mug in the tray, and his overwhelming presence weakens my traitorous knees as he crosses the room to stand over me. All six feet of pure power and testosterone takes my mind back to the night we made love. Scratch that. To the night we had sex. Yeah, lovemaking involves emotions. If there were emotions involved, he wouldn't have walked away the next day, letting me know in no uncertain terms that there was nothing more between us. If only I'd gotten the memo back then, before I went to his hotel room and seduced him.

I lift my gaze to meet his, and even though he's offering me a smile, I catch a hint of uncertainty in his gorgeous blue eyes as they roam my face. Obviously, this is as awkward for him as it is for me. His arms lift, like he's about to embrace me, but professional event planner that I am, I keep it together and hold my hand out.

He stares at it for a moment, his smile dissolving, morphing into confusion, and then he gives me a tight, fast nod as he closes his big hand over mine.

Yeah, that's right. That's the way it's going to be. I'm in charge here.

"Megan," he says, his voice deeper than I remember it. "Nice to see you."

"Alec," I say. "Nice to see you, too. It's been a long time. You're well?" I say, always the master at small talk. A wedding planner has to be a good communicator, and I thank the Lord for my training.

Another tight nod. "Yes, you?"

"Never better," I say and give him my best smile despite the storm raging inside me.

He gestures with a nod to Amanda as she disappears out the door. "Am I interrupting? Granddad told me to be here for two."

"Two is correct and you're not interrupting at all. I was just meeting with Amanda to go over some details for the upcoming Bar Mitzvah I'm planning. She's a caterer. Perhaps you've heard of her business. Kitchen Door Catering, in Hell's Kitchen. I actually rent office space from her."

He gives a slow shake of his head. "Sorry, never heard of it."

I'm not surprised, really; making a name in Manhattan and competing with already established businesses that own the core market share is hard. I can throw money at the marketing budget all day, but the rich and famous prefer the status quo, and rarely give newbies like Amanda and me a chance. Any company used by James Carson, however, will become a household name and that's what I'm banking on.

Alec's gaze moves from my face to my near-empty coffee mug with pink lipstick staining the rim. "I'm going to grab a coffee. Can I get you anything?"

"That's my second cup. I'm already jittery," I say, a little breathless as he gazes at me with those mesmerizing blue eyes.

One brow raises. "Lemon-filled doughnut?"

Okay, now I really can't breathe. Why would he ask that, or even remember that? I open my mouth, but my damn voice is stuck in my tight throat, so I just shake my head no. He hesitates for a moment, and I take that opportunity to lower myself into my seat and dig my planner out from my bag. He smooths his hand over his tie again and turns, giving me a reprieve from his hot stare, and even hotter body. I take a fast breath and fuel my lungs. Honest to God, a man who had sex with me, and then walked away, shouldn't remember my favorite kind of doughnut, or my favorite kind of anything. Damn him for giving me a moment of hesitation, a seed of hope that he might have actually cared about me the night I gave myself to him.

I open my planner with a little too much force, grab my pen and scribble "Alec Carson" on the first blank page. I don't need to look up to know he's back at the table with his coffee. His presence, and the warm enticing scent of fresh soap and something uniquely Alec—a crisp new day after a hard summer rain—reaches my nostrils. My stomach squeezes slightly. I pinch my eyes shut for a second, to darken all the images that are clamoring to resurface. Alec is a world-class jerk, and I'm not going to waste a second remembering the way he touched me that night, with such deft, gentle hands. Or the way he talked to me, using sweet soothing words, as he *fucked* me. Over.

He sits, and my gaze goes to his big hands as he drinks his coffee. Still black, no sugar. Some things never change. Then again, some things do, and maybe that's for the best. I'm not sure I could work with him if I was still harboring a stupid schoolgirl crush.

Oh, but it was so much more than that, Megan.

"Okay," I say, shutting down that inner voice and working not to sound as breathless as I feel. "I want to be honest with you. I'm an event planner, not a matchmaker, but I'll do my very best to set up an appealing online profile for you and help find your soul mate." He goes perfectly still for a moment, and then he laughs, and the dark, jaded sound raises the hair on my neck. "What?" I ask.

"I'm not looking for a soul mate, Megan." He leans toward me. "I don't even believe in marriage."

I sit up a little straighter, and let my gaze roam his handsome face. Every visible muscle is strained, like an overtightened wire about to snap. "If you don't believe in marriage, what are we doing here?"

He goes quiet, thoughtful for a moment and takes a drink from his mug. He sets it on the table, leans back and folds thick arms over his chest.

"I'm here today because my aging grandfather won't stop breathing down my neck. He doesn't like my lifestyle, or my business practices. He says it's bringing a bad name to the Carson family. He wants me to clean up my act and marry a nice girl."

Appreciating his honesty, I tap my pen on my notepad and nod in understanding. The tabloids have been having a field day with Manhattan's most eligible bachelor. He's been photographed with different affluent women—far outside my social circle—on his arm every week. It can't be easy having no privacy.

Don't feel bad for him, Megan.

"I can understand that," I say.

He angles his head, a thick lock of hair falling forward, and I note that he's wearing it longer than usual. He rakes it back and asks, "Can you?"

"Sure," I say and glance at my planner. "But what I don't understand—"

His big warm hand closes over mine. The weight is heavy, and it takes my mind back to the way he once caressed me. Unnerved and aroused by his touch, my gaze flies to his. "It's like this, Megan. I'll get married, but it will be in name only. I'm not interested in anything more. A nice girl will get my granddad off my back, and the stability of marriage will look good to the board of directors who are handpicking Blackstone's next chief financial officer." My jaw drops open as he lays the cold, ugly truth out for me. So, this is what's in it for him? He would actually marry to better his position in the company. What kind of a man would do that? Perhaps the better question is, how did I not see this side of him all those years ago? I pull my hand back fast and wipe my palm on my skirt.

His eyes darken, the black bleeding into the blue as he zeros in on me. "If you have a problem with that…"

CHAPTER TWO

Alec

KEEP YOUR SHIT TOGETHER. *Play it cool. You've got this, Carson.*

Yeah, right!

I can lecture myself all I want, but I don't "got this." Not even a little bit.

I draw in a deep breath. "Do you?" I ask again, working to maintain a rigid, professional-like composure, despite the fact I'm telling the one woman I've always wanted but can never have what I want in a future wife.

How the hell did we end up here, negotiating a wife for me? Granddad, that's how. Now that my cousins Tate and Brianna are married, it was only a matter of time before he came after me. I'm not even sure the man's as weak and frail as he lets on. It could very well be a trick to get what he wants. But can I really take a chance and say no to him? He was there for me my whole life, stepping in to take the place of my dad—his son—when he up and left our family.

I want to make my grandfather happy, and if it means getting married… I clench down on my jaw with an audible click and grind my back teeth together.

I focus back on Megan. She's clearly shocked at what I'm telling her, struggling to digest my words. It takes every ounce of strength, and I mean every ounce I possess, not to press my lips to hers, lose myself in her sweet honeyed taste like I did on prom night.

You can't go there with her.

I stiffen my spine, present cold indifference like I do at every negotiation and study her tense body language. I might not have seen her in eight long years, but I know her well enough to know she's trying to wrap her mind around my need for a loveless marriage. Only problem is, I can't tell her the real truth.

"I… I suppose not." She blinks a few times, picks up her empty cup and sets it down again. "I mean, it's your life." She shrugs. "But I'm not so sure you're going to find a woman who would want a marriage in name only."

I let loose a low, deep humorless laugh. It gives me great pleasure to see that after all these years, little Megan Williams is still as sweet and innocent as the day I met her. I don't ever want her to change, which is one of the reasons I need to keep my hands and mouth to myself. I'm the last guy she needs in her life.

Where the hell was that resolve on prom night?

"You're wrong about that," I say.

Quizzical eyes that once looked at me with adoration narrow, and her thick lashes fall slowly, only to open again. "What makes you say that?"

"Women like power and are influenced by wealth. I'm willing to give whoever we pick exactly that. They can have it all, the money, jets and lifestyle, with the exception of my heart. That's not on the negotiation table."

"What...what about intimacy," she blurts out, then slams her mouth shut and glances around to see if anyone overheard her.

I lean toward her, note the pink flush crawling up her slender neck, pooling on the exact spot I'd like to place my mouth. I take a moment to look her over. At eighteen she was sweet and adorable, but she's grown more beautiful in the passing years. Prominent cheekbones, beautiful full lips, a body any man would kill for. Perfect then, and even more so now.

"Intimacy? Are you asking if I plan to have sex with my wife?"

She takes a deep breath, and as her chest heaves, my gaze slides downward, to her silky white blouse. From my height, and with the top two buttons undone, I'm gifted with a view of her creamy cleavage. I don't deserve to look. Don't deserve anything from her. Despite that knowledge, heat prowls through my blood, and my dress pants become increasingly uncomfortable.

"People…well, people have needs," she whispers.

I lower my voice to match hers. "True, and I'm not ruling sex out, but right now I have other concerns."

"Such as?"

"I'm used to living alone. I need a woman who won't be underfoot in my home. She must be intelligent, likable and a good conversationalist since she'll be attending dinners with board members." She stares at me for a moment, disbelief and a measure of repulsion evident in her big doe eyes. Good, that's the only way I can have her look at me, otherwise… "Perhaps you should be writing this down."

"Oh, right." Her pen flies over the blank pages as she fills it with my criteria. She taps the tip on her chin when done, and stares at her notepad. "Do you care if she works?"

"I'd like for her to have her own life. She won't need to work, but if she chooses to stay home, I'd like to see her involve herself in charitable work." Her eyes lift. "It will look better to the board," I say. Yeah, I get it. I'm coming off like a grade A prick, but that's what I want. That's what I need. If this woman gives me so much as a seed of encouragement, a hint that she might still want me, I could very well lose my shit. I can't—won't—let that happen. She deserves better than that. She deserves better than me.

Last week, when Granddad took me to his study

and plied me with brandy, I knew he was up to something. I agreed to his terms, saw the truth in his words. Sure, I come from wealth, but I want to make my own mark in the financial world, want to become Blackstone's youngest CFO. A wife will help with that and help with my reputation, which will hopefully get the damn paparazzi off my back—Christ knows they destroyed my brother, Will, who is fulfilling the Carson prophecy. But until I walked into this café, I had no idea I'd be facing Megan Williams. The old man never prepared me for her, and I can't help but think he left the event planner's name out on purpose. Smart man, because had I known I'd be coming face-to-face with the sweet girl I screwed over in high school, I never would have agreed to any of this.

I'll never forget the day I met her. It was the summer before our senior year. I was friends with her cousin Sara Duncan, and after Megan's parents died in a car accident, she moved from Philadelphia to Manhattan to live with her aunt and uncle, who are friends of Granddad's. Sara introduced us, and just like that I was lost in her and trying hard to keep it platonic. We were pretty inseparable for the rest of the year, then prom night. Jesus, prom night in St. Moritz. She knocked on my door, and when I opened it…

"Alec?"

Shit.

"Sorry, what?"

"If I'm going to fill out your online profile, I have to know what kind of woman you're attracted to."

Ah. I need to be careful here. My gaze rakes over Megan, and the frizzy state of her auburn hair, my absolute favorite color. It brings a smile to my face. She always hated it when it rained, but I think her wild locks are adorable. With light brown eyes—the color of a root beer Popsicle—fair skin clear of makeup, save for her pink lipstick, she still has that same girl-next-door look going on.

And that, my friends.

Right there.

Is the kind of woman I'm attracted to.

"I prefer blonde," I say, and as she nods her head, her drying auburn locks bouncing, she jots it down.

She plants her elbow on the table and rests her chin in her palm. She goes thoughtful for a long time, then blinks her eyes back into focus. "Can I ask something?"

"Yes, but it doesn't mean I'm going to answer," I say, wanting to be as honest with her as possible, but there are some things I just can't divulge.

"You date all the time. Thanks to the tabloids, I see the gorgeous women on your arm. Why not one of them? If it's to be a loveless marriage, and you think women want you for power and money, and they're probably on your arm because of that, why not just ask one of them to marry you?"

It's a legit question that deserves an honest answer. I might be a tough negotiator, but deep down

I do have morals and I respect integrity as much as the next guy. With Megan, though, I have to be less than forthright with this answer, for her own good.

"The women from my circle aren't suitable for what I need."

"How so?"

"They're glamorous, over-the-top, high maintenance."

"So, you're looking for a sweet girl next door?"

"Yeah."

"The kind of girl you're not really attracted to," she says, her voice so low I have to strain to hear it. But before I can answer—and I have no idea how to respond—she blinks up at me. "Does eye color matter?"

I finish my coffee and check the time. If I'm going to have a nice girl in my home, her appearance at least must be the antithesis of Megan's. Otherwise the daily reminder of what I want and can never have would drive me over the edge. "No, but I do prefer blue."

I watch her throat work as she swallows, and my insides twist. Jesus, that sad look she's trying to hide is ripping me wide-open. Hurting her is the last thing I want to do. But it's also killing me that she looks at me with distaste. Maybe I should put a stop to this. End it now before we go any further.

"Megan," I say.

"Yes."

"Look at me," I command in a soft whisper. Her

eyes slowly lift, lock on mine, and as she stares, a bolt of need grips my chest. I fight it down and ask, "Do you really want to do this? We have a history."

She takes one deep breath, lets it out slowly and lowers her pen. "And that's exactly what it is, a history." The chirpiness is her voice contrasts the visible pain in her eyes. "It's all in the past, where it needs to stay. We're both adults and both professionals and it comes down to this—you're not the only one getting something out of this. You see, Alec, once I find you a wife and throw you the best damn wedding Manhattan has ever seen, I'll be the talk of the town. It will get my business off the ground in a crowded market and skyrocket me into prominence."

"I guess we're both doing this to get ahead, then?" I say.

Her brows knit together. "When you put it that way." She casts her eyes downward for a second. "Looks like we're not so different after all. I'm scratching your back and you're scratching mine, so to speak."

"Tit for tat." As soon as the words leave my mouth, my gaze once again goes down to take in the curve of her breasts. I catch a hint of white lace, and my dick thickens. I want her. I've always wanted her. But am I going to do anything about it? No fucking way. Being around her might just kill me, and I'm going to need a drink, or an entire bottle, by the time we're done here. Because now that I know what's in it for her, I can't walk away and find another event planner. I clear my throat. "Is there anything else you want to know?"

She instantly switches back into professional mode and pulls a laptop from her bag. She sets it between us and boots it up. "Are there any particular dating sites you prefer?"

"Never been on one."

She clicks a few buttons. "I've not had much luck myself—"

"You use dating sites?" Why the hell would a woman like Megan need to use a dating site? She must have men falling at her feet.

"I have in the past," she admits.

I pinch the bridge of my nose, and glance at the barista, anything to keep my mind off Megan in bed with another man. I have no hold on her. She can date any guy she likes, but goddammit, the thought of any man's hands but mine on her still bothers me. Eight years later.

"I see the ads for that Match Made in Heaven site all the time," I say. "Should we try that?"

"It's a good jumping-off point. If we don't get any matches, we can set you up elsewhere. Although I'm sure you'll have a million matches in the first hour."

"What makes you think that?"

"Look at you," she blurts out. Her gaze moves from my chest to my face. "Ah, I mean, you're not bad to look at, and you're successful. All we need is a catchy bio. Let's have a look at it, see what other criteria I might need before I set you up." She points to the seat beside her. "Why don't you sit here, so we can look at the screen together."

"Coffee first. We might be here for a while. Do you want something?"

Her gaze slides to her empty cup. "I guess I'll have another mocha latte."

She reaches for her purse, but I hold my hand up to stop her. "I got it," I say and walk away, needing a moment to pull myself together before I sit close to her.

I order our drinks, and as the barista makes them, I grab a lemon-filled doughnut and a piece of cheesecake. I press my Apple Watch to the payment terminal and hold until it vibrates. After the charge goes through, I carry the sweets to our table.

She shakes her head. "I didn't want—"

"They're for me. I came here straight from the gym and I'm starving. The barista will bring our coffee over."

I lower myself into the seat next to her, and her sweet scent reaches my nose. I devour her with my eyes and throw up a silent prayer. Sweet mother of God, give me strength. Her gaze goes from the pastries, to my fork. Her eyes narrow in on the silverware, and her fingers curls into fists.

"You got something against my fork?" I ask.

"No." She shakes her head as if to clear it. "I was just remembering my mom's Philly cheesecake," she adds, and I get the sense she's redirecting the conversation. "Best in the world, and that's not a very healthy choice for after the gym," she says.

I grin at her. "Yeah, I know, Mom."

"Not funny," she says, and crinkles her nose, those cute freckles bunching together.

"I know but remember when we used to go to my place after school and raid the fridge before dinner. Mom used to—"

"Chase us into your bedroom with her broom, warning we were going to ruin our appetites," she pipes in, finishing my sentence, much like we used to do years ago. "But we were always hungry back then."

We both laugh, but it sizzles out fast, the space between us going perfectly quiet.

"Yeah," I say after a moment, breaking the silence.

"Yeah," she repeats, and then angles her head to glance at my clothes as the barista delivers the coffee. "You put a suit on after the gym?"

"Mmm-hmm." I pick up the doughnut and take a big bite. "Damn, that's good."

"Do you always wear a suit? Everywhere?"

"Yes, always. Except in the gym, the shower or in bed." I wink at her. "I like casual sex, and wearing a suit to bed just makes it formal," I say and wonder what the fuck I'm doing. I shouldn't be teasing her, flirting with her.

Her cheeks darken. "Well, some dates will be more casual than others. What if you go skydiving, or to the movies, or even a romantic hansom cab ride around Central Park?"

"When was the last time you took a horse ride around Central Park?" I ask.

"Ah, well. Never. It's something I've always wanted to do, but I'm not dating right now, and we're talking about you, not me."

A thrill I don't want to feel races through me. "Are you trying to say you want to dress me, Megan?"

"If that's what it takes to find you a wife, then yes. I want complete control."

Megan in bed, completely in control. Yeah, that visual is helping my cock. I take another bite of the doughnut and moan as I hold it out to her. "Try it."

She stares at it for a moment, and her mouth goes slack. "It does look good."

"It is good."

I hold it closer and she bites into it. Her lids close and lemon oozes from the doughnut as powdered sugar gets all over her face and nose.

I chuckle. "You always were a messy eater." I reach out, brush my thumb over her cheek.

She draws in a fast breath, and my hand freezes. Jesus, how can I do this? How can I spend the next month, possibly the next two, with this woman, without giving in to the things I feel?

I'll be fucked if I know, but somehow I have to find a way.

CHAPTER THREE

Megan

"HE SOUNDS LIKE quite the asshole. I think you dodged a bullet after prom. I know it didn't feel like it then, but he did you a solid by walking away," Amanda says, as we toss our damp towels over our shoulders and walk through the gym to the locker rooms.

I nod in agreement and take in the near-empty establishment. I guess it being a Friday night and all, people have better things to do than sweat it out. Although I can think of other, more fun ways to get in a workout. *Good Lord, Megan. Get your thoughts out of the gutter.* It's just that it's been so long since I've been physically touched by a man. I'm sure that's the only reason my body is all amped up. Yeah, it has nothing to do with coming face-to-face with Alec last week.

Liar.

I wonder what he's doing on this Friday night, which glamorous, high-maintenance woman he has on his arm, and whose bed they'll be falling into later. The sooner I get him married, the better it is for my business—and for my sanity. But the questions on the Match Made in Heaven questionnaire that goes with his profile are very personal, and we'll need to fill it out together when he's back from his business trip. I don't know *this* rigid, detached Alec. He's far different from the boy back in high school. Heck, if answering the questions were left to me, he'd probably be matched to a hungry hyena with a toothache.

I snort at that and step into the change room with Amanda.

"Pajamas, romantic comedy and popcorn tonight?" she asks.

"There is no other way I'd want to spend tonight, and no one I'd rather spend it with," I say, and she rolls her eyes.

"I love you, too, but I'm sorry, Megan. I'd take a nice fat dick on a Friday night over a rom-com and popcorn at home, anytime."

I burst out laughing and glance around, but the few women getting changed still have their earbuds in and are paying us zero attention. "Okay, me, too," I admit and instantly hate myself when my thoughts stray to Alec again. Inside my bag, my phone pings, and I dig it out. My heart does a stupid little tumble when the display informs me that it's none other than the man plaguing my thoughts.

Alec: I'm free tonight to plug the holes in the questionnaire. My place, eight?

Swallowing, I tense up and Amanda leans over to see who the message is from. "Hmm," she begins, "Friday night, his place. Sounds like it's not just the holes in the questionnaire he's interested in plugging."

My gaze flies to hers, and I catch her smirk. "Not funny and not going to happen. Not in a million years."

Amanda hikes her bag over her shoulder and blows a wet strand of hair from her forehead. "Whatever you say."

"He doesn't like me that way." I laugh but it comes out sounding like a wounded animal on crack. "I'm actually the complete opposite of the women he's attracted to. Which is fine, because I have zero interest in him either."

"Good, because he hurt you once, and I don't want you to set yourself up for that kind of disaster now that you know what kind of man he is." We push through the locker room door.

"I won't. Fool me once, fool me twice. I get it." We walk through the gym, and step out into the warm spring night. Flowers growing in pots outside the storefronts reach my nostrils and we walk down the sidewalk, passing numerous up-and-coming restaurants on the way to our apartment building.

"If he hurts you in any way…" She stops and

makes scissor motions with her hands. "I will give him an up close view of his farm parts."

"Farm parts?" I laugh and shake my head. Not hard to tell she grew up in Texas's cattle country.

"That's right. Otherwise known as gonads around these parts," she says in her best Texas accent.

I laugh and shake my head. "He can't hurt me if I feel nothing for him. I guess his farm parts are safe."

"Good." She gestures with a nod to the phone in my hand. My God, I'm gripping it so hard my knuckles are turning white. "Now, are you going to answer him, or what?" she asks.

I lift the phone and text back.

Megan: Just finished working out. I'll hit the shower and come over.

Alec: What's your address? I'll send a car.

Am I really doing this? Am I giving the man my address, so he can send a car to drive me to his place, where we'll be all alone? My stomach jumps like I've just eaten a handful of Mexican jumping beans. I give him my address and shove my phone into my bag as we make our way inside. We take the stairs to the second floor, and I give Amanda a hug.

"Movie and popcorn tomorrow night?" I ask.

"You bet, and I want all the details from tonight." She exits the stairwell and I climb to the next floor and enter the apartment right above hers. Amanda moved into this building in Hell's Kitchen a couple years ago, and now is walking distance to her work. When the apartment above hers became available, I jumped on it, and moved my business to one of the spare offices in her warehouse. It's nice to have my best friend close. We're there for each other at a moment's notice, plus she cooks for me all the time. A good thing, considering I'm pretty lousy at it, and she's an amazing chef who is always experimenting and in need of a guinea pig.

I step into my apartment, lean against the door. I probably shouldn't be going to Alec's place, and should have insisted we meet on neutral ground, but I don't want him to think he affects me in any way at all. This is a business relationship, and I plan to keep it that way. My bag rolls off my shoulder when I lean forward, bracing myself.

You got this, girl. All you're doing is finding a wife for the man you once loved. Easy peasy.

On that note, I pull myself up to my full height, and head to the bathroom for a hot shower, even though I should probably take a cold one. Since I have no idea how long his car will take, I soap up quickly and wash my hair. Once done, I give it a fast blow-dry, and pin it to the top of my head in an unflattering mess. I'm not out to impress the man. I'm out to get him married, so I can get my business off the ground.

As I make my way through my small apartment to my bedroom, I can't help but wonder why James

Carson insisted I was the *only* girl for the job. His words not mine. I hadn't seen the elderly gentleman in years, and really, how did he even know I was an event planner? He sold me on the job based on the fact that it would get my name out in the right circles, and while this is a once-in-a-lifetime opportunity, there is a part of this whole thing that just doesn't sit right with me.

I plan numerous weddings, and honest to God, I can tell within five minutes if the couple will make it past the first year. It kind of guts me when I know they won't. Yeah, it's true, I'm a romantic at heart. I want people to find love and live happily ever after. I honestly think there's someone for everyone.

I might not like Alec, but I hate that he doesn't believe in happily-ever-after and has no problem with a loveless marriage. What the hell happened to him over the years? Back in the day he was the sweetest guy, captain of the football team, and always the big brother to all the guys on the team and everyone in our social circle. I never once thought of him as a brother, though. Not even for a second. Which is why during prom in St. Moritz, compliments of a very generous James Carson, I showed up at Alec's hotel room door with nothing but a sexy silk nightie on under my coat. We were friends, close as two people could get, and not once had he tried anything sexual with me. I'd decided to make the first move. Heck, maybe he slept with me out of pity, or had too much to drink. All I know is in the morning, he barely spoke to me, and that summer he made himself invisible before he left for Harvard. Maybe all the blame isn't on him, though. I'm the one who read the situation all wrong. Clearly an intimate relationship wasn't what he wanted, and my stupid actions ended up ruining a good friendship.

But my God, the way he touched me that night, the heated kisses, hungry caresses and a soft touch to soothe the pain that turned to pleasure as he took my virginity. For a brief second I think about running to my room to use my vibrator, but my doorbell chimes.

Dammit.

I tug on a pair of yoga pants and a comfy Taylor Swift T-shirt, then swipe a streak of pink across my lips. I give myself a once-over in the mirror, grab my purse and laptop bag, and head for my door. I retrace my steps down the stairwell and find a tall man dressed in a suit at the security door, both hands clasped behind his back as he rocks back and forth.

"Megan Williams?" he asks when I step outside.

"Yes, that's me," I say, and he holds his hand out and gestures to the sleek, black limousine with its back door open.

"Right this way, Miss Williams," he says with a smile that instantly puts me at ease. The man has a warm, fatherly presence about him, which suddenly has me missing my own. I was fortunate that my aunt Jeannie—my mom's sister—and Uncle Dave took me in after my folks died in the car accident. And while I grew close to my cousin Sara, we're like sisters today, it was never the same as having my own family. I miss that. I want that. Unfortunately, I've been working harder, and dating less. I'm not sure there are any decent guys left in Manhattan.

"Call me Megan." I make my way down the stairs and take in the shiny vehicle that costs more than I make in a year. Yeah, Alec and I really do come from different worlds. But he isn't so different from my adopted family. Uncle Dave is a very successful stockbroker and his family lived a completely different lifestyle than mine. I slide into the backseat. Alec was so kind and caring back then, and there were nights when I was incredibly sad, and Alec and I would text for hours. There was even that one time when he snuck in through my window, held me in my bed while I cried for the loss of my folks.

I swallow down the memories and stare at traffic as the driver takes me to Alec's home. Close to thirty minutes later, we're in New York's Upper East Side. The car slows in front of a luxury Manhattan apartment. Staring out the window, I crane my neck but can't see the top of the building.

The driver takes me to the front entrance, and before I can reach for the handle to let myself out, he's right there, opening the door for me. It feels a little odd to a girl who's used to taking care of herself.

"Thank you," I say. Wait, do I tip him? Cripes, I'm a little out of my element here. I reach for my purse, but he gives me a nod and waves his hand toward the doorman, who seems to be waiting for me.

"The concierge will take you from here," he says.

"Thank you. I didn't get your name?"

His head rears back, just slightly, like my interest in him has taken him by a surprise. Perhaps the women Alec normally has chauffeured to his apartment don't bother chitchatting with the help.

"Phillip Andrews," he says.

"It was nice to meet you, Phillip," I say.

He takes my hand in his and closes both of his palms over it. "The pleasure was all mine, Megan."

He lets me go, and I walk up the marble stairs leading to the massive front entrance. "Hi, I'm Megan Williams," I say when I reach the middle-aged man, with a big toothy smile. I hold my hand out, and he shakes it. "I'm here to see Alec Carson, and Phillip said you'd be taking me from here."

"That's right, Miss Williams, please come in."

"Call me Megan, and you are?"

"I'm Derek," he says, and pulls open the big glass door.

"Nice to meet you, Derek."

"You, too," he says with a nod. "Alec has been expecting you. I trust your drive was pleasant."

"Very," I say, and follow him into the spacious lobby tastefully decorated with glass and chrome that gives the place a welcoming, airy feel. We step onto the waiting elevator, and he puts a key in, and presses the top floor.

"Beautiful night," I say to Derek.

"Spring is here," he says, tugging at the lapels on his black jacket. "My favorite time of year."

"I'm a fall girl," I say. "Sweaters, lattes, falling leaves."

"Tourists," he laments, and we both laugh as the elevator opens on the top floor. "Here we are." He waves his hand and I glance out to find Alec outside his suite waiting for me.

Leaning against the doorjamb, feet crossed at the ankle, he's dressed in a pair of jeans and a comfy-looking blue T-shirt that brings out the color of his eyes. A dressed-up Alec is one thing, but this comfortable, laid-back version has my stupid ovaries doing the *macarena*. He has the sex appeal of a hot fudge brownie delight with a cherry on top, and here I am wishing I had a big spoon.

"Megan," he says, his deep octave throbbing through me and settling at the needy juncture between my legs. "No problems getting here?"

"None whatsoever. Phillip was very nice, and so was Derek."

I turn to see Derek off and give him a little finger wave. He nods before the doors ping shut, locking the world out, and Alec and me in.

"Phillip and Derek," he says. "You know their names?"

I face Alec, and once again I'm blasted with a bolt of lust I wish I didn't feel. "Yes," I mumble.

He swipes his tongue over his bottom lip, his gaze

leaving my face, to take in my T-shirt and yoga pants. In turn, I examine him. "You're not in a suit."

He arches one dark brow, and that's when I notice his hair has been cut. Long or short, he's as handsome as ever. "And you're very observant."

"Did I catch you showering, sleeping or having sex?" I ask.

His grin is so goddamn sexy I reach out and place my hand on the wall to maintain a vertical position. "Well, we might as well be comfortable while going through the forms. I dressed for comfort," I say, and wave my hand over my clothes.

He glances the length of me again and makes a sound. For a brief second I think it might be a moan, but I have to be mistaken. Right? I stash that thought to examine it later as he pushes off the frame and waves his hand to the open door behind him. "Are we doing this in the hall, or do you want to come in?"

Doing this in the hall.

Get it together, Megan. He is not talking about sex.

He turns to his side, and I slide past him, trying to ignore his enticing scent and the heat of his body as I step into his beautiful penthouse suite. I resist the urge to give a low, slow whistle. The door closes and as the lock clicks into place behind me, a warm shudder moves through my body.

"Cold?" Alec asks, mistaking my reaction. "I can turn on the fire."

My gaze goes to the propane fireplace that separates the living room from the kitchen, glass on both sides. "I'm okay, thanks." I scan his place, and take in the amazing view of the Hudson River, the mosaic of stars suspended over the New Jersey skyline. His place looks like it's been professionally decorated in cool grays, and the only homey touches are a picture frame on one of his side tables with a plant beside it. His mother had a lot of plants in the house when he was growing up, but Alec doesn't strike me as the type of guy who could keep one alive. Maybe the designer insisted on it, and his housekeeper waters it or something.

I step up to the table, pick up the frame and smile as I take in a young Alec in his Harvard graduation robe, his arm thrown over his younger brother, Will. Alec has a smile on his face, but it doesn't quite reach his eyes, and for some reason that just doesn't sit right with me. Does he ever laugh anymore, like we used to do when we were teens? God, the times we laughed until we cried. My heart pinches, missing those times.

"How is Will?" I ask, a stupid hitch in my voice as I turn to face Alec. Last I remember was seeing a picture of him in the tabloids in bed with a woman who wasn't his fiancée.

He stares at me a long time before answering. "He's well."

"And your mom? How is she?" I miss his mom. She was always so kind to me, welcoming me into their home, treating me like the daughter she always wanted and never had.

He scrubs his chin. "Mom is well. She stays busy with her charity work. How is Sara, and your aunt and uncle?" he asks.

"Good," I say. "When was the last time you saw Sara?" I ask. They both went to Harvard and maintained their friendship there. I was sure Sara had a thing for him, and there was a time I thought they'd become a couple. Who knows, maybe they did hook up on campus. Then again, Sara is an oversharer about such things and would likely have told me. I never did tell her about what happened on prom night. I was too mortified.

"A few months back. Is she still with Edward and Smith Law Firm?"

"She is. Working hard to make partner," I say, and I'm about to switch the conversation back to him and ask about his dad, but I'm not sure if I should. He left when Alec and Will were young. The guys maintained a relationship with him, but it was strained. How could it not be? He left for a much younger woman. I take in the tension in Alec's body, and sense he wants to get down to business. Ending my trip down memory lane, I turn and place the picture back down.

"Where should we set up?" I ask, and spin back around to find Alec standing right there, so close all I'd have to do is go up on my toes if I wanted to kiss him. Which I don't. At all.

"Why not right here," he says, his voice hoarse, an octave lower as he points to the sofa facing the hearth.

"Okay." I step around him, and plop down on the comfy gray sofa. I set my purse on the floor and tug my laptop from the bag. "These questions are going to take forever, so you might as well make yourself comfortable. We could be here all night." I tuck my legs underneath myself and glance up at Alec. The intensity in his eyes as they roam over my body sends a spark of need rocketing through me. What the hell is going on here? If I didn't know better, I'd think he likes what he sees. But I do know better.

He clears his throat. "I'm going to need a drink." He disappears into the other room, comes back with two glasses. One with white wine, and one with brandy. He swirls the amber liquid in the crystal, and I chuckle softly.

"Something funny?"

"You're so much like your grandfather. You have a lot of the same mannerisms. He swirls his brandy like that and you both have a habit of smoothing down your tie. I noticed you doing that at the café last week."

"Tate does it, too. So does Will. Granddad's clearly rubbed off on all of us." He smiles. "But you always were a people person. Not much gets by you. I'm sure that's what makes you an amazing event planner."

I beam at the compliment. "I am an amazing event planner. It helps when you love what you do."

He hands me the glass of wine. "I like that you own your successes and don't apologize. No point in being modest."

"You own your successes, too," I say, as I recall an article in *Forbes*. He's a financier who restructures businesses and makes no apologies. "Do you like what you do?" I ask.

He eyes me for a moment. "Do you think I'm the big bad wolf, Megan?"

"I never said that."

"You didn't have to, and if you do, you'd be right. I'm not a nice guy."

He might make deals that destroy businesses and people's lives, but I'm not here to insult the man. I'm here to get him married. Changing topics, I sip the wine and the tart flavor bursts on my tongue. "This is delicious."

"Dry, the way you like."

My pulse leaps in my throat. "You remember that?"

"I remember everything," he says, and as he lowers himself beside me, I can't help but think his thoughts have gone to the same place mine have. To the night I seduced him.

I take another sip of wine, stalling before I have to speak, since I'm sure my voice is about to fail me again. "Mmm," I say. I turn on my computer and pull up the profile I began last week. "If we want to match you with the right woman, you have to answer honestly."

"I always try to be honest, and I'm not looking for the right woman," he says, those blue eyes roaming my face, and for the briefest of seconds I wish I were her. Wish I were the right woman for Alec Carson. I practically snort as that stupid thought goes through my head. "I'm looking for a *suitable* woman, remember?"

"You won't at least try?" I say as I shift to face him, legs tucked securely underneath me. "I think everyone has a match, and true love really does exist. You just have to be open to it."

The muscles in his neck bunch as he rolls his shoulders, like the strain of the week is sitting heavily on top of them.

"I'm not open to it," he says, his voice so firm and adamant, it instantly shuts down my rebuttal. "Let's get at this."

Disappointment courses through me but I shove it down. This is Alec's life not mine and if he's against love and marriage, who am I to try to change things. "Okay."

Beside me, he shifts and his leg rubs against my knee as he stretches out and crosses his ankles. He swirls the brandy and takes another drink. The liquid settles on his bottom lip and all I can think about is licking it off. Except he does it for me, and I want to tangle our tongues, taste the brandy from his mouth. A bolt of heat moves through me and I tear my gaze away, try to read the words before me as my stupid libido kicks into high gear.

"Okay, the first set of questions is to generally describe your personality."

"Go on."

"You have three choices for your answers—*not at all*, *somewhat* or *very*." He nods, and I continue with "Bossy?"

He grins, and I click *Very*.

"I'm pretty sure I could have gotten that one right," I say, and rest my head against the sofa pillow. "Remember that time we went to King's Palace amusement park?"

He nods, and looks at the big window, like his thoughts are a million miles away. "It was right after you moved in with Sara."

"You gathered up a few of your football friends, and we all went for the day." He turns back to me and the smile that comes over his face is so genuine and happy, my pulse leaps. As I look at Alec now, I see the boy from my youth. I relax on the sofa and take another sip of my wine. I place it on the table and laugh. "You were so bossy. The guys all wanted to hit the race cars, but you said no, and we did every other ride in the park until it closed and it was too late for any of us to ride."

"Megan," he says, the smile falling fast from his face, a look of horror moving in to take its place. "You'd just lost your parents in a car accident. I couldn't let…what if it reminded…"

"Oh, my God," I say under my breath as the room spins around me. "I... I didn't realize." My heart crashes so hard against my chest, breathing becomes difficult. He did that...for me. "That was so..." Tears prick my eyes and I fight them off. "So considerate of you."

He shrugs like it was nothing.

"The guys were so pissed off," I say, my voice breaking a little. "I thought for sure Dillon Fraser was going to rip you a new one."

"I'd rather that over you..."

"I had no idea." I swallow down the lump in my throat. "Thank you."

He finishes off his brandy and pushes to his feet. "Wine refill?" he asks, and averts his eyes.

"Yeah, sure," I say, certain I'm going to need more alcohol to get through this. "But I'm a lightweight."

"I know." He picks my glass up and leaves, and I press my palms to my eyes hard enough to make me see stars, before I cry over the loss of a young, thoughtful boy who used to watch out for me. He comes back and hands me the wine. I take a huge gulp and find him studying me carefully as I set it on the coffee table.

"You've been asking all the questions, but I have one of my own," he says.

"What?" I ask, unease moving through me.

"Why are you still single?"

Way to get right to the point.

"Well, you see, Alec. There are two kinds of people in this world, those who like Neil Diamond and those who don't." I bite back a grin, and wait for him to get it. When a wide smile splits his lips, we both burst out laughing and the sound is music to my ears.

"How many times did we watch that movie," he says.

"What About Bob?" I shake my head. "It definitely was our go-to movie."

Our laughter dies down, and he turns serious again. "You still want it all don't you. The family, kids, white picket fence."

"You say it like it's a bad thing."

"It's just that it's not for me."

He reaches behind his head and squeezes the back of his neck, and I want to ask why it's not for him, but I don't. When we were young, we shared our hopes and dreams, but having a family of his own was never something he talked about. That didn't mean I didn't think he wanted one, though. I just assumed it wasn't something guys talked about. But I guess in the end it just solidifies that we want different things and would never work out.

"You deserve that, Megan," he says in a voice so soft it wraps around my heart and hugs tight. While we might be different now, he was the one guy who got me, the one guy who understood I needed a family of my own. I can't replace the one I'd lost, but I needed something that was just mine.

"I'm not seeing it happening anytime soon," I say,

and give an exaggerated sigh. "I work long hours and I've pretty much given up dating."

"You haven't been with anyone in a long time?" he asks, quietly.

"No," I say, and look away.

"It's nothing to be embarrassed about. Guys are assholes, I get it."

That makes me laugh. "Takes one to know one," I reply, teasing him with something we used to say when we were young.

"Hey, I resemble that comment."

This time we both laugh, hard, and if I close my eyes really tight, I can almost pretend we're back at his childhood home, hanging out in his bedroom.

But we're not, and I'd be wise to remember this isn't the Alec I once loved.

My heart thuds as I blink up at him. A second passes, then another, and then my laptop fan kicks in, pulling me back. I take a calming breath. "We better keep going," I say, getting the night back on track. I quickly go over the rest of the traits, and avoid reminiscing, even though many of his answers bring back warm memories.

Alec shifts, moving a little farther down on the sofa. "Okay, now we're on to how skilled you are at things."

"Then we're done, right?"

I snort. "No, we have a million more things to answer."

He sighs. "You're right. We are going to be here

all night. In that case, how about a pizza, extra pine-apple even though pineapple belongs nowhere near a pie?"

I laugh. He used to tease me about that so much when we were teens. "We don't have to get pineap-ple. You don't like it."

"Yeah, but it could quite possibly be the only nu-tritious thing I've put in my mouth today."

At the mention of putting things in his mouth, my nipples tingle, and another wave of heat rushes up my neck. Alec's gaze drops to my pinkening flesh, no doubt aware that my thoughts might not be so pure. I bite back a groan, and work for casual when I say, "You used to be so health conscious back when you were playing football." My gaze travels the length of him. "Not that your current diet isn't working for you."

"I work out, try to stay fit, but there isn't much time for eating healthy."

"My best friend Amanda is a chef, remember. We can set you up with healthy meals delivered right to your door."

He gives me a look I can't quite decipher and for a minute I wonder if I'm overstepping boundaries as an event planner/matchmaker. "Not a bad idea," he finally says, and pulls out his phone. He punches a bunch of buttons, and gestures with a nod to my computer. "Pizza will be here in thirty minutes. Next question."

Okay, clearly he wants to get this over with. For

the next half hour we run through the questions, and when a knock comes on his door, I pinch my strained eyes shut for a brief second to give them a break. Alec pushes off the sofa, and his hard body holds my gaze as he pulls his wallet from his back pocket and crosses the wide expanse of polished wood floor. I stand and stretch out my limbs.

A moment later he comes back with the pizza and drops the box onto the coffee table. The smell reaches my nose and I give a low moan. When I look up, I find him standing perfectly still, lips pinched tight, his Adam's apple bobbing as he swallows.

I open my mouth to ask if he's okay, when he bends and flips the box open. "Mario's does great pizza."

"I've never had it," I say, letting my question go as I look at the huge pineapple-filled pizza.

"It's my go-to place. Dig in." He waits until I pull a cheesy slice free, and then he grabs one for himself. We both plop back down on the sofa, a little closer this time, and I bite into my slice. I chew and swallow.

"This is so good."

"Told you."

I make a few more moaning sounds and note the way Alec is shifting uncomfortably beside me. Maybe he has that disorder I recently heard about. What was it called? Misophonia. Yeah, that's it. A hatred of sounds that causes negative emotions, even violence. I stop moaning, and chew as quietly as I can. Heck, I don't want to be the one getting a fork in the eye. I wash my slice down with my wine, and the next thing I know my glass is half full again. A yawn pulls at me, but I stifle it. I want to finish this form here and now. Another hour in his apartment just might do me in.

"Another?" he asks.

"Pizza after the gym, now that's conducive to staying fit."

"You're perfect, Megan."

Perfect? Alec thinks I'm perfect?

Okay, maybe the alcohol is getting to him, and to me. Last time I had too much, I took my clothes off for this man.

I finish off a second slice and wipe my mouth with the napkins. "Should we get started again?" He nods. "Okay, now we're on to, 'How well do each of the following describe you?'"

"Can't wait," he says, and I laugh.

"You answer with *not at all*, *somewhat* or *very*."

"Got it."

"First one—you tell your partner everything. How well does that describe you?"

He goes quiet for a moment and my mind goes back to all the secrets we shared, all the hopes and dreams we only told one another.

"Very," he says, and I like his answer. A person should be open and honest with their partner.

"You are good at keeping secrets."

His hand goes to his jaw and he scrubs it roughly. "Very," he says.

"Me, too," I say under my breath.

"What?" he asks, and my gaze lifts to his.

He leans forward, finishes off his brandy. "Next question," he asks.

All righty, then.

"Monogamous," I say. "Answer with *not at all*, *somewhat* or *very*."

He jumps to his feet, and paces to the window. "Is this all really necessary?" he asks, his empty glass dangling by his side. He angles his head to see me.

I stand and go over to him to take in the skyline. "I… Yes, it's necessary," I say, his blue eyes burning through me. As my body turns traitorous, and I'm no longer able to hold his gaze, I turn my attention back to the sky and work to pull myself together. His glass hits the table, and the noise cuts through the deafening quiet.

"Megan."

I turn to face him, take in the stiffness of his posture. "Yes."

"It's late and you're tired." He leans toward me, and I wobble slightly, partly from the wine and partly from his close proximity. "Phillip has probably clocked out, and I don't want you in an Uber alone this time of night."

"I appreciate your concern, but I'm a big girl."

"I know that but why don't I just drive you home myself."

He's a big guy and the alcohol wouldn't have hit him like it's hit me, but I lost Mom and Dad in a drunk driving accident, and I'm sensitive about touching a single drop and getting behind the wheel. "We've been drinking," I say.

He pauses, and nods in understanding. "You're right. I'm sorry. I wasn't thinking. I never should have suggested that. I know how you feel about it, and I feel the same way." He rakes his teeth over his bottom lip as he takes a measured step closer to me. "I guess the only logical answer here is for you to sleep over."

CHAPTER FOUR

Alec

SLEEP OVER?

Logical?

What the ever-loving fuck was I thinking? I wasn't—can't when she's around—and therein lies the problem. But how the hell can I be expected to have clear thoughts, or reason with any sort intelligence, after all our reminiscing. Not to mention the fact that I no longer have any blood left in my brain. Christ, hanging out with Megan like this, talking and laughing about old times and listening to her make those sweet moaning sounds that have been imprinted in my brain for eight long years, is preventing my synapses from firing.

"I…" she begins, looking about as flustered as I feel.

"I have lots of spare rooms," I say quickly. I don't want her to get the wrong idea here, or the right idea, or… As my blood rushes south, I have no idea what's right and wrong anymore, and so help me, if she gives me one sign, some tiny indication that she might want me to touch her, I'm not sure I have it in me to fight it. "I can call Phillip in the morning, or take you back myself," I say in a firm voice reserved for the boardroom, a reminder to us both that what's going on here is a business meeting and nothing more. "Whatever you prefer. Right now, I don't want you in an Uber alone, and why wake Phillip when we have other options."

She gives a wave toward her computer and stifles a yawn. "We didn't finish answering all the questions. I guess if I stayed over we could do it first thing in the morning. That will save travel time and help get the ball rolling sooner rather than later." She nods, like she's fully convinced and continues with, "I want to get you married as fast as we can this coming summer. A lot of women get engaged in the fall or at Christmas. I want my name to be the one on the tips of their tongues."

"Thinking like a true businesswoman. Then it's settled," I say, a knot in my stomach as the reality of what we're really doing—finding me a damn wife— comes crashing over me. I take a distancing step back before I do something I can only regret later. Something like pulling her into my arms, kissing her sweet mouth and making love to her until morning. "I have some clothes you can wear."

Her back goes straight and she frowns. "Alec, I

don't want to wear clothes that were left here by some woman you dated."

"And I wouldn't want you to either. I have some sweats that tie at the waist, and a T-shirt. It will be big on you, but should be okay to sleep in."

Relaxing slightly, the alarm leaving her pretty face as her doe eyes soften, she says, "Oh, okay, that will work. Thanks."

"For the record, I don't have women's clothes in my place. I've never brought a woman here before..." My home is my sanctuary, the one place where I can lock the world out and just be me, away from the watchful eyes of the paparazzi.

Manhattan's most eligible bachelor. What a load of shit.

She gives me a quizzical look, the freckles around her nose bunching. "I'm a woman."

"I know," I answer. Boy, do I ever know, but no need to go there with her. "Special circumstances and all, plus maybe it's a good idea for me to have a woman here, trying it out for size since our goal is to find me a wife."

The corners of her mouth turn up. "Looks like I'll be popping your cherry." Her brown eyes go wide. "Wait, I mean..."

"I know what you mean," I say, coming to her rescue.

Flustered, her chest rises and falls, and a few curls fall from the clip at the top of her head. Damned if she doesn't make that look sexy. My fingers itch to release that fastener, watch all those silky locks fall—over my pillow.

"My God, I don't know why everything is coming out wrong tonight," she says. "Must be the wine."

"Must be," I say, but I'm a negotiator, a man who reads others for a living, and right now, being alone in my place is fucking with her as much as it is with me, and I need to shut this shit down right now.

"I think I need sleep," she says, and the slight blush that forms on her cheeks has my dick thickening in my pants.

Uh, hello, pal. Didn't you just lecture yourself on shutting this shit down?

I take another measured step back to put distance between us. It's a start, but knowing she's in the next room, sleeping in my clothes, might call for a hot shower, and a little extracurricular activity under the spray. Otherwise I'll never get a wink of sleep, and I have some reports I need to go over in the morning, after we finish the ridiculous questionnaire. What's the point of it, anyway? No way am I going to find the perfect match, not when she's standing right before me and I can't have her. For as long as I've known Megan, she's had white picket fence all over her. She might still be single, and evaded my question on why that is, but she wants—needs—a family of her own. No one deserves it more than her, especially after everything she's been through.

A guy like me, well, I can't give that to her. The men in my family are unable to remain in a monogamous relationship. My father is still in my life since he left, as well as my younger brother, Will's—when he's not off honeymooning with a girl he'll eventually leave. Christ, that man goes through women faster than a drunk goes through one-dollar bills at a strip joint. The mess he made of my mother when he left still haunts me, and no way would I ever want to rip a woman apart like that.

Honestly, I can't even count how many times my father warned me I was just like him—that I didn't have monogamy in me. None of the Carson men do. The sad thing is, my mother said the same, and warned me to walk away from sweet Megan Williams before I hurt her because in the end it was inevitable.

I'm truly holding out hopes for my cousin Tate. He and his wife, Summer, do seem happy together, but the Carson track record is an ugly one. Megan herself said I remind her of Granddad. That man is still going strong in his nineties. I'm pretty sure he hooked up with his old friend Delilah when they reconnected at Tate and Summer's wedding in St. Moritz last summer. Although I really don't want to think too hard on that. At the end of the day, I'm a chip off the old block, unable to be faithful, and I'd never, ever put Megan through that. She's had enough to deal with in life already. It's better for her to think I'm a prick, a hard-assed businessman who isn't interested in love.

"Come on," I say, and she follows me down the

hall to my bedroom. She stays at the door, shifting from one foot to the other as I dig through my closet and come back with clothes for her.

"Thanks," she says. "You wouldn't happen to have a spare toothbrush."

"Yeah, in the bathroom off your bedroom. I keep it stocked for Will. Sometimes he crashes here. You should find everything you need." I walk her to the room beside mine and open the door for her.

She steps in and goes to the window with the view. "This is beautiful."

"Yeah," I say, but when she turns back, it's her I'm looking at. "Do you need anything else?"

She wraps her arms around her slim body and shakes her head. "I don't think so."

"Okay, you know where the kitchen is if you get hungry, and if you need anything through the night, you know where to find me."

I leave her alone to change and make my way to my own room, where I head straight for the shower. I strip off, run the water and climb into the hot spray. As it rains over me, and I envision Megan stripping down in the next room, I take my thick cock into my hand and stroke from base to crown. Hell, it might feel good, but the only thing that could make it better was if I was sliding into Megan with her moaning my name. I take a breath, brace one hand on the wall by the nozzle, and pump a couple more times until I shoot my cum into the stream. Feeling a measure of relief, I rinse off, dry my body and flop down into my bed.

I toss and turn, but sleep continues to elude me. A noise in the other room reaches my ears and I sit up and listen. I kick off my sheets, and tug on a pair of boxers. Is Megan trying to sneak out under the cover of darkness or does she need something? I push open my door, and pad quietly down the hall. When I round the corner, and find her curvy ass aimed my way as she bends over the coffee table, and tucks the tab into the cardboard pizza box, my cock instantly thickens.

"Megan," I say quietly.

She jumps and faces me, and my gaze drops to her breasts, her nipples precisely, and the sexy way they press against the worn material of my white T-shirt.

"Alec, you scared me."

"What are you doing?"

She picks her computer bag up from the floor. "I couldn't sleep, and I came out to get my laptop," she says quickly, her voice breathless, like she's been in my bed, and I've been doing dirty, delicious things to her body.

Get those thoughts out of your head, dude.

"I saw the pizza was still out, and thought I'd put the rest of it in the fridge. Nothing like cold, firm pizza for breakfast," she says, her edgy laugh stroking my balls.

I step up to her and pick up the cardboard box, my

hand brushes hers and she sucks in air. "You always had a thing for leftover pizza with cold cheese, and a firm crust. Must be a weird Philly thing," I tease. She whacks my stomach, and I capture her hand, bring it to my chest.

"It's…it's not weird, and it's not a Philly thing. A lot of people love leftover pizza," she says, her voice hitching as her body vibrates. I step closer, crowd her, brush my thumb over her wrist as I keep her hand pressed to my chest.

"I'm not one of those people. I don't get the appeal." I dip my head and focus in on her wet lips. I drop the box and put my thumb under her chin. Her lips part slightly, and that's exactly the kind of encouragement I want, or rather don't want.

"What's…what's not to get?" she asks, her chest rising and falling faster now, her sweet minty breath washing over my face.

I shrug. "I don't know. I guess I like warm things in my mouth."

Don't do this, Carson. Go the fuck back to your room.

Unable to stop myself, I let go of her hand to grip her small rib cage, and my thumb lightly brushes one hard nipple. "Oops, sorry."

I wait for a kick to the nuts, but instead, she lets loose a sexy moan that fuels the hunger in me. Goddammit, she's as responsive to my touch today as she was all those years ago.

"You asked a lot of questions tonight," I say,

"questions about myself and what I find important in a relationship."

"Yes," she says, and swipes her tongue over her bottom lip.

Want zings through me. "You never asked how I liked to have sex."

"I'm… I'm not sure it's on the form," she says, her eyes dimming with desire.

"What if it is? Some of those questions are pretty damn personal."

"True."

"What if I'm called to a business meeting tomorrow morning and I'm not able to help you finish the questions. The sooner we get this done, the better it is for both our careers, right?"

My gaze roams her face, takes in the need in her eyes. It wraps around my dick and squeezes. I've never needed a woman in quite the same way as I need her. But I should put a stop to this. I have to put a stop to this. I briefly pinch my eyes shut and pray for the strength to walk away.

"What are you suggesting, Alec?" she says in a soft, seductive whisper that nearly makes me come in my boxers.

Fuck me.

"That maybe I should show you." In this moment, as need zaps my balls, every reason I have for staying away from her vanishes into thin air. The only thing I know is if I don't get this woman into my bed this very second, I might just spontaneously combust. "You'll want to find someone who's compatible sexually, and this way you'll know what you're working with when vetting dates. It might speed up the process in matching me correctly."

"It's the logical thing to do," she murmurs, and I swipe her nipple a little harder, and widen her legs with my knee. The laptop bag in her hand falls with a thud and she moans as I shimmy closer, rub her sex with my thigh.

"When you moan like that... Jesus."

"You don't like it?"

I laugh and shake my head. "Oh, I like it. I like it a lot."

A sexy chuckle bubbles in her throat. "I thought you might have had misophonia."

I place my palms over her breasts, give them a little squeeze. This time she emphasizes the moan, and I like the way she's teasing me. "Mis-a-what?"

"Never mind," she whispers, her head rolling back as she moves on my leg, a slight rocking of her hips, enough to rub the swollen little cleft I can't wait to put in my mouth.

"I'm hungry, Megan," I growl into her ear.

"Pizza," she murmurs.

"Haven't we already established that I like to put warm things in my mouth," I say, my voice deeper, thicker, dripping with lust. "Any suggestions?"

Her body stiffens, and her eyes fly open. She pushes away from me, and in that moment, I get it. I hurt her in the past and my question just pulled her from her lust-induced state and snapped her back to her senses. Now she's having second thoughts and I don't blame her one bit. I was a stupid, needy prick for starting this in the first place.

She inches back, her eyes locked on mine, and I swallow as the gap of air between us cools. We stand there for a long time, our eyes locked like we're in a Mexican standoff. I want to speak, say something, do something, anything, but the next move has to come from her.

Her gaze drops to my caged erection, and a visible quiver moves through her body. After a few speechless moments of checking me out, her eyes slowly travel back to mine.

She grips the hem of her too big T-shirt. In one sexy movement she peels it over her head, gifting me with a view of her gorgeous, full breasts and hard pink nipples.

Sweet mother of God and all that is holy.

"Will these do?" she asks.

On that note, I take a labored breath, then another, and in two fast steps close the distance between us. I cup both breasts, revel in the softness of her skin and meet her heated gaze. "Yeah, these will definitely do," I say, and bend forward to take one turgid nub into my mouth. Our moans mingle, and she arches her back as her hands go around my almost naked body. She drags her nails down my arms, palms my muscles, and my dick jumps in my boxers.

The honeyed scent of her skin fills my senses as

her breast fills my ravenous mouth. Greedy man that I am, I suck hard, and widen my lips to take more, until she's writhing and crying out my name. I back off a bit, clench down on one nipple, and her cries of joy burst around me.

I lick and suck and eat at her like she's going to bolt at a moment's notice—leave me starved for another eight long years—but she doesn't. Instead she puts her hand on my cock and gives it a little squeeze.

I release her nipple and give it a soft lick to soothe the sting. Then I scoop her up, ready to make up for lost time, over and over again. I carry her to my bedroom and set her on my bed; she falls backward, and her auburn hair tumbles.

"Look at you," I murmur, taking pleasure in the sight of her. She's so goddamn sexy and I'm the luckiest guy on the planet.

The heat between us, the chemistry that has only grown stronger, flared brighter in our years apart, scorches the air we breathe. I drop to my knees in front of her, lean over her body and press my nose to her stomach, breathing her in. I missed the smell of her.

I go back on my heels, and she sits up, her breathing rough and ragged as she reaches for me, runs her fingers over my flesh. Raw hunger claws at my insides, and I take a breath, work to slow myself down. We both understand there can't be a tomorrow or a next week, we have opposite goals, but we have tonight, and I plan to take things slow, make it last well into the morning.

I untie the oversize sweats and grip the band. She goes back on her elbows and lifts her hips for me. I tug them down slowly, and leave her lacy thong in place. Fucking sexy. I toss her pants away, and slide my finger into the top of her lacy underwear. I swipe it back and forth, coming close, but not quite touching the spot swollen with need, clamoring for my touch.

"Alec," she cries out, and I love hearing my name on her tongue, the sexually frustrated sound as she lifts her hips, trying to force me closer. I tug on her panties and pull them upward until her beautiful lips are hugging the thin band. I wiggle the material back and forth, massaging her clit with the lace.

Her gasp curls around me, her body a quivering mess of need and pleasure. "Oh, yes," she cries out, and as her head goes from side to side, I can't take teasing her anymore. I need my mouth on her body, everywhere, anywhere, all at once—all night long. Delirious with need, I grip the scrap of material in my hand and in one quick thrust tear the flimsy thong from her body.

She gulps and sits up a little straighter. "Alec," she cries out, her brown eyes wide, full of lust and desire.

"Good thing you removed your T-shirt or I might have ripped it from your body, too." Her chest heaves and I bite back a smile. "Now spread your legs," I command in a soft voice and she immediately obliges, offering herself up to me so nicely a groan catches in my throat. I cup her ankles and place her feet on the edge of the mattress. With her knees pointed at the ceiling, I grip her thighs, squeeze slightly and widen her legs even more to accommodate my wide body. Her warm aroused scent turns me on even more, and my heart nearly gives when I glimpse her pink wetness, wide-open and ready for my mouth. I gaze at her for a second, then blink, wanting to capture this moment in a still frame.

"Megan," I murmur, and settle myself on the floor between her thighs, stroking her quivering sex from top to bottom. "So fucking pretty." Her body practically levitates off the bed as I pet her, and my cock throbs, grows another inch until it's bursting through the elastic band of my boxers. Reaching up, I cup one breast and give a squeeze as I slide a finger into her. Christ, she's soaking wet.

A moan rolls out of her throat and a growl catches in mine as her wet heat squeezes around my finger. Her pussy is so hot, tight and beautiful, this could very well be over before it even begins. But I need to hold it together. We're not teenagers back in my room at St. Moritz, where we fumbled and clumsily learned each other's bodies. Yeah, we were young and inexperienced, but up until this moment, it was the best night of my life.

Her sexy sounds of pleasure massage my balls, and my dick throbs even harder, leaving me a little off-kilter. But I can't think about what being intimate with her again is doing to me, how screwed up I'll become tomorrow. No, tonight I just want to feel, and bring her all the pleasure she deserves.

I slide another finger inside her for a snug fit, and small spasms begin at her core. She's already so close, it's insane. Then again, who am I to talk. Pre-cum is pooling from my slit, and my cock is begging me to take her already. But I won't. Not until she comes for me first. I might be called a lot of things, but at the heart of it all, I'm a gentleman and I'm not between the legs of some random woman here. This is Megan Williams, and the fact that she's actually giving herself to me again, when I don't deserve anything from her, well, I don't take that lightly. With her pleasure paramount, I take her swollen clit into my mouth and suck hard as I move my finger in and out. Her pussy grows slicker beneath my ministrations, and I clamp down slightly on her cleft.

Air leaves her lungs in a whoosh, and her whimpering sounds reach my ears as I soften my tongue, lave her aching clit as her body writhes beneath me. I lift my mouth, glance up at her to find her on her elbows, watching me. Our eyes meet, lock, and my heart misses a few beats as I struggle to refill my lungs. My God, she's breathtaking.

"You taste so good," I murmur when I can finally breathe again, and she reaches for me, rakes her hand through my hair and guides my mouth back to her hot core. Loving that she knows what she wants, and isn't afraid to take it, I chuckle against her clit, and fuck her with my fingers, changing the pace, rhythm and depth until she's shaking and crying out my name. I love seeing her like this. Damned if I don't want to make her feel this good every day of my life.

I circle her clit with my tongue, then press against it as I deliver hot, openmouthed kisses to her sweet pussy. She rocks against me, a shameless display of need, as she takes what she wants. Attagirl. She rides my fingers, moving faster and faster and soon enough she's a beautiful hot mess tumbling over the edge.

"Alec," she cries out, the clench of her muscles drawing my fingers in deeper and deeper and making me crazier and crazier. My dick throbs, aching to feel those clenches. "I'm…oh, God, Alec." Her sweetness explodes on my tongue and I drink her in, not daring to miss a drop. I want her flavor in my mouth, want to taste her on my tongue a week from now. She spasms around me, and I stay between her legs and let her ride out the waves until her body goes slack and she's panting for her next breath.

I climb over her body, brush my tongue over both nipples on my way to her mouth. Her legs wrap around me, and through my boxers my cock presses against her hot core. My lips find hers. I kiss her deeply, thoroughly explore her mouth with my tongue, and she kisses me back, the same sweet way she kissed me all those years ago.

I'm about to push off her, grab a condom when

she gives me a hard shove. I roll to my back, and catching me by surprise she climbs over me, strad- dles my legs. "What are you doing?" I ask, my voice rough and labored.

She tugs my boxers down and my cock springs free. She takes me into her hands, weighs me in her palms as she examines the long length of my dick. Her eyes are heavy lidded when her gaze lifts to mine. "Did you miss the part where I said I like firm, too?" she asks.

"Oh, Jesus," I say as she bends forward to lick my cum, like it's her goddamn job. With a slow slide of her tongue, she cleans my crown, before taking me to the back of her throat. "Megan," I croak out, and grip her tumble of hair. I wrap it around my hand and move it to the side to watch my dick slide in and out of her mouth. It's the sexiest thing I've ever seen. "That is so good," I manage to say.

She moans, and the vibrations of her mouth zap my balls. She takes them into her palm and mas- sages gently as her hand works the long length of me and her tongue swirls around my swollen head. The perfect trifecta. Her moans grow louder, more heated, and the way she's worshipping my cock— loving every second of it—fucks me over in so many ways. Blood fills my veins and as much as I like what she's doing, if she keeps it up, I'm going to shoot my load down her throat. But I'm not ready for this to be over. I want, need, other things from her tonight.

"Megan," I growl, and give a little tug of her hair

to pull her off me. Her mouth is wet as I bring her to me for a kiss. "I need to be inside you," I say.

"Yes," she murmurs. I roll until she's underneath me, and then I go up on my knees to reach into my nightstand to pull out a box of condoms. I rip into it, pull out a foil package and quickly sheathe myself. I fall over Megan, who hasn't taken her eyes off me. "You ready for me to fuck you?" I ask.

Eyes heated, she widens her legs and wraps them around my waist, answering my question without words. I position my crown at her entrance and it throbs as I give her an inch. She moans, thrusts upward for more.

"Alec, please," she cries out.

"You need it, Megan? You need my cock?"

"I need you to fuck me," she whimpers, and in one quick thrust I power my hips forward and fill her completely. "Holy God," she cries out, her nails digging into my back. I go perfectly still for a moment, and concentrate on how good she feels as I give her a second to catch her breath. "I feel you, Alec. Feel you throbbing inside me."

"You are so hot and tight, it's all I can do to hang on. I'm already more than halfway there," I groan.

She begins to rock, and I move with her, pulling almost all the way out, only to slide back home again. We move together, each giving and taking, and every time I power into her sweet core, it pulls a cry from her throat. Her hands go to her breasts and she rubs her nipples. Jesus, that's hot. My lips find hers again

as my balls tighten, scream for release. I grind into
her, stimulate her clit with each downward slide, and
soon enough she's chanting my name again, her muscles clenching in an explosion of passion.

"I'm there," she murmurs, her skin warm and slick
as she shatters around me. Her hot cum singes my
cock, drips all over me, and I've never felt anything
more satisfying in my entire life. Perfection.

I change the rhythm and pace, driving deeper,
harder, but unable to get enough. "Yes, yes, yes,"
she chants, and when her eyes roll back in her head,
her body explodes for the third time tonight. There
is nothing in the world better than this. Megan in my
bed, coming all over my cock. Her pussy squeezes
my dick hard, and I can no longer hold on. I throw
my head back and growl as I come high inside her.
My muscles spasm and shudder with my final pulse,
and once depleted, I collapse on top of Megan, press
her into the mattress. Her heart pounds hard against
my chest, and I bury my mouth into her neck, where
I press feather-soft, openmouthed kisses to her deli-
cate flesh. I stay there for a long time, revel in her
scent and enjoy the light caress of her fingers stroking my back. I breathe in contentment as I bask in
my postorgasmic bliss.

Soon enough my cock grows flaccid and with
much reluctance, I pull out of her and discard the
condom. Sprawled out on my bed, her eyes heavy
lidded and struggling to remain open, her hair is a
tangled mess beneath her. I've never seen her look

more beautiful. Her breathing changes, grows softer, and I fix the blankets around us, pulling her into my arms so we can get a few hours of sleep.

She moans, and my pulse beats a bit faster as she snuggles into me, a well-sated woman. I let my gaze fall over her again, and my chest swells, loving that I was the one who did this to her.

I drop a soft kiss onto her forehead, and as reality begins to trickle back in, I struggle to calm my racing heart. Just like eight years ago, Megan rocked my world in a way no other woman ever has or ever will. But it shouldn't have happened then, and it shouldn't have happened now. What the hell is wrong with me? Why can't I be stronger around her? Why would I go and seduce the one girl in the world I need to keep my distance from?

CHAPTER FIVE

Megan

I SLEPT WITH ALEC.

Omigod, I slept with Alec. Last night, after a couple glasses of wine, it seemed like a good idea. I'm a grown woman who's in charge of her sexuality, so why not, right? Why not take what I want from a man who was willing to give it. We're both single, consenting adults and I haven't been touched in a long time. Not that any man has ever touched me the way Alec has, or ever brought me such intense pleasure.

But now, under the stark light of morning, a headache brewing in the back of my head, I'm second-guessing my decision-making abilities. Truthfully, as much as I want to blame it on the alcohol, I can't. I wanted him. I wanted my hands on his body, his on mine. I wanted to feel his hard cock inside me, taking me to places no man has ever been able to take me. But why did he want me in his bed, if I'm clearly not his type?

I guess his cock didn't get the memo.

I lay perfectly still between the warm sheets, sorting things through as I listen to his soft breathing. I told him I hadn't been with a guy in a long time, and Alec and I have a history. Perhaps I reeked of desperation, and he was just doing me a favor. Still, desperation or not, he wanted it, too.

Nevertheless, I should go, get out of here before we have our second—eight years later—awkward morning after. But what are the chances that I can get out of here without waking him, and move to Canada before he figures out I'm even gone?

"You okay?" he asks quietly.

I flinch at the sound of Alec's voice. So much for sneaking out. The mattress moves as he rolls my way, and the warmth of his fingers on my chin as he angles my head until we're eye to eye awakens my body all over again. In his sleep-rumpled state, his hair an unkempt mess, he's even more beautiful than ever.

And I slept with him.

But the real problem is, I want to do it again.

Then keep doing it.

A groan catches in my throat as his gaze moves over my face, assessing me. "Hey," he whispers, the softness in his voice, the genuine concern in his eyes, warming me all over. "What is it?"

"Nothing," I squeak out, but he frowns at the lie.

"Are you overthinking this?" he asks. I can't hide anything from this man. He knows me far too well. And he's right. I'm overthinking this. Like I always do. Heck, for the last eight years I've been overthinking the night I seduced him.

"Actually, I was just thinking about moving to Canada," I say, a successful attempt to lighten the mood, judging by the smile spreading across his face. When that smile reaches his eyes, my heart leaps because in this instant, I realize I'm looking at the boy from my youth, not the anti-love guy who says he's not a nice man. What I'd do to have the old Alec back full-time. I swallow against a tight throat, and it's all I can do not to weep for the loss of our closeness.

He lightly brushes my hair back, those intense blue eyes roaming my face. "Did you enjoy yourself, Megs?"

Megs, oh, God, the nickname.

"Immensely," I say, my sated body aching in all the right places.

"Good. Me, too."

"But we need to make one thing clear. It was just sex. I'm not looking for or asking anything else of you. I don't want you to get the wrong idea about me," I add.

"I won't."

"Good."

"It was just sex," he says. "I get it. Not a problem."

"I shouldn't have seduced you," I blurt out, and avoid adding *again* to the end of the sentence.

A crooked grin curls one corner of his luscious mouth and all I can think about is how his lips felt on my body, between my legs. "You think…" he begins but stops when I pull the blankets up to cover the red blush crawling up my neck. "Hey, wait, no need to be embarrassed," he says. "We're adults, doing what adults do."

"I've been hired to find you a wife and plan your wedding, Alec," I point out. "We shouldn't have done this."

His entire body stiffens at the blunt reminder, and a second later he gives a curt, almost dismissive nod. "You're right, and we have work to do this morning." He tears his gaze away and gone is the softness in his voice, his face…his posture. My God, the man is such a contradiction, soft and sweet one minute, all business the next. If I'm not careful I'm going to end up with whiplash. "Let's chalk it up to a night of fun, and put it behind us."

"That's exactly what we need to do," I say, but my heart is already warning me that it won't be as easy for me as it will be for him. I can't—won't—fall for this man again. I want a loving marriage and family, and his goals are in complete contrast to that. We both know that. Any more time in his bed, fun or not, might just draw me back into a place I simply refuse to go.

From the other room my phone buzzes, the special ringtone letting me know it's Amanda. Great, just great. She's going to want a play-by-play rundown, and no way will I be able to hide this from her. One look at me and she'll know I had sex with

Alec. He'd better hide his farm parts. But oh, what amazing parts he has.

Stop thinking about his equipment, already.

"You going to get that?" he asks, his voice lacking warmth, as he kicks his blankets off, exposing his nakedness to me. He stands and stretches and my goddamn mouth waters.

"Ah, what are you doing?" I ask.

"Going to grab a shower." He glances down at his bare body. "Oh, I didn't think… I mean, you've seen me naked."

"It doesn't mean I want to again."

That's a lie.

I do.

"You better grab your phone. Whoever's calling doesn't seem like they're about to give up." With that he walks to the bathroom, his cute ass dragging my focus the whole way. It's only when he shuts the door that I'm able to think again. "Jesus," I murmur under my breath, and search the floor for the sweatpants he gave me to wear last night. I scoop up my ripped underwear and ignore the quiver careening through my blood. I've never had a man rip my panties from my hips before. Okay, stop thinking about how hot that was.

I scan the floor for my T-shirt and that's when I remember I took it off in the living room. Oh, hell. I open the bedroom door, and dash through the apartment. I grab the shirt and quickly tug it on. Feeling a whole lot less exposed, I dig my phone from my purse and swipe my finger over the screen.

"Where are you?" Amanda asks.

"What…uh…what are you talking about?" I feign innocence, but I'm guessing she won't have any of that.

"I'm standing outside your apartment with two lattes. We have yoga this morning, or did you forget?"

"I forgot."

Silence for a moment, and then, "Oh, my God, you slept with him."

I glance over my shoulder. "Amanda…" I begin quietly.

"Jesus, Megan, what were you thinking?" she huffs out.

"Last night I was thinking, why the hell not," I say.

"And today, what are you thinking today?"

How is it everyone can read me so well? Am I that much of an open book? "I'm thinking I had a great time, and now we're back to business. It won't be happening again. Maybe it was just something we needed to get out of our system." *Okay, girl, get it together. Overthinking and rambling. My two specialties.*

Amanda goes quiet again and I can visualize her rubbing that spot on her forehead. "Are you okay?"

I walk to the window and look out at the Hudson River below. I take a deep yoga breath and let it out slowly, instantly calming myself down. "I'm perfectly fine."

"Don't shit me," she warns.

"I'm fine. We had sex, talked about it, and now we're getting back to the business of finding him a wife."

A pause and then, "One more question?"

"What?"

"Did he make your eyes roll back in your head?"

"Three times," I say, and cover my mouth to stifle a chuckle.

"That's good, then. I'm drinking your latte and going back to bed. When you get back, wake me and I want all the details."

"Everything okay?" Alec asks, coming into the room dressed in nothing but track pants. My gaze falls, takes in his bare chest, the oblique muscles that are guiding my eyes down.

"Yes, it was my friend. I forgot that we had yoga this morning."

He points upward. "I'm doing laps in a few. You can join me if you want to get in some exercise." I look up at his ceiling and he explains. "Rooftop pool."

"It's a bit chilly for that, isn't it?"

"The pool is heated and glassed in. Coffee?"

"Yes, please," I say, and follow him into the kitchen. I glance around the massive space and take in the state-of-the-art appliances as he goes to his coffeemaker, but it's not just any coffeemaker. With all the spouts, buttons and gadgets, it's the fancy kind you'd find at a high-end coffee boutique.

"Mocha latte?" he asks.

"You're kidding, right?"

"I never kid about my coffee," he says, and I laugh. Even when we were teens he loved his coffee. He glances at me over his shoulder. "I need to get my laps in this morning. I have some paperwork that needs my attention this afternoon. To speed things up, would you mind asking questions while I exercise?"

"Uh, I guess not."

He pours milk into a metal cup, sticks it under a spout and steams it. "You're welcome to swim if you want."

"I don't have a suit."

The muscles on his back ripple, the same way they did when I ran my fingers over his body. He finishes making my coffee and hands it to me. I take a seat at the gigantic island and breathe in the welcoming scent.

"If you'll excuse me for a minute," he says. He disappears into the other room and comes back doing something on his tablet. He hits a few buttons, and I assume it must be some work emergency, then he goes back to making his coffee.

"Do you still like Pop-Tarts for breakfast?" he asks.

"No, I kind of gave that up when I became an adult. I usually have yogurt, toast or sometimes just a protein bar." My stomach takes that moment to grumble. "I seem to be hungrier than usual this morning."

Way to bring up all the sex we had, Megan.

"It was a late night," he simply says. "I'm not that well stocked, but I do have bread in the freezer. That will get us by, and after our swim I'll order us in a proper breakfast. We'll have it at the pool."

"You don't have to do that. Toast will do, and I should head out right after we finish the question-naire. I have some work to do on a Bar Mitzvah today."

He makes his coffee, takes a sip and eyes me over the rim. "If you think I'm letting you leave here with-out properly feeding you—"

"Bossy much," I say. "Glad they asked that on the form. We wouldn't want any woman to think you were easy to get along with."

"It's settled, then," he says, not bothering to dis-agree. He opens the freezer, pulls out the frozen bread and places four slices in the toaster. "I have butter, jam and peanut butter."

"Strawberry jam?"

"Is there really any other kind worth having?" he asks, and pulls it from the fridge.

"This coffee is so good," I say, and take a big sip. "I'm going to have to invest in one of those machines. I'll need an engineering degree to figure out how to use it, though."

He chuckles softly. "It's not so hard." He takes

another sip of coffee and goes serious. "How is this all going to work? Once you set up the profile for me, then what?"

"Well, I'm going to pretend to be you online. Vet the women to see if I think they'd be a good match. I'll set up the date, tell you where to be, at what time and what to wear. I probably should check your wardrobe."

"You'll find mostly suits and gym clothes."

"Then we might need to go shopping."

"Do you think that's necessary?"

"Absolutely."

"I don't think—"

I hold my hand up to stop him when the toast pops. "I'm in charge here. That's the only way this is going to work. If you want me to find you a 'suitable' wife…" I pause to do air quotes around that one word "…then you have to put yourself in my hands."

His muscles tighten, and I'm almost one hundred percent sure his cock just twitched at my poor choice of words. He mumbles something under his breath, pulls two plates from his cupboard and slides me two slices. I twist the lid off the jam as he grabs a spoon from his drawer and comes around the island to sit next to me.

"Here's the thing, though. You're kind of well-known, so I was thinking maybe we should use your middle name and we can take a sideways picture or something distant. Give them enough to work with but maybe not identifiable as you."

He hands me the spoon, and my fingers brush his as I accept it. The heat from his flesh trickles through my traitorous body and I work to ignore the frisson of need as I dip the spoon into the jar and come out with a big scoop of strawberry jam. I coat my toast and hand the spoon back, this time taking care not to touch him.

"Are you afraid my real identity will scare them off?"

"I'd just rather a woman walk in without any preconceived notions."

"Makes sense, but I'm not going to hide the fact that I'm looking for a wife in name only."

I open my mouth to ask if he'd at least try, but quickly stop myself. The man is stubborn, and bossy, and when he has his mind hell-bent on something, there is no way I'm going to change it. I'd just be fighting a losing battle.

"Do you have any out-of-town trips that I should know about?" I ask instead.

"Not unless something unexpected comes up."

"I'm going to need a copy of your work agenda and meeting times if I'm going to be scheduling dates for you."

"I'll have my assistant get that to you." He angles his head. "Anything else, boss?"

I roll my eyes at him. "Not that I can think of right now."

"Will you need a key to my place?"

"And risk the chance of walking in on you in the

middle of…" I let my words fall off as I envision Alec
in his bed with another woman, doing all the things
to her that he's recently done to me. *Get it together,
Megan.* "Actually it might be a good idea," I say. It's
best if he doesn't think I care if he's here with another woman, considering that's the whole reason for
me being here in the first place. And really, I don't
care. Not one little bit. "If you bring a woman back
here, I'd like to have your kitchen stocked a bit better, and a few homey touches would be nice. I can
arrange that. I want things perfect. We need this to
work for both our sakes."

"I'll get you a key," he says, like he's not happy
about the whole thing.

I bite into my toast, chew and wash it down with
a mouthful of delicious coffee. Alec does the same
and then turns to me. With a piece of toast halfway
to his mouth he asks, "You're really going to pretend
to be me online?"

"Yes, except more charming."

He goes perfectly still for a second before he lets
loose a laugh. "You don't think I'm charming, Megs,"
he asks, and nudges my chin with his fist.

"I don't really know you anymore, Alec," I say,
and it instantly changes the mood. He pulls his hand
back, more aloof than usual as he finishes his toast.
He stands to put his plate in the dishwasher when
the doorbell rings.

"Expecting company?" I ask.

"Yes," he says, and I check the time as he disappears around the corner. Who could he be expecting on a Saturday morning at ten? I glance at my clothes and jump from the stool, panicked. I'm hardly dressed to greet his guests, and what if it's a woman—one of his many. But then I remember he doesn't bring women into his home, and I'm only here because he's trying it on for size. Maybe that's why my seduction worked. Maybe he was trying a woman out in his bed for size, too.

Okay, Megan, stop overthinking everything.

I'm about to hurry down the hall when the door closes, and Alec calls me into the living room. I peek in to make sure he's alone. "What's going on?" I ask, when I see a dozen boxes sitting on his coffee table. He had a delivery, this time of day?

I slowly walk into the room, and can't believe it when I see the boxes are from Bianca's Boutique, Manhattan's very expensive, very elite lingerie shop.

"These are for you," he says. "Size six, right?"

"I…uh…yes, how do you know that?" He arches a brow at my foolish question. Of course he knows that. His hands were all over my body, and since he's reached out and touched more women than Hallmark, he's probably an expert at guessing sizes. "What have you done?"

"I kept you from your yoga this morning. Now you can swim instead." He settles himself on the sofa, and gestures for me to sit in the cushiony chair across from him. "You don't like Bianca's?"

I step around the coffee table. "I... I've never shopped there?"

"I know Bianca quite well. She's very particular, and her swimsuits are high quality. She personally put this order together for me this morning."

I throw my hands up. "You just called her up and put an order in? This morning? That's what you were doing on your tablet?"

He taps a finger to his lip, like he's amused with all my questions. "Yes."

"I can't believe you did this."

"What's the big deal?"

Okay, this man obviously operates in a different world than I do. "How many did you order?"

He shrugs. "A few. I wasn't sure what fit or style you liked."

"You know you're insane, right?"

He scrubs his chin, and nods. "One of the nicer things I've been called."

"I bet," I say, and he just smirks at me. I lift the lid off one box and pull out a gorgeous designer bikini with a floral print top that ties in the front, and high-waisted bottoms. I've been lusting after a suit like this for a while now, but it wasn't in my budget. "I can't keep all these."

"There's no return on swimwear. They're yours. You're welcome to use my pool anytime. Perhaps your friend Amanda would like to join you sometime."

Flabbergasted I drop the bikini into the box. "That's a nice offer, but this is too much."

"You don't like that one. Try this," he says, and hands me another box. The man is generous, and I have no doubt he'll give his wife all the material things she wants, but is that really enough to keep the marriage alive? Won't she eventually want his heart, too?

I open it, but this time I find a lacey white thong. I pull it from the box, run the expensive material through my fingers.

His grin is sheepish when I glance at him. "Replacement. For the pair I ripped," he explains.

"This is way nicer than what I was wearing."

"I liked what you were wearing," he says almost under his breath, and my gaze shoots to his. He jumps from the sofa. "Did you want to shower before you swim?"

I nod. "Yes," I say. The sooner I get the scent of his skin off mine the better.

He nods. "I'll head up and get some laps in. There's a private elevator in the hall. It takes you up to the roof. No one has access but me."

"The rooftop is just for your use?"

"Yes." He disappears for a second and comes back with a key. He presses it into my palm and closes my fingers around it. "This will get you into my apartment, and to the roof. I'll meet you there."

He heads to his room to get changed, and I open a few more boxes, until I find a pretty black-and-white suit that covers a bit more than the others. Not that it matters. We've seen each other naked. I hurry to the spare bedroom, shower and tug on the suit. Key in hand, laptop bag over my shoulder I make my way to the rooftop, and hurry to the glassed-in pool. Dressed in tight swim trunks, Alec's long, lean body glides through the crystal clear water and he surfaces right in front of me.

"You made…" he begins but his voice falls off as his gaze moves over me, a long leisurely inspection from my dry mouth to the tips of my toes, and all the way back up again, stopping to linger on my breasts—and nipples that are no doubt poking hard against the thin fabric. A moan catches in his throat and my entire body lights, like a match to dry tinder.

Honestly, if he's about to marry someone else, why the hell is he looking at me like he wants to eat me alive?

CHAPTER SIX

Alec

I PICK MY cell phone up from my desk, glance at it and set it down with a little more force than necessary. Fuck. Here it is late Friday morning and I haven't heard from Megan since last Saturday—when she joined me at the pool and I damn near devoured her with my gaze.

Well done, Alec, well done.

I worked to hide my arousal and keep things casual as we did laps, had breakfast and finished the questionnaire. I'm not sure I pulled it off, though. After the round of sex we had, you'd think I'd be sated, gotten her out of my system, but it only made me want her more. How I'm going to get through this and keep my hands to myself is beyond me. She made it clear what we did can't happen again, and I have to agree with her.

I glance at my phone again and check the time. I have a late afternoon meeting, but I need a breath of fresh air before sitting down with the board and hashing out the details on the next deal. My job looks harsh in the eyes of most, I can understand that. We finance investors who buy undervalued assets in companies. Once they secure controlling shares they restructure, changing leadership and management. People frown at what I do, some call me a monster, but I'm good at it—and it's a sure way for me to carve my own way in this world, which is important to me. What they don't know is I always make sure to help those who lose their jobs. Granddad owns half of Manhattan, and with the charity I run, we're always in need of new blood and top management expertise.

I push from my chair and take the elevator down to the main floor. I make my way to my Tesla, press the fob and climb in. Before I realize what I'm doing or where I'm even going, I find myself driving along Ninth Avenue through Hell's Kitchen looking for Kitchen Door Catering.

I slow my vehicle to glance at the storefronts, and a chorus of cars honk from behind. I simply flip them all the finger and pull over to check my GPS. I punch in the name and a second later I'm given directions to the business. I pull back into traffic and follow the route until I'm outside the industrial-looking brick building. I kill the ignition and step out into the warm sunshine and make my way down the busy sidewalk. Delicious scents of ginger and spices reach my nostrils as I enter the shop, and a little bell over the door jingles to announce my presence. Behind the counter, Megan's friend Amanda glances up, and behind her glasses, her brown eyes go wide when she sees me.

"Alec," she says, and wipes her hands on her apron.

"Nice to see you again, Amanda. I never got a chance to say hello at the coffee shop but Megan told me about your catering business."

I quickly catalog the space. The front of the shop has fridges and freezers with take-out food, and behind Amanda there is a wide-open space with three big butcher-block tables, where numerous chefs are working away.

She takes her glasses off and sets them on the counter. "Do you have an event you need catered?" she asks, her eyes wide and hopeful.

"No, but when I do I'll be sure to keep you in mind. Megan also mentioned you do personalized meal delivery. That's something I'm definitely interested in." That brings a big smile to her face. "Speaking of Megan, is she around?" I ask.

She jerks her thumb over her shoulder. "She's in her office. I'll get her for you. In the meantime, why don't you look this over." She hands me a colorful brochure, picks up her phone and presses a button. She turns her back to me, preventing me from hearing her conversation, and I walk over to the fridge to check out today's specials.

I've never really seen an innovative business quite

like this. Not only do they cater events, they make extras and sell it fresh daily. Behind me the door jingles and in walks a woman with four small children, three boys and one girl. They run straight for the cupcake display as Amanda greets the woman, then glances at me quickly. "She'll be right out."

As the kids pick out what cupcake they want, I grin, and think back to my own childhood. How many times did Granddad take me and Will, and our cousins Tate and Brianna, out for treats. The man was a saint and had so much patience with us. Is it any wonder each of us would do anything for him—even get married? Although I still can't quite believe I agreed to it. Must have been all the brandy he used to loosen me up. I must remember to ask him why he hired Megan, or how he even knew she ran an event business. Then again, even at ninety he keeps his ear to the ground.

"Hey," Megan says as she comes around the counter, her hair a tumbled mess, like she's been running her fingers through it. "What brings you here?"

"I thought I'd check out Amanda's kitchen." I wave my hand around the place. "The idea of fresh, healthy home-delivered meals sure would make my life easier." Not a lie. I rub my gut. "Eating out is beginning to take its toll."

"You probably could lay off the doughnuts," she says with a grin. "And stop fishing for compliments." I laugh at that, and she adds, "I'm glad you're here. I was going to text you. It's been a crazy week, and

I should have reached out earlier, but I had a last-minute emergency with the Bar Mitzvah venue. A pipe broke in the yacht club, and I had to scramble to find a new location."

I dip my head and try not to stare at her mouth. "If you ever run into that again, just give me a shout."

"Really?"

"Granddad owns numerous properties that I oversee, and we'd be happy to help you out. Pick up the phone and call me before you take it out on your hair." Her eyes go wide for a second, and then she laughs and finger combs her curls. "I see you never lost the habit of running your fingers through your hair when you're stressed. Remember after exams—"

"Oh, my God, don't remind me. I always came away looking like a sheepdog who went through the dryer without a static sheet."

I laugh out loud. "You were adorable." I glance over her shoulder to see Amanda watching us. "Anyway," I say, and clear my throat, returning to professional mode and getting back down to business. Why does being around her make me forget to keep my guard up? "You were going to text me?"

She pokes my chest and I wish she hadn't. That innocent touch makes me want to pull her into my arms, and kiss the smudged lipstick from her lush mouth. "You have a date tonight, Alec."

While one part of me is happy to get the ball rolling and get this over with, the other part is dreading the idea of picking out a wife. Even if I wanted to back out now—run as far away as possible despite what it could do for my image and career, not to mention pleasing Granddad—I can't. Megan has a lot riding on this, and I can only assume her friend does, too, since she'll be catering my wedding, and getting her food in the hands of some very prominent members of society.

"You found me someone who fits the criteria?"

"Yes. Her name is Danielle. She's an elementary school teacher and she sounds perfect. I made a reservation for seven at Il Mercato. Italian is her favorite. I want to go over some things we talked about so you're up to speed when you meet her."

I gesture with a nod to the door. "Sounds like a good plan. Should we do it over lunch or have you eaten?"

"Lunch is perfect. We can eat in my office where we'll have privacy. How about ginger squash soup, and roasted chicken sandwiches?" She breathes in deep and when she does her chest expands, and behind her silky white blouse, her nipples reach out and taunt me. "It's been cooking all morning and I'm dying to have some."

"We can eat here?"

"Sure. Come on." She glances at her friend. "Amanda, I'm going to grab two bowls of soup and two sandwiches. Put it on my tab," she says. Amanda rolls her eyes at us. I step around the counter, and my gaze travels the length of Megan as I follow her into the kitchen. She's dressed in a curve-hugging skirt that shows off her long, shapely legs and high heels I want her to keep on in bed the next time I put my face between her thighs. Shit, what am I saying? There isn't going to be a next time.

I pull myself together as Megan introduces me to the staff. After an exchange of pleasantries, she goes up on her toes, stretching her hands over her head to pull two bowls from the shelf.

"I could have gotten those for you," I say, as I hover at least a foot over her head.

She shrugs. "It's okay. I'm an independent woman used to doing things myself."

I nod but for some reason that ticks me off. I love that she's independent, but it would be nice if she had someone to rely on, someone to call when, oh, I don't know, when she's stuck and needs to find a new venue. She's so different from the women in my circle, and it makes me want to help her all the more.

She fills the bowls with thick, creamy soup, and hands them to me. "Take them in there," she says, and nods to the office at the end of the hall. "I'll grab us some sandwiches."

I balance the soup and carefully make my way down the hall. I glance in, find a desk scattered with papers, and know I've come to the right place. I set the soup down. One in front of her big comfy chair and one across from her.

"I see you're still messy," I say when she comes in.

"Excuse me," she says, pretending she's offended

by the remark, but the grin lingering on her lips tells another story. "It's called organized chaos."

"Oh, is that what we're calling it now? I'll be sure to remember that." She sits across from me, and smiles. My God, she is so beautiful. "Amanda has a nice setup."

"She's really hoping to grow. If we pull off the wedding of the century, her business is going to sky-rocket. I really want that for her."

I dip my spoon into the soup and taste it. "If everything she makes tastes this great, I'd be happy to hand her name around."

"You'd do that?" she asks, beaming, and for some reason being able to make her this happy thrills me and fucks me over at the same time.

"Yeah, sure," I say, like it's nothing, but it's obviously not nothing to Megan.

"Thank you," she says, and I love how much she cares about her friend's well-being. She always was kind and thoughtful, a giver. My mind rewinds to the way she gave me her body, and my cock thickens. Shit.

"Okay, so fill me in on what I need to know," I say, getting us both back on track.

As we eat, Megan opens her laptop and turns it my way. I read through the conversation and get myself up to speed. "I must say. I'm impressed. You're pretty good at pretending to be me."

"After going over all those forms I think I know you better than I know myself."

We both nod at that, and I lean back in my chair and bite into my sandwich when her phone rings. "Excuse me for a second." She swipes her finger across her phone. "Hey, Sara, what's up?" she asks. I busy myself with the brochure Amanda gave me and listen to the one-sided conversation. It doesn't take long to figure out Sara is putting together a last-minute anniversary party for her folks, and Megan is organizing it.

"You're never going to believe who is sitting across from me this very minute," Megan says, glancing at me. "Nope...nope...nope," she says, and winks. "You give up? Okay, I'll give you a hint. He helped me get you home from that party when you thought it would be a good idea to drink too much and dance on the table." She laughs and nods her head. "That's right, none other than Alec Carson." A moment and then she responds, "He's good. Yeah, sure we can all get together soon, talk about old times." She goes quiet for a minute. "Well, I can ask him, but I'm not sure he'd be interested. He's a busy guy." Megan grabs a pen, takes a couple notes as Sara talks, then she responds with, "I'm, ah... working on an event for him. I'll explain the details later, over drinks tonight at Onyx when we hash out the details for the anniversary party."

After she ends the call, she crinkles her nose. "Sorry about that."

"She wants you to invite me to the anniversary party?"

"Ah, yeah. You don't have to go, of course."

"I'll go."

Her brow furrows.

"Sure, why not," I say. "I always liked your aunt and uncle. It would be nice to see them again."

"Oh, okay. Sara was out of town on business, and I'm scrambling to pull this off in two weeks. Thank God, Amanda could fit us in and cater the event."

"About this schoolteacher," I say.

"Right." She shows me the woman's picture, and with blond hair cut short, she's cute enough in that girl-next-door way, but she's no Megan.

Megan frowns and glances at me. "I'm not sure you should wear a Gucci suit. I'd like for you to dress just a bit more casual for your first meeting."

I arch a brow. "Is this where you take me shopping?"

"Do you have the time?"

I check my watch. "I have a couple hours."

She grabs her purse from beneath her desk. "Then we should get at it."

"What did you have in mind?"

She tosses her purse over her shoulder and gives me a once-over. "Casual pants, shoes, sweater. A little more of a relaxed look, I think. Why don't we hit Fifth Avenue?"

"Shopping is not my favorite thing, especially on Fifth Avenue."

She plants her hand on her hip and arches a brow. "Alec—"

"Fine, fine," I say, and hold my hands up in sur-
render. "You're the boss," I say, following her out
of her office.

"We're off to do some shopping," she says to
Amanda, and I tuck the brochure into my pocket.

"You'll be hearing from me soon," I say, and open
the door for Megan. She squeezes past me, and her
warm scent reaches my nostrils. I breathe her in,
and work to marshal my desire as I step outside and
guide her to my vehicle.

Two hours later, shopping bags in hand, she points
to one more store. "Let's go in there," she says.

I hold the bags up; I'm so over this. "You don't
think I've bought enough?"

She pouts, and her pink painted lips pucker as she
blinks up at me. "Just one more," she says, her voice
a pleading whisper, and I shake my head, unable to
say no when she begs like that. Fuck, what I'd do to
hear her beg like that in bed, let me know all the dirty
things she'd like for me to do to her. We head inside
some new trendy store and she gasps when she sees
a blue sweater on sale. To her it's clearly something
special; to me, it's a blue sweater.

"Try this on for me." She grabs a casual dress
shirt from the shelf. "This, too."

"That's it," I say, giving her a warning glare. "No
more after this."

"Go," she says, and waves me toward the changing room as she browses a few more items. I reluctantly walk to the back of the store and the sales clerk

opens the room for me. I slip out of my suit jacket, unbutton my shirt and pull on the sweater.

"Can I see?" Megan asks.

I open the door, and her gaze falls over me. She makes a little noise, and I'm almost positive I see desire in her eyes. "That's it. That's the sweater you're going to wear tonight. Along with the new boots and chino pants. It's perfect." Her eyes move to mine, and hold for a second too long. "There's no way school-teacher Danielle won't fall for you," she says, almost regretfully.

"That's not really the goal."

She rolls her eyes at me. "You know what I mean." She steps into the change room with me. "Hang on," she says, then puts her arms around my neck to adjust the sweater on my shoulders and tuck the tag in. Her hair tickles my face, and when I catch her honeyed scent again, my traitorous hands slide around her waist, pull her against me. She gives a small gasp, and when she lifts her face to mine, confusion mixed with need brimming in her dark eyes, I can no longer fight the battle. I dip my head, press my lips to hers.

At first her mouth is pinched tight, and I'm about to pull back, curse myself for my weakness, but then she softens against me, and I slide my hands down, run my palms over the curve of her gorgeous ass. She moans into my mouth, and I slide my tongue to hers, taste her warm sweetness. My cock grows in my unforgiving dress pants, and she moves against me, massaging my dick with her stomach. I back her up, push her against the mirror and practically dry hump her right there in the changing room with the damn door open.

Someone clears their throat and we break apart, fast. I spin and tuck her behind me as I come face-to-face with the sales clerk. "Perhaps you two should get a room," he says, and I nod.

"Sorry about that." I grin at him. "She liked my sweater. A lot."

"You'll be taking it, then?" he asks, and folds his arms, his foot tapping a steady rhythm on the carpeted floor.

"I'll take ten. Mix up the colors," I say. "Toss in a couple of the dress shirts, as well." My way of apologizing for our inappropriate behavior.

A smile lights up his face. "You got it," he says, and steps away. I turn back to Megan. Her hands are covering her face and she's peaking at me through her spread fingers.

"Oh, my God, how mortifying."

"It's fine, and don't worry. He's getting a big commission because of our PDA."

Her hands fall, and her eyes narrow. "Why did you do that?" she asks, her brow crinkled. "Why... why did you just kiss me?"

"Because I have a date with a 'girl-next-door' schoolteacher," I say, doing air quotes around the words.

She smooths her sexy mess of hair down. "That still doesn't explain—"

"I don't usually date nice girls, remember? It's been a week since you were in my bed, and I needed a reminder on how nice girls kiss, so I don't screw tonight up."

Lame, Carson. So lame.

She's not buying it any more than I'm selling it, but she nods her head. "You're up to speed now?"

"Yeah," I say, even though I want to kiss her some more—everywhere, all afternoon.

"Then we probably shouldn't do it again."

"You're right." She's about to move past me when I block the door. "Can I ask you something?"

"Yes, but it doesn't mean I'm going to answer," she says, throwing my words back at me.

I grin. "You're going to Onyx for drinks with Sara. It's across the street from Il Mercato. Did you choose that lounge so you could keep tabs on me?"

"That's exactly why I chose it."

"Are you worried I'm going to screw things up?"

"I'm worried about a lot of things, Alec."

CHAPTER SEVEN

Megan

YEAH, I'M DEFINITELY worried about a lot of things, especially this afternoon's heated kiss in the men's change room. My God, what was he thinking, and then to play it off as practice? I don't know what was going through his head, I only know what was going through mine, and that was to shut the damn door and finish what he started.

I toy with my wineglass and stare out the window as I wait for Sara to arrive. I came to Onyx a bit earlier, wanting to catch a glimpse of Danielle, and possibly to see Alec dressed in the clothes we picked out for him today. I have no doubt he's going to charm the pants right off the sweet schoolteacher, or rather the pretty blue dress, as that's what she was wearing when she got out of the cab. She came here alone, but I have a feeling she won't be leaving solo.

Shoes tapping on the floor catch my attention and I turn to see Sara rushing toward me, dressed in a pencil skirt similar to mine, and a blue blouse similar to my white one.

"Sorry, I'm late," she says, and leans down to give me a hug. "I got caught up at work, and you know how that is." She sits across from me, and the hostess lets us know our server will be with us shortly. "Are you eating or are we just having drinks?" Sara asks as she flicks her auburn hair from her shoulders. We might be cousins, but we look so much alike we could easily pass as sisters.

My stomach grumbles, a reminder that I haven't eaten since lunch with Alec. "I could use some food," I say, and flip open my menu. The server comes, and Sara orders a glass of white wine, while I get a refill on mine. Maybe alcohol will help me forget I just sent the man I used to love, and recently had sex with, on a date in his quest for marriage.

"Tell me, what is this event you're setting up for Alec?" Sara asks, and I angle my head, glance across the street again when the front doors of Il Mercato open. Alec arrived before Danielle, dropped off by his driver, and they've been in there for a half hour now. I shouldn't expect them to be finished so soon but I can't help myself from checking every five seconds. "Something interesting over there?" Sara asks, and scans the street.

I take a sip of wine. "Very," I say.

She leans toward me, almost conspiratorial. "Do tell."

"New York's most eligible bachelor is in that restaurant, with a woman who might be his future wife."

Sara's jaw drops open, and she blinks several times. "Alec is getting married?"

"Something like that."

"Wow, I never thought I'd see the day." We both go quiet when the waiter returns with the wine. She takes a sip, waits until he leaves and then asks, "Who's the lucky girl?"

"Don't know yet."

She toys with the stem of her glass and gives me a look that suggests I might be losing my mind.

"Wait, I'm confused—"

"That's because it's confusing," I say, and lower my voice. "Alec hired me to find him a wife. Technically his grandfather hired me."

"That's insane," she says. "Alec has no trouble finding women on his own. I read the tabloids."

"Yeah, but he wants a nice girl, a girl-next-door type. Tonight he's on a date with an elementary schoolteacher. I set it up."

"Since when did you become a matchmaker?"

"If I find him a woman I get to plan his wedding. Imagine what that will do for my career."

"That's amazing," she says, "but a nice girl doesn't seem like his normal type. Not anymore, anyway."

"What do you mean?"

"When you came to live with us, you had girl next door written all over you, and I assumed he liked that since you two were inseparable."

"We were just friends," I say.

"Yeah, tell that to the million girls who wanted to go out with him senior year, but he only had eyes for you. We all had a crush on him."

"He never once hit on me. We were friends." I learned that the hard way. "I kind of thought you had a crush on him."

"Who didn't. I wasn't going to do anything about it, though. You're my cousin and I'd never do anything to hurt you. I thought you liked him."

I loved him.

"I didn't know," I say.

"So why is he looking for a nice girl now? I don't get it."

"He needs a 'suitable' wife if he wants to step into the CFO position at Blackstone. He doesn't believe in love or happily-ever-after. He wants a wife in name only."

"I never knew he was so romantic," she mocks.

"Right?" I give a sad shake of my head.

She snorts out a laugh. "Oh, well, at least whomever he marries will get good sex out of it. I'm sure that man fucks like a god," she says, and I nearly spill the wine in my glass as I bring it to my lips.

Don't blush, Megan. Don't think about the way he fucks and give yourself away.

Too late.

Fortunately, before Sara notices the color on my face, the waiter comes and takes our order. He jots it down and I close my menu and hand it over. When he disappears, I turn my attention to Sara. "How are things with Doug?"

She groans. "We're done. Doug turned out to be a dud." She gives a humorless laugh. "Maybe Alec is on to something, because I'm beginning to believe there is no such thing as love or happily ever after either." She glances out the window. "What about you? How's your love life going?"

"Let's just say I'm about to buy shares in Duracell." She laughs at that, and I pull a notepad from my purse. "How's work going?" I ask.

"Busting my ass 24/7, but the senior partners keep overlooking me. I have more experience than Laura Sweeny, but her husband golfs with them, so she got the last promotion." She scoffs. "I need a husband who golfs. Maybe that will help me get ahead, but there are just no decent guys out there and I've given up on trying to find a needle in a haystack."

"I hear you. Okay, so two weeks to plan a party. You're not giving me much time."

She crinkles her nose. "Sorry, I was out of town for work, and time just got away from me. Will you be able to pull it off?"

"I'll get the invitations out the second we secure a venue, which might be hard this late in the game."

"Don't kill me, but I was actually hoping to have it at the Skylark."

"Sara—" I'm about to tell her there's no way in hell I could get that last minute when she blinks at me and cuts me off.

"I told Mom, and now she has her heart set on it."

I groan and sit back in my chair. "I'll see what I can do, but Amanda won't be able to cater. They don't allow that."

"You'll make it up to her with Alec's wedding."

"True," I say. "I'm not making any promises. But I'll make some calls first thing tomorrow."

I open my notepad and we spend the next fifteen minutes going over the guest list, the menu and decorations. Our meals arrive and after every bite, both Sara and I glance out the window, looking for lover boy and his date.

I tap my pen on the table. "Oh, I forgot to tell you. Alec said he'd come to the anniversary party."

"Maybe he'll bring his fiancée," she says, and wipes the corner of her mouth with her napkin. But as I think about Alec showing up with his fiancée, the chicken I just swallowed sits like lead in my stomach. "What?" Sara asks me when she notices I've gone quiet.

I blink. "Nothing."

"Megan, please don't tell me you're still hung up on him."

"I was never hung up on him," I say. I glance out the window again and sit up a little straighter in my chair when the door opens, and the handsomest guy I've ever set eyes on steps outside.

"It's them," I say, and hope Alec can't see us staring. Or can he? His head lifts and his gaze zeroes in on me. Surely he can't see me watching from the dim light in the restaurant. He lifts his hands and gestures for a cab. It arrives, and he pulls money from his pocket and hands it over as Danielle gets in the backseat, no kiss goodbye.

The cab drives off, and he immediately starts our way. "What's he doing?" I ask.

"I think he sees us," Sara says. "He's on his way over here. I don't think the date went well."

"Great," I say, hating the relief I feel. I don't want Alec. I don't even really like the man he's become. I don't think.

I grab my napkin, twist it in my hands and scan the restaurant to find Alec stalking toward us. He doesn't look angry, and I'm glad for that. Maybe the date went better than I thought.

"Megan," he says, and steps up to the table. He bends, drops a kiss onto Sara's cheek and flashes her a smile. "Nice to see you again, Sara. I'd like to get caught up, but right now I need to talk to Megan. Would you mind?"

Sara drops her napkin onto the table. "Actually, we're finished here." She checks her watch. "I need to get going. Work never stops. Megan, I'll grab the bill on the way out."

Sara snatches up her purse and leaves, and I sit there staring at Alec. What the heck is going on? He's scrubbing his chin, his gaze latched on to mine.

"Have a seat," I say.

"Can you come with me?"

"I… Sure." I stop twisting my napkin and reach

for my bag. Alec slides his hand around my body and places his big palm at the small of my back as he leads me out. "Where are we going?"

"I need air," he says.

He guides me to the limousine that picked me up that first night and opens the door for me. I slide into the back.

"Hi, Phillip, it's nice to see you again."

"You as well, Megan." He gives me a big smile, like he's actually delighted to see it's me getting into the backseat.

"What's going on?" I say to Alec as he climbs in beside me. I scan his face, still unable to read him. He clearly has his guard up. "Did the date go well or not?"

"Not," he says. "Phillip, how about a drive through the city."

"Very well, Alec." With that Phillip presses a button on the dashboard, and the privacy divider goes up.

"What happened with Danielle?"

"She was a good choice. I can see why you picked her. She fit my needs, but when I came right out and told her I wasn't looking for love, things fizzled from there." He shakes his head. "Here I thought it would be easy."

"Maybe girl-next-door types aren't impressed by your wealth." Is it weird and awful that I'm happy he didn't go home with her tonight? *Yes, yes it is, Megan. You need to get him married. Not just for your business but for Amanda's, too.*

He moves closer, and his thigh touches mine. The air around us instantly charges. I suck in a fast breath, sexual tension arcing between us. "Yeah, maybe," he says, his voice dropping an octave.

"We'll keep trying." Dammit, I hate how raspy my voice sounds. "There has to be a nice girl out there who will be happy with the lifestyle you're willing to offer."

"Maybe I need to switch tactics, figure out how to impress a nice girl."

"That's probably a good idea."

"Are you willing to give me a hand?" he asks, his voice low and husky, and so goddamn sexy my nipples harden, and I grow damp between my legs. How can this man turn me on with a simple question? That in itself is a huge problem, and if I knew what was good for me, I'd knock on the glass and ask Phillip to pull over so I can run far away from this man, and this spell he seems to have over me.

I open my mouth, about to end this, but instead find myself asking, "What do you have in mind?"

Good Lord, girl.

He reaches into a cabinet and pulls out a bottle of my favorite white wine. He opens it and hands me a glass. I take a sip and moan. "Mmm, delicious."

"Impressed?"

"I'm impressed that you knew my favorite kind of wine. I've always liked dry white, but my favorite brand has changed over the years, so how did you know?"

"I asked Amanda when I called her shop to put an order in."

"Ah, I'll have to talk to her about telling my secrets. What else did she divulge?"

"Nothing, and I'd rather find out your secrets myself. A nice girl would like that, right?"

"She probably would, and thank you for supporting Amanda's business. I really appreciate it."

"You're a good friend. We should all be so lucky."

I'm about to ask him about his friends when another thought hits. "Wait, why do you have my favorite wine in the car. Were you planning this?"

Instead of answering, he presses a button and the moonroof opens. A cool night breeze brushes over us, but my body is so hot, it's refreshing. I glance out to take in the mosaic of stars shining in the velvet sky.

"Wow, so pretty."

"Want to be really impressed?" he asks, and takes my wine from me.

"Sure."

"Stand up," he says, and shifts to the seat across from me. I stand, and poke my head through the opening in the roof as his hands go to my waist to balance me. Wind rushes through my hair, but fortunately we're going slow enough that it doesn't steal my breath. I glance around, take in the traffic and all the bright lights of the bustling city. I'm about to duck back inside when Alec's hand dips beneath my skirt, and slides upward, dragging the fabric with it.

Oh, my God.

As he exposes the lower half of my body, I flatten my hands on the roof of the vehicle and can't believe that I'm shifting my stance, giving him access to the spot that has been craving his touch since we parted last Saturday. Okay, that's a lie. I've been craving his touch since our night in St. Moritz. Still, this is wrong. He had a date with another woman tonight. A date *I* set up.

His hand slides a little higher and a moan catches in my throat. Okay, maybe I'll just let him touch me for a second, give me one glorious orgasm, because goddammit, I'm fighting a losing battle here. He rubs my clit through my lacy underwear, the panties he bought me last week. If I didn't know better—and I'm not entirely sure I do—I'd think I wore the thin lace on purpose, in case something exactly like this might happen tonight.

He tugs the panties to the side, and cool air washes over my pussy, but the second his mouth closes over me, my temperature skyrockets. "Oh, yes," I cry out, as he licks me from top to bottom, circling my clit in that little way that makes me insane.

He dips one thick finger inside me, and rubs the bundle of nerves that takes me higher and higher. He pulls his finger out and slides two back in, filling me so nicely. "Please," I murmur, even though I'm sure he can't hear me, but then he changes the pace and depth, touching me places so deep, I can barely fill my lungs.

From the sidewalk, a group of teens raise their fists and pump air as they cheer me on, like they're privy to what's going on down below, and for some reason, I'm not even embarrassed. This man, the lust he arouses in me is melting all my reserve, not to mention my brain cells. Seriously, though, I can't for one minute believe I'm in a limo, driving through New York, as Alec finger fucks me from the backseat. Does it get any better—any dirtier—than this? Jeez, maybe deep down, this girl next door is a little more adventurous and a whole lot more naughty than she ever knew.

In a fast move, he rips the material from my hips, and I can't believe how much I like his impatience. The soft blade of his tongue swipes over my clit, a hot stimulation that curls my toes and my fingers.

"Yes," I moan, and lift my gaze to the sky, not able to focus on anything but the pleasure coursing through me. He takes his fingers from my pussy, and I groan, but when he pushes his tongue in and slides his hands around my backside, massaging my cheeks and spreading them, a new kind of need takes hold.

Is he going to…

He touches my back opening, rolling his finger around the rim, and dipping in slightly, and the sensations are so foreign and so delicious, my entire body pulses. What the hell? With his tongue inside me, his finger gently probing my backside, I buck forward and grind my clit on his face. His growl of approval reaches my ears, thrills me, and a second later a gasp crawls out of my throat, and I grip the hood of the vehicle as a powerful orgasm tears through me, stealing my ability to breathe as well as to stand. As my hot release drips down my thighs, my legs weaken, and Alec pulls me in.

His eyes are dark, intense, but there is a small smile playing on his gorgeous face. He likes playing with me, likes trying new dirty things to gauge my reactions. Well, if that orgasm didn't tell him I liked it a little filthy, nothing would. And who knew? Surely not me. My sex has always been vanilla. How could I ever go back to boring missionary after this?

I'm about to fall back onto my seat when he pops the button on his chinos, and pulls out his cock. My mouth waters as I take in his huge thickness, and before I can even think about what I'm doing, I straddle his lap, and sink down until every inch of him is buried deep in my body.

"Alec," I cry out, and press my mouth to his, taste myself on his tongue.

"You feel so fucking good," he murmurs into my mouth. He cups my breasts through my blouse, and brushes his thumbs over my aching nipples. I arch into him, and his big fingers fumble with the buttons. "I want to rip this off you," he growls. While I want that, too, I don't want to be caught exiting the vehicle with my clothes torn apart. He finally gets the buttons opened, and unhooks my bra from the back. I shrug out of it and as I move up and down, slide his cock in and out of me, he clamps down on one nipple and I go perfectly still.

"So good," I moan, and as he sucks on me, his other hand massages my breast. He growls and my sex muscles ripple around his pulsing cock. I want to feel him. That's when some small working brain cell reminds me I jumped on his cock without a condom.

"Alec," I say, a hint of panic in my voice. There is more than pregnancy to consider here. "Protection."

My nipple pops from his mouth, and he curses. Before I can think better of it, even though there is a part of my lust-induced brain warning this is a bad idea, I cup his face, and say, "I'm clean and I'm on the Pill."

He exhales, almost painfully. "I'm clean, too, Megs. I always use a condom. I promise."

"I trust you," I say, shocking myself with that admission. He might be a lot of things but the Alec I knew and loved would never do anything to hurt me.

"I don't want to stop," he says, his cock still buried deep inside me. "I want to fill you with my cum."

"I want that, too," I say, even though I'm not sure why. Maybe it's because I want to do something special with him, something I've never done with another man. Or maybe it's because I want a part of him in me, a reminder of this night when I watch him walk down the aisle with another woman.

"Good," he growls.

"Then we can do this?"

He grips my hips, lifts me up and then pulls me

back down again. Heat and need roll through me. "Yeah, we can fucking do this."

I gasp and press my forehead to his. We breathe together as he repeats the movement, and lifts his hips to power into me. My hands go to his shoulders, palm his muscles through his sweater.

"You are so overdressed," I say, almost giddily as he takes me higher and higher.

"I'll get naked for you later," he says, and shifts me to take my other nipple into his mouth.

Later, yes. Later I can spend time with my mouth on his body, his beautiful cock. Wait, no, there can't be a later. Later I'll be stronger. Later I'll somehow find the willpower to stop this from happening. I lift my arms, brace them on the roof, as he licks, nibbles and sucks on my turgid nipples, each slide of his tongue so beautiful and artful, I feel the pull deep between my legs.

"I'm so close, Megs," he says, and pulls me to him, his arms wrapped tight around my body, his mouth buried in my neck.

"I feel you. You're throbbing." I moan, lift high and when I sink back down, I come all over his cock.

"Jesus, you're so hot."

His teeth scrape the tender flesh of my shoulder as he powers into me and goes completely still as he finds his release. I hold my breath, concentrate on each pulse, as well as the sensations he rouses deep inside me.

When he finishes, I suck in a gasping breath and

he cups my face. "Breathe, Megs. Breathe with me."
I gulp and he inhales, and I follow his lead for a few
minutes until I'm no longer panting.

Catching me by surprise, he brings my mouth to
his for the softest, sweetest kiss. The tenderness in
his lips wraps around my heart and squeezes. Damn,
that is not good.

"I see you have a thing for ripping panties," I say,
trying to make light of this.

He chuckles. "Just yours."

I lift myself from his cock. He groans, and opens
some compartment and pulls out a tissue. He wipes
me between the legs and my heart wobbles at the gesture. I fix my skirt as he cleans himself and disposes
of the tissue, and that's when a bit of reality creeps in.

"Do you think he heard?" I ask, staring at the
privacy panel.

"No, it's soundproof." He zips up and leans toward
me, a dirty, wicked grin on his face. "I would never
put you in a situation where someone could hear or
see you, Megan. Not unless you wanted that."

"Oh," I say for lack of anything else as I put my
bra and blouse back on. This guy really is kinky, and
I kind of like that.

He presses a button, and says, "We can head to
Central Park now."

The vehicle turns, and I sway into Alec as he
comes to sit beside me. He glances out the window,
and from the heavy way he's breathing, to the way
he's gone quiet and pensive, I get that he has some-

thing on his mind. Maybe he, too, is trying to figure out why we keep doing this. As though moving of its own accord, his hand closes over mine and squeezes. I swallow against the tightness in my throat.

"Central Park?" I ask. "Why there?"

"Something I want to show you," he says quietly without taking his gaze from the road. We sit in silence and a few minutes later, the car stops. Alec opens the privacy barrier. "Thanks, Phillip, we shouldn't be too long."

"Take as long as you like, Alec."

Alec nods, climbs from the car and holds his hand out to me. I accept it and slide out. "Come on," he says, and I follow him blindly through the park, toward the crowd gathering at the pond.

"Oh, my God, we're here to see the Mandarin duck, aren't we?"

He grins. "You ruined the surprise."

I plant one hand on my hip and eye him. "I've really been wanting to see it. Did Amanda tell you about this, too?"

"No, I figured this one out all on my own. You always used to love coming here to feed the ducks." A chill goes through me, and he tugs me to him. One arm circles my body and he runs his hand up and down my arms to warm me.

"You remembered," I say quietly, touched that he took me here—then and now.

"I remember."

My heart pinches. On my saddest days missing

my parents, Alec used to take me to the pond. It was a distraction, and it always helped me clear my head, get it on straight and figure out my future.

We make our way to the edge of the pond to see the beautiful, multicolored duck. "How do you suppose an Asian duck made it to Central Park?" I ask.

"Don't know. He's kind of mean, though," Alec says as the duck nips at a local mallard.

"He's probably just unsure and feeling lost and territorial," I say, understanding those emotions exactly after seeing Alec with Danielle tonight.

I glance up at Alec, and his eyes are serious and intense when they meet mine. If I'm not careful, this man is going to ruin me. I turn back to the pond and once again, as I stand here, I realize what's real, what's not and what my future holds.

"Let me just say, I don't really think you have a problem impressing nice girls. I've been chatting with another woman online. I'll set you up a date for next week." Forcing a smile, I add, "She's a librarian. Maybe she's one of those women who are all quiet during the day and real wild at night." It's cliché, but I thought that would pull a smile from him, but no, he's still staring at me like he wants to eat me alive again.

Okay, I get it. There is tension between us, enormous tension, enough to light up Central Park in a blackout, for a week. Maybe Sara was right. Maybe he did like me back in the day, but decided not to start anything because he wasn't the marrying type, and I wanted the family and kids. Fine, I can live with that rejection now, especially knowing he doesn't believe in marriage, or love. But at the end of the day, why can't we continue to have some fun together until I find him a wife. We're both single, and we clearly fit in the bedroom—or the back of a limo. The man drove straight for my sex when I poked my head through the roof, and I'll be damned if I didn't want that. Why deny myself earth-shattering orgasms? If I keep my heart out of it, I can't see why I should.

"I was thinking," I say.

"About?"

"You might need more help than I first thought. Maybe it's a good idea if I continue to be of assistance. You know, to give you practice impressing the girl next door."

His nostrils flare and even in the dim light I can see the black of his eyes bleed into the blue. "Do you think that's a good idea?" he asks, and I get it, he wants me physically but he's as unsure about this idea as I am.

"No, not even a little bit."

CHAPTER EIGHT

Alec

WITH THE MORNING board meeting finished, I tug on my jacket and I'm about to push from my chair and leave the boardroom when Malcolm Blake, CEO and chairman of the board, holds his finger up to me.

"Can you hang back a moment, Alec," he says, and I give a curt nod as everyone exits the room.

"What can I do for you, Malcolm?" I ask when we're alone.

He crosses the room, leans against the massive table and puts his hand on my shoulder. "I had a drink with your grandfather on Sunday."

"I'm sure he enjoyed the visit. Was he his usual pleasant self?" I ask, thinking about how he grumped about the stock market after my last visit. He might be in his nineties, but he keeps up with the news, and watches his investments closely. I'm pretty sure he's on the ball way more than he lets on. He might fool the other grandkids, but he's not fooling me.

He laughs, like he's privy to some inside joke, and says, "He told me you're getting serious with a woman. That we should be hearing wedding bells in the near future."

"He did, did he?" What. The. Fuck.

"You know, James never was much good at keeping secrets."

Or keeping his nose out of his grandkids' business. But it's best I don't say that.

"We'd love to meet this girl," he says. "Stability goes a long way with the board of directors, and that will definitely come into play when we choose the next CFO. Karl will be retiring in the fall, and of course we have a few other candidates, but marriage will definitely give you a leg up. You'd be the youngest CFO in Blackstone's history."

I grin. "It would be my honor."

He slaps my shoulder. "Summer is just around the corner and you know what that means."

"Blackstone's annual golf tournament." Every year the event is held at Malcolm's own personal golf course, and the members and their families all convene, eat and drink. I usually play a round of golf and hightail it out of there before every grandmother tries to set me up with their granddaughter.

"That's right, and we expect you to bring your young lady."

"We'll be there," I say.

"That's what I wanted to hear," he says. He pushes off the table and I stand. He walks me to the door and I can't help but want to strangle Granddad for telling him I was getting serious. Well, not really, but shit, did he have to tell Malcolm?

I nod to my assistant, step into my office and close the door. Circling my colossal desk, I sit, and stare out the window to take in all that is New York. The sun is warm today and getting warmer as summer approaches. I tug my phone from my pocket and it buzzes in my hand. My heart leaps, hoping it's Megan. When I see her name, I want to kick my ass. I shouldn't be this happy to hear from her, and agreeing to sleep together the other night, yeah, not my brightest moment. But I can't seem to keep my hands off her. Maybe this is for the best. Keep having sex with her and get it out of my system once and for all. Like I actually believe that's going to happen. But what choice do I have? Keeping my hands to myself clearly isn't working.

Megan: I hate to ask, but can you help me with something?

Alec: Does it involve getting you naked?

Megan: Is that all you ever think about?

Alec: No sometimes I think about other things too. Want to hear?

Megan: I bet and no, I don't want to hear.

Alec: Hey, what is it you need help with and why do you hate to ask?

Megan: I am trying to secure Skylark as the venue for my aunt and uncle's anniversary party, but I keep getting the answering machine. Time is short. I was wondering…

Alec: Yes, I know the owner, but it's going to cost you, and if you think I'm talking about the venue being expensive, you'd be wrong.

Megan: That's blackmail.

Alec: That's right.

Megan: You didn't forget about your date tonight did you?

Alec: How could I when you keep reminding me. What should I wear?

Megan: I'm going to swing by your place around 4. I have a client I need to meet near your place. I'll lay out your clothes. Karla the librarian loves sushi, so pretty casual.

Alec: Give me the details on Skylark. I'll make some calls, and don't ever worry about asking me for a favor.

Megan: Thank you Alec.

I stare at my phone as she sends me the details, my heart pounding a little faster. When we finish texting, I pinch the bridge of my nose, and open my laptop. I have a ton of work to get through this afternoon, but now my thoughts are filled with Megan, and doing things for her, making her life a bit easier. I make a few calls, talk to the right people and in no time at all I secure her venue. I could call her and tell her, of course. But I'd rather do it in person so I can see her smile, her reaction.

Head down, I bury myself in my work, ordering in a sandwich for lunch, and eating at my desk. When late afternoon rolls around, I power down my computer, shove it into my bag and head outside. I find my Tesla in my designated spot and jump in. Maneuvering through the busy afternoon traffic, I make my way home, my pulse jumping in anticipation as I get closer.

I hit the button to open the garage door and drive into the well-lit underground parking area. The smell of gas and fumes lingers in the air as I wait for the elevator to arrive. When it does Derek greets me and waves his hand for me to enter.

"You're home a bit early today, Alec," he says, making small talk like we always do.

"I have some things to take care of at home," I tell him, and he grins at me like he knows exactly what I'm up to.

"Miss Williams has already arrived," he informs me.

I scrub my face to hide my smile. "Yes, we have some business to take care of." Derek puts his hands behind his back and whistles softly as we make our way to the penthouse. "How's Peggy?" I ask. Last time we talked about his wife, she was in the hospital with complications from pneumonia. At the time, it was easy to tell Derek was distressed, and worried about the hospital bills.

He gives me a toothy smile. "She's doing well. She's back to work, and feeling herself again."

"Glad to hear that."

"We sure would like to thank whoever took care of our medical expenses."

I nod. "I'm sure if they wanted a thank-you, they would have given you their name."

"You're probably right about that. Best I let it go."

"For the best, I think."

When the elevator stops at my penthouse, I practically leap off.

Derek chuckles slightly. "I don't remember ever seeing you this happy," he says, and that's when it occurs to me that I am happy, and haven't been this happy since…high school. "You have a wonderful day," he adds before the doors ping shut.

"You, too," I say, and pull my key from my pocket. I open the door quietly, not wanting to startle Megan but wanting to surprise her just the same.

I drop my laptop bag and kick off my shoes. From my bedroom, she's humming something and I pad quietly down the hall, following the sound as it wraps around my dick and strokes hard. I stop at the doorway and damn near swallow my tongue when I find Megan bent over my bed, arranging clothes for me to wear. From my viewpoint, I take in the soft swell of her ass in her sexy black-and-white-striped dress, which rides up her creamy thighs as she moves my clothes around.

I clear my throat and she spins around, her hand going to her chest. Eyes wide, she stares at me. "Alec, you scared me half to death."

"Sorry," I say, as my gaze races over her, my dick thickening even more.

"What…what are you doing here?"

"I live here, remember."

She plants a hand on her hip, and glares at me. Damned if that doesn't turn me on even more. "I told you I was going to take care of your clothes."

"There's something else that needs taking care of," I say, and she gives me a quizzical look.

"Oh, what might that be?" she asks, but the blush crawling up her neck lets me know she gets it.

"You, Megs. You need to be taken care of." Christ, all I can think about is laying her on that bed and giving her a dozen orgasms.

"Me? What do I need taken care of?" she asks, her chest rising and falling a bit faster.

"I secured your venue. Skylark is booked for the party," I say, and my heart crashes against my chest when her eyes go wide and a huge smile splits her lips. Catching me by surprise, she rushes across the room and throws her arms around me. I pick her up and her legs go around my back. Fuck, yeah.

"Alec, this means the world to me. My aunt and uncle will be so happy." She hugs me tight and her breath is warm on my neck. "I have no idea how to thank you."

"I do," I say, my voice a little deeper. Her head slowly inches back. Our eyes meet and her expression is filled with equal amounts of curiosity and desire.

"Do you now?" she asks, her lips quirked, and I love that she's playing along. "Care to explain?"

"It involves hot water, and soap." I shift my hands under her ass to hold her, walk to my bathroom and set her on the counter. Her arms fall to her sides as I step back, and let my gaze race over her beautiful face and body. God, she's so perfect.

I shrug out of my suit jacket and loosen my tie. "I need to wash up and get ready for my date. I haven't showered with a good girl yet, and I believe I'm going to need your assistance."

"Oh, well." Her legs widen on the counter, and her dress rides farther up her thighs. Fuck, she is so sexy. "Yes, we did agree that I would help you practice impressing nice girls." She gives a sigh. "The things I do for you, Alec."

I remove my tie and unbutton my shirt. Her eyes drop, take in my near nakedness. Christ, I love the way she looks at me. "I think it might be beneficial to us both." I remove my shirt and tug open my pants. Her fingers go to the small buttons lining her dress, and man, do I ever want to rip it off her. She toys with the top button, but doesn't open it, and I can't help but think her thoughts mirror mine.

"Yes, that's right. You get to become CFO, and I get all the perks that come with planning your wedding."

I kick off my pants and socks then remove my boxers. Her breathing changes when I take my hard dick into my hand and start stroking. "Well, yes, there's that," I say, and step up to her. I slide my hand up her thighs, and push her panties to the side. "But maybe a few other perks, too."

"Such as," she asks breathlessly, her hips moving, squirming, as her hot core beckons my touch.

I slide a finger into her. "An orgasm or two."

"Alec," she gasps, her hands going to my shoulders as I fuck her soaking wet sex with my finger. I love finding her like this, love how aroused she gets for me. Her eyes slip shut and her lips part as she tosses her head from side to side, her hair a tumbling mess over her shoulders. With my finger moving in and out of her, I slide my tongue over her bottom lip, then lean in for a taste. She kisses me back, her soft sexy moans of excitement curling around my cock.

She reaches down, takes my thickness in her hands and I let loose a loud growl. "This is very impressive," she says, and as she strokes me, her pussy grows wetter. I chuckle and slide another finger in, wanting to bring her to orgasm so I can taste her. I press my palm against her clit, and stimulate it as I finger fuck her and her hands grip my dick tighter. Her pussy starts rippling and I pull out of her. Her hands fall from my cock, and she braces them behind her and lifts herself slightly as I slide her panties down. I toss them away, grip her legs and widen them even more. Desperate to taste her, make her come all over my tongue, I bury my face between her legs. I lick her, put my tongue inside her and circle her clit with my thumb.

"Alec," she cries out, and a second later her hot juice spills from her beautiful pussy. I growl and lap at her, drink her in, not wanting to miss a damn drop.

"You taste so good, Megs," I say as she continues to ripple and ride out the pleasure. Her hips move, buck against my face, and when her body stops spasming, I stand and wipe my wet mouth with the back of my hand. Her eyes are glazed, and her chest rises and falls.

Fucking sexy.

As she sits there, struggling to catch her breath, I turn on the shower, and come back to lift her from the counter. Her body slides down mine, the tiny buttons on her dress scraping my flesh.

"Are you fond of this dress?" I ask.

"I have another just like it," she says, her eyes dimming with desire.

"Good." In one quick tug, I rip it open and the buttons fall to the floor and scatter. She gasps and

I tear it from her body and let it fall to her feet in a rumpled heap. "But I'll still replace it."

"You don't have to do that."

"Want to," I say.

I reach behind her and unhook her bra, freeing her beautiful breasts. "I haven't spent enough time here." I brush my thumb over her hard nipple, and bend to take it into my mouth. I lick softly, and squeeze her breasts together so I can taste both at the same time. "I'm going to fuck you here," I say, and she whimpers in response. "I'm going to fuck you everywhere."

"I don't see as we have a choice," she says playfully. "We have to cover everything so you're ready for your dates."

"Exactly," I say and back up, stepping into the stream and bringing her in with me. The warm, needlelike spray falls over us and I grab the bar of soap. I lather my hands and run them all over her body, and she moans as I touch her. I remove the nozzle, rinse her off and spend a few extra minutes with the spray between her legs. She's a quivering mess when I replace the nozzle and she reaches for the soap, washing me in turn. My dick is a steel rod by the time she takes it into her hands. Bubbles form as she soaps me, and I move my hips, power into her hand, but I don't want to come, not yet. There are so many things I need to do to her first. I grab the nozzle again and rinse my body, but before I can turn the spray off, she drops to her knees and takes my dick into her mouth.

"Fuck, Megs," I say as she takes me to the back of her throat and chokes a little. I push her wet hair from her shoulder, revel at the way she sucks me deep. One hand goes to my balls, and she gently massages. She works her mouth over me, taking me closer and closer to the edge. I need her to stop as much as I need her to continue. I fuck her mouth a few more times, and then pull back. She moans at the loss.

"I want you to come in my mouth," she says.

"Me, too. Come on."

I grab a towel and wipe her down, then quickly dry myself. Reaching for her hand, I take her back into the bedroom.

She sits on the edge of the mattress, and widens her legs to show me all her pretty pink wetness. I remove the clothes she laid out, and nearly bite off my tongue as she showcases her body.

I step up to her, push my thumb into her mouth and she sucks me so hard, I nearly shoot off. "You want my cum?" I ask, and she nods. "You want me to fuck this pretty mouth and shoot my cum down your throat?" She nods and squirms on the bed. "Is that what nice girls want?" I ask pulling my thumb out so she can answer.

"It's exactly what nice girls want," she says.

"Get on the bed, and squeeze those gorgeous tits together. I want to fuck them," I say, and she visibly quivers. She goes down on her hands and knees, pointing her sweet ass my way as she crawls to the middle of the mattress. I growl. "Megs," I say.

She looks at me over her shoulder. "Yes," she asks innocently.

I take my dick in my hand and stroke. "You shake your ass at me like that and it makes me think you want it fucked."

She drags her teeth across her bottom lip. "Maybe I do. Maybe I don't," she says, and I shake my head. This woman is going to be the death of me.

Pre-cum pools on my crown and I rub it around to lubricate my cock as she sprawls out, offering herself up to me completely. I climb over her and she squeezes her beautiful breasts together just like I asked. I place another pillow under her head and angle it, so her mouth can take my dick.

"Perfect," I say, and straddle her body. I slide my cock between her tits, and she opens her mouth when my crown presses against her lips with each forward thrust. I rock into her, and she swirls her tongue over me. "Yeah, just like that, baby," I say. "Show me how much you want my cum."

She quivers at my words, and I love the dirty side of this sweet girl. In fact, I love everything about her. But I can't think about that, not when her tits are squeezing me so tight, and her mouth is doing crazy things to my dick. I thrust into her harder, faster, chasing an orgasm as she moans around my crown, the vibrations going right through me.

"Yes," she cries out between each thrust.

"You've got me right there, baby," I growl, every muscle in my body tightening, as my orgasm mounts.

"You ready to taste me?" She nods and I reach down, slide my hand around the back of her neck and fill her mouth with my hot cum. She swallows and drinks me in, but I come so much she can't take it all. It spills from her lips and when I finally drain myself and pull out, she licks her mouth, cleaning every last drop.

I can barely catch my breath as I watch her. When she licks the last of my release, I turn her around and put a pillow beneath her hips, to lift her ass. "I plan to fuck you here," I say, and slide my finger between her sweet cheeks. I circle her tight opening, probe slightly. "It won't be tonight. It will take time to prepare you properly." She moves against my finger, and writhes on the bed and even though I just came, my cock grows hard again. I can't get enough of this woman. I slide a finger into her hot core, and she cries out my name. "Do you need my fat cock in here?" I ask.

"Yes, please," she says, and I chuckle.

"My dick is hard for you again," I say. "And this is exactly where it wants to be."

She wiggles her ass and I push my finger in as I position my cock at her dripping opening. In one hard thrust I drive home and she lets loose a cry.

"Alec, yes," she says, and reaches up to grip the headboard to hang on for the ride. I pull out and drive back in again. I slide my hand between the pillow and her body to stroke her clit.

"You like that, baby? You like my cock in here?"

"I do," she cries out, and I work my finger in her ass, stretching her, letting her get used to the new sensations.

"And my finger. You like my finger in this sweet virgin ass of yours?" Her reply is muffled as she buries her face in her pillow and comes all over my cock. Her muscles ripple around me, and I can't even believe I'm coming again. I spurt into her, and after filling her beautiful body, I fall over her back.

I push her hair to the side, and press kisses to her shoulder. She goes still beneath me, sated and spent, judging by the soft sounds of contentment crawling out of her throat. Not wanting to crush her, I roll over and pull her with me. She snuggles into me, and her hair tickles my face. I take deep breaths and let them out slowly as my heart rate settles to normal.

She lifts her face to mine, her gaze roaming over me, her smile, soft and seductive. "You keep looking at me like that, and we'll never get out of this bed," I say.

She chuckles slightly. "How exactly am I looking at you?"

I coil a strand of hair around my finger and give it a tug. "You know exactly how you're looking at me."

"Sex has never been this good," she admits.

"Impressed?" I ask, to stop myself from telling her it's the best sex I've ever had, too.

She laughs. "Very." But then all humor disappears from her face. "It's getting late, and I need to get you up to speed on Karla before your date."

I nod, but what I really want to do is crawl under the covers and spend the night with her. Except I can't do that. I'm not the guy for her and we both know it. Right? Wait, am I seriously thinking I am the guy for her? That I might have staying power?

Just then my cell rings…and rings and rings.

"You should probably get that," she says.

I go in search of my phone, and find it in my pants on the bathroom floor. I slide my finger across the screen. "Hey, Mom."

"Is it true?" she asks.

I pinch the bridge of my nose. "Is what true?"

"You hired Megan Williams to find you a wife?"

"Technically Granddad hired her."

A beat of silence then, "Alec…"

I can hear the worry in her voice, the fear… maybe even a hint of disappointment. She always liked Megan and was the one who warned me to distance myself from her all those years ago. Honestly for as long as I can remember, my mother criticized the Carson men, and constantly reminded me that I'd grow up to be no better, and would only end up breaking a woman's heart. It wasn't easy to hear I was cursed when I was just a boy, when I didn't really understand the history of my family. The older I got, the more I struggled with it, and I swallowed it down until I met Megan. I was so goddamn scared of hurting her, I had no choice but to walk away, even though it was, by far, the hardest thing I ever had to do.

"Mom…"

"Alec, do you still have feelings for Megan?"

"I need to get married and she's helping me."

"You didn't answer the question."

"She's a nice girl and—"

"And you'll just end up breaking her heart." I swallow. Hard. "Have you talked to your father lately?"

"No, why?"

She snorts. "He's got a new young thing on his arm."

"I didn't know."

"How could you at the rate he goes through them. The Carson men just can't commit, Alec. I'm sure you don't need me to bring up Will and the splash done on him in *Starlight*."

"No. I remember it well."

"Thank God, Naomie found out and left him before she became other casualty." She makes a tsking sound. "How embarrassing for him, and the entire Carson family." She goes quiet for a second. "Alec, honey," she says, softening her voice. "You know I love you. I'm just trying to save you from falling into your father's footsteps. I want you to be better than that, and I don't want to see your private *affairs* made public."

I cringe. She has about as much faith in my ability to remain monogamous as the rest of the Carson family. "I'm looking for a wife in name only," I tell her.

"I see."

"I know what I'm doing," I tell her, even though I'm pretty sure I don't. "I have to go. I'll talk to you later." We say our goodbyes and I end the call. I make my way back to Megan, who is looking at me with concern.

"Everything okay?"

"Yeah, you were going to tell me about Karla. Karla the librarian, who wants to go out for sushi on a Tuesday night. Although I shouldn't complain. The sooner I find someone, the better, right?"

"Right," she says, and pulls the blankets up to cover herself. Now, why did that feel more like a kick to the nuts? Oh, maybe because someplace deep inside me I want her to tell me not to go out, that she's the girl for me and we can make forever work. But there is no forever in my world, as I was just re-minded, and I'd be wise to remember that.

Yeah, I'm totally fucked.

CHAPTER NINE

Megan

IT'S BEEN FOUR WEEKS. Four glorious, yet horrible weeks and not one of the dozen women I've set Alec up with have been "suitable." While one part of me is far too thrilled about that—seeing as I end up in his bed every night—the other part of me is distraught. The clock is ticking, and Blackstone's annual golf tournament where Alec is to introduce his fiancée is coming up fast. He needs to have a woman on his arm, and a ring on her finger, if he wants to impress the aging board of directors, with their old-fashioned values.

I rush around my apartment and get ready to meet Alec. At least I've convinced him to stop scaring the women off by blurting out that he wants a marriage in name only, and he promised he'd at least try to find common ground and give the relationship a chance. Yet none of the women have measured up to what he needs. Or so he says. I have the feeling he's not try-

ing hard enough, and the women are the ones backing away, which is why I am now stepping in to go
on a date with him. I want to see firsthand what he's
like, how he acts and treats his dates. If he's coming off as some hard-assed, guarded businessman,
no wonder he can't get a second date.

We're going to my favorite Mexican restaurant,
and with the weather warmer and the nights growing longer, I slip into one of my favorite dresses, a
little black number that can be dressed up or dressed
down. As it slides down my sides, the soft material
scraping my skin, the sudden visual of Alec tearing
it from my body sends heat to my core.

"Oh, my," I say under my breath as I fasten the
button at the back and contort my arms to zip it up.
I put on a bit of mascara, a light dusting of blush
and swipe my favorite pink lipstick across my lips,
which are still kiss-swollen from last night, and all
the nights before.

The buzzer sounds, and I rush to my front door
and press it, giving Alec access to the building. A
moment later a knock comes on my door, and I take
a deep breath. Why the hell am I so nervous? This is
Alec, and I've been in bed with him numerous times.

You've never gone on a date, though.

But it's not even like it's a real date. We both know
that. I'm only doing this to critique him. Right?

Okay, stop overanalyzing things, Megan.

I slip on my shoes and smooth my dress down, and
pull myself together as I walk to the door. I swing it

open, and when I find Alec standing there, looking casual and yummy in his chinos and button-down shirt, I nearly falter in my heels.

With one hand behind his back, he reaches out, touches the tumble of hair flirting with my shoulders. "You're beautiful," he says, his gaze slowly sliding down the length of me.

"You are, too," I say for lack of anything else.

He grins at me, a grin so sexy and so full of mischief and promise, I almost forget how to breathe. Surprising me, he produces a bouquet of flowers from behind his back.

"Nice touch," I say. Jeez, I can't remember the last time a guy gave me flowers, a real date or not.

"I thought so."

"Modest, too. For the life of me I don't understand why you can't get a second date," I tease.

"I'm not sure I'd use the word *can't*."

"Your ego won't allow that?" I tease.

"I told you, those women weren't right. You're doing a good job picking them. They fit all my criteria on paper, but there's something missing when we meet face-to-face."

"You have to stop being so picky," I say as I take the flowers into the kitchen. I fill a vase with water and drop them in. I turn back around and reach for my purse. "Ready?" I ask.

"Yeah," he grumbles, and follows me to the door. We step into the hall and I lock up. A few minutes later we're in his Tesla heading to Lindo's. Alec finds a parking spot and comes around my side of the car to let me out.

"So far, so good," I say to him. "That would impress any woman, I'm sure."

He grins. "I'm not an ogre. I do have manners. Plus, you're grading me, so I'm pulling out all the stops." He slides his arm around my body, placing his hand on the small of my back, and a fine shiver moves through me. "Cold?" he asks, his brow furrowed with genuine concern, and I hate how much I like that.

"Not really." No sense in lying. The man is well aware of what his touch does to me.

"Ah," he says, his grin widening. "We could skip dinner and head straight to my place."

"Alec," I warn, even though I'm in love with the idea. "We need to focus."

"Fine, fine," he says, and opens the restaurant door. I step inside and breathe in the delicious scents as I glance around the dimly lit, cozy and somewhat romantic restaurant. Alec stands close as the hostess comes our way, so close I can smell his freshly soaped skin as well as the aroma that is uniquely Alec.

Alec gives his name and reservation time, and the hostess checks her tablet before leading us to a small table in the back corner. Light from the candle dances across his handsome face as we take our seats.

"Nicest table in the place," I say to him, and look

around, noting the way some woman keeps casting glances our way. A former lover? My stomach knots at the thought and I push it down. Not my business, nor my issues.

Alec opens the wine list and hands it to me. "What would you like?" he asks.

"I'd love a glass of chardonnay," I say, and hand it back. The waiter comes to take our drink orders, and Alec orders wine for me and a soda for himself.

"You're not having anything?" I ask.

"I'm driving," he says and my heart wobbles in my chest.

"I wish you would have met my parents, Alec. You would have liked them."

"I'm sure I would," he says. "I feel like I know them anyway, from all your stories."

I swallow down the lump in my throat. "You were always such a good listener, so patient with me when I was sad. You barely knew me, and yet you took such good care of me. I don't think I would have made it without you." I pause for a moment as my mind trips back to high school. "In thinking back, I don't think it was fair of me to put that burden on you. I wasn't your problem."

His hand slides across the table and captures mine. "Megs, come on. You were going through a hard time, and I wanted to be there for you."

"Why?" I ask, and hold back the question I really want to ask.

Why did you leave me after prom?

"Sara and I were friends, and you were her cousin. You were like a lost puppy and I kind of have a thing for puppies," he says with a grin.

"You just lost points."

He sits up straighter, his shoulders square, and I can't help but grin at his cute yet confused expression. "What did I do?"

"Somehow in there, I think you called me an ankle biter."

He bursts out laughing, and I laugh with him, the mood around us softening, mellowing. The waiter comes with our drinks, and we place our food orders, and fall into easy conversation. The woman two tables over, however, keeps an eye on Alec and I do my best to ignore her.

Our meal arrives, a dinner for two, and in the center of the table the waiter sets out an enchilada, a burrito, a taco and a chimichanga for us to split.

"Looks amazing," I say as Alec slices the enchiladas in half and divvies them up on our plates.

"I haven't had Mexican in years," he says.

"Remember when we used to eat it every weekend?" I ask him. "It was always between pizza and Mexican."

"And nine times out of ten you always won the thumb war and got your way," he says.

I glance at his big hands. "Wait, did you let me win on purpose?" I bite into my food and moan at the delicious flavors.

"Me, let you win?" He arches a brow. "Are you forgetting how competitive I am?"

"Nope, you were competitive."

"Still am."

I take a sip of wine. "Win or die trying, right?"

He laughs. "Something like that?" He forks the enchilada into his mouth, and nods. "This is good," he says.

"Try this one." I cut the chicken burrito into two and put half on his plate. He takes a generous bite, and moans. "I think this beats pizza every day."

"Pizza has its place," I say, remembering the first night we shared a pie at his apartment and the way we played afterward. *Okay, get your mind off sex before your nipples poke through your dress. It's all fun and games until someone puts an eye out.* Changing topics, I ask, "You're still coming to the anniversary party tomorrow night?"

"Still planning on it, unless you're sending me out on another date."

"I'm not. I figured you needed a night off."

"I'm looking forward to catching up with Sara." A little sound escapes me when he brings up my cousin. "What?" he asks, and takes a drink of water.

"Did you know back in high school all the girls had a crush on you."

"Nope. Didn't know."

"Apparently they wanted a piece of Alec Carson." I lean toward him. "But they all thought we were an item."

He doesn't laugh at that, like I thought he would. Instead he says, "I can see that. We were pretty inseparable."

I dig deep, gather courage, and I'm about to ask him what happened to us, when the woman who's been staring takes out her phone and aims it our way.

"I think that woman just took a picture of us," I say to Alec.

"Shit," he says under his breath.

The woman pushes her chair back and steps up to our table. "Alec," she says. "Alec Carson."

He angles his head. "What can I do for you?" he asks, and from the way he's looking at her I get the sense they don't know each other.

"Rumor has it New York's most eligible bachelor is soon to get married." Her gaze slides to me, and she has a weird smirk on her face. "Are you the lucky lady who's finally pinned him down?"

"If you'll excuse us, we're in the middle of dinner," he says, his voice hard and agitated but holding a measure of politeness, even though the woman doesn't deserve it.

"But it's breaking news, Alec." She bats wellpainted eyelashes at him, and does a flirty toss of her red hair. "I'm sure *Starlight* would love to do a spread."

Starlight is a tabloid magazine that emphasizes sensationalized crime stories and gossip about celebrities. It wasn't long ago that Will was on the cover…in bed with a woman who wasn't his fiancée. He must have gone into hiding, keeping his head down and nose clean, because he hasn't been in the news for a long time. Could this be the reporter who outed him?

The brazen woman turns to me. "And what is your name?"

"Her name is none of your concern," Alec answers through clenched teeth. His jaw is so tight, I'm sure he's going to crack his back teeth.

My pulse beats a little faster, and my heart goes out to Alec as I take in the tension in his body. I've seen the pictures of him in the papers, of course. But never knew how aggressive and downright rude the paparazzi could be—to his face—until this very second.

"Don't worry, I'll find out who she is." She laughs as her gaze moves over me. "Although you don't really seem like his type." She taps her finger to her chin, and puckers her lips. "Tired of playing with models, going for the plain Jane instead?" she asks, her gaze zeroing in on Alec.

Alec stands so fast, his chair shoves backward, but it doesn't faze the woman at all. "Don't you dare talk about her like that."

"Oh, my. I've never seen this protective side of you before, Alec. She must be pretty special," she says, giving me another glace before walking away.

Alec slowly sits back in his chair and smooths his hand over his chest.

"I'm sorry. It's awful what you have to put up with. Do you want to leave?"

He takes a deep breath, lets it out slowly. "Let's finish our meal and not give her that kind of power over us."

"Do you think she'll print the picture?"

"I don't know. We're having dinner. Nothing to really sensationalize over that."

"Does this happen a lot?" I catch a glimpse of the woman as she breezes out the door, looking quite smug with herself. "When you were on other dates, were you harassed?"

"Sometimes."

Perhaps that's why things never worked out. No one wants to be accosted, photographed or belittled during dinner.

"She's wrong, you know," he says.

"Wrong?"

"You're not a plain Jane. You're beautiful."

I set my fork down, my pulse jumping in my neck. "Thank you," I say quietly as he divides the taco, and puts half on my plate, but I no longer have an appetite. "How do you think she found out? Who would have said you were soon to get married?"

"Granddad is spreading it all around town. I'm going to have a talk with him."

"Don't be too hard on him. He's just excited for you. I think…" I let my words fall off. I don't want to say anything to upset him.

"You think what?" he asks, pushing the matter.

"I don't think he's very well, Alec. He was doing a lot of fading in and out when he hired me, like he was forgetting his words, and I think he just wants to see his grandkids happy and settled down before…" I can't bring myself to finish the sentence. I've always loved Alec's granddad. He was so good to me when we were younger, and the thought of losing someone else I care about cuts me deeply.

"Yeah, I guess." Alec pinches the bridge of his nose. "I'm not so sure his mind is going, though."

"Really, why?"

"He had enough wits about him to convince me to get married, and drag you into it all."

"He didn't drag me. I went into this willingly."

"Even though you knew it was me."

"Yes."

"Even after…" He looks down, like his thoughts are now a million miles away. Or more like eight hours away by plane. The amount of time it takes to go from New York to St. Moritz.

The waiter comes, interrupting the moment, and asks if I'd like a refill on wine. I decline, and set my fork down, finished with dinner and wanting to leave, just to go somewhere we can be alone.

"Ready to go?" Alec asks.

"Yes. You?"

He gestures to the waiter to bring the bill, and after he pays, we make our way out into the dark night. I breathe in the fresh spring scents before climbing into the Tesla. Alec circles the car, his strong, confident movements drawing my attention, and a few minutes later, he pulls into traffic, but instead of taking me back to my place he goes in the opposite direction.

"Where are we going?" I ask.

"It's a surprise."

"I don't like surprises," I say.

He laughs. "Like hell you don't. You screamed your head off when I got you those Rolling Stones concert tickets for your birthday."

"Well, okay maybe I do," I say. "As long as it's a good surprise."

His hand slides across the car and sits heavy on my thigh as he gives it a squeeze. His warmth seeps through me, and my insides quiver with all the crazy things I feel for this man. All the emotions that have resurfaced in his presence. Suddenly I'm not so sure any of this was worth it. Not if it means I spend another eight years mending a broken heart.

I stare out the window, take in the pedestrians and shops as he drives, and soon enough we're at Central Park. "Are we here to feed the duck again?" I ask.

"Nope." He parks and comes around to my side of the car. I climb out, and he hits the fob to lock the doors. "Let's go," he says, taking my hands in his. A breeze blows over us as I follow him through the lit park and he stops at the hansom cab.

"A carriage ride? Are you serious?" I ask.

"You said you've never been in one but would like to." He grins. "How many points does this get me?"

"A lot," I say, a little touched and surprised that

he remembered. He boosts me up until I'm situated on the seat. He talks to the driver for a second, and then climbs in beside me. I snuggle close, and he wraps his arm around me.

The buggy starts, and I glance around to admire the sights and the people. "This is so nice," I say.

"Yeah, it is."

His mood is mellow, but there is heat in his eyes as he gazes at me. His hand brushes my hair from my face. "I want to be inside you," he whispers.

My heart stalls. "I want that, too."

"My place or yours?" he asks.

I grin at his cheesiness. "How about winner chooses," I say, and take his hands in mine for a thumb war. He laughs out loud and the sound takes me back, reminding me of the Alec I once knew. Only problem is, I'm beginning to like this version of him a little too much.

CHAPTER TEN

Alec

PHILLIP PULLS THE limo up to the curb, and I thank him as I exit the vehicle.

I step inside the building where the anniversary party is well underway and take the elevator to the top floor. I'm a bit late but I had some last-minute things to take care of that kept me tied to my desk. When I enter the Skylark, I look around and finally spot Megan talking to Sara. My heart kicks into gear the second I see her, but then worry seeps into my bones. I can't tell what they're discussing but from Megan's body language, I'd hazard a guess that it's something very important. I take a step toward her when I'm stopped by Megan's aunt and uncle.

Jeannie opens her arms wide, her smile sincere and genuine. I always loved that about her. She was down-to-earth, and very motherly, which was something Mcgan needed after losing her folks.

"Alec," she cries out, ecstatic to see me, and I

bring her in for a big hug. "I understand you're to thank for all this," she says, widening her arms and glancing out the floor-to-ceiling window, with the view of the Hudson River, Empire State Building and Midtown Manhattan.

"Just made a call. This is all Megan," I say, giving her the credit.

"How are you, son?" Dave asks, and gives my hand a shake.

"Doing well. How about you?"

"Counting down the days to retirement," he says, and we both laugh. "Come on, what are you drinking?" He puts his hand on my shoulder to lead me to the bar. I excuse myself from Jeannie, who is already greeting other arriving guests, and take in the cozy atmosphere as we head to the bar at the back. We both take a seat and I order a brandy.

"What's this about you getting married?" Dave says, and I laugh. He always was one to get right to the point, much like Granddad, which is why they've always hit it off.

"I guess you've been talking to Granddad."

"Ran into James on the golf course the other day."

"Granddad was playing golf?" I say. Yeah, he's far more agile and sly than he's letting on.

"Winning, too," he says with a chuckle. "He told anyone who would listen that his grandson would soon be making a big announcement."

"I bet he did."

"Who's the lucky girl?" he asks, and my gaze instantly goes to Megan. Dressed in a sexy black cock-tail dress, with her hair pinned up, showcasing her neck, she's the most stunning woman in the room. Jesus, I've never seen her more beautiful. Maybe that's not entirely true. A well-sated Megs in my bed, all sleepy, and warm. Yeah, that's one hell of a look on her. But those days must come to an end. My own brother couldn't keep his dick in his pants—the spread in *Starlight* proved that—and he was engaged to a woman he loved. We just don't have it in us and I can't—won't—hurt Megs like that.

I turn back to Dave, who is watching me care-fully, and try to get my shit together. "We'll be mak-ing an announcement soon," I say. "Right now, it's hush-hush."

Dave laughs at that. "Well, it's nice to see you and Megan together again. Here I used to think you'd one day put a ring on her finger."

I give a humorless laugh. "We're just friends," I say, the lie catching in my throat.

"That's what she says, too." He takes a long drink from his glass, draining the amber liquid. "James also told me about the great things you're doing at the university."

Fuck, are none of my secrets safe with that man? And honestly if he's so disgusted with my lifestyle and what I do for a living, why is he talking about my charity work. I keep that private.

"There you are," Megan says, coming up to us.

Her gaze goes back and forth between the two of us. "Wait, what was that about the university?"

"Nothing," I say quickly.

"Oh, okay," she says, my words taking her back a bit, judging by the way she's blinking rapidly. "I was beginning to think you changed your mind about coming."

"Just had some last-minute things to take care of," I tell her.

She gives me an odd, almost edgy look, and I frown, hoping everything is okay between her and Sara.

Dave stands. "Well, I must go mingle," he says. He gives Megan a kiss on the cheek. "Thanks again for all this, sweetie. Your aunt is over-the-moon happy."

"My pleasure," Megs says and hugs him.

When he's gone, she turns to me. "What's going on?" I ask, my gaze raking over her face and taking in the tension in her body.

She shakes her head. "Am I that easy to read?"

"Yes."

I finish the brandy in my glass and gesture the bartender for another. "What are you having?" I ask.

"White wine."

I get her a glass, and say, "Want to step outside, get a breath of fresh air."

"Yes," she says quickly, her voice almost breathless.

We maneuver through the guests, and we end up

stopping at least a dozen times to make small talk. When we're finally outside alone, Megan takes a deep breath, and looks at the view.

"Gorgeous," she says, and I shift closer, pressing the side of my body to hers.

"Yeah," I agree, my gaze focused solely on her. She glances up at me, that odd worried look back in her eyes.

"I was talking to Sara."

"I saw that when I came in."

"She's smart, a lawyer as you know. A great conversationalist, too. She hasn't had much luck with men, and is pretty much done with the dating scene."

I eye her. Where the hell is she going with this?

She takes a drink of her wine, and I toss back my brandy.

"She's pretty, too. She doesn't have blond hair and blue eyes, but she does have those girl-next-door looks you mentioned."

I nod as understanding dawns. "What are you saying, Megan?" I ask, just to make sure.

"She's game, Alec."

"Game?" Why is it she can't quite bring herself to just say Sara wants to be my wife in name only?

"She's up for a sex-only marriage."

I rock back on my heels, toss the idea around in my brain. "I see. What are your thoughts?"

"I think it's an excellent idea. I mean, it's Sara. You two go way back so a fast engagement and marriage will be more believable, right?"

"True."

"Plus you've gone on numerous dates and can't find anyone suitable. Time is also of the essence."

"Yeah" is all I say.

"You were right, you know," she says so low I have to strain to hear her.

"About what?"

"She likes the idea of your wealth and power. It surprised me. But I guess there really are girls out there enticed by such things." She gives a humorless laugh. "You won't have to worry about her falling for you and asking for your heart."

"I guess I won't."

"Anyway, I changed the seating arrangement, and put you next to her. You guys can treat it like a date, get reacquainted and see if she's right for you."

She sips her wine, and it takes every ounce of strength I have not to bend forward and lick the moisture from her lips. Instead, I harden myself, and take a measured step back.

"We should get inside." She checks her watch. "Dinner will be ready in a minute."

She makes a move to go, and I cup her elbow. She spins back to face me. "Megs," I say.

"Yes?" As she looks up at me, with those big inquisitive brown eyes, I want to tell her the truth. I want to tell her she's the one for me, but I can't bring myself to do it. I love her and don't want to hurt her.

"Thanks."

"You're...you're welcome," she says, stammering a bit, and I hate myself even more.

"I'll leave you two to catch up."

I swallow down the bile punching into my throat as she pulls her elbow away and disappears inside. I follow her in, and make my way to the tables set up for dinner. I find Sara and she waves me over. She pulls the chair out for me and I sit next to her.

"Sara," I say.

"Alec." She shifts a bit closer to me. "It's so good to see you again."

"You, too."

"So," she begins. "Have you talked to Megan?"

I give a nod. "Is this something you want to do, Sara?"

She gives a laugh, and tosses her hair over her shoulder in a flirty manner. "I am so done with relationships, and I've been working my ass off at the firm, trying to make partner. Like your old-school board of directors, marriage and stability go a long way with my senior partners. It's the only way a partnership is going to happen for me, and I like the perks that come with being on your arm." I nod, not at all certain about this. Mcgan was right about everything. Sara is smart, and a great conversationalist, but looking at her reminds me of the woman I can't have. "But we don't have to rush into anything just yet," she says, as if she can read my hesitation. "Let's go on a few dates, see how compatible we are." She gives me a come-hither smile and I instantly understand she's talking about bedroom compatibility.

Megan takes a seat at the other side of the table, a few chairs down, and some guy who looks about her age, pounces into the seat next to her. He instantly engages her in conversation, and I wonder how well they know each other. Did she put him next to her on purpose? Is she interested in him?

Fuck me.

I tamp down the raging jealousy taking up residency in my gut. I want her happy, and if that guy can do that for her, give her the family and happily-ever-after she wants, then I need to stop being a selfish prick and get on board.

Soon enough our meals are served, and we all make small talk and dig in. Once dessert arrives, Dave stands, taps his spoon on his stemware to gain everyone's attention and smiles at those around the table.

"I would like to thank everyone for being here tonight to celebrate this special occasion," he begins. "Or maybe you're all here to give pity to Jeannie for putting up with me for the last twenty-five years." Laughter erupts and when it dies down, he says, "She wasn't an easy one to catch, I tell you. But she was worth the chase." He bends down and gives his wife a kiss. "Jeannie," he says, "you are the best thing that has ever happened to me. You're kind, thoughtful, generous, have given me a beautiful family." I glance at Megan who has tears in her eyes. "Every day my love for you grows stronger, and every day my belly grows bigger, thanks to all the amazing meals you put on my plate." We laugh as his gaze moves around the table, and I swear he's talking to me and me alone when he holds my gaze and says, "If you're lucky enough to find someone who gives your life purpose, someone you can't wait to fall into bed with every night, and more importantly wake up to every morning, then hang on to her with everything in you, and if she doesn't see it your way, and she's worth the fight, then for God's sake fight." As we chuckle, he lifts his glass and we all follow suit. "Here's to the best twenty-five years of my life, and here's to many more."

After his speech, guests are socializing while dessert is being cleared, when Sara's phone rings. She reaches into her bag and checks the display.

"Shoot, I have to get this." She rolls her eyes. "Work."

"No problem," I say.

She excuses herself from the table and finds a quiet place to take her call. My gaze slides to Megan's and I find her talking to the guy beside her, but his gaze keeps drifting to her breasts. Son of a bitch. I push from my chair, and I'm about to grab him by the scruff and tell him to get some goddamn manners, when Sara touches my arm.

"I have to go." She goes up on her toes and puts her mouth to my ear. "This is so not how I wanted tonight to end."

"Yeah," I say as Megan excuses herself. She gives her aunt and uncle a hug, and heads toward the balcony. I relax slightly when douchebag doesn't follow. I turn back to Sara and try to focus on what she's saying to me.

"I'll call you tomorrow, and we'll make plans," she says. "I'm really looking forward to getting reacquainted." She gives me a slow, simmering smile, one that tells me exactly how she wants our next date to go.

"I'll see you soon, Sara," I say, and bend to kiss her cheek. She's an attractive woman, but I feel no spark. I guess that's a good thing since I want a marriage in name only. We get a few raised eyebrows from those around the table and I suppose if we do go through with it, the display will go a long way.

After she disappears, others rise from the table, and I head to the balcony in search of Megan, but she's not there. If she's gone, there's no sense in me staying any longer. I say my goodbyes, head to the elevator and shoot Phillip a text. I step out into the chilly night and find Megan standing on the curb, hailing a cab and shivering in her tight dress.

"Hey," I say, and she turns to face me, a fake smile on her face.

"Oh, hey," she says as I step up to her, my body so close tension arcs between us.

"Did you like that guy?"

She frowns. "You mean the guy talking to my breasts?"

"Yeah, him."

A sound crawls out of her throat. "He's the son of my aunt's friend."

I nod and glance past her shoulder. "Where are you going?"

"I'm exhausted. I thought I'd call it a night, get to bed early. Wait, where's Sara?"

I dip my head, touch a strand of her hair and consider tugging on it until her mouth is open, mine for the taking. "She had some business to attend to."

"What do you think? Is she suitable?" Megan asks.

"Too early to tell."

"Oh."

Just then Phillip pulls up to the curb. "Come on," I say to her.

"No, it's okay. I can get my own lift."

"Get in the car, Megan."

"Alec—"

"In the car."

"You—"

"I'm still a single guy, Megan, and you're a single woman. Let me put my cock in you. One last time."

She blinks several times, and her body vibrates when I put my hand on her waist. "I... I..."

Even though she's stumbling over her words, she doesn't pull away, she steps closer to me. Taking that as a yes, I guide her to the car and open the door.

She aims her sweet ass my way as she climbs in and shimmies to the other side to make room for me.

"Hi, Phillip," she says, her voice as shaky as her body.

"Megan, always a pleasure."

"My place, please," I say and put my hand on Megan's leg, holding her in place. Tonight I want—no need—to be with her. Need to own and claim every inch of her body before I set her free again.

We sit in heavy silence as Phillip drives us home, and what feels like a lifetime later, he finally pulls up in front of my building. I open the door and Megan follows me out, the tension so thick between us, it's almost suffocating. I loosen my tie, and capture her hand to lead her up the front steps to the main door where Derek is standing guard.

"Good evening, Alec, Megan." He gives us a big toothy smile, and presses the button to the elevator. I clench down on my teeth when it takes too long to get here. We finally get on, and Derek inserts his key and takes us to the top floor. He doesn't make small talk like usual. I can only guess he feels the tension in the air.

We reach our destination, and we both hurry off, thanking Derek as I insert my key and drag her in with me. Finally alone, I push her against the door, and trap her body with mine.

"I've wanted my mouth here all night," I say, then press my lips to her, desperate to taste her. Her soft lips open, and she moans for me as I feed my starvation. Her hands slide around my body, and grip my ass. I chuckle slightly and push against her, rubbing my hard cock on her stomach. Our tongues tangle and her moans grow needy.

"You want my cock."

She nods, and I push my leg between hers to widen them and rub her hot pussy on my thigh. I slide my hand around her neck, undo the small button and unzip her dress. Not wanting to break contact, but wanting her naked, I step back. "Take it off," I say.

She wiggles her hips, a vicious little tease, and the dress slides down her body. I drink her in, devour her with my eyes as she stands before me in a matching bra and panties. "Turn around," I say. "Hand on the door."

She turns from me, and I close the distance, putting my hand on her ass to squeeze. I touch the tiny lace thong, and slide my hands around the front to dip into the lace. Her sex is sopping wet and a growl I have no control over comes out of me.

"I love that you're always ready for my cock," I say, and she breathes rapidly as she wiggles against my finger.

"Please, Alec," she begs. She pushes backward, and rubs that sweet ass of hers against me.

"I'm going to fuck you, Megan. I'm going to fuck you everywhere tonight," I say, and her body vibrates in anticipation. I slide my other hand around her body and up her breasts. "Tell me you want that."

"I want that," she says, as I tug her bra down and brush my thumb over her hard nipple.

"First I want you on my face. I want to eat you, while you rub that sweet pussy all over my mouth." She cries out my name, and I go to my knees to tug her panties down her legs. "The shoes stay on," I say. She lifts one leg and then the other and I tuck her panties into my pocket. I stand back up, and unhook her bra. "Face me."

I step back and she turns slowly. The heat in her eyes, glazed with lust, as her beautiful creamy flesh beckons my touch nearly has me coming in my pants. Her shaky hands reach for my suit jacket and she pushes it from my shoulders. It falls off and her fingers work the buttons on my shirt. I hiss when her fingers touch my flesh, burn through me. I unbutton my pants and kick them off. Her hand goes to my cock, and she rubs me through my boxers. "Fuck, yeah," I say, digging my fingers into the soft warm flesh of her ass. I pick her up, and her legs go around me as I carry her to the bedroom.

I set her on the bed. "Up on your knees." Her beautiful tits bounce as she positions herself, and I tug off my boxers and take my throbbing cock into my hand. Her gaze drops, and she wets her mouth. So sexy. "Touch yourself," I say.

She quivers and her small hand slides between her open thighs. When she runs her fingers over her hot pussy, her head rolls back, her little gasps and moans making me insane. I climb onto the bed with her, and flatten myself out. "Come here," I say. "Come ride my mouth."

She straddles me, and I grab her hips, position her right where I want to, right where I can worship her. I pull her down onto my face, and her sweet scent and flavor fill my senses and push me closer to the edge. She shamelessly grinds her sex on my face and I eat her, run my tongue over her clit and shove it inside her tightness.

"Oh, God, Alec," she says, and puts her hand on the headboard as she grinds harder, taking what she needs. That's a girl. She rolls her hips, a sexy move as she whimpers and chases her orgasm.

I pull her ass cheeks open, and slip a finger into her back passage. Over the last couple of weeks I've been preparing her, and tonight—the last time I'll ever have her in my bed—is the night I'm going to take her, everywhere.

She bounces on my mouth, her clit so hard and inflamed I take it between my teeth, roll my tongue over it, and she cries out as a hot gush of liquid heat dribbles into my mouth and over my chin, announcing her orgasm.

I growl and lap at her sweetness, tasting the depths of her as she rides out the waves. Panting and quivering, she needs time to come back down, but we're far from done here. I grip her hips and lift her from my mouth.

"Slide down," I say.

She shimmies down, and I position her so she's

on her knees, straddling my hips, her hot sex wide-open for me. So pretty. I slowly lower her onto my hard dick, and her hot tight walls hug me. Perfect. So damn perfect. I stretch her hot slick flesh with my girth and she wiggles, trying to force more of me inside, but I hold her hips and control the depth, even though I'm near delirious with need.

"Alec," she murmurs.

"You want it all?"

"Yes," she cries out.

"Don't worry, baby, I'm going to give you everything."

Her eyes flash to mine, and my heart thuds when I see the need reflected there. I pull her down a little more, sinking in a few more inches, and as she opens wider for me, I wish to God I could give her everything. But I can't. I just fucking can't.

Her body shakes all over and she gets hotter and wetter as I fill her. My balls ache and I power up, giving her every last inch of me, and she moans as I stretch her walls. She lifts up, sinks back down again, and as her pretty pussy devours my cock, the world around me melts away.

"Ride me, Megs. Work your sweet pussy over my cock. I want you to come again. I want you to drip all over me." Her movements become fast, more frenzied, and I inch up to take her bouncing breasts in my hands. She lifts up, sinks down and rubs her clit on my pelvis, and her entire body tightens around my cock. Jesus, it's the hottest thing I've ever seen.

I close my eyes, struggle to hang on as her release coats me and drips to my balls.

"Yeah, baby," I say.

The second she stops spasming, I sit up and lift her from my cock. Her face is flushed as I reposition her on the bed, until that sweet ass is in the air. Her body tightens, and I run my hand along her back to reassure her.

"Hey, Megs. Do you want this?" I ask.

"Yes," she cries out.

"I won't hurt you. I promise."

"I know. I just… I've never done this before."

I run my fingers over her spine, then gently slide them between her creamy ass cheeks. "I know." Christ, the fact that she trusts me with her body like this. It's an honor. "I can make it good for you," I assure her.

"I like the sensations when you put your finger in me," she says, and I love how open and honest we're being with each other.

"If at any time you don't like it, I'll stop."

"I want this, Alec," she says quickly, a new sort of desperation in her voice. "I want you to do this."

My pulse leaps. I get the sense that she needs to have me everywhere as much as I need to be everywhere. I lean over her, drop a soft, tender kiss on her cheek and slip a pillow under her hips. "So pretty," I say, and sweep my fingers over her flesh until goose bumps form.

I grab a bottle of lube from my nightstand, having bought it specifically for this occasion. I squirt a generous amount into my palm and rub it until it's warm. I touch her cheeks, widen them and put my finger inside her. She begins to writhe and I move it in and out, desperate to mark this beautiful woman everywhere. "Feel good?" I ask.

"It feels different, but nice. I like it." Her body relaxes, opens.

"Look at you," I say. "All warm and ready for me." I add another finger, and her breath rushes. I'm so goddamn hard just from touching her my balls are ready to explode. I spend a long time preparing her, then pour lubricant on my throbbing dick. I fall over her body, position my cock at her tight entrance and put my mouth near her ear. "Baby, you ready for me?" I ask.

She pushes back, and my cock breaches her opening. "Yes," she cries out. I glance down, revel in the way her beautiful body is taking me.

I go painstakingly slow, giving her time to adjust to each inch, until I'm finally balls deep inside her, my eyes practically roll back in my head. She sucks in a breath and my cock aches with the need to release, but I won't, not until I make her come for me one more time.

She moves against the pillow, rubbing her hot pussy over the cotton, but I slide a hand between her legs, and take control of her stiff clit. I press against her slick cleft, and apply pressure as I work my cock in and out of her ass. She rocks against me, and when she cries out and starts coming all over my hand, I nearly lose my mind. I pump deep, once, twice and on the third time, I spurt my cum high inside her, giving her everything I can give her.

"I feel you," she cries out.

I fall over her, press kisses to her back, and she softens beneath me, all warm and sated and sweet. We stay like that until I grow flaccid, and her breathing changes, slows.

"Don't move," I whisper, and dart to the bathroom. I come back with a warm cloth to clean her. "Roll over," I say quietly, and she's like a rag doll as she slowly goes to her back. I inch her legs open and wipe her with the warm cloth. She moans in contentment and I crawl back in beside her, pull her close. Her soft brown eyes close slowly, sleep pulling her under. I tuck her against me, and cover us up, as my mind goes back to what her uncle said about falling in bed together every night, and more importantly waking up together each morning. Yeah, I want that. I want it with Megan. Is there a chance I could be a better man for her? That I could find happiness, like my cousin Tate has.

Can I take that chance?

Can I not?

CHAPTER ELEVEN

Megan

IT'S NOT LIKE me to sneak out in the middle of the night—after the most intimate sex of my life—but that's exactly what I did after Alec fell asleep in his bed beside me. No way could I be there come morning, have him tell me to my face that our time together was over. I knew what I was getting into before I even went to his place.

Let me put my cock in you. One last time.

Before he committed to Sara, which we both knew he was going to, he wanted to have a little fun in the sack with me, a girl he wasn't worried about losing his heart to. Now that he's found a wife in name only—he made the decision Sunday morning, hours after I'd left his bed—I need to pull myself together. It's been two weeks since I fled, two weeks where he and Sara have been photographed together numerous times, even at the annual golf tournament, and I need to get my head back in the game and start thinking about their wedding plans, because any day now, they're going to announce them.

Amanda sticks her head into my office. "Lunch?"

Ignoring the storm stirring up my stomach, I give her my best smile, but she can see right through me, see the pain beneath the surface. Why oh why did I go and fall for him again?

Again?

Who am I kidding? I never stopped loving him.

"Actually, I had a late breakfast, so I'm going to pass," I say. I honestly haven't had much of an appetite lately.

She eyes me for a moment. "Hey, are you okay?" she asks, folding her arms as she leans against the door frame.

"Perfectly fine," I say, and lift my chin an inch, to prove I have it all together.

"Megan," she begins. "If you love him you need to tell him."

"I don't love him." I sigh and lean back in my chair. "Even if I did, I couldn't just tell him. It's a little more complicated than that," I say.

"What I don't understand is all the sex you two were having. He must have deeper feelings."

I think about that for a minute, remember the feel of his lips on mine, the way he took such good care of my body. Would a man not feeling something deeper be so gentle, so tender, so eager to mark every inch of me?

"It's just sex, Amanda. Two people having fun

while they're passing the time. Even if I did love him, we have different goals in life," I say to remind myself. "And I'd never tell a guy I loved him when he's made it perfectly clear he doesn't believe in love or happily-ever-after. After so much loss, having my own family isn't just something I want, it's something my heart needs."

She frowns. "Okay, I'm here if you need to talk."

Just then my phone rings, and I'm grateful for the distraction, until I see who's calling. "Thanks, Amanda," I say, and slide my finger across the phone. "Sara, hi."

"We finally set a date," she says. "And it's soon."

I grab my pen, and note the way my stupid hand is shaking. "Okay, give me the details."

"It's going to be a very formal wedding at the country club in two weeks. It's the perfect spot."

Funny, Sara and I have different opinions on the perfect spot. I want my wedding to be casual, my groom dressed comfortably, and I'd prefer it to be at a beach or a lake, not some snobbish country club. But it's not my wedding, so I have no say.

"Two weeks," I say, not at all surprised they're moving quickly.

"No sense in wasting time."

I begin to tell her all the things that need to be done ASAP, like the menu, cake, dress, invites, photographer, flowers, etc., but Sara goes silent on the other end.

"What's the problem?" I ask.

"The problem is that I have to be away for work." Her voice sounds distant, like she's driving through a tunnel. "Will you be able to just plan these things without me? Oh, as far as bridal party goes, I'm going to ask my best friend to be my maid of honor, and that's it. No bridesmaids. I would have asked you but with you planning everything, there would be way too many complications."

"I totally understand," I say. No way could I stand for her while she marries the man I'm in love with. "So you asked Jessica?"

"Yes, and Alec is having Will as best man. All of New York's most important people will be there. This can only do good things for my career," she says, a hint of excitement in her voice.

I still can't quite believe the two are marrying for their careers. Doesn't anyone believe in love anymore? I pinch the bridge of my nose. "Are you telling me you don't care about the menu, or, or—?"

"Not really. This is your area of expertise, you know what to do better than I do."

"What about the guest list?"

"I'll email you mine, and you can work with Alec for his and all the other things you mentioned. The two of you can pull it together, I'm sure of it."

Work with Alec?

That's the last thing I want to do.

With a headache brewing, I shake my head no, even though she can't see me. "Sara, I don't know—"

"I'm going to be away for the next week. Maybe

more. I have a convention in Atlanta. The firm is sending me, and I have no choice."

"What about your dress?"

"Ah, can you just pick something for me? We're the same size."

My head begins to spin and I take a deep breath. "I can't pick out your wedding dress for you."

"Sure you can. We're the exact same size. If it looks good on you, it'll look good on me. I want to be a princess on my special day, so as long as it's a ball gown, I'll like it."

Years ago when I envisioned my wedding, I pictured myself in a ball gown. A real Cinderella. Now, however, I'd like something a little more streamlined.

"I... Is Alec okay with me planning everything?"

"I haven't had a chance to run it by him. Would you mind? I need to get packed and catch a flight."

"I don't think—"

"I just arrived home. I have to run."

My God, what kind of marriage are they going to have?

One in name only.

"Gotta go. Thanks, Megs, you're the best."

I sit there, dumbfounded as the line goes dead. She seriously wants me to pick a wedding dress for her. The menu and other things I can understand, but a dress? That's completely insane. I shake my head, and stare at my phone. How the heck is Alec going to feel about working closely with me. I haven't talked to him, or set eyes on him in weeks. I take a deep fortifying breath, and shoot him a text.

Megan: Sara has to be away for a convention, and she asked that I work on the wedding plans with you.

I stare at my phone, watch three dots appear and then disappear. He must be writing and deleting, unsure of what to say. His response finally comes in.

Alec: What do you suggest?

Megan: I'll need to meet with you to go over menu, guest list, etc. The sooner we get started the better. Do you want to come by my work, and we'll put together a menu to start things off?

Alec: Four o'clock okay?

Megan: See you then.

I must be out of my mind. With no time to waste, I pick the phone back up and start making calls, to set things in motion, and before I know it, the day is almost over.

I glance up when I hear footsteps in the hall— heavy steps that can only be Alec's. I smooth my hand over my hair after running stressed-out hands through it all day. I stand to greet him when he comes into view, his large frame eating up the doorway and completely overwhelming me. My mouth instantly goes dry. He does a quick sweep of my clothes, and in turn I look him over. Hair cut short, face clean-shaven, he looks handsome, composed...guarded.

Keep it together, Megan.

I give him a huge smile, and resist the urge to hurtle myself at him, and show him I'm the girl for him. But I won't. Because I'm not. It's over between us, and I need to remember that. "Have a seat," I say, and gesture to the chair across from me, thinking about the last time he was in this office with me, and the limo drive we took later that night.

Dressed in a suit that showcases his broad shoulders and fit body, he smooths his hand over his tie.

I sit, and I'm about to make small talk when he gives a curt nod. "You wanted to talk to me about a menu?" he says, getting right down to business.

All righty, then.

"As you know, Amanda will be catering, and thank you for that, by the way. She's thrilled."

"Her food is amazing. I've been getting deliveries to my door for the last week."

"She is amazing, and this is a once-in-a-lifetime opportunity for her."

"For you, too," he says, his blue eyes intense when they latch on to mine. "That's why you agreed to this, right? Because of what it could do for your career?"

"I... Yes," I say, but there is a part of me that's not one hundred percent sure of that. Maybe it was the thought of seeing Alec again, getting a glimpse of the young boy I once knew, and always loved, that had me agreeing. "Yes," I say again, not wanting him to think there were other reasons. He continues to stare at me, and I reach for the menu. What the hell is going on with him?

"Here is Amanda's menu. I'd suggest a beef, chicken and fish dish for the mains, and she does some lovely hors d'oeuvres to start the night." I glance up, but he's not looking at the menu, he's looking at me. The intensity in his eyes sucks the oxygen from my lungs, and nerves flutter in my belly. I wipe my suddenly wet palms on my skirt.

"I'm sure she does."

"Do you want to take a look?"

"No, I trust your judgment."

"Oh, okay," I say. "I won't let you down. This wedding will be talked about for years to come." He nods, and I wait for a response. When none comes, I say, "I hope your week isn't too busy. I've booked us for cake tasting, flower shopping—"

"Text me the times."

"What about tuxedos? I scheduled an appointment. Will you and your brother want my help with that? Oh, wait. Sara didn't tell me a color scheme. Her favorite color was always lavender, but I'll have to double-check that. You'll want your tie and cummerbund to match."

"You'll probably want to come to make sure we get the colors right. I know how you like to pick out my clothes."

Wait, was that a hint of humor? If it was, his face certainly isn't showing it.

"I have an appointment to look at dresses right afterward, so that shouldn't be a problem."

"Sounds like you have everything under control," he says.

"It's what I do." I stand and he stands with me. I walk around my desk to open the door, and his body brushes mine. Sparks arc between us, and I suck in a fast breath when he cups my elbow, a show of possession. I spin to face him. His head is dipped, eyes glossy, like he's a million miles away as his gaze fixates on my mouth.

"Alec," I say, my voice a breathless whisper.

"Yeah," he murmurs.

My entire body responds to the need in his voice. But we can't do this. He's engaged now. "I'll text you that schedule," I say in my best professional voice, and his head snaps up, like he's just been slapped.

"Right." He lets go of my arm and walks into the hall. I'm seconds from collapsing in a mess of hot tears and need when he turns back around.

"Megs," he says softly.

"Yes."

He opens his mouth, hesitates and scrubs his hand over his face. "I'll be waiting on that schedule."

CHAPTER TWELVE

Alec

FOR THE LAST WEEK, I've been everywhere with Megan, and so help me fucking God, it's been torture. Torturous not to kiss her at whim, not to pull her into my arms, carry her to my bed. I'll be glad when this wedding is done and over with and I won't have to spend every second with her. But will that stop me from spending every second thinking about her, fantasizing about her being in my arms, between my sheets.

Probably not.

Christ, I should have kept my mouth and hands to myself. Never should have given in to weakness. The last time she was in my bed, I was beginning to believe there could be more between us, but when I woke up and she was gone, it was the slap in the face I needed. I can't be the man she needs.

As I stand in the dressing room trying on my tux, my brother, Will, in the room beside me, and

Megan standing outside waiting, I think back over the week. Megan managed to get the invitation out in record time, considering the sizable crowd we're having. Since I cared little about the details, we picked peonies for the flowers, and vanilla for the cake, a popular crowd-pleaser and both Sara's favorites. I consider that a moment longer. I'm sure if it were Megs's wedding she'd pick daisies for the flowers and lemon for the cake.

I tug on my jacket, and glance at myself in the mirror. I'm not in love with the lavender color, but in the end does it really matter?

"Almost done?" Megan asks.

I open the door and her eyes go wide as she takes me in. "You look amazing," she says under her breath. Just then my cell pings, and I grab it from my pants on the chair.

"It's Sara," I say, and frown at the phone. "Shit."

"What?" she asks.

"She's stuck in Atlanta for the next couple days."

Will comes from his dressing room and smooths a hand over his lapels, breaking the moment.

"I'm not so sure about this color," he says scrunching up his face.

"Not your choice, bro," I say, with a slap to his back.

"Are you whipped already, Alec?" he teases. "Light purple. Couldn't we have at least picked something a little more manly?"

"Like soft blue," Megan says, and I take in the soft

blue dress she's wearing. I'm guessing that would be her color of choice.

"That would work," Will says, and gives himself a once-over in the mirror. "You owe me for this, bro."

I laugh. "When you get married, I'll wear pink."

Will's face drops, and he grumbles under his breath, something that sounds like "never going to happen," when the clerk steps up to us.

He pulls out a measuring tape and gets to work on sizing us up. Once we're both back in our regular suits, I step from the change room and find Megan on her phone. She glances up at me and smiles. "I guess you don't need me anymore."

Oh, how wrong she is.

She gestures with a nod. "I have to head next door to do a dress fitting."

"You're picking out Sara's dress?"

"Crazy as it sounds, I am. All designers want to be worn by your bride, so they're bending over backward for me."

Bending over backward.

Kill me now.

I check my watch. "I can come help, if you want."

"I'm sure you must have more important things to do on a Friday night."

"This is the highlight reel," I say, and she laughs.

"What about Will?" she asks, pointing a finger back and forth between the two of us as Will checks his phone. "You two must want to hang out."

She's giving me an out, and if I knew what was

good for me, I'd take it. I'm about to agree because any more time with her is going to do me in.

"Can't," Will pipes in. "I'm off to St. Thomas."

Megan frowns. "You have work in the US Virgin Islands?"

"A little work, but I plan to take some much-needed rest and relaxation before Alec's wedding," Will says.

"Why not go to St. Moritz?" Megan asks, and I note the way her gaze darts to mine at the mention of the ski resort. Have her thoughts gone back to the night she came to my room? "Your grandfather owns half the place."

"All the more reason for me to go to St. Thomas, where I have my own private villa," Will says.

"He likes his privacy," I say, and Megan nods.

"Okay, well, if you have nothing better to do, then come help me pick out a dress," she says to me. I shouldn't go. I should just go home and down a few brandies and forget all about Megan, but I'm clearly some kind of masochist, because I nod and follow her out of the store. We go to the bridal boutique one shop down and I open the door for her. Her body brushes mine and I bite back a moan of want as she slips inside.

We head to the back of the store where there's a dais and a series of mirrors. Megan introduces us to Maria, who will help her try on gowns, and I pick up a magazine and flip through it blindly when she's led into the change room. A few minutes later Megan comes out looking elegant in a big ball gown. While it's nice, and it fits her beautifully, it's not something I can see her wearing on her wedding day. Then again, it's not her who's going to be wearing it and walking toward me as I wait at the altar.

She steps up onto the podium and examines herself in front of the mirrors. I lean forward, brace my elbows on my knees. She's frowning when she turns to me.

"What do you think?"

"You look beautiful," I say. She smooths her hand over the big skirt, and the bling on her waist glitters. "Although the bling isn't you," I say.

"I know, but I think Sara would love it." I sit back and nod. "Wait, let's take a picture," I say, "and I'll send it to her." I pull my phone out, snap a picture and send it to Sara. As we wait to hear, Maria suggests we try on another.

Megan continues to try on different styles and send pictures to her cousin. But still no response from Sara. After the tenth dress, Megan comes from the change room and I nearly bite off my damn tongue.

"Holy shit," I say, as she walks to the podium in a strapless, body shaping gown that showcases her beautiful curves and creamy skin. I stand before I even realize what I'm doing and walk up to her.

"This one," I say. "This is the dress." I run my hand along the exposed skin on her back and when a shiver moves through her, Maria makes an excuse and rushes off.

Megan turns to me, a flush on her cheeks, her eyes wide as I touch her. "When we were kids you talked about a ball gown princess dress—"

"You remember that?" she asks, cutting me off.

"Yeah. But I have to tell you, Megs. This is the one. It's stunning. I've never… What made you try this on?"

"I just… It was a mistake." She lets her words fall off, turns from me fast, averting my gaze, but there is a hitch in her voice when she says, "I need to get out of this." She nearly falls as she steps down from the podium. I hurry to her, catch her in my arms, and when I do, everything I feel for her comes racing to the surface. I dip my head and at the same time she swipes her tongue over her lips like she's preparing her sweet mouth for me.

"Megs," I whisper, just as my damn phone pings.

Megan pushes away from my arms. "That's probably Sara," she says, her voice rough and breathless.

I glance at my phone. "She said to pick whichever one you like best. She has no preference."

"Oh, okay," she says, then disappears into the changing room. I sit back down and restlessly flip through the magazine, every nerve in my body agitated and on fire. When she finally comes out, her face is pale and she looks like she's just seen a ghost.

I jump from my chair, close the distance between us. "What is it?" I glance at the phone in her hand.

She's gripping the thing so hard her knuckles are turning white. "Are you okay?" She blinks once, then twice, then shoves her phone into her purse so I can't see what has her so rattled. "Megs?" I ask again.

"Everything is…fine," she says, but I know her well enough to know she's lying.

CHAPTER THIRTEEN

Megan

I'VE HAD A KNOT in my stomach since I received that text from Sara at the bridal boutique.

Sara: Met the hottest guy at the convention. He's a god in bed. Won't be home for a couple more days. Hope the planning is going well. You look amazing in all those dresses.

I didn't respond. Didn't know how. Jesus, she's engaged to Alec and having hot sex with a guy at her convention. Something tells me the convention was long over, and she was hanging back just to have a little bedroom fun. How the hell could she do this to Alec? Okay, yes, I get it. Alec and I have been having sex like bunnies, but the key words here are *have been*. We stopped the second he got engaged to Sara. Alec might be a lot of things. A LOT of things. But he's no cheater. He once told me he wasn't a nice guy. Fine. Maybe he does deals at work that destroy businesses and livelihoods, but when it comes right down to it, I know in my heart he's monogamous.

"What are you going to do?" Amanda asks from the chair facing my desk as she sips her latte. I reach for mine, grateful that I have a friend who knows when I need my favorite drink.

"I don't know what to do," I say. I'm an honest girl. At least I try to be. I only fib when I have to, when I know it's for my best and someone else's. When was the last time I fibbed? Oh, when I thought I could have sex with Alec and not feel anything more.

My lips tingle with the memory of him, and the intimate way he always claimed my mouth.

Stop thinking about him already.

I push from my chair. "I can't tell him."

"If it's a marriage in name only, will he even care?"

"I don't know. I mean eventually they'll have sex, right?" Unease worms its way through my veins. "I'm sure they're already having sex, actually."

"It's not too late, you know."

Pacing in my office, I spin to face my friend, who is staring at me with those astute brown eyes. "If you're suggesting I tell him how I feel, yes it's too late. He's getting married in less than a week, Amanda. Everything is set. I'm not about to jump in now and ruin this. Think about what this wedding will do for your business."

"If you're worried about me, don't. Some things are more important than fame and the bottom line."

I take a big breath and let it out slowly, wishing I'd gone to yoga this morning.

The bell over the front door jingles, and I plop back down into my chair as Amanda excuses herself and darts to the front. I put my head on my desk, but perk up when a familiar voice reaches my ears. Amanda pokes her head in, her eyes wide.

"Someone here to see you," she says.

I stand when James comes in, his cane banging on the floor.

"James, what are you doing here?"

"Now what kind of greeting is that, child?"

"Sorry. It's nice to see you. Please have a seat. Can I get you a coffee, tea?"

"Any brandy?" he asks and I grin.

"No sorry."

He waves a dismissive hand. "No matter."

"What can I do for you?"

"Just checking in to see how plans are going? Haven't seen Sara in some time now." His eyes narrow and I almost squirm under his scrutiny. It's like the man can see through me, see how I feel about his grandson.

I nibble my lip, and hate to lie to the man but say, "She got tied up at a conference in Atlanta."

"Tied up, huh?" he says, like he's privy to something I'm not.

"Can I ask you something?" I say, calling on all my bravado.

"Yes, but it doesn't mean I'm going to answer," he says, and I laugh.

"You sound like Alec."

"That boy means the world to me."

"I know he does and he'd do anything for you, James."

"He's one of the good ones."

That gives me pause. If he thinks he's one of the good ones, why did he tell Alec his image was hurting the family? Why is he pushing him to marry to clean up his act?

"How so?" I ask.

"Did he ever tell you about his grandmother?"

"When we were younger, he mentioned her. She was gone when I came into the picture."

"I'm not sure what it was, but out of all the grandchildren, they had a special bond. Oh, don't get me wrong, he treated all the grandkids the same, but she said there was a different light inside Alec." He pauses and smiles as if recalling and relishing an old memory. "They spent a lot of time in the garden. Did he ever tell you he has a green thumb?"

"No," I say, and smile at that. I couldn't keep a plant alive to save my soul. But then I remember the one plant at his place. I thought it seemed out of place, surrounded by his cool gray decor.

"Oh, yes, he spent a lot of time with his grandmother in the garden. He took it the hardest when she died."

"How…" I shut my mouth, not wanting to dredge up sad memories, but James's eyes flicker.

"Ovarian cancer," he says, frowning. "Damn cancer. That's why he set up a trust fund."

"Trust fund?"

"He didn't tell you."

"No."

"He finances a dozen deserving medical school students each year. Pays the entire shot. He's determined to find a cure. He's quite the philanthropist, that one."

If I wasn't seated, my knees would have given out on me. "He does?" My mind races, back to when he told me he wasn't a nice guy. Why would he do that? "Why wouldn't he tell me about this?"

"He's secretive. Very private. All my grandkids are. Not much wonder with the paparazzi in their faces all the time." James laughs, but it holds no humor. "The loss of his grandmother hit him hard, though and if the media found out about the charities, they'd dig deeper. His grandmother guarded her private life, and Alec goes to great length to ensure it remains protected, even after all these years."

"What do you mean?"

"Damn media will start asking questions on why he finances students, and he doesn't want any of his grandmother's business made public." A warm smile touches his mouth. "Deep down that boy is soft."

"He is?" I ask, even though I know it's true.

"Every time Blackstone puts someone out of work, he secretly makes sure he finds a position for them." He puts his finger to his lips. "That's a secret, too, though."

As my heart pounds behind my eyes, I try to make sense of this. Alec is a good guy, and his granddad knows it. Then why did Alec tell me otherwise, and why did James specifically ask me to find his grandson a wife and get him settled because his lifestyle looked bad on the family, dragged down the Carson name?

"James?"

"Yes, child?"

"Why me? Why did it have to be *me* to find Alec a wife and then plan his wedding?"

"How else was I going to get you two lovebirds together?"

CHAPTER FOURTEEN

Megan

I'VE BEEN WALKING around in a daze for the last few days, pulling together the last-minute details for tomorrow's wedding as I try to process what James told me. Lovebirds? Alec and *me*? He can't be right. If he is, then why is Alec marrying Sara?

Restless and on edge, I walk to my window, peer out at the street below, then go back to my sofa. Even though everything is set and I'm about to pull off a grand wedding that will make everyone stand up and take notice, I grab my journal and go through tomorrow's arrangements one more time, until a knock sounds on my door. My heart jumps into my throat, desperately wanting it to be Alec. For the last week I've wanted to talk to him, tell him what James said to me, but I couldn't bring myself to do it. The man rejected me once, all those years ago, and I'm pretty sure I can't go through that kind of humiliation again.

Stop being a chickenshit.

I shut down that inner voice, stand quickly and take a couple deep breaths. I don't want to appear too anxious or needy.

I pad softly to my door, pull it open and frown when I find Amanda standing there. "Oh, hi."

She huffs. "Nice to see you, too."

"I'm sorry." I widen the door to welcome her. "Come in. I am happy to see you."

"Are you expecting someone else?"

"No."

She lifts a bottle of wine. "Then maybe you'll want to drink this with me tonight."

I grin, even though I don't feel like smiling. "You know me too well."

I shut the door, set the lock and follow my best friend into the kitchen. She roots through my drawers, pulls out a corkscrew and opens my favorite wine, but when she does, my thoughts go back to Alec, and when he had my favorite brand of vino in the limo. God, that limo drive. Not only was the sex amazing, but when he took me to the duck pond, it touched my heart on a whole new level. The man knows me well, that's for sure.

But what I don't understand is why he told me he wasn't a good guy. Did he not want me to like him?

I reach for the stemware, and Amanda adds a splash of wine to each glass. We walk back to the living room and she moves wedding magazines and papers to sit in the comfy buttery-yellow chair across from me, then tucks her feet underneath her. I do the same. Once comfortable, Amanda takes a sip of wine and rubs the line on her forehead. I brace myself.

"What?" I ask.

"I spent the last week trying to wrap my brain around your relationship with Alec."

My stomach cramps, and I set my wine down, ready to straighten out my friend on where Alec and I stand. "Amanda—" I begin, but she cuts me off.

"No, really stop, Megan. Think about it. None of the women he dated were suitable. He couldn't commit. Maybe he was holding out for you. I mean he did ditch that one girl and take you on that dirty limo ride."

"Amanda—" I try again but she stops me.

"Maybe he's in love with you, but is afraid to commit for some reason. Something is holding him back, I feel that in my gut and my gut never lies. Maybe he settled because he was desperate with the golf tournament coming up. Maybe he had no choice. I've seen him and Sara together, Megs. There is zero chemistry, whereas you two damn nearly vibrate when you're near each other. The sparks. Insane." She puts her hands by her head and makes an explosion sound.

I pause for a moment, look past her shoulder and consider the heat between us. My entire body warms when I reminisce about the way he touched me, in and out of the bedroom. The stolen kisses, the way he couldn't seem to keep his hands or his eyes off me whenever we were together. His touch was so achingly tender and at times possessive. The last time we were in bed it was like he needed to mark every inch of me. I quiver just thinking about it.

Could Alec feel the same way about me as I do about him? Is something holding him back? If so, what? I let out a frustrated growl and I drop my head back on the sofa.

"Maybe I'm just clinging to something that isn't there. You of all people know I have a hard time letting go. Maybe I was good enough to have sex with, but not to marry. Maybe I don't fit the criteria of what he needs in a wife."

"Maybe you need to talk to him to find out." She sips her wine and swirls it in her glass. "Did you ever tell him you wanted more?"

"No, actually I told him I didn't want more from him."

"Maybe he's working with that information."

My heart beats a little faster in my chest. Is there really a chance that Alec and I can be together? Is something holding him back, some deeper fear?

"He's getting married to Sara tomorrow," I announce, my hope dwindling.

Amanda sets her glass down, and meets my gaze unflinchingly. "I want you to answer me seriously, Megan. Do you love him?"

Oh, God, I do. I love him so much. He's the best guy I know.

"Yes," I answer honestly, and Amanda stands.

"Get your purse," she says, pulling her phone from her back pocket.

"What?"

"Get your purse. I'm getting you an Uber. You and Alec need to talk."

"Amanda—"

"Stop overthinking this, girlfriend. Car's on its way. Move it."

I climb from the sofa and stand on shaky legs. The truth is I do love Alec, and before he goes through with this sham of a wedding tomorrow, I have to talk to him, tell him how I feel. Otherwise I'll spend the rest of my life regretting it and wondering what if…

"Okay," I say, my voice as shaky as my legs. I grab my purse, and feel equal measure of excitement and fear as Amanda walks me out the door, down the stairs and to the front of the building. As I stand there, I start to get cold feet. "Maybe this isn't a good—"

"Overthinking again," she says, and holds her hand up to stop me. "You have to know, Megan. You can't spend the rest of your life wondering what if."

"You're right. I can't."

An inky black car pulls up, and I slide into the backseat. "Text me," Amanda says. "I've got a good feeling about this."

I give the driver directions, and fold nervous hands on my lap. *Breathe, Megan, just breathe.*

I stare out the window and try to calm myself, a difficult task considering what I'm about to do. Will he be happy, mad? What about Sara? She's looking forward to being on Alec's arm. Can I do this to her? But Sara loves and cares about me. Surely if she knew how I felt, she'd want me to be with him. A short while later we pull up in front of his building, and I get out. My heart is in my throat as I walk up the stairs, forcing one foot in front of the other. Derek greets me at the door, but this time he doesn't offer me a toothy grin. No, this time he looks a bit confused.

"Megan, I wasn't expecting you tonight," he says, as he opens the glass door for me.

"Some last-minute wedding things I need to discuss with the groom," I say.

"Very well." He walks me to the elevator, inserts his key and I force myself to make small talk on the way up. I stammer a bit, and trip over my words. Is it any wonder? My damn brain is racing a million miles an hour.

"Thanks," I say when I step off. The elevator doors ping shut, and I stand in the hall and take a minute to pull myself together before I knock. I wait, but the door doesn't open. Has the groom gone to bed already so he'll be refreshed for the big day? I knock again, a bit louder this time, and slip my hand into my pocket to grab the key he gave me. Should I? I wait a few more minutes and when he doesn't answer, I decide to let myself in.

I open the door, and peer into the dark. "Alec," I call out quietly. If he's asleep, should I wake him? I tiptoe down the hall, and when I hear noises coming from his bedroom, I hurry my steps, but when I peer through the crack in his door, and find Sara in his arms, my vision goes fuzzy around the edges and I falter backward.

I lean against the wall, brace my hands on my knees and mentally berate myself. Why, oh why did I come here? Alec isn't in love with me. He currently has his arms wrapped around my cousin—his fiancée—like he's anxious to get an early start on their honeymoon.

Tears fall, and I swipe at them, hate them. Hate myself for believing there could be more between us. Amanda was wrong. James was wrong. Everyone was wrong, including me, and I never should have spent one minute thinking Alec could want me. I struggle to pull myself together, and when I finally get my legs working again, I retrace my steps, go out into the hall and lock up behind myself. I press the button for the elevator and pull my hair forward, not wanting Derek to see my red eyes. Grabbing my phone, I shoot Amanda a text.

Megan: Still have that bottle of wine.

Amanda: Oh no. Are you okay?

Megan: Not even a little.

Amanda: I'm so sorry Megs. I thought…

Megan: Not your fault.

I shove my phone back into my pocket when the elevator arrives, and I force myself to smile when the doors slide open.

"That didn't take too long," Derek says.

I clear my throat and hope to pull off casual. "Nope, all is good."

As if sensing my dark, shaky mood, Derek goes quiet and when we reach the lobby, I wave good-night and rush outside to draw a breath. I call for an Uber and by the time I reach my apartment, I've pretty much cried myself out. I slide from the vehicle and find Amanda waiting for me.

"Hey," I say, and when she pulls me in for a hug, more tears fall.

"Come on. I have wine, and ice cream."

I let her guide me to my apartment, where we—and when I say "we," I mean *me*—finish the bottle of wine, and eat the ice cream. The next thing I know, I'm waking up with a killer headache, the sun shining in through my open curtains. Beside me, Amanda is asleep, and my heart misses a beat, thankful that she stayed to take care of me.

I glance at the clock and jolt upright. "Damn," I say, and give my head a minute to settle. With so many last-minute things to pull together before the ceremony this afternoon, I shake Amanda.

She groans, and I say, "We need to get moving."

Her lids flutter open. "Right," she says. "I'm moving."

"I need to shower," I say.

"Me, too." She sits up and rubs her eyes. "You okay?"

"Fine," I lie, wanting to busy my mind with the ceremony.

"You want to ride to the country club in the van with me? I'll make Jeremy sit in the back with the food and you can ride up front with me."

"No, I need to go earlier. I'll Uber and meet you there." I turn from her, unable to face the worry in her eyes as she looks at me.

I make my way to the shower to clean myself up, and once I'm washed and dried, I slide into a dress—presenting professional event planner—and glance at myself in the mirror. Ugh. With dark circles under my eyes, I look like a raccoon with a bad case of food poisoning. I stick my tongue out, groan some more and reach for my toothbrush. Feeling a little more human, I grab my purse, and make my way to the country club to ensure all the details are perfect for the wedding of the century.

I busy myself, checking on the photographer, flowers, table settings, minister and everything else. It's the only way I can get the image of Alec with his arms wrapped around Sara out of my mind. Soon enough the guests begin to arrive, and I hide in the back and help Amanda in the kitchen. Even though I'm probably more of a nuisance than an assistant.

She's got this catering thing down to a science and everything is warming in chafing dishes.

"Stop worrying about me," I say to Amanda, when I catch her watching me from the corner of her eye.

"Okay, okay," she says, and turns her attention to plating the hors d'oeuvres. I check my watch and leave the kitchen when I spot Sara, her maid of honor, Jessica, and Aunt Jeannie and Uncle Dave pull up in a limo. I swallow down the knot in my throat as she waves to me and I put on my best happy face.

Looking gorgeous and radiant in her ball gown, the one I picked for her, she comes toward me. "We need to get you inside," I say. "We can't let the groom see you." A groom I've been avoiding all day. I know he's here, I feel his presence, can almost smell his hypnotizing scent. I usher Sara and Jessica inside the country club, while her mom and dad head off to mingle before the ceremony begins in less than fifteen minutes.

"We need to talk," Sara says to me, the serious-ness in her tone sending sparks of worry down my spine. "Jessica, do you mind. I need to talk to Megan alone."

"No problem," Jessica says, and steps away, her pretty lavender dress swishing as she turns.

Sara puts her hands on my shoulders. "I can't go through with this," she says. "In fact, I never ever planned to go through with it. I didn't even think things would go this far."

I shake my head, incredulous. "What are you talking about? You're here, you're dressed." I wave my hand toward the window. "Alec is outside waiting for you."

"You don't understand," she says, shaking her head, almost panicked. "I never wanted to marry him."

I pinch the bridge of my nose as the room spins around me. "What are you talking about?"

"I don't need to be married to make partner. I made that up."

"Sara, you're losing me."

"This you'll understand. He's in love with someone else. He always has been."

"Sara—"

"Why do you think I had you go dress shopping for me? Why do you think I went away for so long, or texted you to tell you I was sleeping with someone else? I wanted to wake you the hell up, so you'd see what that man means to you and vice versa. I thought spending time together would do it, but you're both so stubborn and dense."

I back up, stumble a bit and grab the nearest chair. "You set all that up on purpose."

"Of course. I wanted you two together. Heck, everyone knows you two belong together."

"Sara," I say. "I saw you two last night. I saw you in his arms. I went to Alec's apartment to talk to him and I saw you two together in his bedroom."

Her head jerks back, her eyes wide in surprise,

then she laughs. "I seduced him last night." My stomach knots, and I place my hand over it, fearing I'm going to be sick. "I did it to prove a point."

I shake my head, unable to wrap my brain around all the things she's saying to me. "He pushed me away, Megan. He rejected me because he's in love with you. I kissed him on purpose, to show him we have nothing together. I jumped in and said I'd be his wife, because I didn't want him marrying some schoolteacher or librarian or anyone but you. He loves you, Megan, and you need to be the one walking down that aisle." She reaches behind her head and begins to unbutton her dress.

"What are you doing?" I ask.

"Changing clothes with you."

"You can't be serious."

"Of course, I am. Now go out there, and show that man you love him. Isn't that how it's done in those romance movies you watch?"

"It's called the grand gesture, and for the record, I knew he loved her," Amanda says from behind me.

I spin to face her, catch her grin. God this is all happening too fast, I don't even have time to think it through. Amanda comes up and starts unbuttoning my dress, and the next thing I know, before I can even catch my breath, or get a word out, I'm being zipped up in Sara's wedding dress.

"This is insane," I say. "I can't do this. He's expecting you."

"And he'll be thrilled when he lifts this veil and finds you behind it," Sara says.

My heart beats like I've just had a triple shot of espresso. Could Sara be right? Does Alec love me? "He said he didn't believe in love or even want a family. Those are all the things I want."

"He wants it, he just doesn't know it," Sara explains. "You're going to show him he does. Now stop overthinking this."

I'm in a complete daze as my best friend and cousin practically drag me outside. I stand there looking at Alec through my veil as I try to catch my breath. Looking amazing in his tux, his brother, Will, beside him, he's rocking back and forth on his heels, the guests sitting in lavender colored chairs all stand when the wedding march begins. It's a beautiful wedding, a wedding of the century, and what's about to happen next will either make or break my business. But I can't think about that right now. I'm about to give Alec the shock of a lifetime.

Am I really going to do this?

Uncle Dave steps up to me. He grins, like he's in on all this, too. Has everyone been matchmaking? Sara shoves me from behind, to set me into motion, and I can barely make my legs move as I walk toward the man I love. From the corner of my eye I spot James, and he's grinning. He knows it's me!

Does Alec?

God, what will he do when my veil is lifted? I hesitate. I can't do this, it's insane. I'm about to bolt, but Uncle Dave holds my arm, to prevent me from fleeing. My heart pounds so hard, I can't think, can't hear, can't breathe.

When I finally reach Alec, I step up to him. His jaw is clenched tight, and the muscles are rippling. He reaches out, and I tense when he lifts my veil.

A gasp sounds in the crowd, and he goes perfectly still. Too still. His expression darkens, and deep blue eyes—angry eyes—narrow.

"Alec," I whisper.

"No," he says, and shakes his head as he backs away. "Not you, Megan. Never you."

CHAPTER FIFTEEN

Alec

"IF YOU'RE GOING to get married, you should at least marry the woman you love," Granddad says as he swirls his brandy in his glass and relaxes into his recliner.

I pace around his den, so goddamn mad I can barely see straight. "I can't believe you set this all up. Just to get Megan and me together."

"You've been in love with her since high school and I'm not the only one who knows you two belong together," he says. "Look at what Sara did." He chuckles, but I find no humor in the situation.

I close my eyes, and my heart aches when the vision of Megan dressed in that wedding gown fills the darkness. The horrified look on her face, one I put there, rips a hole in my gut. It's been three days since she bolted from the country club, and I holed myself up in my penthouse until Granddad insisted on seeing me. Megan is the last person in the world I ever meant to hurt, which is why I can't marry her.

"You don't understand," I say through gritted teeth.

Granddad pushes from his chair, saunters across the room and refills his brandy. He pours a splash into another glass and hands it to me. "Then make me understand," he says.

I swirl the brandy, swallow it in one gulp and welcome the burn as it goes down my throat. I set the glass down, run my hand through my hair and walk to the window to glance out.

"I love her, Granddad," I finally admit out loud.

"I know."

"And that's exactly why I can't be with her," I say quietly.

"Now that makes no sense."

I spin, frustrated with this whole situation. "The Carson men have a hard time with commitment, you of all people know that. Even Mom warned me to stay away from her. If my own mother doesn't believe in me, how can I possibly believe in myself."

"Ah, I see," he says, and nods his head, like he just solved all the problems in the world.

I smooth my hand over my tie and pace back to the sofa across from Granddad. I drop into it, and brace my elbows on my knees. "What do you see?"

"You don't think you have it in you to be loyal."

A noise crawls out of my throat. "Name a man in our family who's been loyal," I say. "Christ, Will was in love and even he couldn't stay loyal. We just don't have it in us and I can't—won't—hurt Megan like that. She deserves someone better."

"You're wrong you know."

"What am I wrong about?" Restless and edgy, I shake my foot.

"I was loyal, son. I was very loyal to your grandmother. She was my everything."

I sit up a little straighter. "You've been with a lot of women, Granddad."

"I grieved for your grandmother for many years, Alec. But I knew she didn't want me to spend the rest of my life alone. It was many, many years after she was gone that I started dating again."

"Yeah, I guess I never really thought about that."

"You have a lot of me in you, whether you believe that or not. So does Tate. Look how happy he and Summer are. They're in it for the long haul. You'll see."

"They do seem happy." A sound catches in my throat. "And Megan did say I remind her a lot of you. She said we have the same mannerisms."

Granddad leans forward. "You don't think you can be loyal?"

"Not really."

"Let me ask you this. Have you slept with Sara?" I groan. In no way do I want to talk about my sex life with my ninety-year-old grandfather. "Answer me, son."

"No, I didn't sleep with Sara. She tried to get me into bed, but I pushed her away."

His brows arch. "Even though she was your fiancée, you pushed her away."

"Yeah."

Cloudy blue eyes lock on mine. "Why do you think that is?"

I shake my head. "I just...it didn't feel right."

"Why didn't it feel right?" he asks, and I wish he'd stop pushing.

"Granddad—"

"Answer the question, Alec."

I briefly shut my eyes and take a deep breath. "Because I'm in love with Megan, and being with someone else felt wrong."

"And there you have it," he says, and leans back in his chair, a smirk on his face.

I mull that over for a moment. I couldn't sleep with Sara, not after I'd had Megan in my bed. In fact, I made the decision to have a celibate marriage, because it felt wrong...disloyal to Megan.

Holy shit.

"Granddad...what have I done?"

"Nothing you can't fix."

I shake my head. "You're so wrong about that. Megan must hate me. Did you see the tabloids, see what they're saying about her and her business? Jesus, no one will ever hire her again. She has every right to hate me."

"Yeah, you were quite the dense ass," he says.

I scoff. "Why don't you tell me what you really think?"

"All right I will." He waves his hand toward the door. "Get up off the sofa, get out there and go fight for the woman you love."

"How?"

"You're a smart man, most times," he says with a grin. "I'm sure you'll figure it out."

I jump from the sofa, my heart and mind racing a million miles an hour. I need to make this right. I need to show Megan what she means to me. As an idea forms, I glance at Granddad. "I'm going to need your help."

"I thought you might say that."

CHAPTER SIXTEEN

Megan

"I CAN'T BELIEVE I let you talk me into this," I say to Amanda and give a slow shake of my head.

"When someone offers you a free vacation, you don't turn it down," she counters.

I glance out the window, take in the beautiful mountains, with their snow-peaked caps. The last time I was here, in St. Moritz, it was after prom, when I seduced Alec. I never, ever thought I'd find myself back in the place that holds so many glorious, yet painful memories. But James called me a few days after I ruined Alec and Sara's farce wedding, offering me use of his private jet and his villa here in the Alps. I flat out refused. But Amanda begged and pleaded with me, which is a little uncharacteristic of her. In the end I caved. Her business went down with mine last week. This is the least I could do to make it up to her.

The cab driver whistles from the front seat, and

I fold my hands on my lap, my heart still raked raw from Alec's rejection. But I don't want to think about him. This vacation is about getting him out of my mind and heart once and for all.

"I did a bit of research on this place," Amanda says. "Before we go to the villa can we go to Lej da Staz?" She blinks hopeful eyes at me.

I shrug. "Fine by me." I remember that lake. It has a long boardwalk out over the water, with the mountains as the backdrop. It's a beautiful spot. A perfect wedding venue, one I would have picked over a country club. But now, well, now I no longer believe in true love and happily-ever-after. I might as well start collecting cats.

Amanda leans forward and talks to the driver as I check my phone. No messages, no brides calling to book their future weddings. And why would they? They probably think I'm going to try to steal their grooms. I groan low in my throat and rest my head against the back of the seat.

A short while later the cab stops, and I'm grateful. After the long flight, I need to stretch my legs. I'm about to get out of the backseat, but out on the boardwalk there appears to be a wedding. My heart climbs into my throat and tears threaten as painful memories from last week bombard me.

"We should go," I say to Amanda. "Looks like a wedding and I don't want to disturb them."

"Let's just stretch our legs. We'll be quiet." She

opens her door and jumps from the cab. Unsure about this, I quietly open mine and slide out.

I shade the sun from my eyes and kick out my cramped legs. I glance around and see numerous tents set up. Under one, food is being laid out for the reception and it smells divine. In the distance I glance at the guests milling about, and note the soft blue colors and decorations.

"Come on, let's get a closer look."

"I think I've crashed enough weddings this week," I say, but Amanda, being a little pushy and persistent, grabs my arm and practically drags me along. As I get close, I slow my steps.

"Is that Uncle Dave?" I ask, my head rearing back in surprise. The sun is in my eyes, and I haven't slept for a week, so there is a good chance I'm hallucinating.

"You tell me," Amanda says, her voice a little amused.

I scan the crowd, and when I see my family and friends, my heart leaps. "What's going on?" I ask, but when I turn to Amanda, she's backing away. "What are you doing? Amanda, what the hell?"

"It's the grand gesture," she says. "The way it was meant to be."

I turn back to the wharf and when I see Alec coming toward me, dressed casually in a white shirt, beige pants and barefoot, tears sting my eyes. "Alec…" I choke out. "What's…going on?"

He steps up to me, takes my shaky hands into his.

"What's going on is that I was a complete idiot. But I plan to fix that."

"What…what are you doing?" I ask when he pulls a box from his pocket.

"Megan, I love you. I've always loved you."

Tears fall down my face. "You said never me, Alec. You looked me in the eye and said never me."

"Haven't we already established that I'm an idiot," he says. I nod, in agreement, and he laughs softly. "Megan, I've wanted you my whole life, but I never thought I could be loyal. The men in my family, well, you know all about them. I thought I was no different. Even my mother…" He swallows. "You're the woman I want."

"Alec," I say again, my brain trying to process.

"You were right when you said I was like my grandfather. He was loyal to Grandmother, and I am loyal to you. I know that because Sara seduced me and I couldn't touch her. Couldn't be disloyal to my love for you."

"You…love me?"

He laughs and goes down on his knees. "I love you, Megan. I want you to be my wife. Please say yes."

I look past his shoulders, take in all my family and friends, watching us. Amanda is nervously shifting from one foot to the other. I guess now I know why she was so adamant that we come here. "You did this? You set this up?" I choke out, returning my gaze to Alec.

"When we were teenagers, you described your perfect wedding to me. Do you remember that?"

"I do," I say. "I can't believe you remember, though."

"I remember everything, Megan. I remember every detail, right down to the casual way you wanted the groom to dress." He goes quiet for a moment, thoughtful, and I listen to his throat work as he swallows. "I remember the night you came to me in my room after prom. It was the best night of my life."

I nod. "Mine, too, until the morning."

"I'm sorry. I handled it badly."

"No, I understand now. You were trying to protect me." My heart swells as my throat tightens with all the things I feel for this man. All these years he was trying to protect me from himself, when all he wanted to do was love me.

He holds the ring out. "I will love you forever if you let me."

"I don't love you like you think," I say, and his face falls, sadness backlighting his gorgeous blue eyes.

"Megan—"

I press my fingers to his lips to quiet him. "You think women love you because of your power and wealth. I don't love you for that."

A relieved smile lights up his face. "So you do love me?"

"Of course I love you, you big dummy."

He laughs and tears fall down my face as he pulls the ring from the case, but I back up.

"Megan...what?" he asks.

"I wish I had my dream dress."

Once again relief moves into his eyes. "Sara," he calls out, and she comes forward with the strapless gown I tried on and fell in love with at the bridal boutique.

I give a big hiccupping sob. "Alec, I can't believe..."

"Marry me, Megan. Make me the happiest man on the planet."

"Yes," I say, and he slips the beautiful ring on my finger. A moment later he stands, and turns to the crowd.

"Whew," he says, wiping his brow. "It was touch and go there for a while but she said yes."

As everyone claps, he picks me up and spins me around. "I love you, Megs. I promise to be the best husband in the world."

"I love you, too," I say as he puts his mouth on mine for a deep, intimate kiss full of love and promises.

"Okay, let's get this show on the road," I say, as he laughs and pulls me to him, renewing my belief in true love and happily-ever-after.

* * * * *

COMING SOON!

We really hope you enjoyed reading this
book. If you're looking for more romance,
be sure to head to the shops when new
books are available on

Thursday 20th March

To see which titles are coming soon, please visit

millsandboon.co.uk/nextmonth

MILLS & BOON

LET'S TALK
Romance

For exclusive extracts, competitions
and special offers, find us online:

 facebook.com/millsandboon

@MillsandBoon

@MillsandBoonUK

Get in touch on 01413 063232

For all the latest titles coming soon, visit
millsandboon.co.uk/nextmonth

MILLS & BOON
A ROMANCE FOR EVERY READER

- **FREE** delivery direct to your door

- **EXCLUSIVE** offers every month

- **SAVE** up to 25% on pre-paid subscriptions

SUBSCRIBE AND SAVE

millsandboon.co.uk/Subscribe

WANT EVEN MORE
ROMANCE?
SUBSCRIBE AND SAVE TODAY!

'Mills & Boon books, the perfect way to escape for an hour or so.'

MISS W. DYER

'Excellent service, promptly delivered and very good subscription choices.'

MISS A. PEARSON

'You get fantastic special offers and the chance to get books before they hit the shops.'

MRS V. HALL

Visit millsandboon.co.uk/Subscribe
and save on brand new books.

JOIN THE
MILLS & BOON
BOOKCLUB

* **FREE** delivery direct to your door

* **EXCLUSIVE** offers every month

* **EXCITING** rewards programme

50% OFF
YOUR FIRST
PARCEL

Join today at
Millsandboon.co.uk/Bookclub

MILLS & BOON

THE HEART OF ROMANCE

A ROMANCE FOR EVERY KIND OF READER

MODERN

Prepare to be swept off your feet by sophisticated, sexy and seductive heroes, in some of the world's most glamourous and romantic locations, where power and passion collide.
8 stories per month.

HISTORICAL

Escape with historical heroes from time gone by. Whether your passion is for wicked Regency Rakes, muscled Vikings or rugged Highlanders, awaken the romance of the past.
6 stories per month.

MEDICAL

Set your pulse racing with dedicated, delectable doctors in the high-pressure world of medicine, where emotions run high and passion, comfort and love are the best medicine.
6 stories per month.

True Love

Celebrate true love with tender stories of heartfelt romance, from the rush of falling in love to the joy a new baby can bring, and a focus on the emotional heart of a relationship.
8 stories per month.

Desire

Indulge in secrets and scandal, intense drama and plenty of sizzling hot action with powerful and passionate heroes who have it all: wealth, status, good looks…everything but the right woman.
6 stories per month.

HEROES

Experience all the excitement of a gripping thriller, with an intense romance at its heart. Resourceful, true-to-life women and strong, fearless men face danger and desire - a killer combination!
8 stories per month.

DARE

Sensual love stories featuring smart, sassy heroines you'd want as a best friend, and compelling intense heroes who are worthy of them.
4 stories per month.

To see which titles are coming soon, please visit

millsandboon.co.uk/nextmonth

MILLS & BOON
MODERN
Power and Passion

Prepare to be swept off your feet by sophisticated, sexy and seductive heroes, in some of the world's most glamourous and romantic locations, where power and passion collide.

Julia James
Heiress's
PREGNANCY
SCANDAL
MILLS & BOON
Modern

Jennie Lucas
Chosen as the
SHEIKH'S ROYAL
BRIDE
MILLS & BOON
Modern

Kim Lawrence
A WEDDING
at the
ITALIAN'S DEMAND
MILLS & BOON

Sharon Kendrick
The
SHEIKH'S
SECRET BABY
MILLS & BOON
MODERN

Eight Modern stories published every month, find them all at:

millsandboon.co.uk/Modern